Scene

by Suzan

'If we made love,' she said to him, 'Would you be bored with me after only one hour?'

Matthew choked on the air he was breathing, exhaling sharply. *'What?'*

Maggie felt her cheeks grow hot. She couldn't believe she'd actually said that!

'Never mind,' she mumbled.

'*Not* "Never mind,"' Matthew insisted. 'You just asked me if I thought you'd be boring in bed.'

Maggie avoided his eyes.

He pulled her chin so she was looking up at him. 'I do *not* think making love to you would be dull. I would not be bored after one hour or even one hundred hours. And this is something that would *not* be difficult to prove.'

The look in his eyes was unmistakable. Fire. But was it passion for her or passion for a challenge?

'What would you do if I said, "OK, prove it"?'

A Bachelor and a Baby
by Marie Ferrarella

ᴆ ᴕᴕᴐ ᴄ

'Rick? What are you doing here?' Joanna asked.

The desire to kiss her was almost overpowering to Rick. But it was at odds with the renewed feeling of betrayal that seared through him. She obviously had moved on with her life and was now carrying some other man's child.

'Are you all right?' he asked, his voice harsh with anger, with hurt.

She started to say something and had her breath stolen away before she could utter an intelligible sound. Her eyes widened as her hand flew to her abdomen.

'What's the matter?' On his knees beside her, concern pushed aside his anger.

'The baby,' Joanna gasped, pushing the words out as best she could. 'I think the baby's coming.'

'You mean later.'

'I mean *now*.' Joanna clenched his wrist.

'Hold on,' Rick told her, beginning to rise to his feet. 'I'll get help.' The death grip tightened on his wrist, yanking him back down to her.

'Rick, you *are* help.'

Available in June 2004 from Silhouette Desire

Scenes of Passion
by Suzanne Brockmann
and
A Bachelor and a Baby
by Marie Ferrarella
(The Mum Squad)

Her Convenient Millionaire
by Gail Dayton
and
The Gentrys: Cal
by Linda Conrad
(The Gentrys)

Warrior in Her Bed
by Cathleen Galitz
and
Cowboy Boss
by Kathie DeNosky

Scenes of Passion
SUZANNE BROCKMANN

A Bachelor and a Baby
MARIE FERRARELLA

SILHOUETTE®
DESIRE™

DID YOU PURCHASE THIS BOOK WITHOUT A COVER?
If you did, you should be aware it is **stolen property** as it was
reported *unsold and destroyed* by a retailer. Neither the author nor
the publisher has received any payment for this book.

*All the characters in this book have no existence outside the
imagination of the author, and have no relation whatsoever to anyone
bearing the same name or names. They are not even distantly inspired
by any individual known or unknown to the author, and all the
incidents are pure invention.*

*All Rights Reserved including the right of reproduction in whole or in
part in any form. This edition is published by arrangement with
Harlequin Enterprises II B.V. The text of this publication or any part
thereof may not be reproduced or transmitted in any form or by any
means, electronic or mechanical, including photocopying, recording,
storage in an information retrieval system, or otherwise, without
the written permission of the publisher.*

*This book is sold subject to the condition that it shall not, by way of
trade or otherwise, be lent, resold, hired out or otherwise circulated
without the prior consent of the publisher in any form of binding or cover
other than that in which it is published and without a similar condition
including this condition being imposed on the subsequent purchaser.*

*Silhouette, Silhouette Desire and Colophon
are registered trademarks of Harlequin Books S.A.,
used under licence.*

*First published in Great Britain 2004
Silhouette Books, Eton House, 18-24 Paradise Road,
Richmond, Surrey TW9 1SR*

The publisher acknowledges the copyright holders of the
individual works as follows:

Scenes of Passion © Suzanne Brockmann 2003
A Bachelor and a Baby © Marie Rydzynski-Ferrarella 2003

ISBN 0 373 04986 2

51-0604

*Printed and bound in Spain
by Litografia Rosés S.A., Barcelona*

SCENES OF PASSION
by
Suzanne Brockmann

SUZANNE BROCKMANN

lives just west of Boston in a house always filled with her friends—actors and musicians and storytellers and artists and teachers. When not writing award-winning romances about US Navy SEALs, among others, she sings in an a cappella group called Serious Fun, manages the professional acting careers of her two children, volunteers at the Appalachian Benefit Coffee-house and always answers letters from readers. Send an SAE with return postage to PO Box 5092, Wayland, MA 01778, USA.

For Melanie and Jason.

One

――――――

Traffic on Route 95 was in a snarl again.

Maggie Stanton sat in her car, too tired even to flip radio stations to find a song that annoyed her less than the one that was playing. She was too tired to do much of anything besides breathe.

Or maybe tired wasn't the right word. Maybe discouraged was more accurate. Or downtrodden.

No, downtrodden implied a certain resistance to being trod upon.

Maggie was just plain pathetic. She was a doormat. A wimp without a life of her own.

She was twenty-nine years old and she was living at home. Yes, she'd moved back in with her parents because of the fire in her apartment.

But that was three years ago.

First her mother had asked her to stay to help with Vanessa's wedding.

When 9/11 happened, her father had asked her to keep

living at home a little longer, and somehow another year had passed.

Then right after Maggie had found a terrific new place in the city, her grandmother had died, and she couldn't leave while her mother was feeling so blue.

It was now way past time to leave—a quarter past ridiculous—and her mother was making noise about how silly it would be for Maggie to get a place of her own when she was on the verge of getting married.

Uh, Mom? Don't get the invitations engraved just yet. The bride kind of needs to be in love with the groom before that happens, doesn't she?

Although, like most of the major decisions in Maggie's life, it was possible that this one would be made by her parents, too. And she would just stand there, the way she always did, and nod and smile.

God, she was such a loser.

Maggie's cell phone rang, saving her from the additional tedium of self-loathing. "Hello?"

"Hey, pumpkin."

Someone kill her now. She was dating a man who called her *pumpkin*. No, she wasn't just dating him, she was—as her mother called it—preengaged.

Yes, Brock "Hey, Pumpkin" Donovan had actually asked her to marry him. Maggie had managed to stall for the past few weeks—which turned out to be an enormous mistake. She should have said no immediately, right before she ran screaming from the room. Instead, because she was a wimp and rarely screamed about anything, she'd put it off. Her wimp thinking was that she'd find the right time and place to let him down without hurting his feelings. Instead, he'd gone and told Maggie's older sister Vanessa, who was married to Brock's former college roommate, that he'd popped the question. And Van had told their parents, and...

Segue to Mom buying *Bride* magazine and starting negotiations with the Hammonassett Inn.

Maggie's parents had been so excited, they'd wanted to throw a preengagement party, for crying out loud. Fortunately, the only date Mom had had available was this Saturday—the day that Eastfield Community Theater was holding auditions for their summer show.

And they knew not to schedule something on *that* day.

Maggie's involvement in theater was the only thing she had ever put her foot down about. Her parents had wanted her to go to Yale, so she'd gone to Yale instead of Emerson's performing arts school. Yale had a terrific drama department, but her parents had made so much noise about starving artists needing a career to fall back on, she'd majored instead in business. After college, the noise had continued, so she'd gone to law school instead of moving to New York City and auditioning for a part on a soap opera. Her father had wanted her to work for his lawyer buddies at Andersen and Brenden here in New Haven, and here she was.

Stuck in traffic after putting in a twenty-seven-hour day at A&B. Preengaged, heaven help her, to a man who called her pumpkin.

Living her life vicariously through the roles she played on stage at ECT.

Because God forbid she ever say no and disappoint anyone.

Wimp.

"I'm still at work," Brock told her now, over the phone. "It's crazy here. I'm going to have to cancel, sweetheart. You don't mind, do you?"

Maggie had actually taken her gym bag with her to work despite the fact that she and Brock were supposed to have dinner. More often than not, Brock canceled or arrived at the restaurant very late.

Of course, tonight was the night she'd planned to let him down. Gently, with no screaming and relatively little pain.

And yes, that *was* relief flooding through her, chicken that she was. There was also annoyance, she realized. This man allegedly loved her. He said he wanted to marry her, for crying out loud.

And yet his idea of wooing her was to repeatedly break dinner dates at the last minute.

She could imagine their wedding day—Brock calling her as she sat dressed in her wedding gown in a sleek white limo being driven to the church.

"Pumpkin!" he'd boom over the cell phone's little speaker. "Something's come up. Compu-dime's systems have gone haywire! They need me in Dallas, pronto. We're going to have to reschedule—you don't mind, do you?"

And there it was—one of the reasons Brock wanted to marry her. She was so completely, idiotically compliant.

Of *course* she didn't mind. She *never* minded. She always did what was asked or expected of her, with a smile on her idiotic face.

She was *such* a loser.

"I'll call you tomorrow," Brock said now. "I've got to run."

And he was gone before she could say anything at all.

With his curly hair and Hollywood-star cleft in his chin, Brock was a good-looking man. And, as Maggie's mother kept pointing out, he got six weeks of vacation each year.

Yeah, *there* was a reason to get married—for a man's extensive vacation time.

Be careful, Angie had said the last time they'd talked on the phone. Maggie's best friend from high school was convinced that if Mags didn't stay alert, she'd wake up one morning married to the Brockster. Kind of the same way she'd woken up one morning with a law degree, a job at A&B and living at home again at age twenty-nine.

But Angie was Angie. Her goal in life was to make waves. She'd just gotten married herself to a man from England, and was living now in London, working as a stage manager in the theater district. She had a dream job and a dream husband. Freddy Chambers, a seemingly straitlaced Brit, was the perfect match for Angie Caratelli's rather violently passionate nature.

Kind of for the same reasons quiet Maggie had gotten along so well with Angie.

It had been more than ten years, but Maggie still missed high school. She and Angie and Angie's boyfriend, Matt Stone—all part of the theater crowd—had been inseparable and life had been one endless, laughter-filled party. Well, except when Angie and Matt were fighting. Which was every other day, because Matt had been as volatile as Angie.

Life had been jammed with anticipation and excitement and possibilities. There was always a new show to put on, a new dance to learn, a new song to sing. The future hung before them, glowing and bright.

Matt would have been as horrified as Angie if he knew Maggie was a corporate lawyer now, and that her office didn't even have a window. But he'd disappeared over ten years ago, after graduation. His and Angie's friendship hadn't survived that one last devastating breakup, and when he'd left town, he hadn't come back.

Not even a few years ago, when his father had died.

No, Maggie was the only one of them still living here in town. Wimp that she was, she *liked* living in the town she'd lived in most of her life. She just wished she weren't living at home.

"Help," she said to the woman in the car in the next lane over who looked nearly as tired as Maggie felt. But with the windows up and the air-conditioning running, they might as well have been in different rockets in outer space.

Angie repeatedly suggested that Maggie quit her job, dump Brock and run off to live in a recreational vehicle with that really gorgeous, long-haired, muscular Tarzan lookalike Maggie had caught glimpses of while at the health club. The *jungle man,* she and Angie had taken to calling him since he first appeared a week or so ago. She'd first noticed him hanging from his knees from the chin-up bar, doing midair sit-ups.

He had long, straight, honey-brown hair, and as he effortlessly pulled himself up again and again, it came free from the rubberband and whipped in a shimmering curtain around him.

Maggie had never gotten a clear look at his face, but the glimpses she'd seen were filled with angles and cheekbones and a clean-shaven and very strong chin.

She could picture him now, walking toward her, across the tops of the cars that were practically parked on Route 95.

He would move in slow motion—men who looked like that always did, at least in the movies. Muscles rippling, T-shirt hugging his chest, blue jeans tight across his thighs, hair down around his shoulders, a small smile playing about his sensuous mouth, a dangerous light in his golden-green eyes.

Well, Maggie hadn't gotten close enough to him to see the color of his eyes, but she'd always had a special weakness for eyes that were that exotic, jungle cat color.

Oh, *yeah.*

He'd effortlessly swing himself down from the hood of her car, and open the driver's side door.

"I'll drive," he'd say in a smoky, husky, sexy half whisper.

Maggie would scramble over the parking brake. No. No scrambling allowed in this fantasy. She'd gracefully and somewhat magically find her way into the passenger's side as she surrendered the steering wheel to the jungle man.

"Where are we going?"

He'd shoot her another of those smiles. "Does it matter?"

She wouldn't hesitate. "No."

Heat and satisfaction would flare in his beautiful eyes, and she'd know he was going to take her someplace she'd never been before. "Good."

The car behind her hit its horn.

Whoopsie. The traffic was finally moving.

Maggie stepped on the gas, signaling to move right, heading for the exit that would take her to the health club.

Maybe, if she were really lucky, she'd get another glimpse of the jungle man and her evening wouldn't be a total waste.

God, she was *such* a loser.

Two

Matt Stone needed help.

He'd been back in Eastfield—he wasn't quite ready to call it "home"—for less than two weeks, and he could no longer pretend that he was capable of pulling this off on his own.

His father had been determined to continue messing with Matt's head even after he was dead. He'd left Matt a fortune—and the fate of two hundred and twenty employees of the Yankee Potato Chip Company—provided he was willing to jump through all the right hoops.

As far as Matt was concerned, his father could take his money straight to hell with him.

But for two hundred and twenty good people to lose their jobs in *this* economy…?

For that, Matt would learn to jump.

Still, he needed a lawyer who was on his side. He needed someone with a head for business. And he needed that person to be someone he trusted.

He needed Maggie Stanton.

He'd seen her a time or two at the health club. But she was always in a hurry, rushing into the locker room. Rushing to an aerobic dance class. Rushing back home.

He'd seen her last night—checking him out. She was very subtle. Maggie would never leer or ogle, but she was definitely watching him in the mirrors as he did curls.

She didn't recognize him. Matt didn't know whether to be insulted or glad. God knows he *had* changed quite a bit.

She, however, looked exactly the same. Blue eyes, brown hair, sweet girl-next-door face with that slightly elfin pointy chin, freckles across her adorable nose…

It was a crime to humanity that she'd gotten a law degree instead of going to New York and working toward a career on Broadway. She had a voice that always blew him away, and an ability to act. And, oh yeah, she could dance like a dream.

She'd won all the leads in the high school musicals starting when she was a freshman. She was Eliza Doolittle to his Henry Higgins when he was a junior and she was a sophomore.

The following year, they were Tony and Maria in *West Side Story*. It was the spring of Matt's senior year, and the beginning of the end of his friendship with both Angie and Maggie.

Because Angie knew.

As Tony and Maria, he and Maggie had had to kiss on stage. It was different from the polite buss they'd shared as Eliza and Henry the year before. These were soul-sucking, heart-stopping, full power, no-holds-barred passionate kisses. The first time they went over the first of them, Matt had followed the director's blocking with his usual easy confidence, pulling Maggie into his arms and kissing her with all of his character's pent-up frustration and desire.

Maggie had become Maria, kissing him back so hotly, pressing herself against him and…

And Matt had to stop pretending to himself that he hadn't fallen for his girlfriend's best friend.

And of course, Angie knew. The only person who *didn't* know was Maggie.

It was entirely possible she never knew.

Or maybe she *did* know, and she had been as angry with him as Angie.

In which case she probably wouldn't return his phone call.

Which meant that he'd just have to keep calling.

Because he *needed* Maggie Stanton and this time he wasn't going to take no for an answer.

Laden with files, Maggie staggered back into her office at five o'clock the next afternoon after a six-hour meeting with a client.

She pulled the wad of phone messages off her spiked message holder with a sigh, taking them with her into the former closet that was her office. She closed the door, dumped the files in the only other chair in the room, and, sitting at her desk, spread the message slips on the desk in front of her.

Brock had already called twice. Seven of the messages were from clients she knew, three were names she didn't recognize.

There was a brand-new pile of files on her desk, with a casually scrawled note atop saying, "Deal with these before tomorrow, will you?"

Oh, yeah, sure. No problem—if she stayed here at the office until midnight.

Maggie let her head fall forward onto the desk. "I hate this job," she whispered, wishing she were brave enough to say it loudly enough for either Andersen or Brenden to hear.

There was a knock on her office door.

Maggie lifted her head. This was where he'd make the scene. Her jungle man. She'd say, "Come in," and the door would open and he'd be standing there, just looking at her with those golden-green eyes.

He'd step inside and close the door behind him and say, "Ready to go?"

And she wouldn't hesitate. She'd say, "Yes."

And he'd smile and hold out his hand and she'd stand up and slip her fingers into his and...

The door opened a crack and Janice Greene, the firm's receptionist, peeked in. "You *are* still here."

"Oh, yeah," Maggie said. "I'm still here."

"You missed one," Janice told her, handing her the phone message slip.

"Thanks," Maggie said as Janice went back out the door. She glanced down at the slip and... "Whoa, wait a minute, please—didn't he leave a number?"

Matthew Stone, read the slip in Janice's neat handwriting.

"He said you would know it," Janice said. "I'm sorry, I should have—"

"No," Maggie said. "It's all right." The only number she knew for Matt was the one for the big old house he'd once shared with his father, down by the water.

As Janice shut her door, she picked up her phone and started to dial.

But then hung it back up.

She'd always felt a little funny about the fact that she'd taken Angie's side during her and Matt's last big fight—the one that broke them up for good and even managed to disrupt Maggie's own friendship with him.

Angie had never gone into detail about what it was that Matt had supposedly done.

All Maggie knew was that Matt and Angie had had the mother of all fights shortly after rehearsals for *West Side Story* had started. And that was saying something because theirs was a very stormy relationship, filled with conflict.

Angie had come running to Maggie's house for comfort. And soon after, Matt had shown up, too.

Maggie could tell he'd been drinking from the aroma of

alcohol that surrounded him. It had been whiskey she could smell, which alarmed her. Usually he only drank beer.

"Are you okay?" she'd asked him, coming out onto the front stoop.

He sat down heavily on the steps, and she knew as she sat next to him that something was really wrong. In addition to having too much to drink, he looked anxious and ill at ease.

He couldn't quite meet her eyes. "Mags, there's something I have to tell you," he said

"Get the hell out of here, you creep!"

Maggie turned to see Angie inside the front door. Her eyes were blazing and her arms were crossed as she glared down at Matt.

He swore softly. "I should have figured you'd be here."

Maggie had looked from Angie to Matt, feeling hopelessly caught in the middle. She stood up. "Look, you guys, why don't I go inside? This doesn't have anything to do with me."

Matt started to laugh, and Angie kicked him, hard, in the back. He fell off the steps, landed in the shrubbery and came up mad.

"*Damn it!*"

"Stay away from me," Angie shouted back at him. "And stay away from Maggie. I'm warning you, Matt!"

Maggie had never seen such venom in her friend's eyes.

Matt turned deliberately away from her and looked at Maggie. "I would like to talk to you. Alone. Will you come for a ride with me? Please?"

"I wouldn't let her go for a ride with you even if you were sober," Angie shouted. "Get lost, you son of a bitch!"

"I wasn't asking you," Matt shouted back. "Just shut the hell up!" He turned back to Maggie. "Come on, Mags. If you don't want me to drive, we could take a walk."

"I'm sorry," Maggie said as Angie pulled her back into the house.

After that, she'd only seen Matt at rehearsals.

She'd urged him to patch things up with Angie, but he simply smiled. "You still don't get it, do you?" he asked.

Finally, she *did* get it. Matt and Angie were through, and their three-way friendship was over.

The next year, Matt went off to college. Angie found a new boyfriend and life went on. Maggie had kept track of Matt for a while.

The last address Maggie had had for him was from nearly seven years ago, when he was living in Los Angeles. Since then, she'd heard nothing of him, as if he'd dropped off the face of the earth.

But now he was back.

Maggie picked up the phone and dialed.

It rang four times before a breathless voice answered it. "Hello?"

"Hey, Matt."

"Mags!" he said, genuine pleasure ringing in his voice. "Thanks for calling back so quickly. How are you?"

Awful. "I'm fine. Welcome back to the East Coast."

"Yeah, well," his voice sounded subdued for a moment. "I, uh, actually, I'm back in Eastfield on business and, um, that's partly why I called. I mean, aside from just wanting to see you. God, it's been forever."

"You sound exactly the same," she said.

"Yikes," he said. "Really? That's kind of scary."

Maggie laughed. "So what kind of business are you in these days?"

"The inheritance business," he told her. "Can you meet me tonight for dinner? I'm going to ask you to do me a giant favor and I'd rather not do it over the phone. I need the opportunity to use visuals—you know, so I can properly grovel."

He *did* sound exactly the same. "How giant *is* this favor?"

"It's about twenty-five million dollars giant."

Maggie choked. "What?"

"I really want to wait and talk to you about this in person," Matt said. "How about if I pick you up at six-thirty?"

Maggie looked at that new stack of files on her desk. "Let's make it later. I'm going to be here for a while, and I was hoping to hit the health club tonight. I want to go to a class that ends at eight. Is that too late?"

"That's right. Tonight's that dance class you like to take. I've seen you over there, you know."

"You're kidding. You saw me at the club and you didn't bother to say hello?" Maggie couldn't believe it. "Thanks a million."

"You didn't see me?" he asked.

"If I had, I would've said hi. Jeez, Matt."

He laughed. "It makes sense that you wouldn't recognize me. I've put on some weight."

"Really?" Maggie tried to picture Matt carrying an extra fifty pounds around his waist. Oh, dear. He was probably balding, too. No doubt it was his cosmic punishment for being too gleamingly handsome as a seventeen-year-old.

"Look, why don't we meet at the club?" he asked. "We can get something healthy to eat in the café."

Maggie snorted. "Yeah—since when do *you* eat anything healthy, Mr. Cheese Fries?"

Matt laughed. "I'll see you a little after eight."

Thanks to the files on her desk, Maggie missed the dance class. It was eight-fifteen before she pulled into the health club parking lot.

And there he was. Her jungle man. Hanging out right by the door, leaning against the wall. Dressed in jeans and that white T-shirt, just like in her fantasy.

Only this was real.

He was just standing there, as if he were waiting for her. And she was going to have to rush right past him, because she'd already kept Matt waiting.

Boy, she hated being late.

But as she moved toward him, the jungle man pushed himself up and off the wall. His hair was down around his shoulders, shiny and clean. His shoulders and chest were unbelievably broad, and the muscles in his arms actually strained against the sleeves of his T-shirt.

His face was twice as handsome as she'd imagined—although the twilight still made it hard to see him clearly.

He smiled as she drew closer, and she realized that his cheekbones were indeed a work of art. And his chin and his smile with those gracefully shaped lips, and those golden brown eyes that were—oh my God!—*Matthew*'s eyes…

Maggie couldn't remember the last time she'd been completely speechless. But she sure as hell was speechless now.

Matthew.

Her fantasy jungle man was actually her old buddy *Matthew*.

He'd put on some weight, all right, but it was all solid muscle.

"Hey, Mags," he said—Matt's voice coming out of this stranger's mouth. He was laughing at her. He knew damn well that she'd noticed him in the club but hadn't recognized him.

Come on, Maggie. You're an actor. *Act*.

"Hey, Matt," she said, her voice coming out perfectly matter of fact. "I'm sorry I'm running late."

"That's all right," he said. "I'm just glad you're here. You look great, by the way."

"I still look fourteen," she told him. "*You* look great. God, Matt, I've seen you around here for days, but I didn't know it was you."

"Yeah, well, I've changed a lot," he said, his eyes suddenly serious.

Maggie had to look away, suddenly uncomfortable with this new man-sized Matthew Stone. Somehow, she'd been expecting the kid she'd known in high school. This man was not only taller and broader, but he'd also lost the nervous energy that had ruled the teen. Young Matt had never sat still for longer than a few minutes, hopping from chair to chair around the room, smoking one cigarette after another.

This man exuded a quiet strength, a steadfast calmness. And that was really why she hadn't recognized him—never mind the long hair and muscular body.

Matt smiled at her, not one of his old devil-may-care grins, but a gentle smile of genuine pleasure.

"I really missed you," he said.

"I missed you, too," she told him. "But right now I have to visit the ladies' room. It's a long drive from New Haven at this time of night."

"No problem. I'll go up to the café. Want me to order you something?"'

"Yeah, thanks," she said as he held the door open for her. That was a new one, too. Matt—holding a door? "Will you get me a salad?"

"Italian dressing on the side," they both said at the same time.

Matt grinned. "Some things never change."

Three

———

When Maggie walked into the café, Matthew was standing at the juice bar, talking to three healthy, young college girls. What was it that he'd said? Some things never change.

He turned, as if he'd felt her eyes on him and quickly excused himself. Coming toward her, a smile lit his handsome face. "Hey."

Their food had already come out, and he pulled her by the hand to a table. And held her chair for her.

She looked up at him as she sat, half expecting him to pull it out from underneath her, so he could laugh as she hit the floor.

But he just smiled at her, and sat down. Behind a huge salad and a plate of steamed vegetables. The hamburger kid was eating *vegetables*.

"Before we get down to talking about twenty-five-million-dollar favors," Maggie said, "I'm dying to hear what you've been up to this past decade."

And where was the beer? Even at seventeen, Matthew

Stone never sat down to eat dinner without a cigarette and a bottle of beer.

"It would take a full ten years to tell you the whole story," he said with a smile, digging into his salad.

Maggie looked around the open, airy café. The ceiling was high, the colors were muted grays and maroons. A sign on the wall proclaimed that there was absolutely No Smoking.

"Do you still smoke?" she asked.

"Nope. I quit three years ago," he told her. "I also stopped drinking and started eating vegan. See, I, um… Well, I got sick, and I needed to take some kind of action—feel like I was doing something to help myself get better. I don't know if it really helped, but it certainly helped my head, you know?"

"How long were you sick?"

He shook his head. "A long time. Do you mind if we don't talk about that? It's not… I have these superstitions about… Well, I'd rather not—"

"I'm sorry," she said. "Of course, you don't have to… I had an address for you in California."

"Yeah," he said. "Yeah. I was, uh, all over the southwest for a while. Right after dear old dad gave me the boot. He kicked me out—did you know about that?"

She shook her head. "No."

"Yeah, there was trouble at one of the colleges and he wouldn't even hear my side of it. I mean, sure, it was the fourth college I was…" he cleared his throat. "Politely asked to leave, but… That time it really wasn't my fault. Still, I got the 'never darken my door again' speech."

"That's terrible," she said.

"It was good actually. I finally learned to take care of myself. I kind of floated for a while. I actually did some acting—and got paid for it. My most legit job was at this dinner theater in Phoenix. I did two shows with them—*Cat on a Hot Tin Roof,* and *Guys and Dolls.*"

"That's great—getting paid for acting?" Maggie smiled at him, and he smiled back.

"I guess. It was… It really wasn't that great. They didn't pay very much. I had to wash dishes, and…" He shrugged. "Their leading lady had nothing on you."

Yeah, right. "Thanks."

When he looked at her, something sparked. Maggie felt it deep in the pit of her stomach, and she had to look away. She'd trained herself for so long to feel nothing more than friendship for Matt that this kind of physical attraction seemed odd and unnatural.

His eyes gleamed with humor. "Oh, here's a story you'll really like. When I was in L.A., I managed to get this agent. What a sleazeball. He told me he could get me some work in the movies. Nothing big, you know—bit parts. But still, it was the *movies.…* Anyway, he sent me on an audition, right?"

Maggie nodded, watching Matt's face as he talked, the corners of his mouth quivering with restrained laughter. It was hard to believe that it had been ten years since she'd seen him. It just seemed so natural, sitting here together.

"So I go into this place," he said, "and I realize that it's not a cattle call. You know, there're not four hundred other guys that look sort of like me lining up to audition for the part of the store owner who says 'A dollar fifty,' to Keifer Sutherland when he comes into the convenience store to buy a pack of cigarettes. The director actually comes out and shakes my hand—if you can believe that—and he takes me into the studio. I was so jazzed. They had cameras set up on a soundstage, along with this living room set. It looked like a stock American home set—something out of a sitcom, you know?"

He paused, taking a sip of water. "Well, imagine my surprise when the director told me to go ahead and take off my clothes."

"What?"

"Yeah." Matt grinned. "It didn't take me long to figure it out. I asked to see the script and it was called—I'll never forget this—*Sleazy Does It.* It was a porno flick, Mags. It wasn't an audition—they were just going to shoot the film that same day. Is that too scary or what?"

Maggie had to laugh. Poor Matt. Thinking he was going to get a part in a major motion picture... "Did you do it?"

He choked on his water and glared at her, mock outrage on his face. "Thanks a lot. No, I did *not* do it."

She was still laughing. "Your past ten years have been much more exciting than mine."

"You graduated from Yale, went to law school and managed to get an M.B.A. at the same time. You had a fire, moved back in with your folks. You dated someone named Tom for four years, now you're seeing a guy named Brock Donovan. You've had the lead in *Oklahoma, Carousel, Paint Your Wagon, Showboat, The Boyfriend, Superman, Anything Goes, Guys and Dolls, Lil' Abner* and one more.... What was it?"

"*Annie, Get Your Gun.*" Maggie couldn't believe it. "How do you know all that?"

He closed his eyes, placing his fingertips on his forehead. "Matthieu senses all," he said with a heavy Eastern European accent. "I also know that Angie's married now," he added in his regular voice.

There was something in his face, in his tone, that Maggie couldn't read.

"Yeah," she said. "Freddy's great. You'd like him. But it's kind of a drag—they live in London."

"That must be tough," he sympathized. "You and Angie stayed close, didn't you?"

Maggie nodded. "I miss her."

"Did she ever tell you..."

"What?"

He shook his head. "Why we broke up. I don't know. It all seems so silly now."

He was looking at her, and she felt herself blush under his scrutiny.

"Why did you break up?" she asked.

"Maybe I'll tell you some other time," he said. His eyes were warm. Hot, almost…

Where are we going?

Does it matter?

No.

Maggie cleared her throat. "Are you going to audition for the summer musical? I mean, are you going to be in town for a while?"

"Yeah, I'll be here at least three months," he said. "I don't know about the show, though. I saw the audition notice in the paper. It's tomorrow, right? But the show was one I didn't recognize."

"It's called *Day Dreamer*. It was written by this local team of writers. It's not… It's really funny. And the music's good, too.…" Maggie felt herself babbling in an effort to keep the conversation pointed securely away from the physical attraction that seemed to simmer between them.

But she lapsed into silence as he sat back in his chair, his eyes still glued to her face. As he moved, the muscles in his arms and chest moved, too. It was hypnotizing. With a motion that was clearly well-practiced, he tossed his hair out of his face, back behind his shoulders.

"I guess I'll audition," he said. "If you're going to…"

"Matt, why do you wear your hair like that?" she asked. "I mean, it's beautiful, but you always had short hair. In school, you used to make fun of the boys who wore their hair long.…"

"It's a complicated story," he said evasively. He sat forward, pointing at her salad. "Are you going to eat that?"

She wasn't very hungry. "Do you want it?"

"No, I want to get out of here," he told her. "I want to take you to see something."

He stood up, tugging down on the thighs of his jeans in a

movement that was all Matthew. How many thousands of times had she seem him do that?

But going vegan and quitting drinking and smoking, and the new super healthy body...

As they left the café and walked down the stairs to the lobby, he caught her puzzled look and said, "What?"

It was remarkable, really. With his dazzling white T-shirt tucked into the top of his blue jeans, his long hair cascading halfway down his broad back, he was an odd mixture of her friend Matt and her fantasy jungle man. He looked sort of like Matt and he moved and talked sort of like Matt, but there was so much more that was different about him now. She could see so many changes in him, the most startling being his confidence, his solid, quiet strength.

Again, she found herself attracted to him, and that felt strange.

"I'm trying to figure out exactly who you are," she said bluntly, "just who it is you've become."

He looked startled for a moment, and then he laughed. "You know, Mags," he said, "I really did miss you. You and your honesty."

He opened the door leading out of the club. With a grand gesture, he motioned for her to go through.

Outside, the night air was cool, and Maggie shivered slightly. Matt casually draped an arm around her shoulders.

His touch was warm, and Maggie felt the urge to lean against him, to rest her head on his shoulder, wrap her own arm around his waist.

But he was just being friendly old Matt. Wasn't he?

She pulled away. "Your car or mine?"

Matt turned around and gave her such a look that she had to laugh. "I assume that means you still *have* to be the driver, right?" she said.

He grinned. "I've got the old man's Maserati. He never drove it anywhere. What's the point in having a car like that if you never use it?"

"Do you remember when you stole it and used it to drive Angie to the junior prom?" That was one of the best times they'd had together and one of the worst.

He unlocked the front passenger side door of the gleaming black sports car and opened it for Maggie. "How could I ever forget? I spent four days in jail for that one. God, my father was such a bastard."

Matt got into the driver's seat and closed the door. He looked over at Maggie, real sadness in his eyes. "I was such a disappointment to him. Right up to the end."

She didn't know what to say, and then there was no reason to say anything because he put the key into the ignition and started the engine with a roar. "Oh, yeah," he said, flashing her a smile. "This is a very nice car."

Maggie wanted to ask about his father, but she held her tongue. Mr. Stone had died over a year ago, and even though he and Matt had never gotten along, she'd been surprised when Matt didn't show up for the funeral.

She shook free of the thought, fastened her seat belt, and got ready to hang on for dear life as he pulled out of the parking lot. But he drove almost slowly.

"Where are we going?" she asked.

Does it matter?

She loosened her fingers from her grip on the handstrap as she realized he was going to stay under the speed limit.

"Out to my father's office," Matt told her. "*My* office," he corrected himself with a laugh. He shot her a look. "Can you believe I have an office?"

Maggie was confused. "You mean, over at the factory?"

"No," he said. "The main office was in our house."

Matt glanced at her.

Maggie's face was lit in regular intervals by the street lights. The pale yellow glow made her seem unearthly.

She was prettier than ever. She still had the biggest, bluest eyes he'd ever seen. They were surrounded by thick, dark lashes. Her complexion was fair—a fascinating contrast to the dark brown of her soft, wavy hair. Her nose was small and almost impossibly perfect, her lips soft and full, and always quick to curve into a smile.

For the first time since he'd hit town, he was honestly glad to be back.

Very glad.

"I want to offer you a job," he told her as they neared the house. "I'd like to hire you as my corporate attorney and business advisor—for three hundred thousand dollars a year."

She stared at him.

She didn't say a word as he pulled into the driveway of his father's huge white Victorian house. All the outside lights were on, spotlighting it against the darkness of the night.

He'd grown up in this house, playing on the vast lawns that overlooked the Long Island Sound, scrambling on the rocks at the edge of the shore. It was a wonderful old place, full of nooks and crannies. It had rooms that weren't perfectly square, windows that opened oddly, and closets that turned out to be secret staircases.

"What's the catch?" Maggie finally found her voice.

After Matt's mother died, his father had had the house renovated and restored. And although he knew his father hadn't intended for it to happen, the renovations removed every last trace of her, every homey, motherly touch, leaving the house as impersonal and empty as a museum.

Matt pulled around to the back, where the office was, and parked the Maserati under another bright spotlight.

"The catch," he said, turning toward her in the sudden silence after the car's powerful engine had been shut off. "Yeah, there's definitely a catch. You know my father had money. Big money."

Maggie nodded. The Yankee Potato Chip Company, the mansion, the twelve-car garage with the twelve cars to go in it.

"Dear old dad decided to leave it all to me—all twenty-five million, if—'' Matt took a deep breath ''—I can show that I can run the business within a three-month time period—which started last week. If I can't—adios to everything. The executor of the estate will shut down the business, auction off the factory, and all the money will go to charity. If that happens, I'll get nothing. And if I get nothing, your job—and everyone else who works for YPCC—will be terminated.'' He looked at her. ''How's that for a catch?''

Maggie nodded again, her eyes serious. ''That's some catch. What exactly does the will stipulate?''

Matt opened the car door. ''I've got a copy inside. I'll let you take a look at it.''

She got out of the car, too, staring up at the house. ''You know, Matt, all those years we were friends, I never went inside your house.''

''That's because my father hated Angie,'' Matt told her. Angie had taken Mr. Stone's crap and handed it straight back to him. ''He would've really liked you, though.''

''Is that a compliment or an insult?'' she asked with a laugh.

''Oh, it's a compliment,'' he told her. And wasn't that strange? He and the old man would've finally agreed on something.

Maggie followed him up the path to the office door and into the house.

The outer office was large and spacious, with rows of file cabinets along one wall. There was a huge oak conference table in front of enormous bay windows that looked out over the water. The hardwood floors glistened, as did the intricate wood molding that surrounded the windows and door. It was a modern office with computers, copy machine and fax, but the feel of the room was Victorian. It was gorgeous. And in the daytime, with the view of the sun sparkling on the water, it would be even more beautiful.

Matt led the way to a dark wooden door and, pushing it open, he turned on the light.

Maggie had to laugh, looking around at the late Mr. Stone's private office—Matt's office now. "Oh, Matt," she said. "It's *you.*"

He grinned.

Thick red carpeting was underfoot. The walls were paneled with the same dark wood as the built-in bookcases. Row upon row of books lined the wall, and Maggie glanced at the varying titles and subjects. Mr. Stone had a few books on astronomy, several on geology, an entire shelf of medical books on cancer, many titles on the Second World War, but the vast majority of the books in the room were fiction—mysteries.

Matt's father had been into whodunits. He had always seemed so practical and down-to-earth, with no time for non-sense of any kind. She just couldn't picture him biting his fingernails in suspense as he read faster and faster to find out who was the killer.

The inner office had big windows but they were shuttered with elaborately carved wood. The centerpiece of the room was a massive cherry desk and what looked like a black leather Barcalounger behind it.

Maggie slowly circled the desk. It was quite possibly as large as a queen-sized bed, its rich dark wood buffed to a lustrous shine. She picked up the single item that rested on its clean surface—a photo of Matt at about age six, clinging possessively to his smiling young mother's neck.

"Why didn't you come to his funeral?" she wondered.

He turned away.

"I'm sorry," she said swiftly, putting the picture down. "I shouldn't have asked—"

"I saw him about two weeks before he died. I was in the hospital—it was back when I was sick. Somehow he'd managed to track me down and he came to see me."

He was leaning against the door frame now, arms crossed. His pose was relaxed, but Maggie could see tension in his jaw. And she could hear it in his voice.

He laughed, but it didn't have anything to do with humor. "I don't know how he did it, but he managed to pick a fight. I mean, I'm lying there, dying for all he knows, and he's telling me I never did anything worthwhile with my life."

Maggie didn't hesitate. She crossed toward him and put her arms around him. "I'm so sorry."

"I told him to go to hell." Matt rested his cheek on the top of her head. "I told him to stay out of *my* life, because no matter how short it was going to be, it was my life. So he got up to leave, and I thought he was just going to walk out, but he turned and he told me that he loved me, and that he didn't want me to die. I told him—"

His voice broke, and Maggie held him even more tightly. She felt him take a deep breath, then exhale loud and hard. "I told him that I hated him," Matt said, "and that I couldn't wait for him to die." He made another noise that wasn't quite laughter. "God. *Why* did I *say* that? Of course, two weeks later the son of a bitch went and had a massive coronary. It was his ultimate revenge—he couldn't have planned it better if he'd tried."

She looked up at him. "Matt, he loved you. He knew you didn't mean what you said."

He sighed. "I hope so."

In this light, from this angle, flecks of color made his eyes look more green than gold. Green, and very warm. As he looked down at her, his face held something—a sadness, a sweetness, and also a tenderness—that she hadn't ever seen there in all the years she'd known him. At least not when he wasn't acting.

It was entirely possible that back then, he simply hadn't let it show.

His arms were still around her, and she was still holding him. They'd stood like this, leaning against each other, so many times—Matt had always been very casual with affectionate embraces. But everything felt different now, and as she looked into his eyes, she knew he felt it, too.

Attraction. Desire.

It seemed inappropriate. It had been years, but it was still hard not to think of Matt as Angie's boyfriend.

Except Angie was married now to someone else. And this new, fantasy jungle man version of Matt was here, looking at Maggie as if he were thinking about kissing her. Not just a Matt kiss—he'd always been generous with friendly kisses on the cheek, too—but a real, on the mouth, tongues in action kind of kiss.

Like the way Tony had kissed Maria. Maggie's stomach did a flip as she remembered kissing Matt on stage. Except that hadn't been them—it was the characters they were playing who had kissed so passionately.

Still…

She pulled away from him and went to stare once again at the books on the shelf. This was just too weird.

"I'm sorry," he said quietly. "I shouldn't have laid all that on you."

Maggie shook her head. "Oh, no, I'm glad you told me," she said as she turned to face him. "That's what friends are for, right?"

Their eyes met. And Maggie felt it again, that spark of sexual energy that seemed to flow between them. Friends.

"You were going to give me a copy of that will," she reminded him breathlessly, reminded herself, as well.

He took a step toward her, and another, and she knew he was going to kiss her.

But the kiss he gave her was only a Matt kiss, on the cheek. He stepped past her, going into the outer office. She followed, feeling oddly disappointed—was she insane?—as she watched him switch on the copy machine.

"You can take this home and look it over," he told her as he opened one of the file cabinets and took out a manila folder. "Let me know what you think by Monday. I know it's short notice, but I need you to decide by then because if you aren't interested in the job, I'll have to start looking for someone else to help me right away.''

Maggie watched as he copied the document.

A three-hundred-thousand-dollars-per-year job, guaranteed to blow up in three months if she didn't help Matt become a businessman.

Was it exciting? Absolutely. Was it crazy? More than absolutely. What would her mother, her father, God, even *Brock* think?

They'd think she was irresponsible, silly, reckless, wild.

But what did *she* think? How about answering *that* question for once?

Sure, there was a chance this decision would backfire, leaving her without a job and laughed at by her friends and family. But there was a chance that something special was going on here—that she finally had an opportunity to take control of her life, to get out of her cell and make a difference in some way, even if only in her life and Matt's and the people who supported their families from the Yankee Potato Chip Company.

To do something she wanted to do, something *she* would be proud of...

But the risk...

There were butterflies in her stomach—just like when she was little and in line for the Ferris wheel at the firemen's carnival. As the line got shorter and the moment of truth approached, she would nearly sweat with anxiety. Would she do it or would she chicken out?

She would look up at the seemingly shaky structure that would take her on a ride fraught with danger, up to terrifying heights. Then she'd remember the exhilaration of the wind in her hair as she looked way, way down at the little people below and out at the horizon that seemed to stretch on forever.

It had been worth it. It always had been worth it.

She looked at Matt as he shut off the copy machine, as he stapled together the copies he'd made, as he put the original back in the folder, back in the file cabinet.

Where are we going?

Does it matter?

No.

"I'll take the job," she told him.

He turned and stared at her. "But you haven't even read the—"

"I don't care," she said. "You offered, I'm taking it."

Matt laughed. "Since when do *you* make a decision without forty-eight hours of soul searching?"

"Since right now," she said.

"Are you sure?" He looked worried.

She felt a twinge of uncertainty. "Are you sure you want me?"

"Absolutely!"

"Then I'm sure."

Matt just looked at her. With that same, disconcerting heat in his eyes. She had to turn away, look out the window at the night.

"I've been thinking for some time now about making some changes," she confessed. "It occurred to me that if I took your offer I wouldn't have to go back to that horrible office without a window."

"You don't have a *window?*"

She glanced at him. "You've got to earn a window at Andersen and Brenden."

"God."

"I wouldn't have to make that awful commute, I wouldn't have to wear uncomfortable shoes—would I?"

"No way." He was grinning at her. "If you work for me, you don't have to wear shoes at all. Of course in three months you won't be able to afford to *buy* shoes...."

"Not if I can help it," she said. "This is a beautiful office. It's ten minutes from home, inches from the ocean...." She made a face. "Although, telling my dad that I'm leaving A&B isn't going to be fun...."

His smile had faded. "Maggie," he said, seriously. "I don't want to pressure you." He paused. "Don't get me wrong. I want you to say yes. I *really* want you to say yes. But this isn't going to be easy. Your job will be to help me figure out how to run this business. At this point, I can barely remember how to add or subtract. It'll mean really long hours. I've only got three months, and right now, quite frankly, I couldn't run a business if my life depended on it. So if you aren't absolutely sure or if you're doing this just to help me out of a tough spot or if you're going to regret this tomorrow..." He looked searchingly into her eyes. "I want you to be really sure."

She looked back at this man who was half Matt, half her fantasy man and didn't hesitate. "I'm sure."

A flood of emotions crossed his face. "Well, all right," he said and handed her the copy of the will. "Let's have dinner tomorrow after the auditions. We can start work then."

Maggie glanced through the will—it was fourteen pages long. "We should forget about the auditions. If we only have three months—"

"No," Matt said. "I'm not giving up a chance to be in another show with you. And rehearsals are only, what? A couple evenings a week?"

"Except for the last week before it opens," she chided him. "Then it's every week. We really can't—"

"Yes, we can," he said. "The show won't open until the end of my fiscal quarter. If we haven't succeeded by then..." He shrugged. "It'll be too late."

"I just don't think we should take on too much at once," Maggie told him.

The smile he gave her was beautiful. "You worry too much."

"You don't worry enough," she countered.

"This is going to work out just perfectly."

Four

The air in the community theater auditorium was cool compared to the outside warmth of the sunny spring morning. It smelled like sawdust and paint, musty curtains, a little bit of sweat, and a whole lot of excitement.

It smelled like a show.

Maggie smiled and waved to friends from past productions as she put her gym bag down on one of the seats in the first row.

There was an audition sign-up sheet posted on the apron of the stage, and she signed in.

"Sign me in, too."

She looked up to see Matt leaning over her shoulder to look at the list. His hands were on the stage, on either side of her, effectively pinning her in.

His teeth flashed white and perfect as he grinned at her. He was standing so close, Maggie caught a whiff of the spearmint toothpaste he'd used, probably right before leaving his house. He was wearing all black—a snugly-fitting T-shirt, sweats, and a pair of jazz shoes that had clearly seen a lot of use. Howard Osford, the slightly balding, slightly overweight tenor who usually won the romantic leads out of lack of competition didn't stand a chance today.

"What are you singing?" she asked as he watched her add his name to the list.

Matt shrugged, straightening up and freeing her. He followed her back to her gym bag, throwing himself casually into the seat next to it. "Want to do a duet?" He stretched his long legs out in front of him, and looked up at her, a glint in his eyes.

Maggie stopped taking off her street shoes to glare at him. "That always really pissed me off."

"What?" He grinned, knowing darn well what she was talking about.

"The way you could come into an audition totally unprepared and walk away with the lead."

Matt tried not to be obvious about watching her as she pulled off her T-shirt and adjusted her sports bra. She was wearing tight black pants that flared and a colorful dance top that left her midriff bare.

"You should get a belly button ring," he said.

She rolled her eyes. "Ouch. No thanks."

"You know, it's been more than three years since I've gone on an audition," he said. The room was filled with dozens of hopeful singers and dancers. It didn't matter the town or the state—the hope that hung in the air at an audition was always the same.

"Are you scared?" she asked.

Matt tried to look frightened. "I won't be if you sing a duet with me."

She just laughed. "Not a chance. I, for one, worked hard to prepare a song."

"Then let me use you as a prop."

Maggie crossed her arms. "Come again?"

Ooh, he loved it when she put on a little attitude. Sweet

Maggie had a backbone beneath that soft outer layer. "A prop," he repeated, working hard not to smile. "You know, a warm body to sing to. I always do much better when I'm not up on stage all alone."

She laughed in his face. "Tough luck. That's what an audition is all about—being on stage all by your little old self. You can sing to me all you want, but I'm going to be right down here." She shook her head in disgust. *"Prop."*

"Okay," Matt said.

"That's it? No fussing? No begging? No whining? Just, okay?"

He tipped his head back and smiled up at her. "It's only an audition."

"I hate you," she said, and walked away.

Ten minutes later, the first trembling victim stepped onto the stage, and Matt joined Maggie at the back of the room.

"I'm up twentieth," she whispered. "You're twenty-first. Have you decided what to sing?"

He nodded yes. "I'm doing something from my favorite show."

"What is your favorite show?"

"West Side Story. It was the most fun I've had on stage in my entire life."

Maggie looked at him, perplexed. "You mean, back in high school?"

"Yup."

He looked up at the stage, watching as the director cut the singer off midsong. Maggie studied his profile, remembering the turmoil of his senior year.

Another singer mounted the stage and made it through about sixteen bars before being stopped and thanked for coming.

"Sheesh." Matt glanced at her. "This director is brutal. They're dropping like flies. He doesn't give anyone time to warm up. At this rate, you're going to be up there in less than a minute."

"He is pretty harsh," Maggie agreed, then asked, "How could *West Side Story* be your favorite show? You were miserable the entire time. You had that big fight with Angie...."

"As Matthew I was miserable," he told her. "But I sure loved being Tony."

He had a funny little half smile on his face, and a look in his eyes that made her heart beat faster.

He looked back at the stage, and Maggie watched him watch the auditions.

"Maria was a great part," she told him softly. "But it was very hard each night to watch you die."

He glanced at her, and the look on his face was one she absolutely couldn't read.

"Maggie Stanton," a stout woman with cat-eyed glasses and a clipboard finally called. "You're next."

Yikes.

Matt caught her arm as she started for the stage, pulling her into his arms for a hug. "Break a leg, Mags."

She looked up at him, and the realization hit her hard, leaving her feeling weak. She wanted him to kiss her.

He was handsome and vibrant and so very alive and she wanted him to kiss her.

He wasn't Angie's boyfriend anymore and *she wanted him to kiss her*.

And he did.

On the cheek.

She swallowed her disappointment as she walked down the theater aisle toward the stage. Those sparks she'd thought were flying all over the place must've been only in her mind.

Or else he would have really kissed her, wouldn't he?

He saw her as a friend, a buddy to hang with.

Which was a good thing. Matt had never been cut out for anything but short-term, intensely passionate flings. True, they wouldn't leave his bedroom for a week, but after that week, it would probably be over. Any kind of romance with him would definitely be a mistake—particularly since she was going to be working with him.

She *was* going to work with him.

She'd called her boss at A&B this morning, and he'd accepted her resignation gracefully. In fact, he'd told her he didn't even need the usual two weeks notice. Times were tough all over, Maggie knew, and business had been off lately, even at the big law firms.

She just had to go in some time next week, clean out her desk and drop off the company cell phone.

She handed her music to the accompanist with a smile, moved center stage and nodded to the director. He was someone she'd never worked with before, someone who didn't know her from Eve. She could see him glancing through her resume, and she turned back to the piano player and nodded.

As the first strains of music surrounded her, Maggie closed her eyes and took a deep breath, letting herself become the character—a thirtysomething dancer pleading for a second chance on the stage.

As Maggie started to sing, Matt looked up from his search through the piles of sheet music that had been tossed on a table in the back of the auditorium. God, she was good. He'd forgotten how good. He'd never understood why she hadn't studied acting, gone professional.

He had to laugh. Yeah, he'd met her parents many times. He did understand. And it was a shame.

She sang the first part of the song standing absolutely still, but with tension in every part of her body. When she reached the refrain, she exploded, both in volume and movement. She was fantastic, her voice clear and true, her body graceful.

Matt moved closer to the stage and sat on the arm of a chair. He could see the back of the director's head, and the man hadn't moved once since Maggie started singing. He grinned as the director let her sing the entire song, right down to the very last note.

The entire room burst into applause, and Maggie—typical—actually looked surprised. She blushed—also typical—and bowed.

"Very nice," the director called, his usually bored voice actually showing interest. "Don't go anywhere. I want you to read for me."

She collected her music from the piano player and went down the stairs as Matt went up. He gave her a high-five.

"Your turn to break a leg," she said.

"You're a hard act to follow."

Maggie sat down in the front row, feeling the last surges of adrenaline leaving her system. Matt came center and looked down at her and smiled, and somehow the adrenaline was back, making her heart flip-flop.

The music started and Maggie recognized the song instantly. "Something's Coming." Of course. Matt had always loved that song. It was all about hope and excitement and limitless possibilities. She had to smile. It was practically his theme song.

"Hold it," the director called, and the accompanist stopped. "Matthew Stone?"

"That's me," Matt said.

"From Los Angeles?"

"Yeah, I lived there for a while." Matt squinted slightly, looking past the bright lights at the director. "Dan Fowler? Is that you?"

"Yes. Thank you. Next," the director said in a bored voice.

Matt's eyes flashed. "What, you're not even going to hear me sing?"

"I don't want you on my stage," Fowler said.

The room was dead silent. No one so much as moved.

Maggie stared up at Matt, holding her breath, waiting for him to explode. But he merely crossed his arms.

"Mind telling me why not?" he asked, his voice almost too calm.

"Because the last time I cast you in a show, you disappeared off the face of the earth halfway through rehearsals. That screwed me up pretty badly."

"I called," Matt countered. "I apologized. But I had to go into the hospital."

"A detox center, wasn't it?" Fowler countered.

"Detox?" Matt laughed. "Yeah, I guess it kind of was." He looked out at the director. "That was three years ago, Dan."

Detox. God. Maggie had always known that in the past Matt had lived recklessly, always pushing the edge. It wasn't hard to believe that somewhere down the line he'd become addicted to either alcohol or drugs.

"It's still fresh in *my* memory, Stone."

"I'm not leaving this stage until you let me audition." Matt said the words easily, evenly, but in such a way that left no doubt in anyone's mind that he would not give in.

Fowler scowled. "You can audition until your face is blue. I'm not going to cast you. You're wasting everyone's time."

Maggie stood up, grabbing her gym bag. "Matt, let's go. There'll be other shows—"

"Hold it," Fowler said. "Maggie Stanton?"

There were a few moments of whispering as Fowler leaned over and spoke with his producers and assistants.

"Come here for a sec," he finally called.

Maggie looked uncertainly at Matt, who nodded to her, telling her to go ahead. He then sat as if unconcerned, on the apron of the stage.

She left her bag on the seat and made her way to the director. She was outraged at the way he was handling this situation. To publicly humiliate someone like this was unprofessional. It was rude, inexcusable....

Dan Fowler was about thirty-five years old, but he had streaks of gray in his full, thick beard that made him seem at least fifteen years older. His eyebrows were large and bushy, making him look as if he had a permanent scowl. He didn't speak until Maggie stood directly in front of him.

"You with him?" he asked quietly, motioning up to the stage and Matt.

"Yes," she said tightly. "I don't know what happened three years ago, but right now he's clean."

Fowler tapped his fingers on the table in front of him, looking from Maggie to Matt and back again. "Will he agree to urine testing?"

"For *drugs?*" Maggie asked in amazement.

Fowler nodded.

"You can ask him," she said, "but I doubt he'll go for that."

"Hey, Stone," the director called. "I'm willing to audition you if you consent to drug testing."

"I meant, ask him *privately,*" Maggie hissed, throwing up her hands in despair. She risked a look at the stage, fearful of Matt's reaction.

But he pushed himself to his feet and looked out at them serenely.

Only Matt knew how difficult it was to appear that calm. Inside, his blood boiled. He may have played hard and fast at one time with drugs and alcohol, but that had nothing to do with his admission into the hospital. But he wasn't about to go into those details here. Not in front of a crowd, and especially not in front of Maggie.

He looked out at her. He could tell from the tightness of her shoulders that she was mad as hell. But he knew that she really wanted this part—she *deserved* this part—and he didn't want her to lose it on account of him. And if he walked out of there, she'd go with him. He knew that. On top of that was the fact that he desperately wanted to play opposite her again....

"Okay," he said, keeping his voice light.

"Good," Fowler said. "Sing your damn song and get your ass off my stage."

Matt snapped out a count and the accompanist played the introduction. He started to sing, his eyes following Maggie as she moved down the aisle, back to her seat. He could see the shine of unshed tears in her eyes, and he knew she'd realized that he'd let Dan Fowler push him around because of her. And she would, no doubt, chalk it all up to friendship. He was just her good old pal Matt, doing something nice for his buddy Maggie.

And yet there was attraction simmering between them. Although if it scared her even a third as much as it terrified him, was it any wonder she kept trying to ignore it, to push it aside?

But, God, imagine if she could let herself love him....

She looked up at him, and he channeled everything he was feeling into the music. Like most actors, he could be super critical of his own performance, but this time...well, even he would have cast himself.

He stopped the song halfway through, looking out at the director. "That's enough, don't you think, Dan?"

"Thank you," came the standard reply. Then, "Stick around to read."

Victory. He was going to get a chance to read lines. Whoopee.

Matt swung himself gracefully off the stage to find Maggie waiting for him. She silently took his hand and pulled him down the aisle to the back of the auditorium, ignoring all the curious eyes that were on them. She led him out the closed double doors into the lobby and started for the door to the street.

"Whoa," he said. "Where are we going?"

"We're leaving."

He planted himself. "No way."

"*Yes* way. That man is a creep." She was seriously angry.

"He's a good director, though. Wait and see."

Now she was angry with *him*. "You're only doing this for me, aren't you?"

Yes. And he'd do far more for her, too, if she'd only let him. "Nope," Matt told her. "I'm doing it for myself."

Maggie didn't buy it. "Matthew, you've had enough crap dumped on you from your father—with the will and everything. You don't need to deal with this, too."

"Hey!" He grabbed her by the shoulders and shook her gently. "It's okay. Really. It's just my lurid past catching up with me. It happens. I don't mind drug testing—"

"Liar."

Matt laughed at the look of intense indignation on her face. God, she was wonderful.

"Well, okay," he admitted. "It sucks. But life's not always fair, and it's no big deal." She started to react, and he put one finger on her lips. "Really. If there's one thing I've learned over the past few years, it's to know the difference between big problems and little problems. And Dan Fowler is definitely a little problem."

The woman with the clipboard and the cat glasses poked her head out of the door. "Stone and Stanton?" she said. "He's looking for you. On stage, to read."

"I want to do this," Matt said, looking into Maggie's eyes. "Let's do this, okay?"

Maggie nodded, letting him drag her back into the auditorium. He took the bag from her shoulder, put it onto a seat and pushed her up the stairs to the stage.

"Take a few minutes to read it over," Fowler called out from his throne behind the bright lights, a benevolent monarch lazily granting the peasants some crumbs from his table.

Maggie quickly skimmed the scene. And oh, God. She could feel herself start to blush. Of course. It had to be *this* scene. She glanced up to meet Matt's eyes. He raised an eyebrow at her, then looked back at his script.

Oh, God.

"Whenever you're ready, boys and girls," Fowler's indolent voice commanded.

"I read the entire play last week," Maggie quickly told

Matt. "This scene is part of a fantasy that my character is having. She's just imagining that you're there in her bedroom, okay?"

"Got it," Matt said. He looked out toward the director. "We're ready, Dan."

"Quiet," Fowler roared, and suddenly the room was still.

Sieg heil. Maggie couldn't believe they were still here, auditioning for this tyrant. But then Matt read his first line, and she thought of nothing but the script.

"Lucy, are you still awake?" he read.

"Go away," Maggie read, with weariness and annoyance in her voice.

"Hey," Matt read, throwing up his free hand. *"I don't really want to be here. I'm just part of your overactive imagination. You want me to leave, you have to imagine me gone."*

"All right. I will." As the script directed, she squeezed her eyes shut, concentrating for a moment. When she opened her eyes, he was still standing there, of course. *"Oh, damn,"* Maggie read.

"Cody Brown, at your service," Matt read.

"What kind of name is Cody, anyway? It's a ridiculous name for a man born in Manhattan. You sound like a cowboy or a rodeo rider. What were your parents thinking?"

"Aha," Matt read. *"So that's why I'm here. You want to insult both me and my parents. Well, go for it, Luce."*

"I'm much too tired to be properly insulting," Maggie sulked.

"Why else would you have imagined me here in your bedroom at one o'clock in the morning?"

Maggie looked up at Matt, her alarm not entirely feigned. He smiled, a smile that started very small and grew across his handsome face. *"I know why I'm here,"* he said as he advanced across the stage toward her.

Maggie stared at him, frozen in place. Was he really going to...? *"No..."*

"You're wondering what it would be like to kiss me," he read, moving closer to her. *"Aren't you?"*

"No!"

As Maggie stared up at him, he came closer, until they were less than an inch apart. But he still wasn't touching her.

Matt had the next line, but he waited a moment before reading it. The look in his eyes was remarkable as he gazed down at her, the perfect mix of nervousness and desire on his face. Oh, he was such a good actor. *"You're wondering what it would be like if I put my arms around you, like this,"* he read, then tossed the script onto the floor as he did just that.

"And you're wondering what it would be like to put your arms up around my neck." Matt was going on memory now, but the lines were easy from here on in.

Maggie let her own script slide to the floor as she, as if almost in a trance, put the palms of both hands on Matt's chest and slowly slid them upwards. She felt him inhale, as if he found her touch exciting. It was a nice addition to what was already fabulous acting.

Her hands met behind Matt's neck and she could feel his long, soft hair against her bare arms. She was Lucy. And this was make-believe. They were acting. *Acting.*

"And you're wondering what it would feel like," Matt said slowly, *"if you brought your lips up, like this—"* and he gently pulled her chin up, then tenderly pushed the hair back from her face *"—and if I brought my lips down, like* this…"

Maggie was expecting a gentle kiss, but the moment his mouth found hers, something exploded. She felt his arms tighten around hers as he kissed her, and she kissed him, as she opened her mouth to him and…

Oh, God. She was lost.

But just as suddenly as that kiss began, it ended. Matt pushed her away from him and took several large steps to the other side of the stage.

"Well, forget it," Matt said, his voice perfectly hoarse

with emotion as he turned to look at her. *"Because I'm not going to kiss you."*

They stared at each other, both breathing hard.

"Very nice," Dan Fowler's voice cut in. "Stick around for the dance audition."

Maggie's hands were shaking as she bent down to pick up her script. Matt took it from her.

"You okay?" he asked, concern in his eyes.

"Sure," she lied, looking up at the man who seemed intent on turning her world inside out. "I'm…just fine."

Five

Maggie dragged herself up the stairs to her bedroom. The dance audition had been grueling. A sane person would take a hot shower and curl up in bed with a good book. But somehow she'd let Matt talk her into having dinner with him, as they'd planned the day before.

"Nothing fancy," he'd insisted, with that little smile that could turn her to jelly.

Did he know? Could he tell that she'd finally succumbed to Matthew Fever? That's what Angie had scornfully called it back in high school when one after another pretty young girl had fallen prey to Matt's charms and followed him around adoringly, sighing soulfully.

"Everyone gets it," Angie had insisted.

"Not me," Maggie had said.

Now she wondered if it were like other childhood diseases—much more dangerous if contracted when an adult.

She closed the door to her room and undressed quickly, slipping into her bathrobe.

There was a soft knock on her door, and she opened it cautiously, not wanting to get into another discussion with her mother about the pros and cons of an October wedding.

But it was her little brother, Stevie, who stood there, yawning, as if he had just gotten out of bed.

"Morning," he said, scratching his head, making his short dark hair stand up straight.

"It's five in the evening. Don't tell me you slept all day."

"I cannot tell a lie," Stevie said, a weak smile on his still-boyish face. "Your evening is my morning."

"That's pathetic." She softened her words with a smile.

"I didn't get home last night until noon," he told her. "That is noon, as in this morning."

"Are you kidding? Are you grounded for the rest of your life?"

"It was prom night." Her brother grinned. "It was very wholesome. I went to two different after-prom parties, and there was absolutely no alcohol served at either one. I felt like one of *My Three Sons*. Believe it or not, it was fun. And I'm not hung over. What a bonus."

"How'd it go with Danielle?"

Stevie rolled his eyes. "Great—if my goal was for her to still not realize that I'm alive."

"It must run in the family," Maggie said. "I know what you mean."

He narrowed his eyes at her. "You can't accuse the Brockster of not knowing you're alive. He wants to marry you. What's doing, Mag-oid? You got a boy toy on the side?"

Maggie smacked him on the rear with her towel. "None of your business, Dr. Love. Outa my way. I need to take a shower."

"Be nice to me," Stevie said. "I came here to warn you. I overheard the 'rents talking, and it sounds like Her Royal Highness, Queen Vanessa, is coming over for dinner tonight."

"Oh, thank God," Maggie said. "I've already got an excuse. I'm having dinner out with a friend."

"Lucky you, you'll miss *that* magic. Give a shout when you're out of the shower."

As Maggie was putting the finishing touches on her makeup, the doorbell rang. It was only 6:18. She'd never known Matt to be early, but he was doing an awful lot of things differently these days.

She stood back and looked at herself one last time in the mirror. Jeans and a red tank top, sandals on her feet. Who'd've thought she'd ever wear something this casual to a dinner meeting with her new boss?

A boss she happened to have the screaming hots for. And *that* was something she couldn't let happen. Talk about ways to destroy a friendship. And what would *Angie* say?

The doorbell rang again, and she clattered down the stairs, throwing the door open.

"Hi." She smiled, expecting Matt.

Brock looked back at her, his arms filled with suitcases. Vanessa stood behind him, also laden with luggage.

Uh-oh.

Maggie's sister never traveled light, but seven suitcases for a two hour dinner...?

"My arms are breaking here," Vanessa said, and Maggie stepped back, holding the door open for them.

Brock piled the suitcases near the stairs, smiling at Maggie. "Hey, kiddo." His deep voice boomed in the small foyer. "Bet you didn't expect to see *me* tonight."

"No," Maggie said faintly. "I didn't."

Stevie came down the stairs, his hair still wet from his shower. He stared from Van to Brock to the large pile of suitcases to Maggie. *Uh-oh.* He was thinking the same thing she was.

Maggie's dad came out of the den and shook hands warmly with Brock. "Glad you could join us," he said, then turned to Maggie. "Van told us Brock was giving her a ride over tonight, so we invited him to stay for dinner."

"Oh." Maggie looked back at Stevie.

He shrugged. "I didn't overhear *that* part," he mouthed to her. "Yo, Van," he said out loud. "You planning to change your clothes between every bite of your roast beef?"

"I'm staying for a while." Van's voice sounded brittle.

"Oh, wow." Stevie looked at Maggie again. They both loved their sister, but it was much easier to love her when she lived under a different roof. "What, is Mitch away on business or something?"

"Or something."

Uh-oh.

The phone rang.

"I'll get it!" Maggie and Stevie said in unison.

But their mother picked it up in the kitchen. "It's for you, hon," she called to their father.

"I'll take it in the den." He disappeared down the hall.

"Help me get this stuff upstairs," Vanessa commanded.

"Yes, sir!" Stevie fired off a salute as Vanessa and Brock led the way. "She's staying for *a while*," he muttered out of the side of his mouth to Maggie.

"Matt's going to be here any minute," Maggie muttered back.

"*Matt?*" Stevie was delighted. "The friend you're having dinner with is a *Matt.* Oh, boy."

"Dinner's almost ready," their mother called from the kitchen.

"I'm going out. I've got a business dinner," Maggie called back, loudly enough for Brock to hear. Except he was leaning close to Vanessa, listening intently to whatever she was saying.

"I can't hear you with the water running!" her mother called back.

"What are you going to do?" Stevie whispered to Maggie. "I know—you could invite him to stay for dinner, too."

"Bite your tongue!"

Stevie was laughing. "It's the only solution. You know, this evening is turning out to be much more interesting than I thought."

Maggie rammed Vanessa's suitcase into the back of his leg.

"Ouch!" he yelped.

"Margaret!" their father shouted from the bottom of the stairs. "I want to talk to you. Now."

Maggie froze, looking at Stevie. Uh-oh.

"God, what'dya do?" he asked, sotto voce.

"I'm almost thirty years old," she whispered back. "Why do I feel as if I'm thirteen and I've left the basketball out in the driveway?"

The doorbell rang.

Uh-oh. "I'll get it," Maggie called, desperately trying to sound normal as she hurried down the stairs.

"I'll help!" Stevie dropped Van's suitcase and scrambled after her.

They both nearly crashed headlong into their father, who seemed to materialize out of thin air. He had on his fighting face.

"Maggie, that was just Bob Andersen on the phone," he said. "He just happened to mention that you *quit* your *job* this morning!"

"Yo, Mags! Finally makin' that rockin' career move?" Stevie said approvingly.

"You did what?" Vanessa came down the stairs, followed closely by Brock.

The doorbell rang again.

"She quit her job at Andersen and Brenden." Her father shook his head in disbelief.

"Will someone please answer the door?" Maggie's mom came out of the kitchen, wiping her hands on a dishtowel.

"I'll get it," Maggie said again, hurrying to reach the door before her mother got there. She took a deep breath and pulled it open.

Matt was standing there, wearing his usual jeans and white T-shirt, his hair loose, looking like a dream date from a music video. "Hey," he said with that smile that lit his entire face.

She reached for his hand and pulled him into the foyer. His smile turned to surprise as he saw her entire family staring at him.

"Everyone," Maggie said in her best stage voice. "I'd like you to meet my new boss, Matthew Stone."

"Oh, my *God,*" Vanessa said.

"Your new *what?*" Brock asked as he sized Matt up.

"Intense." Stevie was impressed.

"Close the door, dear," Maggie's mother said, her voice faint with shock, "or bugs will come inside."

Maggie sat at the dinner table, buzzing with nervous energy. How did this happen? She'd thought she'd been in control. She'd intended to stick to her plans and go out with Matt. After all, it *was* business, right? Instead, they'd ended up here, in one great big, hostile room.

She looked across the table and met Matt's tranquil gaze.

Well, the *entire* room wasn't hostile.

"You have *how* long to do *what?*" her father was saying as her mother passed Matt a plate heaped with mashed potatoes, vegetables…and a large slice of roast beef.

And he was a vegetarian. She opened her mouth to protest, but Matt caught her eye and shook his head very slightly, taking the plate with a graciously murmured thanks.

"We have a fiscal quarter," he told her father. He seemed entirely at ease with the fact that everyone was staring at him. "And I'm not really sure *what* I have to do in order to inherit the business." He smiled at Maggie. "That's one of the things we're meeting to discuss later this evening."

"Let me get this straight," Vanessa said. "You've actually hired Maggie to do…what?"

"She's going to be both my lawyer and my business partner," he said.

Maggie glanced down the table at Stevie, who was looking at Matt in something akin to shock. Her brother looked at her, realization in his eyes and a rapidly growing grin on his lips.

Oh damn. Stevie had figured out that Matt was the man who had come up in their earlier conversation. What was that phrase Stevie had used? *Boy toy.*

She looked down the table at her brother, promising him with her eyes that the wrath of Satan and the winds of hell would be nothing compared to her if he let this one slip. He smiled at her and made a zipping motion across his mouth.

Yeah, you better keep it zipped, junior....

"Maggie, aren't you hungry? You haven't touched your plate," her mother said.

She stared down at her dinner, her appetite gone. Her stomach churned nervously at the sight of roast beef congealing in a puddle of gravy. "Um," she said.

Brock slipped his arm around her shoulders and he gave her a squeeze. "You know how girls are," he said. "Always dieting."

Matt send Maggie a disbelieving, amused look. She knew what he was thinking. *Girls.* Brock's feminist awareness quotient was a shade lower than a Neanderthal's.

And she really wished he wouldn't touch her.

"I'm curious as to why you didn't discuss Matt's job offer with Brock before you took it," Vanessa asked. "I mean, you *are* planning to get married, aren't you?"

And now everyone was looking at Maggie.

But oh, my God, she was *not* going to turn Brock down in front of her entire family.

"Um," she said.

Steve had his glass of milk in his hand, and Matt, who was sitting right next to him, elbowed him.

No one else saw it. Just Maggie.

But the milk went everywhere. "Whoops," Stevie said as Vanessa jumped up to avoid getting drenched.

"Clumsy me," Stevie said as Maggie's mom ran for the kitchen towel.

Matt threw his napkin down to start soaking up the spill. He looked up at Maggie and smiled as Stevie kept on making noise. "Wow, how did *that* happen?"

No one was looking at her anymore. "Thank you," she said silently to Matt.

He blew her a kiss.

Which Vanessa, unfortunately, saw.

"Didn't you date Maggie back in high school?" she asked Matt after the worst of the spill was cleaned up and they were all sitting back down.

He shook his head. "No. I went out with Angie. You know, Caratelli, off and on for a couple of years."

"But you *wanted* to date Maggie," Vanessa persisted. She laughed. "Date being the euphemism that it is in high school." She looked at her brother. "Right, Steven?"

"Has anyone seen the new James Bond movie?" Stevie asked brightly.

"Am I right or am I right?" Van asked Matt.

"Van," Maggie said. What was her sister doing? As if Brock weren't already prickly enough just at the sight of Matt. "Don't."

"Matthew's not denying it," she pointed out. She'd had far too much to drink tonight and Maggie's heart broke for her. Her mother had pulled her aside to report that Van was home because Mitch had made it official. He was filing for divorce.

Maggie met Matt's eyes again, across the table, and the look on his face was…

God, was it actually true? Matt had wanted to go out with…

But…

"I was seventeen," Matt said to Vanessa. "I wanted to *date* everyone."

Maggie stood up. Enough already. "We have to get to work."

"For the record," her father said. "I'm not happy about this job change."

"For the record," Maggie said, "I am."

Matt leaned against the Maserati, watching Maggie say good-night to Brock, who was going to stay and keep Vanessa company for a little while longer.

He clenched his teeth as he watched the other man kiss Maggie. True, she turned her face away so that first kiss landed on her cheek. But Brock was a persistent bastard, and…Matt had to look away.

He jumped slightly, surprised to see Stevie leaning next to him. He hadn't heard the kid approach.

"So. You're a millionaire."

"Not quite." Matt glanced at Maggie. She'd pulled away from Brock, but he still held her hand.

"Answer me honestly," Stevie said. "Are your intentions toward my sister honorable?"

Matt looked at Stevie in surprise. The kid was already as tall as he was, but he was lanky with that big-boned pony look that teenage boys so often had. He wore his dark hair buzzed at the back and sides, with a long lock of curls in the front that flopped down over his eyes. His face was just starting to lose its boyish prettiness as he began to fill out.

"I guess that's not really my business, is it?" Stevie continued with a shrug. "You know, she's as much as told me that she's not going to marry the Blockhead."

"She did?"

Stevie smiled. "Yeah, well," he imitated Brock's deep voice. "You never know with girls. They're always changing their minds."

Matt laughed. "God, he's a jerk."

"Who's a jerk?" Maggie said, joining them.

"No one," Matt and Stevie said in unison.

"Oh, great," Maggie said, looking at their matching Cheshire cat grins. "That's all I need. You two as cohorts. As if I didn't know who you were talking about. Come on, Matt. Let me grab my briefcase from my car, then we can go."

"Have fun," Stevie said. With his back carefully to Matt, he dropped her a wink that was loaded with meaning.

Maggie let her own smile drip saccharine. "You have fun, too, Stevie-poo. Maybe if you're lucky you can get Vanessa and Brock to play Monopoly with you."

"Sounds real neat, but no," Stevie said. "I've got plans. I'm going to go drive past Danielle's house, oh, twenty-eight, twenty-nine times." He glanced at Matt. "Unrequited love."

Maggie got into Matt's car as Stevie leaned over to look in the window. "Maybe you can offer me some advice," he said to Matt, "you know, with the wisdom of your great age and all. There's this girl, see?"

"Danielle," Matt clarified, looking up at Stevie.

"Check. She's the most fabulous, beautiful, wonderful…well, you know. But she doesn't think of me as a *guy*. We're friends, that's all."

Maggie leaned forward to look out Matt's window at her brother. "Just go knock on her front door and tell her that you love her, for crying out loud!"

"Oh, no way," Matt said.

"God!" Stevie reeled back in shock. "That's very uncool."

"Yeah, and potentially humiliating," Matt said. "If I were you, I'd take my time. Go slowly. You know, don't scare her away."

"Meanwhile the captain of the football team takes the more direct approach and ends up taking her to the prom," Maggie said.

"Oh, no." Matt cringed.

"Oh, yes." Stevie nodded. "Pathetic, but true. And on that cheerful note, I'll bid you good night." He vanished into the shadows.

Matt glanced at Maggie. "Your little brother isn't so little anymore."

"Scary, huh?"

He started the car, shaking his head. "Sometimes I wish I could be eighteen again. Man, what I'd give to be able to go back and do it over."

Maggie groaned. "Not me. Once was enough, thanks."

He pulled out of the driveway. "There are definitely some things I'd do differently."

"Like what?"

"Like, I wouldn't start smoking. I wouldn't drink or do drugs. I would've taken better care of myself." He glanced at her. "I would've asked you out."

Maggie looked back at him, but now his eyes were firmly on the road. Vanessa had been right. Matt *had* wanted to date her in high school. *Date.* Right. Wow, she'd never known. "Why didn't you?" she asked.

He glanced at her with a smile. "Would you have gone out with me if I had?"

"No." Her loyalty to Angie had been too strong. She never would have risked that friendship. Even for… "Matt, to be honest, I never thought of you as anything but a friend."

Ten years ago. Now she was aware of him to the point of distraction.

He smiled at her again. "That's why I never asked you out. I wasn't a big fan of rejection."

They rode in silence for a few miles, then Maggie said, "I'm sorry about dinner. Are you sure you still want me to work for you? It's obvious that insanity runs rampant in my family."

He just laughed. "And it doesn't in mine?"

He was pulling into the parking lot of Sparky's, the town

watering hole. "What are you doing? Why are we...? You don't drink anymore. Do you?" she asked.

"No, I don't," he said. "But *you* do. And after that dinner you definitely need something with a kick."

"Roast beef," Maggie shook her head. "I can't believe my mother served roast beef to a vegetarian. Why didn't you let me say something?"

He pulled her out of the car. "Because people tend to feel embarrassed and rejected when you don't take what they offer for dinner. I took the plate and didn't hurt your mom's feelings." Still holding her hand, he led her across the parking lot and into the dimly lit bar. "But I didn't eat the meat. It's an old trick I learned in California. Cut it up and move it around the plate and no one notices that you didn't eat it. Everyone's happy."

Maggie hadn't been inside Sparky's in close to seven years, but the place hadn't changed. It was dark and it smelled like a frat house basement.

Matt pulled two stools out from the bar, then stepped back so Maggie could climb up. He sat next to her, pulling his stool so close that his thigh brushed hers. He caught the bartender's eye. "Coupla drafts."

The touch of his leg against hers was making her crazy. Matt had never been careful with her personal space, constantly draping an arm around her, often coming up behind her to massage her shoulders or braid her hair.

His casual, friendly touch had always been part of the package. True, Maggie had heard tell that a friendly backrub had at times led to far more friendly activities, but she had never been subject to his amorous advances.

Or had she? Maybe she'd been too naive to realize....

He leaned against the bar and his shoulder grazed hers and she nearly jumped off the stool.

The bartender slid two foaming mugs of beer in front of them, and she gratefully took a long swallow. And risked a look at Matt.

His elbows rested on the bar and his T-shirt was pulled tight across his strong back. He was watching her, his face shadowy in the weak light, his eyes reflecting the yellow of a neon sign. It made him look otherworldly and alien, reminding her that he was in some ways a stranger, after all that time away.

Ten years ago, she never would've dreamed of kissing Matthew Stone. Tonight, she was having trouble thinking about anything else.

Maggie remembered her own words, spoken only minutes before to Stevie, realizing how impossible her advice had been. There was simply no way on earth *she'd* ever be able to turn to Matt and tell him that she was falling in love with him.

But she was.

But she couldn't. What would Angie say if she knew? What would *Matt* say?

She stared morosely into her beer, taking another sip and feeling its coolness and accompanying warmth course through her.

Matt drew lines in the frost on the outside of his glass of beer. *His* glass of beer? What was a guy who'd been in a detox center three years ago doing with a glass of beer?

"You're not going to drink that, are you?" she asked.

"No." Matt laughed. "I'm not an alcoholic, despite what you heard from Dan Fowler today. I don't drink because I *choose* not to, not because I can't."

He met her gaze steadily, and she felt herself blush. "I'm sorry."

What had happened to him three years ago? She wished he would talk about it, but he didn't. And she was afraid to push.

He reached over and pushed her empty glass toward the bartender, then slid the full glass in front of her. "I ordered this for you. Let's go play pool."

"I thought we were going to talk business."

"I'd rather play pool. We can talk business tomorrow."

"Tomorrow's Sunday," she said. "I'm having dinner with Brock."

Matt let his opinion of Brock show on his face. "Why do you waste your time with him?"

"I'm not," she said. "I mean, I won't be anymore."

There was a flare of something in his eyes. Satisfaction. And something else. "Good. Because he's…" Matt laughed. "Don't get me started. I can't believe you've been dating him for, what is it? Six *months?*"

"Five months," she corrected him. "And we've never actually…*dated.*" At least not according to Van's definition.

Matt knew what she was saying. "Wow," he said. "That's… Wow." He laughed. "So okay. If his being fabulous in bed *wasn't* the reason you were with him… Why the hell did you go out with him more than once?"

Maggie closed her eyes. "Because he wanted to be with me," she told him. "Because nice men don't exactly fall out of the sky. Because I hoped he'd grow on me. Because I want a family. I want babies. Did I tell you that Angie is pregnant?"

She looked at him, expecting to see disbelief on Matt's face. Angie. Pregnant. Instead, he was looking at the floor, real sadness in his eyes.

Was it possible he still loved her?

Maggie touched his arm. "Are you okay? I mean I know it must be a shock. Angie always swore that she'd never have kids, but…"

Now he looked perplexed. "What did you say about Angie? I think I missed something."

"She and Freddy are going to have a baby," Maggie repeated.

"No kidding? That's great."

Okay, now *she* was the one who was confused. If it hadn't been the news about Angie, what *had* made him look so unhappy?

"Angie's going to be a really cool mom," Matt said. "Although I can't picture her changing a diaper."

She finished her second beer and, almost magically, another appeared. She narrowed her eyes at Matt. "Are you trying to get me too drunk to talk business? Another beer and we'll *have* to play pool. I won't be coherent."

"I'm trying to get you relaxed," he admitted. "You're wound pretty tight."

He slid off his seat and, standing behind her, he slipped his hands under her hair and began massaging the muscles in her neck and shoulders.

God, it felt good. Too good. Maggie felt herself get even more tense.

"Man, you have to loosen up. Is this what being a high-powered attorney does to you?"

No, it was what *he* did to her. She closed her eyes, letting his fingers work their magic, letting herself pretend that they were in an alternate time line—one where Matt was more than just a friend.

Matt could see Maggie's face in the bar mirror. Under his hands, her shoulders were starting to relax. Her eyes were closed, her lips parted slightly.

Oh, brother. That was just too inviting. He was dying to kiss her the way he'd kissed her that morning at the audition. She'd actually commended him on his fine acting job, unaware that he hadn't been acting at all.

He was praying that they'd both get the leads so that he'd be able to kiss her that way again and again. And again.

It was an odd blend of torment and delight. Delight that she could kiss him and make his heart pound and his blood rush. Torment that she could seem so unaffected by it herself.

And, oh my God, she'd never slept with Brock.

"We should talk about work. What time do you want to start tomorrow?" Maggie murmured, her eyes still closed.

"What time is your dinner with Brock?" he countered.

"We made plans to meet at six," she said.

"Then let's start early," he leaned close to her ear to say. "Eight o'clock. Let's have breakfast together, okay?"

It was an innocent enough suggestion, but somehow with his hands on her shoulders, his fingers caressing the bare skin of her neck, it seemed like a different sort of invitation. Maggie's heart nearly stopped when she felt him lean forward and kiss her just below her ear.

He spun her bar stool so that she faced him.

He was going to kiss her. Wasn't he? As Maggie looked up into his eyes, she only saw uncertainty. Oh, boy, she was probably looking at him as if she wanted to gobble him up, which would freak him out if he'd only intended that kiss on the neck—as sensual as it had felt—to be friendly.

"As your lawyer," she said, half to fill in the sudden odd silence, "I recommend that we gain access to any other papers that might be in the court's files."

Matt backed off. "Other papers?" He was puzzled.

"Your father's will states only that you must, and I quote, 'improve the business,' within a three-month time period. It's much too vague. What exactly did your father mean by 'improve the business'?"

"Make more money," Matt said. "That was always the bottom line for him."

Maggie frowned. "I'm going to need to look at the company's yearly financial statement, as well as the last few years' quarterly reports. As far as we both know, Yankee Potato Chip is thriving despite the recession. I'd bet that gross profits aren't going to vary from quarter to quarter."

And it wouldn't be easy to improve a healthy business in only three months. Any action made by an increased, aggressive advertising campaign wouldn't bring about increased sales within three months. Maggie put her chin in her hand and stared into space.

"What are you thinking?" Matt asked.

She looked at him. "I was just wondering what could possibly be in that codicil."

"What's a codicil?"

"It's an addendum to a document. There was a note at the bottom of your father's will, with your father's signature, saying that his will has a codicil. It was dated only a few weeks before he died, but it wasn't included in the other pages you gave me. The court has a copy. We'll need to see it," Maggie told him.

"You think it's going to be any help?" Matt asked.

"I don't know. There's probably a copy of it somewhere in your office. We should go back and start looking for it." She slid off the stool and nearly landed on the floor.

"I'll look for it later," Matt told her as he caught her. "I think you're ready for a game of pool. You want to break or should I?"

Six

_____

Maggie unlocked the kitchen door and went into the house without turning on the light. She was feeling wobbly from all that beer she'd had. She normally didn't have a single beer, let alone _four_. Or was it five?

It was after midnight, and her parents had gone to bed. The house was dark, so she locked the door behind her and crept into the living room and…

And there, on the stairs, in the glow from the streetlight, was Vanessa.

Kissing Brock.

She was in her nightgown.

His jacket was off and his shirt was unbuttoned.

And it was pretty damn obvious that he'd been with her, up in her bedroom.

"Wow," Maggie said. "_That_ was fast."

Her sister and the man who'd asked her to marry him just a few weeks ago—never mind the fact that she was intending to tell him no tomorrow—leapt apart.

"God," Vanessa said. "Maggie, you scared me to death."

Maggie turned on the light. Brock, at least, had the decency to look embarrassed.

Vanessa, from the looks of things, was even more drunk than she was.

Maggie sat down on the couch. "Your car's not out front," she said to Brock.

"I, uh, parked it down the street," he admitted. "Look, Maggie, I'm sorry—"

"I thought you were Mitch's friend," she said.

"I am."

"Some friend."

Vanessa took offense at her tone. "Mitch is a son of a bitch who should rot in hell," she said, sitting down on the step between the entryway and the living room.

"Who filed for divorce because *you* were cheating on *him*," Maggie said. She looked at Brock. "Did you know that?"

"Because *he* was cheating on me!" Vanessa started to cry. "You're so self-righteous."

"Hey," Maggie said. "I think I'm allowed a little self-righteousness when I come home to find out that you slept with my boyfriend."

"I didn't think you'd be coming home," Vanessa countered. "Out with Matthew Stone? No woman in her right mind would make him drive her home. Except you. You're so perfect, Margaret. So perfect and proper and *cold*."

"This probably isn't a good time to be having this conversation," Brock said.

"Shut up," Vanessa said, just as Maggie said, "Zip it, Brockster."

"Maybe I should go…"

"How could you sleep with her?" Maggie asked him. The answer was right there on his face. All along, he'd wanted Vanessa. Even drunk, with her makeup faded and her hair a mess, Maggie's sister was hot. All along, Brock had just wanted to get close to Maggie's hotter sister. She looked up at him in amazement. "Maybe the question I should ask is how could you ask me to marry you, when you're in love with *her?*"

"I'm sorry," he said. "I thought…" He shook his head. "I'm sorry."

This was why he didn't push when she'd said she wanted to wait before they spent the night together. She'd thought he was just nice. But oh, my God… "Have you been sleeping with her all this time?"

"No," Brock said. "Absolutely not."

"No," Maggie echoed. "You just *wanted* to sleep with her." God, she'd almost spent her life married to a man who really wanted her sister. She stood up and looked at Vanessa. "And you knew it. You *bitch.*"

"Fine," Vanessa said. "I'm a bitch. I'd rather be a bitch than little miss no-no-no we've only been going out for four months, we can't possible have sex yet."

"Oh, my God," Maggie looked at Brock. "You discussed our sex life with my *sister?*"

"What sex life?" Vanessa laughed. "You don't *have* a sex life."

"Not like yours," Maggie said hotly. "No. I don't have sex with strangers in the parking lot of a bar."

"Yeah," Vanessa shot back. "Miss Goody-Goody. You just don't have sex, period. I can't imagine why Matthew Stone even bothers to look at you. Sure, he'll sleep with anything female, but the way you dress it's hard to tell you're actually a woman. If you *did* sleep with him, I'd give it one week. Although I'd bet big money that Matt would be bored to tears after only one *hour* in bed with *you.*"

Maggie gasped. "That's an awful thing to say!"

"Van," Brock said.

"It's true." Van started to cry. "You're so perfect. I *hate* you."

"And I won't live in this house with you," Maggie told

her sister. "I know you say things like that because *you're* the one who's messed up, and because you can't deal with Mitch's leaving you, but I am *so* out of here. Tell Mom and Dad I've moved out. For good," she added, the words making her feel remarkably light, despite her anger and hurt, despite the growing nausea from her churning stomach.

"Maybe this conversation should wait for the morning," Brock said again.

"Maybe you should go to hell," Maggie told him, and, grabbing her briefcase, she went into the kitchen and out the door.

She got into her car, but her head was spinning and her stomach definitely felt sick.

She was going to throw up.

She stared down at her car keys. How many mugs of beer did she drink?

Too many to drive.

Savagely, she opened the car door and got out.

As if on cue, the skies opened and it started to rain.

Maggie squared her shoulders, and still carrying her briefcase, started the long walk into town.

Stevie cranked up the volume of the radio and switched on the windshield wipers as the rain came down harder. He flipped his bright lights lower as he saw someone walking along Route One.

Poor wet son of a bitch. Didn't need to be blinded, too.

But then Stevie hit the brakes and did a one-eighty, tires squealing. That was no ordinary son of a bitch. That was his *sister!* He pulled up alongside her and rolled down the window.

She didn't stop walking.

"Yo, Mags." He slipped the car into first to keep up with her.

She didn't look at him.

She was soaked to the skin and dripping wet, hair plastered

to her head. And she was carrying her briefcase, like some deranged zombie commuter.

"So where you going?" Steve dared to ask.

"Into town," she said, as if it were a perfectly normal answer.

"You, uh, want a ride?"

"No, thank you."

Stevie pulled his car to the side of the road and got out, trotting to catch up to his sister. "Maggie, are you okay?" He stood in front of her.

She stopped. "Stevie, if you don't move, I'm going to throw up on you."

He moved, fast, and Maggie kept walking.

"Maggie, come on," he called, but she didn't look back.

Maggie was walking to the Sachem's Inn Motel, one step at a time. She didn't feel good, but she felt a whole lot better since she'd stopped at the corner of Lily Pond Road to throw up behind the O'Connor's shrubs.

It was another few miles into town, another mile after that past the harbor to where the motel overlooked the water.... She couldn't handle the thought of walking three more miles. But she could walk one step. One step and one step and one step. Eventually, they'd all add up to three miles.

She stopped short.

Matthew.

Steam rose from the cooling hood of his car, creating a wall of mist behind him. He was wearing only a very small khaki-colored pair of running shorts. Light from a street lamp glinted off the moisture on his bare skin. It was cold enough so that his breath hung in the air, but he stood still, just watching her.

"Hey jungle man," Maggie said. "I've run away from home."

"So I've heard," Matt said. "Steve called me. It's about time you moved out of there. Can I give you a lift?"

Maggie looked at him, at his bare feet and athletic legs. Bare skin started again on the other side of his shorts. His stomach was a six-pack and his chest was… Fantasy material, indeed.

Vanessa was right. This was not a man who would ever want to be anything more than friends with Maggie. "Will you take me where I want to go?" she finally asked.

"Depends."

"Then forget it," she said. "I'll walk."

She stepped around him, but he caught her arm. "If you're walking, Mags, I'm walking with you." It was not an idle threat.

It was freezing. "You're not exactly dressed for a stroll in the rain."

"Neither are you. Come on, get into the car."

Maggie looked at him for several long moments.

"Please," he said.

"I look like I've really lost it, don't I?" she asked.

He smiled. "Kind of. But I figure you must have a good explanation. Why don't we get into the car and you can give it to me."

"Will you take me where I want to go?" she asked again.

"Yes," he said this time.

Maggie got into the car.

Matt turned the key and cranked up the heat.

"I'm ruining your leather seats," she realized with dismay, reaching for the door handle.

He hit the lock button and slipped the car into gear. "That's okay. In a few months I'm going to be a millionaire. I'll buy new ones."

"I want to go to the Sachem's Inn Motel," she said.

"Really?" He gave her a sidelong glance. "With me?"

"Very funny. Just take me there."

Matt sighed. "I'm not going to take you there and simply drop you off."

"You *promised*."

"Did not."

"You *said* you'd take me where I wanted to go."

"Yeah, but I didn't *promise*. I'm taking you home with me."

"You *jerk*." Maggie started to cry. She'd finally left home, and damn it, she'd left it under her own power, despite the fact that she'd had too much to drink to drive safely.

But now she'd gone and gotten rescued. Well, she didn't want to be rescued, not even by Matthew Stone, jungle man.

Matt stopped at a red light and turned to look at her.

"I want to do it my way, Matt." Her blue eyes were swimming in tears. "Let me. Please?"

The traffic light turned green, but he ignored it. He took a deep breath, hardening himself against her tears. "I don't think it's a good idea for you to be alone tonight," he told her. "If you insist on going to the motel, I am coming with you."

"I insist," Maggie said, wiping her eyes and sticking out her chin. "And I don't need a baby-sitter."

"Too bad, because I've made up my mind."

"Well, *I've* made up my mind, too, and I'm staying there alone."

Their eyes locked and held. And the traffic light turned red again.

"Let's compromise," Matt told her. "First come home with me. We can get warmed up, maybe get something to eat, and talk—"

"I don't want to talk." She crossed her arms, staring straight ahead.

"Fine," he said. "We can sit in silence in the hot tub. After that, I'll take you over to the motel. If you still want to go there."

Maggie looked at him. "Hot tub?" she said.

* * *

"You already turned it on," Maggie said, wonder in her voice. "It's already hot."

She stood shivering in the bathroom in Matt's house, staring at the steam rising from the hot tub.

"I was sitting in it when Steve called." Matt tugged impatiently at the zipper on her jacket. It stuck slightly, but he finally got it down, and peeled the wet sleeves off her arms. Her skin was icy.

He reached for the button on her jeans, but she pushed his hands away. "I can do that."

Yeah, but it had always been one of his fantasies. Not a good time to tell her that. "Then do it," he countered. "Come on, let's get you in there before you die of hypothermia."

She hesitated. "I don't have a bathing suit."

Matt laughed. "You don't need a bathing suit for a hot tub. For God's sake, Maggie, I'll turn around. Just get in, will you?"

He pointedly did just that and she peeled off her clothes. Yeah, she was definitely tanked—otherwise she surely would have noticed that the room was filled with mirrors and his turning his back was useless. He could see her from all angles, and, oh, mighty God... A more chivalrous man might've closed his eyes but life was just too short.

Matt watched as she slipped into the water, and... Wasn't that just perfect? Now it was his turn to get naked. But maybe that was good. Let her see what she did to him.

But, "Eek," she said, as he started to pull off his shorts right in front of her. She closed her eyes until he was sitting across the tub from her. "Doesn't this strike you as weird?"

Matt stretched out his legs to get more comfortable, and brushed against her. All right. Don't do that. He was purposely sitting over here so there'd be no contact. "What's weird about it?"

Her eyes were so blue and her face was pale and she was still shivering slightly. The last thing he should do was go over there and put his arm around her. He drew an imaginary line around her. Whatever happened, he was *not* going to cross that line. Not tonight, anyway.

"Well, to start with, we don't have any clothes on," she told him.

He shrugged as the water bubbled around them. "Personally, I'd find it much weirder if we did."

She narrowed her eyes at him. "It's weird and you know it."

Matt nodded. "Yeah, it's weird. That doesn't mean it's not nice, though."

"I have this fantasy," she told him, "where this perfect stranger just kind of holds out his hand to me, and takes me away from my life."

Oh, man. "That's, uh… That's probably one a lot of people have."

"It's pretty wimpy," she said. "Like, I just want to lie back and be rescued."

"Nothing wrong with that," Matt said.

"No," she said. "Because who's to say that his choices would be any better for me? My fantasy should be that I go up to the jungle man and say come with me—let's escape, but let's do it *my* way."

Jungle man. That wasn't the first time she'd mentioned this jungle man. "That's a good fantasy, too." He laughed. "Mags, I get the feeling that you're telling me something, but I'm not sure if I understand exactly what it is. Can we stop talking in code? I really want to talk about what happened tonight after I dropped you off."

She sank down so that the water covered her mouth. Okay.

"Steve said he thought you and Vanessa got into a fight or something?"

Her eyes filled with tears.

"Talk to me," he said.

She lifted her mouth above the water line. "If we made love, would you be bored with me after only an hour?"

Matt choked on the air he was breathing. *"What?"*

Great, now he'd embarrassed her. She closed her eyes. "Nothing. Never mind."

"No," he said, moving across the tub to her. Mistake, mistake, *mistake.* He moved back, just not as far as he had been, but still safely on the other side of his line. *"Not* never mind. You just asked me if I thought you'd be boring in bed, didn't you?" *Damn.* "Did Vanessa say that to you? Mags, she already had too much wine at dinner. And she's nuts on top of that..."

But Maggie was just sitting there, eyes closed, looking like she actually thought...

"To answer your question," he told her, "no. No, I certainly don't."

She opened her eyes and looked at him, looked away. "It was stupid to ask. I mean, what are you really going to say? 'Yes, sorry, I think making love to you would be dull?'"

Okay. Game over. Matt crossed his line, moving so that he was sitting right next to her. "For the record," he said, pulling her chin up so that she was forced to meet his gaze, "I don't think making love to you would be even remotely dull. I would not be bored after even a hundred hours. And this is something that would *not* be difficult to prove."

"What would you do if I said, okay, prove it?" She was looking into his eyes, no longer needing his hand under her chin to meet his gaze, but he didn't move. Her skin was so soft, and she was finally warm. Her lips were slightly parted, her cheeks charmingly flushed, her eyes bright.

Too bright.

No, no, no. No. He wanted to cry. Instead, he shook his head. "I can't," he said. "Not tonight, anyway. You're drunk. It wouldn't be fair."

"I'm *not* drunk," she said with the kind of indignation that only someone who'd had too much to drink could pull off.

"I think you are," Matt countered. "But okay. Let's take

that off the table. Even if you're not drunk, you're upset. I don't want to sleep with you because you're mad at your sister.''

"There." Maggie pulled away from him. "You don't want to sleep with me. You just said it."

"No way! Misquote! Sound bite attack! Take it back, or you're going to get dunked!''

She'd moved all the way to the other side of the hot tub, but as he advanced on her, she actually came toward him.

"Matt, kiss me."

That he could do.

He leaned forward, moving slowly now, until his mouth met hers in the sweetest of caresses. Her lips were soft and warm, and oh, Lord, so willing.

Matt carefully kept himself from touching her, aware once again that they were both naked, knowing that if he felt the softness of her body against his, he'd be lost.

And oh, although it was careful and gentle, it was the kiss he'd been waiting for, for a lifetime.

Maggie was kissing him. She wasn't pretending to be someone else who was kissing the person he was pretending to be.

It took his breath away.

It was hard as hell to pull back, to stop kissing her, and he had to turn away to keep her from seeing the tears that had jumped into his eyes.

He forced a smile.

Maggie didn't know whether to laugh or cry. Matt was treating her the way everyone always treated her—as if she might break. And if she were going to feel embarrassed about this in the morning—and she knew she was—then, damn it, she wanted the kind of kiss Matt had been legendary for in high school, the kind of kiss that would knock her socks off.

Provided she had socks on.

"I think we should try that again," she said.

"I think I need to get out of this tub," he countered.

"I think there's suddenly some doubt as to who would bore whom in bed," she told him, amazed at the words coming out of her mouth.

"Oh really?" he said. There was an odd light in his eyes as he looked at her. He didn't move, he just sat there, very, very still.

She shifted slightly, so that the water barely covered her breasts. Matt's gaze flickered down and then back to her face.

"I'm not going to take advantage of you," he said, but he still didn't move.

"It's not taking advantage if it's what I want," she countered. She stood up, water sheeting off her.

Matt stood, too, and scrambled out of the tub, grabbing a towel and wrapping it around his waist. "You're too angry and drunk to know what you want."

"I am not!"

"Please, just—"

"For the first time in ages, I'm actually making my own decisions—"

"This is no decision. It's a knee-jerk reaction." He raised his voice to interrupt her. "If we make love tonight, everything changes between us. Maybe it would be great. Maybe you'd wake up in the morning and still want me. Maybe we'd be lovers until the day I die. But maybe not."

He handed her a towel. "Maybe it wouldn't be anything more than a one-night stand," he continued, the lateness of the hour suddenly evident in his voice. "I really don't mind if you use me, Mags, but I'm not going to let you use me up. I value your friendship too much to throw it away for just one night."

"I'm sorry," she whispered.

He headed for the door. "Dry off. I'll go find you some clothes. Then we can duke it out over whether or not I'm going to drive you to the motel."

* * *

Matt came back into the bathroom with his smallest pair of shorts, a T-shirt and a sweatshirt.

Maggie was gone.

He'd walked right past her—she was curled up in the middle of the bed. It wasn't his bed, but she probably didn't know that.

He sighed, moving closer, but then realized she was fast asleep.

She clutched the sheet to her chest, and her dark hair fanned out against the white pillow. He stood looking down at her, at her long, dark eyelashes that lay against her fair skin, at the smattering of freckles that ran across her cheeks and nose. She looked like the teenage girl he'd first met so many years ago.

As a seventeen-year-old boy, he wouldn't have been able to resist shedding his own clothes and climbing into that big bed with her.

As a thirty-year-old man, he swore softly, then picked up the towel she'd dropped on the floor. He carried it into the bathroom and hung it up to dry, tossing the clothes he'd brought with him on the back of a chair. He covered the tub and turned off the light.

Okay. Leave. Walk away. Go upstairs.

Instead, he came back to look at her in the light from the hallway.

Instead, he sat on the edge of the bed. He'd leave in a minute.

God, he was a fool. He could have had her, made love to her. He could have been lying next to her right now, basking in the afterglow.

But tomorrow was coming with a vengeance. And tomorrow they both would've had to live with the consequences.

Maybe he could make her fall in love with him. Maybe. And wouldn't that be nice. Then she'd be in love with someone who could make her no promises. Maggie wanted a family—babies and a husband who was going to stick around. Matt could give her no guarantees.

But he knew what he wanted. For the first time in years, he was certain. He wanted *her*. After all this time, he still wanted her.

He remembered the day more than a decade ago that he'd realized he was in love with Maggie Stanton. He'd been shocked, horrified, disbelieving. The great Matt Stone, slayer of hearts, did not fall in love. Then, as time passed and he realized that he had, indeed, succumbed, he'd had to face the fact that she didn't see him as anything more than a friend.

When he'd left for college, he'd partied hard, sure that now that he was away, he'd forget about Maggie. It was only a high school crush, right?

He'd dated a long line of long-legged blondes, he'd drunk hard and had been horribly unhappy.

Somewhere down the line, he'd stopped missing her.

At least he thought he had.

Matt reached out to touch her. Her skin was so smooth, so soft. He wanted to kiss her, taste her, inhale her....

He'd leave in a minute. Really.

But he swung his legs up onto the bed, leaning back, resting his head on his hand, propped up by his elbow. He leaned forward to kiss her shoulder, and she smiled in her sleep and snuggled against him.

He knew then that he wasn't going anywhere, and he put his arms around her.

Tomorrow Maggie would wake up and find him there. And if she still wanted him in the light of morning, there'd be no holding him back, regardless of the consequences.

Seven

Maggie awoke to the sound of the window shade rubbing against the sill in the gentle ocean breeze.

The room was dim, but bright sunlight seeped in around the edges of the shade. She could tell from the brightness that it was late morning, possibly even past noon.

She stretched and her leg bumped something very solid and memories from the night before came roaring back to her.

It was indeed Matt, lying beside her, fast asleep. His long hair was tangled around his face. He was on his side, one arm tucked under his head, his legs kicked free from the sheet. He was wearing a pair of shorts—what a relief. Maggie was hyperaware of her own lack of clothing.

She'd tried to seduce him last night, but he'd refused.

Her face heated. She'd thrown herself at him, but he'd made it clear he didn't want to be anything more than friends.

So what was he doing in bed with her?

The phone rang, suddenly, shrilly, and Matt stirred. His

eyes opened and focused on her for one brief moment before he turned and picked it up from the bedside table. "Hello?" His voice was husky from sleep. He sat up, pushing his hair out of his face, swearing softly. He listened for a moment longer, than handed the phone to Maggie. "It's your brother."

"Stevie?" she said, clutching the sheet to her. Her own voice was rusty sounding, and God, her head was throbbing.

"Yo, Mags," he said, wonder in his voice. "Are you guys still in *bed?*"

"Well, sort of," she told him. "But it's not what—"

"I'm very impressed. I'm also very glad I called. Mom and Dad are on their way over."

"Oh, God!" Her eyes met Matt's and from the look on his face, she knew he'd heard what Stevie had said.

"I'm going to shower," Matt told her. "I left some clothes for you in the bathroom."

"They're coming out to have a little chat, if you know what I mean," her brother said. "Hang tough. And don't let 'em get close enough to throw the straitjacket around you."

"Very funny," Maggie said. "Stevie, thanks for calling."

"Anytime. Good luck. And don't forget to practice safe sex."

She and Matt had had the safest kind of sex there was— none. But if he wanted to keep their relationship limited to friendship as he'd claimed last night, why was he sleeping in her bed?

Maggie hung up the phone and went into the bathroom. She drank directly from the sink faucet, trying to rehydrate and make her head feel a little less like it was about to explode.

She dressed quickly—her underwear was mostly dry, but everything else was still damp. She put on Matt's clothes— which made her look like a kid playing dress-up. And her hair...

Nothing like falling asleep with a wet head to create a

noteworthy style. Her only chance at looking seminormal was to put it into a ponytail.

She went in search of Matt who surely had a vast collection of ponytail holders.

Following the sound of running water, she went up a huge curved staircase to the third and then the fourth floor.

The fourth story of this old house wasn't a full floor. There was a very small landing at the top of the stairs and a single door. Maggie knocked, but there was no answer. She tried the knob and the door swung open.

Another door was off to the immediate right. The bathroom—she could hear the sound of the shower. More stairs led up, and she climbed them.

This was Matt's room—Maggie knew it without a doubt.

It was the tower room, large and airy. Its octagonal walls were all windows. There were no curtains, only miniblinds and they'd all been pulled up.

Sunlight streamed in from all angles, and the hardwood floor gleamed. The woodwork around the windows was white, as was the ceiling and all the furniture and the spread on Matt's double bed. There wasn't much color in the entire room. There didn't need to be. Nature provided all the color anyone could possibly want.

The view was breathtaking. The sky—and there was so much of it—was a brilliant blue. She could see the deep blue-green water if she looked in one direction. When she turned she could see the gentle hills that led into town, covered with the new green leaves of early summer. The white steeple of the Congregational Church peeked up over the treetops.

A wind chime of fragile white shells hung in front of an open window, and it moved in the breeze, creating a delicate and soothing cascade of music.

The bathroom door opened, and Matt came into the room. Maggie blushed—he was wearing only a white pair of briefs.

"Nice room, huh?" he said, unfazed at the sight of her, as he rubbed his hair with a towel. He made no attempt to cover himself, as if it were entirely normal for her to be there in his room while he was in his underwear.

"It's beautiful," she said. "I'm actually looking for a ponytail holder."

"In the bathroom drawer," he told her.

She went down the stairs. The bathroom air was still heavy with moisture, the mirror steamed up despite the fresh air from an open window. It was a modest little room, nothing like the bathroom with the hot tub, downstairs.

She fished through a drawer jammed with combs and razors.

"I think you should tell your parents that you're going to live here for a while," Matt told her, coming to stand in the doorway.

"I don't think that's a good idea." She used his brush to attempt to tame her hair. "And I don't think my parents will, either."

"I've got eight empty bedrooms," he pointed out. "They don't have to fear for your virtue."

And neither did she, obviously. Maggie put his brush back on the edge of the sink.

"Mags, we have to talk about what happened last night," he said as if he could read her mind.

"What's to say?" She pushed past him and headed down the stairs to the main part of the house. "Except I guess I should probably apologize. And thank you. I would have been *really* embarrassed this morning if we'd actually, you know…"

She would have been *beyond* embarrassed and well into mortified. If he'd made love to her, it would've been as a favor.

Matt followed her down the stairs.

She turned to face him. "You *are* a good friend," she said. "And you were right. Our friendship is too valuable to risk losing."

His expression was unreadable.

The doorbell rang.

"We should talk more about this later," he said. "Right now it's showtime."

He brushed past her as he went down the stairs, and Maggie had to cling to the thick oak banister, shocked at the way her body responded to even such casual contact. It was a symptom of Matthew Fever.

Could she really live in a house with him? Without embarrassing herself further? On the other hand, could she pass up the opportunity to be near him?

And she wanted to be near him—desperately. Maybe it would pass. Maybe this illness would leave as quickly as it had struck.

Her parents were dressed in their church clothes. They peered at Matt and Maggie through the screen.

"Mr. and Mrs. Stanton," Matt said graciously. "Please come in."

"Maggie, are you all right?" her father asked.

Her mother came and hugged her. "My poor baby. Get your things. We'll take you home."

"I don't want to go home," Maggie told her.

Her father glanced at Matt. "Honey, we want to talk to you, and it'll be much easier at home."

"Anyone thirsty?" Matt asked. "I'll go get some lemonade."

"No," Maggie said sharply. "I'm not thirsty and neither are my parents."

"Mags, I was trying to be polite—give you some privacy."

"We don't need privacy." She turned back to her parents. "I'm going to stay here for a while."

Her parents both started talking at once.

"Margaret, I understand how unhappy you must feel about Brock and Vanessa—"

"Vanessa's gone to Brock's," her father told her. "What's

she's done is inexcusable. It's not fair that you should be the one to leave. And moving here seems rather sudden and—''

''Wait a minute,'' Maggie said. ''Don't get the wrong idea. Matt has lots of room here, and he offered me a place to stay. We're friends, Dad. It's like me moving in with Angie.''

Her father glanced at Matt again, this time sizing him up. ''You don't really expect us to believe that, do you?'' He turned to Matt. ''Maybe you should get that lemonade, son.''

But Matt, thank God, knew that she desperately didn't want to be alone with her parents. ''Sure,'' he said easily, but then turned to Maggie. ''Want to give me a hand?''

She nearly bolted toward the kitchen.

''Go on into the living room,'' she heard Matt say, before he followed her and shut the kitchen door behind him.

''What's this with Vanessa and Brock?'' he asked, as he crossed to the cabinets and took out four tall glasses.

''I got home last night just in time to see Brock kissing Vanessa good night,'' she told him, sitting at the kitchen table and putting her head in her hands. ''She actually slept with him.''

Matt swore. And then he put a couple of aspirin on the table in front of her, along with a glass of water.

''Thank you. Apparently Brock's been interested in Van all along,'' Maggie told him. ''She and I had a little confrontation.''

''What a jackass,'' he said. ''So that's what last night was about, huh?''

Maggie nodded, unable to meet his eyes. ''I can't believe I was too stupid to notice that I wasn't the one he really wanted.''

Matt took a pitcher of lemonade out of the refrigerator and stirred it with a long spoon. ''Maggie, the man wanted to marry you.''

''Until Vanessa became available. Then it was no contest.''

"But you didn't want to marry him—"

"That's not the point," she nearly shouted at him. "God, how many times back in high school did boys ask me out because they wanted to get closer to Van?"

"Too often," Matt said quietly. "It sucked. I remember how hurt you used to be."

"I thought that was over with," she admitted. "I thought people were finally interested in me, for who I am, not for whose sister I am. But I was wrong. I feel...insignificant and...worthless and *stupid*."

And when she'd come to him, he'd rejected her, too. Matt's heart sank. Damn, he'd thought he was doing the right thing last night, and it had been exactly, perfectly wrong.

"Maggie—" he started, but she cut him off.

"I'll get over it," she said. "I always did before. But I've got to confess, I'm seriously considering moving someplace where no one's ever heard of Vanessa Stanton."

"Maybe that's not a bad idea," Matt said. "I'll make a deal with you. In three months, if I don't win my inheritance, we'll get one of those big camper things and cruise the United States."

Maggie looked up at him with the most peculiar expression. "You mean a...recreational vehicle?"

"Yeah." He grinned at her. "It'll be a blast. What do you say?" It was always good to have a plan B. Especially since he really didn't expect plan A to work.

She put her face in her hands. It was hard to tell whether she was laughing or groaning.

"As for right now, I know what to tell your parents." He handed her the pitcher of lemonade. "Carry this out, will you?"

"What?" asked Maggie. "What are you going to tell them?"

Matt picked up the tray with the glasses. "They're not going to believe that there's nothing going on between us.

We can deny it until the end of time, but they're going to think you're living here with me. You know, *with* me.''

''But it's not true.''

''I know that and you know that, but I'm telling you that denying it will only make them crazy. Just follow my lead,'' he said with a smile. ''Think of this as an improvisational skit.''

''I *hate* improv,'' Maggie muttered, following him out of the kitchen.

The Stantons looked up as Maggie and Matt came into the living room. They were sitting stiffly on those chairs his father had bought—the uncomfortable ones with wooden legs that were curved into bird's claws. Matt put the tray down on top of the coffee table.

''Just set the lemonade over here, then come sit next to me, babe,'' he said to Maggie.

Babe? She didn't say it, but the look she was giving him nearly made him laugh out loud.

He poured the lemonade, handed glasses to Mr. and Mrs. Stanton, and then patted the couch next to him.

Slowly, she approached. Slowly, she sat down. And he draped an arm around her shoulders. ''Mags and I discussed it in the kitchen,'' he told her parents, ''and we decided that you should know the truth.''

Mr. Stanton nodded. ''That would be appreciated.''

''Last night I asked Maggie to marry me,'' Matt told them. He could feel disbelief radiating out of Maggie, and it was all he could do not to laugh.

''What?'' said Mrs. Stanton.

''What?'' said Mr. Stanton.

''Matt!'' said Maggie.

He shut her up with a quick kiss. ''It's no secret that I've been crazy about her for years,'' he told them, then looked at Maggie. ''Right, babe?''

The Stantons—all three of them—wore identical looks of

shock. Matt knew not to kiss Maggie again. If he did, they'd all fall out of their chairs.

Mrs. Stanton looked at Maggie. "But…"

"She said yes," Matt said, squeezing her shoulder.

"I said no," she countered, elbowing him in the ribs.

"Obviously, we're still working it out," he said quickly, putting his hand on her knee, and sliding it up her smooth, bare thigh. His shorts looked good on her. "You can understand her hesitation. She's not sure if this is the real thing or if she's just on the rebound."

"I see." Mr. Stanton was staring at Matt's hand, still moving north on Maggie's thigh.

Out of desperation, Maggie grabbed Matt's hand and held it tightly. But that was, of course, exactly what he'd wanted her to do, since it looked as if she'd taken his hand intentionally, instead of in self-defense.

"We've decided the best thing to do is to live together, see how it goes," Matt said.

Her parents, of course, were appalled.

"You must know that we don't approve."

"I realize that, sir," Matt said solemnly. "But I want Maggie and I'm afraid if she goes back home with you, she'll never make up her mind."

Hey. Maggie shot him a look, but he refused to look at her. The muscle in the side of his jaw was jumping, though. Matt was clenching his teeth to keep from laughing. He actually thought this was funny! She squeezed his fingers, wishing she actually had nails to dig into him.

Her father shook his head. "Well, decision making's never been her strong suit," he said ruefully.

They were talking about her as if she were a horse being sold or a child or a…a…houseplant.

"I can make up my mind quite easily," she said hotly. "In fact, there's absolutely no decision here. This is ridiculous and…"

And she stopped, suddenly realizing that if she said no, she'd end up going back home with her parents.

They were all watching her, her parents with anticipation, Matt with one eyebrow lazily lifted, his expression carefully bland. But his eyes were sharp and he was watching her as if he were trying to read her mind.

What would he do if she said yes? Wouldn't *that* scare him to death? She smiled, imagining his frantic backpedaling as he tried to keep her mother from pulling out her Polaroid camera to snap an engagement photo to send to the society page of the *Shore Line Times*.

Matt watched Maggie smile and realized that she was actually considering saying *yes*. The shock value would be tremendous—it would blow her parents right out of the water. Come on, Mags, say it.

Except, God, he'd have to tell her the truth about where he'd been, what he'd been doing these past three years. If they were going to get married, he'd *have* to tell her all that, and more—Whoa, Stone, slow it down. This was fiction. This was acting. This was not real life.

Still, he leaned toward her. "Say it," he whispered.

She stared at him.

"Say it," he repeated. "Come on, Maggie. Marry me." He slid off the couch onto his knees on the floor in front of her and brought her hand to his lips as the audience—her parents—watched in undisguised shock. "Please?"

Maggie couldn't believe him. *Oh, overacting!* she wanted to shout. God, she *hated* improv because she was never really sure how the other actors wanted her to respond. Now, did Matt really want her to say yes, or did he want her to say no? Or was he too caught up in the drama of the scene even to think rationally?

Didn't it occur to him what would happen if she actually said yes?

She looked down at Matt, still waiting on bended knee like

some kind of fantasy husband-to-be. Damn him for making her wish this wasn't just a game. She almost smacked him.

"This is silly," she said. "Matt, get up off the floor. We have to tell them the real truth."

Whatever he was expecting her to say, it wasn't that. Matt covered a laugh with a cough. "The real truth." He pulled himself back onto the couch. "Oh, you mean the *real* truth."

She looked at him expectantly, innocently, waiting for him to take the lead. Which of course he couldn't take since he had no idea what she had in mind.

She threw him a bone. "The Internet thing," she said, "www.VegasWedding.com?"

He almost completely lost it, and he covered by kissing her. In front of her parents.

"God, I love you," he said, with so much emotion in his voice, she almost believed him, too.

Her father cleared his throat. "What Internet thing?"

"You don't have to go to Las Vegas anymore for a quickie wedding," Matt explained to her parents, taking her cue and running with it. Were they actually going to believe this? "You just go online and visit the Web site, and you can actually get married in a virtual ceremony." He kissed Maggie's hand. "We did that last night."

"Is it legal?" her mother asked.

"Absolutely," Matt said. "They send the marriage certificate in the mail. It takes a couple weeks, though, because they, you know, laminate it first."

Her father looked as if he were going to protest, and Maggie cut him off. "Dad, I'm twenty-nine years old."

He nodded. "You are. I think your living here is a mistake, and I think rushing into marriage with someone you haven't seen in ten years is also a mistake. We would like it if you came home. That's what we came here to say. That and we love you." He looked at Matt. "And if you hurt her, I'll make you wish you were never born."

He stood up, and held out his hand for Matt to shake, then

gave Maggie a hug. "This is the biggest barrel of crap *I've* ever heard," he whispered to her. "But your mother believes you. You just decide whether or not you're going to marry this guy, and you do it *fast,* you hear me?"

Maggie nodded, and he kissed her cheek. Her mother hugged her, too, and then they were out the door.

Matt put his arm around her as they watched her parents drive away. "How about another kiss for show?" he asked, nuzzling her neck.

She elbowed him hard in the ribs. "You had your chance last night, *babe,*" she said. "Matt, how could you tell my parents that we were going to *live* together? Didn't it occur to you that my mother might have a heart attack right there on the living-room rug?"

"And I'm telling you they weren't going to believe that we could live here in platonic harmony," Matt said, rubbing his side. "I can't believe you came up with www.VegasWedding.com. It was beautiful—I wish I'd thought of that. You know, this was the best improv I've been in in a long time. Did you see their faces?"

Maggie glared at him. "That was no improv, Matt, that was my *life*. Now my mother thinks we're *married!*"

"But it worked," he pointed out. "You didn't get pressured to go back home."

"She's going to want a look at our laminated wedding certificate," she said. "Jeez! Laminated. Very classy, Matt!"

"I was thinking on my feet," he said as she pushed past him into the house. "Give me a break!"

She turned back to him. "Give me the keys to your car."

He went into the kitchen and came back with the keys to the Maserati. "Where are you going?" he asked as he handed them over. "Can I come along? After all, it *is* our honeymoon."

"Shopping," she said. "No. And stuff it."

Eight

The sun was sinking in the sky by the time Maggie returned from the mall.

Matt was out on the front-porch swing. He watched as she unloaded one huge shopping bag after another from the car.

"Honey, I'm home," she singsonged.

"Well, if it isn't the little wife," he said, coming to help her. "Thank God you've got your sense of humor back."

"Nothing like a little shopping to ease the soul."

"A little?" His arms were piled high with packages. "You're going to be paying off your credit cards until you're eighty years old."

"*Your* credit cards," she said smoothly. "We're married now, remember?"

"Oh, good, I'll keep that in mind, later, when it's time to go to bed," Matt said in his best Groucho Marx imitation.

"I was kidding," Maggie said darkly.

Matt wasn't.

"I paid cash for this stuff," Maggie told him. "I worked

at A&B for three years. Remember me? I used to live at home. I saved all my money all that time. I can afford to splurge. I wanted to splurge. So I bought myself clothes that I like." She hadn't bought one single corporate clone suit.

Matt pulled a sundress out of one of the bags. "Put this on," he said, draping it over her shoulder. "I'm taking you out to dinner. We're celebrating."

She shot him a look. "Celebrating what? And if you say 'Our recent marriage,' I'm going to smack you."

"How about celebrating our getting the leads in the summer musical?"

"No kidding?" Maggie's face completely lit up.

"Nope." He smiled back at her. "Dan Fowler called while you were out. You got Lucy. And I'm 'Cody Brown, at your service.' First rehearsal's tomorrow night."

"This is great!" Maggie did a victory dance around the entry hall. "I'm so jazzed—I really, *really* wanted this part."

Matt grinned, watching her. But then she stopped and stared at him accusingly. "Why didn't you tell me right when I got home?" she asked.

"I did. I mean, I am. I mean, this *is* right when you got home. So you want to go out and celebrate?" Dinner—and then maybe another, less public celebration…

"Definitely." She beamed at him.

"Get dressed," he ordered her. "I'll meet you on the porch in twenty minutes."

Maggie pushed open the screen door and stepped out onto the porch. The last traces of the sunset were facing from the sky. Matt had lit a citronella candle and was sitting back in one of the rocking chairs, his cowboy boots up on the rail.

"You look great," he said simply, getting to his feet.

"You do, too." Maggie laughed. "I thought you only wore T-shirts and jeans."

He had on a pair of brown pants and a soft, white poet's

shirt with full, billowy sleeves. With his hair down, he looked like a time traveler from the past.

"This is about as dressed up as I get," he said. "I mean, aside from a tux."

It was plenty. Matthew Stone in a tux would create riots. Women would faint in the street.

In fact, more than one female head turned as they walked into the little harborside restaurant that was only a few miles from Matt's house.

Maggie was much too aware of his fingers on her back as the hostess brought them to a table overlooking the water. He's just a friend. He's just a friend. He's just a friend. Maybe if she chanted it silently, she wouldn't do anything stupid.

Dinner was lovely, and Matt carefully kept the conversation on safe topics—movies they'd seen, books they'd read, and since they had ten years of catching up to do, they never ran out of things to say.

As they were finishing dessert, the waitress brought over a florist's box and handed it to Maggie with a smile—and an appreciative glance at Matt.

Maggie gave him a quizzical look, but he just smiled.

She untied the ribbon and lifted the lid.

A dozen roses—deep red and gorgeous. "They're beautiful."

"Only eleven," he said quietly. "You make it a dozen."

There was a card among the flowers, and she opened the tiny envelope.

Make Love To Me Tonight was printed in plain block letters on the card.

She looked up at Matt. His face looked mysterious in the candlelight. Shadows accentuated his cheekbones, giving him an exotic look. His eyes glittered slightly, looking more golden than usual in the dim light.

Maggie felt like crying, because she knew exactly why he was doing this.

But she must have hidden what she was feeling, because he reached across the table and took her hand, raising it to his lips and kissing her softly on the palm.

It was the perfect thing for him to do. He was perfect. Everything was perfect. Except none of this was real. He was only doing this out of pity.

"Matt," she started, but he shook his head.

"Don't say anything now," he said. "Let's take a walk."

He tossed a small wad of bills onto the table, and held out his hand for her. She let him lead her out of the restaurant and onto the sidewalk that led to the marina.

The sky was clear and the moon was up.

Maggie shivered in the cool air, and Matt moved to put his arm around her shoulders, but she sidestepped him.

He caught her arm. "I made a mistake last night," he said, breaking their silence.

"Matt, I know—"

"Wait. Just hear me out, okay?"

She nodded, moving over to the railed fence that lined the edge of the seawall. She couldn't meet his eyes, instead looking at the moonlight reflecting off the surface of the water.

"I was trying to be noble," he told her. "I thought I was protecting you. But I was wrong, and I want to rewind and take it from the hot tub, okay?"

She closed her eyes.

"Come on, Maggie, look at me."

Slowly, she turned.

"I want to make love to you." He pulled her toward him. She didn't know how he did it, but he actually managed to make his eyes hot with desire.

"Matt—"

"I've wanted to make love to you since we were in high school," he said as he pulled her close, as he kissed her neck, her throat, her jaw.

"Please stop," she said weakly. If he kissed her on the lips, she wasn't sure if *she'd* be able to stop.

And then he did. His lips found hers, and he kissed her slowly, languidly, his tongue exploring her mouth and…

Maggie smacked him on the butt with the cardboard flower box. He let go of her, staring as if she were insane.

Maybe she was. Anyone who would willingly stop a man from kissing her like that had to be more than touch crazy.

"I know what you're doing." She backed away so that there was distance between them. "I thought you'd try something like this. When you found out today about Vanessa and Brock… You feel sorry for me and you're trying to make me feel better."

He laughed. "Yeah, I don't think so—"

"It's not working," she told him. "You can turn off the act."

"This isn't an act." He reached for her, but she brandished the flower box again. He laughed. "Maggie, I swear—"

"And I've kissed you often enough on stage to know that you can play the part of the passionate lover with your eyes closed and both hands tied behind your back."

"Oh, come on—"

"Please, Matt," Maggie begged. "I'm exhausted. I don't want to fight with you right now. Don't make this worse than it already is."

He shook his head and started to speak but stopped himself. Without another word, he led her back to his car.

They drove home in silence, but as he pulled into the garage, he looked at her. "It's not an act."

"Good night," she told him, and nearly ran into the house, into the room she'd claimed as her bedroom.

She locked the door behind her. But she wasn't sure if she was locking him out—or herself in.

Nine

Matt's eyes opened as the sun streamed into his tower bedroom.

He glanced at his clock: 6:18. Four hours of sleep. Not bad. Not great, but not bad, considering…

Maggie was only one floor beneath him, but after last night, she might as well be a million miles away.

He'd spent most of the night tossing and turning, trying to ignore how much he wanted her, trying to figure out how he'd be able to return to his status of *friend* after tasting her lips. But he'd done it before. He'd fallen desperately in love with her more than ten years ago, and he'd survived.

Or had he?

Matt had spent the night alternately praying that it would simply be a matter of time before she came to him, and praying that he would have the strength to keep his distance from her.

It was probably a good thing that she'd told him no last night.

It was ten days and counting until he was scheduled to go back to the hospital for a checkup. He'd all but decided not to go, thinking it was little more than a visit to a high-tech fortune teller. Whether he was going to live for one year, ten years, or a hundred years certainly mattered to him, but knowing wouldn't change the way he lived his life.

Except now everything had turned upside down, and now he desperately wanted to know.

He pulled himself out of bed.

He had work to do.

Maggie grabbed an apple from the refrigerator, still humming the melody from the summer musical's closing number.

The first rehearsal—a read through of the script—had gone well, except for the fact that she'd counted seven different times she was going to have to kiss Matt on stage. Each kiss would have to be set up, blocked and rehearsed. Over and over again. She wasn't sure whether to laugh or cry.

As she took a bite of the apple, she opened up the connecting door to the office and turned on the lights.

"Whoa," Matt said. "What are you doing?"

"I want to look over those numbers some more," she said.

She held her apple in her teeth as she used both hands to clear a stack of file folders from one of the chairs. The conference table itself was stacked high with files and bound reports and computer printouts. They had worked hard all day, right up to the rehearsal.

"It's nearly midnight." Matt cleared off another chair so he could sit, too. "This will still be here tomorrow."

"These numbers are bad," Maggie said. "I've looked at the quarterly reports for the past four years, and the gross profits have remained pretty darn constant, even after your dad died. There's not a lot of room for increased profits here, Matt."

"So what do we do?"

She stretched her arms over her head. "I guess we have to start thinking creatively."

"Oh, good."

"Good?" She looked at him in disbelief.

He grinned. "Quarterly reports and gross profits make my head spin. But creative thinking is something I can handle."

It was true. Even back in school, Matt had never had the patience for math. He hadn't been very good at following rules. But in terms of creativity, he was a pro. Put him in an empty room with a canvas and paints, and you'd get a masterpiece. Most likely the canvas would remain blank and the masterpiece would be painted on the wall, but it would be truly magnificent.

"Tomorrow we should go down and take a look at the plant," she said. "Maybe that will trigger your creative process."

"Okay," he said easily, idly picking up a thick file folder and leafing through it. "God, can you believe a temporary secretary costs more than forty dollars an hour from some of these agencies? *That's* not within our budget, is it?"

Maggie searched through the piles of reports for the current year's annual budget. "Actually, it is. But we can cut costs. I mean, jeez, we could hire Stevie to be our slave for fifteen dollars an hour."

Matt smiled. "That's a great idea. Let's hire Steve."

She looked at him in exasperation. "I was kidding."

"Can he type?"

"Probably. He's always online."

"I'll call him tomorrow."

"Matt, sometimes I think you're totally nuts." She rubbed the back of her neck, twisting her head to stretch the muscles. She'd have to make time tomorrow to get in a workout at the club.

With a start, she felt Matt's hands touching her shoulders. She stood up quickly, breaking free. "Don't," she told him.

"Mags, lighten up. I was trying to help you relax."

"Well, just don't, okay?"

He didn't say anything then. He stood there, looking at her, his eyes guarded, his face nearly expressionless.

"I'm sorry," she said. "I don't know what's wrong with me. I know it must have confused you when I…did what I did the other night. I was upset and angry and I wasn't thinking clearly. Sometimes I wonder if I'm still not thinking clearly. But I do know that you were right. Our friendship is far too valuable to throw away for a little sex."

She risked a glance at him, and found he'd turned to stare out the window. Part of the lawn was lit by spotlights aimed at the house, and the semicircles of bright green grass stood out as islands in the surrounding sea of darkness.

"I'm still feeling really vulnerable," she said softly. "Every time you touch me, I question your motivation. And damn it, I don't want your pity, Matt."

He just shook his head. "You know, if I'm feeling sorry for anyone here, it's myself."

She rolled her eyes. "I need you to give me some space so we can get things back to normal." Sooner or later she'd start feeling human again. Sooner or later, she'd be able to accept a back rub from him without wanting his hands to caress her entire body.

"All right." He glanced at her and forced a smile. "I'm going up to bed. I'll see you in the morning."

He made a wide circuit around Maggie, careful not to get too close, and went out of the office without looking back.

Wait, she wanted to say, but she kept her mouth tightly shut.

"You did *what?*" Angie's voice sounded remarkably clear over the international connection.

Maggie smiled, imagining the look on her friend's face. "I moved out. It was right after I had a fight with Van, who moved back home because she and Mitch are getting a divorce, and now she wants to go out with Brock, so he dumped me, but that's okay because he was a jerk, and this all happened on the same day I quit my job because I'm working full-time for Matthew now.''

Angie's stunned silence was extremely impressive because she was Angie and rarely stunned or silent.

"So what else is new?'' she finally asked.

"I got the lead in the summer musical,'' Maggie said.

"I was kidding,'' Angie exploded. "Damn, Mags is that all?''

"That about covers it.''

She sat in her nightgown, with her feet up on the late Mr. Stone's big desk, talking on his private line. She'd gotten up very early to give Angie a call. It was already lunchtime in London, and she knew her friend was rarely home in the afternoon.

"Let me get this straight. You're working for Matthew?''

"Yep.''

"He's paying you?''

"What, do you think I'd do it for free?''

"You? Yes.''

Maggie laughed. "Yeah, you're probably right.''

"How is he?'' Angie asked.

"He's fine,'' Maggie told her friend. "He's great, actually. He's changed an awful lot, Ange.''

She snorted. "Don't count on it. With Matt, you never know what's reality and what's just an elaborate song and dance. My guess is right now he's taken on the role of the prodigal son. He's probably imitating his dear departed father, dressing like a businessman and saying things like, 'Let's do lunch.'''

"No,'' Maggie said. "He's not. I don't know exactly what happened, but he went through some very tough times over the past few years. He's different now. You'd probably have trouble recognizing him.''

"Now *that* I refuse to believe,'' Angie said. "Hey, tell me what happened with that jungle guy from the club. You meet him yet?"

"Um," Maggie said cautiously. "Yes, I did."

"And…?"

"And… I don't know." She couldn't tell Angie that her fantasy man and Matt were one and the same. She just couldn't.

"Is he human?"

"Extremely human," Maggie said. "Totally, absolutely human. Incredibly human."

"Uh-oh." Angie laughed. "You've got it bad, haven't you?"

"It's terrible," Maggie admitted, pulling her feet off the desk. "I may never recover."

"That's the way I felt when I first met Fred. Obviously you don't have a choice. You've got to marry the guy."

Maggie closed her eyes. "I don't think so. Angie, look, I've got to go. I've got to go down to the courthouse this morning, and there's a ton and a half of paper sitting in the office waiting to be read. I'll call you again soon, okay?"

"Mags, where are you staying?" Angie said. "You told me you moved out, but you didn't say where you're living now."

"I'm staying with a friend," Maggie told her, feeling doubly dishonest. "I've got to run. See you, okay? Bye!"

She hung up the phone and put her head down on the desk.

She should have told Angie the whole truth, but she couldn't deal with the thirty-minute lecture on the evil of Matthew Stone that would have been sure to follow.

Maybe she wouldn't ever have to tell Angie. Maybe her feelings for Matt would conveniently vanish. But her own words came back to her. *I may never recover.*

She had to smile, thinking of Angie's solution. Marry the guy. Ange would be horrified to know that she'd even inadvertently advised her best friend to aim for marriage with Matthew Stone.

Angie would be even more horrified to find out that Mrs. Stanton thought Maggie and Matt were already married.

Married. To Matt.

She'd have a better chance of winning the lottery. Matt simply wasn't the marrying kind.

He *was* however, the hot sex in the hot tub kind.

She had to stop thinking about that.

The clock on the wall said six forty-five. She was too wired to go back to sleep. She might as well get to work.

On her way through the kitchen, she put on the tea kettle and searched the cabinets for the tin of tea bags. Hoping against hope, she opened the refrigerator, looking for a lemon.

There were five in the lower drawer.

That was odd. Fresh fruit and vegetables filled the refrigerator. She'd been here for two days now, and she hadn't noticed anyone delivering groceries. And Lord knows she hadn't had time to pick anything up. Yet the refrigerator was packed with food—

"Hey, you're up early." Matt came into the kitchen. His skin was slick with perspiration and his shorts and T-shirt were soaked through. He was still breathing hard, as if he'd just finished some strenuous exercise.

"So are you," she managed to say.

Matt wiped a bead of sweat that trickled down his face as he looked at her. She was backlit by the light from the refrigerator, and her nightgown had become diaphanous. Her hair was still messy from sleep, and without makeup, her face looked fresh and young. But her body was all woman.

She had no idea of the show she was putting on for him. And wasn't that a shame. At first glance, he'd dared to hope that she was purposely trying to drive him crazy, that maybe she wanted him to pick her up and carry her into the nearest bedroom and make love to her.

God knows that was what he wanted to do.

"I didn't expect you to be up so early," she said, clutching a lemon to her chest.

Yeah, no kidding. She didn't move, so he reached past her into the open fridge for the orange juice. He drank directly from the plastic container. "I was out running," he told her. "I try to do five miles a day, but sometimes I miss."

"You've *already* run five miles this morning?" The tea kettle began to howl, and she closed the refrigerator door—too bad—and carried her lemon to the stove. She took the kettle off the burner, then turned to look at Matt skeptically. "Sometimes I think aliens have invaded your body. The Matt I know had to be dragged out of bed every morning to make it to school on time. I remember when noon on a Saturday was unbearably early for you."

"It's not a Saturday," Matt pointed out, finishing off the juice.

Maggie shook her head as she filled her mug with steaming water. "What time *did* you get up?"

"Four-thirty," Matt told her. "Usually I don't wake up till six o'clock, but for some reason I've been having more trouble than usual sleeping."

And guess what—or rather who—that reason is?

She didn't meet his eyes, because she knew.

"So far this morning," he told her, "I've memorized the first ten pages of my dialogue for the show, and I've gone grocery shopping."

"Grocery shopping this early?"

"The Stop and Shop is open twenty-four hours." He shrugged. "Sometimes if I can't sleep, I'll go over at three a.m." He smiled. "No crowds, you know."

"If you write out a list, I'll get the groceries next time we need them," Maggie volunteered.

But Matt shook his head. "No, that's okay. I like to do it."

She took her mug of tea and headed for the door. "Aliens have *definitely* invaded your body."

* * *

The Yankee Potato Chip factory was a huge brick building on the other side of town, surrounded by a parking area that was almost entirely filled with the employees' cars.

Maggie flipped through her file as Matt pulled up in front of a parking spot marked President near the main door.

"I don't know if I can do this," he said.

"Of course you can." She glanced up from the papers. "You own this company. You're perfectly within your rights to inspect—"

"No, I mean, I don't know if I can park here."

Maggie looked at the parking spot, then at Matt.

"I mean, that word *president,*" he said. "It implies a certain dignity, a certain knowledge. Maybe I should have them paint over it with Ignorant Son."

Maggie laughed. "I can think of better ways to use the money."

"So can I."

Inside the plant, the manager gave them a complete tour, explaining as they went what he saw as the strengths and weaknesses of the operation. Matt grasped each issue quickly, asking probing and intelligent questions. He stopped frequently as they walked, speaking to the employees, listening intently as they talked. By the time they were through, five hours later, Maggie was exhausted.

And Matt was silent in the car on the way home. It wasn't until an hour later that he turned from staring out the office window to say, "Have you come across blueprints and specs for the construction of the plant?"

"I just saw them." Maggie dug through the piles of papers and files, and found the thick three-ringed binder. She hefted the blueprints onto the table. "What do we need these for?"

"Hmm," Matt said. He punched the speaker phone and dialed. "Hey, Steve, it's Matthew Stone."

Steve? As in Stevie? As in her brother? She hadn't thought Matt was serious about...

"Yo, Matthew Stone." It was indeed Stevie. "'Sup, my man?"

"How are you at Internet research?"

"I think I once surfed around looking for historical information on the Ramones," Stevie said. "Why?"

Maggie rolled her eyes. "He got 1520 on his SATs."

"Hush there, Mags," Stevie said. "If you say that too loudly, you'll ruin my rep. Chicks don't dig the brainiacs."

"You want to bet?" Maggie countered.

"Steve, you want to earn twenty bucks an hour?" Matt asked.

"Tell me who to kill," her brother said. "I'll ask no questions."

"Consider yourself hired," Matt said.

"When do I start?"

"Now. I need you to get me all the information you can find about…got a pencil?"

"No," Stevie said, "but for twenty bucks an hour, I'll open a vein and write with my own blood."

"Get a pencil," Matt said. He looked up at Maggie and smiled. "I think I can improve this company."

"Okay, boys and girls." Dan Fowler raised his voice and the actors immediately fell silent. "Break's over. We've got mucho work to do tonight, so don't turn off your brains yet. Let's walk through the blocking for the opening number. Places on stage!"

The cast scrambled for their spots.

Maggie moved center stage. So far Dan's storm-trooper attitude was working. He was among the most efficient directors she'd ever worked with.

"Okay," Dan called. "Lucy is center. Spot comes up on her. The stage is dark and misty. Creepy crawly things start moving behind her…."

As he spoke, the cast walked through their on-stage movements.

"Lucy says, *Stop,* and the creepy things scramble away. Lights come up. Out from the wings come my men in top hats and tails. They pick her up and carry her around...."

Maggie looked nervously at the eight men who would be hoisting her onto their shoulders in this part of the opening number. They didn't lift her now, since it was only a walk-through, but they were going to spend a great deal of time rehearsing this particular move, to make it look effortless.

"On comes the full chorus, including all four secondary leads. We talk, talk, talk, sing, sing, sing. The stage is packed but the crowd parts as Cody enters upstage center."

This was as far as they'd got before the break.

"Okay, Cody," Dan ordered Matt. "You come directly downstage to Lucy. You sing your bit of the song and then you talk. Lucy, don't back away, I want you directly center stage for the kiss that's coming."

Maggie nodded, glancing up at Matt, who was making notes on his script.

"This kiss has to be very 1940s Hollywood," Dan continued. "Very big screen passionate. The music underneath swells, so you've got to time it just right. I think you've got eight bars of music to fill. Rhonda, dear, play it for them, would you?"

The accompanist played as Maggie and Matt listened. God, eight bars was an awfully long time.

"Try it with the music," Dan ordered. "Whenever you're ready."

Matt tossed down his script and positioned himself next to Maggie. "Your last line is what? *So go away,*" he remembered. "You should turn your back to me, as if you're going to walk away, stage left. I'm going to grab you by the arm and swing you back around toward me, okay?"

Maggie nodded, suddenly frightfully nervous.

"Give us about four measures before the kiss," Matt called to Rhonda, who began to play.

Maggie listened for the musical cue, then turned away

from Matt. He pulled her hard toward him, and she slammed into his chest. As Matt's lips met hers, she couldn't keep from giggling.

"Wrong!" Dan's nasal voice interrupted. "Stanton, you're as stiff as a board. Get into character! Think about your motivation! This is one of Lucy's fantasies, and she's as hot as hell for Cody, even though she won't admit it. Come on, people, what happened to that chemistry I saw at your audition? I want steam! I want pheromones! Try it again."

Once again the music started. Matt pulled her toward him, more gently this time, but she knew she was still too tense.

"I'm sorry," she said, pulling away before he kissed her.

"Can we take a few minutes?" Matt called to Dan.

"Not right now," Dan's bored voice intoned. "Work on it at home. We've got to move on."

"I couldn't get into character tonight," Maggie said in the car on the way home from rehearsal. "What's wrong with me?"

Matt glanced at her. Her expression in the dim reflection from the dashboard light was woeful. She was stuck inside of her own head, that's what was wrong.

He spun the steering wheel hard to the right, pulling into a side street. Maneuvering the car to the side of the road, he cut the engines and the lights, and they were plunged into total darkness.

"Matt—"

He grabbed her and kissed her.

"There," he said as he let her go. God, he didn't want to let her go. But that was probably why she was freaking out about kissing him in the first place. "*That's* how long those eight bars of music are. That wasn't so terrible was it?"

"No," she said faintly.

"Good," he said as matter-of-factly as he could manage. He started the car and did a one-eighty to get them back to the main road, glad that the car was too dark for her to see his face, because his eyes surely would have betrayed him.

Ten

Maggie read another selection from the endless pile of business reports as she ate a bowl of oatmeal. Matt sat across from her with a giant bowl of fruit.

She glanced up at him, and he smiled.

"Don't you ever eat anything but fruit for breakfast?" she asked.

Matt laughed. "Wow, we wouldn't do too well on the *Newlywed Game,* would we? No. The only thing I eat before noon is fruit."

"Why?"

"Because it makes me feel healthier."

Maggie gazed across the table at him, wishing he'd tell her why he'd been in the hospital three years ago. But whenever she brought the topic of conversation even vaguely in that direction, he changed the subject. Like right now.

"Speaking of newlyweds, your mother left a message on the answering machine. She wants us to come for Sunday dinner sometime next month. Talk about advance notice—I guess she figures this way we can't make up an excuse.''

Maggie sighed.

"Also, we've got a rehearsal tonight," he added.

She nodded. Great.

"We're doing a run-through of the first four scenes," he reminded her.

She nodded again, focusing her attention on her oatmeal.

He didn't get the message. "You know that means we've got to go in there and do that kiss from the opening scene."

The kiss. Oh, God.

"We should practice it," Matt said. "Don't you think?"

Maggie took a deep breath. "Yeah. We should. How about after lunch?"

"How about now?"

She looked at him, looked at the clock. Stevie was due to arrive in about fifteen minutes. "Okay." Somehow that made her feel safe.

Safer.

She stood up and headed toward the stairs.

Matt followed. "Where are you going?"

"To brush my teeth."

He caught her arm, pulled her in to him, and kissed her. His mouth tasted sweet, like watermelon and bananas with a hint of peaches thrown in.

"Yum," he said. "Brown sugar is definitely better than mint at this time of day."

Maggie's insides were doing flip-flops. He hadn't touched her since that kiss in his car after last week's disastrous rehearsal. She'd thought she was getting over him—or at least *used* to him. But if all it took was one little nothing kiss to make her knees feel weak, she was in big trouble.

"Here's what I'm going to do," Matt told her. He maneuvered her around as he spoke, going through it in slow motion, putting her into the right position for the best angle for the kiss. She tried to pay attention, but couldn't. "Lucy is really nuts about this guy, despite everything she says. We should show that right from the start."

As Maggie looked up into Matt's golden-greenish eyes, she realized that she understood Lucy's motivation perfectly. Because, damn it, she wanted Matt, no matter how hard she tried to deny it. Maybe that was her problem. This role was hitting too close to home. But maybe if she kissed him not as Lucy, but as *Maggie*—Maggie kissing Matt. He'd never know the difference, and she'd bring a certain authenticity to the role.

"Ready?" Matt asked.

"Yeah." She smiled. She was ready.

She stepped away from him as per the stage directions, and he pulled her toward him. This time, her movement was fluid, and she seemed to flow into his arms. Her lips went up to meet his, and she kissed him with all the fire in her soul. Unable to remember any of the blocking he'd just explained, she put her arms around his neck and pressed herself against him.

She heard him groan, and felt his hands move down her back to the curve of her derriere, as he kissed her harder, more deeply. His thigh pushed against her, and she opened herself to him, wrapping one of her legs around his. The sensation of her bare skin against his made her ignite, and she pulled him even closer.

And still she kissed him. The eight bars of background music could have played over and over and over again.

He slipped his hand up underneath her T-shirt and she shivered at the touch of his fingers against her skin. But then his hand cupped her breast and her heart nearly stopped beating.

"Yo, dudes— Oops, looks like I've come at a bad time."

Maggie and Matt jumped apart to see Stevie backing out of the room.

"We were just rehearsing," Maggie said breathlessly, her cheeks heating.

Matt sat down at the kitchen table and put his face in his hands. When he glanced up at Stevie, his expression was black, with only a hint of amusement in his eyes to offset it.

"Oh, gee, I just remembered, uh," Stevie said, "I've got to run some errands—"

"Oh, knock it off." Maggie was annoyed. "It wasn't what it looked like." She turned to Matt, blushing again as she remembered the feel of his hand on her breast, but determined to be professional. "I think we sort of overshot the mark, but at least I wasn't stiff."

Matt fought the urge to laugh at her word choice. *She* may not have been stiff....

"Do you want to try it again?" she asked.

"No," Matt said. He couldn't. He couldn't even stand up right now. "Maybe later."

Steve followed Maggie into the office, turning back to give Matt one last apologetic look. Matt made a face at him, shaking his head and rolling his eyes in frustration.

Stevie glanced in the direction Maggie had disappeared, then came back into the kitchen. "Maybe this is none of my business," he said quietly to Matt, "but she's in love with you."

"I wish."

"I'm telling you, it's true." Steve was serious. "I know her. She's... Just don't hurt her, okay?"

Matt was silent as he met the kid's gaze, uncertain how to respond. He couldn't decide himself which was worse torture—thinking she didn't love him or thinking maybe she did.

As usual, Maggie and Matt rolled into rehearsal several minutes early.

The assistant director, the stocky woman with the cat eyeglasses and the clipboard—her name was Dolores, but Dan

Fowler called her *Hey!*—approached Matt immediately, holding out a plastic-wrapped cup with a screw-on lid.

Maggie's stomach took a downward plunge.

"Time for you-know-what," Dolores said, tossing the cup to him. "The rules are I've got to walk you into the little boys' room."

Matt was serene. He just laughed. But when he glanced at Maggie, she knew this bothered him more than he was letting on.

She watched him walk away, wondering how it would feel to be haunted by a bad reputation. It didn't seem fair that people didn't notice how much he'd changed.

"Stanton!" Maggie turned to see Dan Fowler waving to her from up on the stage. "Come here for a sec."

"What's up?"

He was sitting on one of the chairs that served as makeshift scenery, and he motioned for her to sit, too. When she did, he crossed his arms and looked at her.

And she panicked. He was having second thoughts about casting her. He didn't think she was going to be able to do those kisses, and he was figuring out the best way to break the news....

"How long have you been seeing Stone?" he finally asked.

She blinked. Stone. Matt. "I'm not... I mean, we're not dating or anything, if that's what you mean."

"You always show up with him. And leave with him."

What was this leading up to? Maggie didn't have a clue. "We're housemates," she told him.

"You live together."

"Yeah, but as friends," she clarified. "We went to high school together."

"And you're not involved with him?"

"No." Why was he asking this?

Dan smiled, his beard parting to expose white, even teeth.

His eyes were warm, the dark brown flecked with gold. When he wasn't frowning, he was actually quite handsome.

"I was wondering if you'd have dinner with me tomorrow night," he said.

They ran through the opening number, even daring to hoist Maggie onto the shoulders of the men's chorus. It was awkward and she giggled, but they were on their way.

Then the dread kiss approached. Matt gave her hand a reassuring squeeze as they began the sequence.

He pulled her to him, and instead of kissing her immediately, he gazed down into her eyes for several beats. When his lips finally met hers, Maggie melted. She forced herself to keep the embrace open, only putting her arms around his neck at the very end of the musical phrase.

When he pulled back, he didn't immediately move away. He looked into her eyes again, and smiled.

"Perfect!" Dan shouted. "That's *exactly* what I wanted."

Maggie finished up the song on a cloud of relief and desire.

Al, the choreographer, was nearly as much of a slave driver as Dan Fowler. Sweat dripped off Maggie's face as they stopped for a break.

"One of these days," she swore as she threw herself onto the stage next to Matt, "I'm going to be in a show that rehearses in a theater that has air-conditioning."

The dance they were doing was a blend of athletic street dancing and graceful jazz, with several steps reminiscent of the old dirty dancing craze thrown in. Most of the steps had no body contact—instead they had to maintain eye contact. Maggie found that almost more dizzying than when Matt actually touched her.

Almost.

She rolled onto her stomach and put her chin in her hand. "Matt? How well do you know Dan Fowler?"

He turned his head to look at her. "I don't know. Well

enough. I know he's a good director—he gets the job done, and his end result is better than average. Why?''

She shrugged.

''Why?'' Matt asked again, his eyes narrowing. ''What aren't you telling me?''

God, he knew her too well. ''Nothing,'' she said.

''*Tell* me.''

She laughed. ''No.''

''Tell me.'' He rolled onto his side, head propped up on one hand. She could tell from looking at him that he wasn't going to let this slide.

And okay. Maybe she could actually get a rise out of him. She glanced around to make sure no one else was in earshot and Matt leaned in closer as she said, ''Dan asked me out.''

He laughed. ''You're kidding.''

Was that jealousy in his eyes, or just amusement? ''No,'' she said. ''He asked me to have dinner with him.''

''Dinner with Dan,'' Matt mused. ''Do you think he takes the time to eat anything but fast food?''

No, it definitely wasn't jealousy. Was it possible he really didn't care if she had dinner with Dan…? ''I'll let you know,'' she said, even though she'd turned down the director.

Matt froze. ''You're *going?*''

Okay. *That* was a slightly better reaction.

''Actually—'' she said, but he cut her off.

''I'm sorry,'' he said. ''I didn't mean to… He's great. He's perfect for you, Mags. He's honest and solid and…''

''Oh,'' Maggie said.

''Break's over,'' Dan announced.

Matt gave her a smile as he pulled himself to his feet.

She'd been hoping for jealousy—not for Matt to give her and Dan his blessing.

Eleven

At 1:00 a.m., Matt rose stiffly from his seat at the conference table.

He'd worked muscles in that dance rehearsal tonight that he'd forgotten he had.

The evening had been an emotional workout, too.

The more he thought about it, the more he was convinced that Dan Fowler was perfect for Maggie. The guy was honest and dependable and basically decent. Not too tactful, but that was mostly by choice, since being tactful took too much time.

Matt also knew that Dan had a strict personal policy of never, *ever* dating the women from his shows. His feelings for Maggie had to be pretty intense if he was willing to break his rules to ask her out. Of course that didn't surprise Matt at all. The surprise would have been if Dan *hadn't* fallen instantly in love with her.

If he had to handpick a guy for Maggie to become involved with, Dan would be at the top of his list. It couldn't have turned out better if Matt had planned it.

So here he sat, sick with jealousy, knowing without a doubt that no one, not even Dan Fowler, could love Maggie more than he did.

But he also knew that his love for her would do her absolutely no good if he wasn't around.

Matt stretched, knowing that he wasn't going to sleep tonight. Instead of lying awake in bed, he might as well make himself as comfortable as possible. He went into his father's master bedroom—the room Maggie had fallen asleep in, that first night she spent here—and into the bath, where he uncovered the hot tub.

He tried to be quiet as he took the stairs up to his room. There was a paperback book up there he'd started reading several nights ago. He'd finish it long before dawn, but at least he'd fill a few hours.

He paused as he reached the landing on the third floor, looking at Maggie's closed door. Slowly, he moved toward her room, stopping outside, staring at the doorknob, wishing for the first time in years for a beer.

If he had a beer or two or four, he could use the alcohol as an excuse for reaching out and opening that door. Without the beer, the responsibility was all his.

Maggie sat up in bed, her heart racing. As she listened, Matt's footsteps faded back down the hallway and up the stairs to his bedroom.

With a sigh of frustration, she sank back in the bed. She couldn't take much more of this.

Then she heard him coming back down the stairs, and again, she held her breath. But he went past her door without stopping this time.

Don't think. Just do it.

But even as she threw back the covers and opened her door, she couldn't help but think.

If she went to him, and threw herself at him again, they would probably make love.

Still, she went down the stairs, down the hall past the dining room, past the living room, to the master bedroom. The connecting bathroom door was ajar.

Quietly she went to the door and peeked in. Matt crouched next to the tub, dipping his fingers in to test the temperature.

She closed her eyes and pushed the door open. "Hi," she said, and he jumped to his feet.

He didn't say a word. He simply looked at her.

Now that she was actually here, her confidence faded. She crossed her arms in front of her, suddenly aware that she was wearing only her nightgown. "I heard you going up and down the stairs," she said. "I know you can't sleep. I can't, either."

And still he didn't say a word, didn't move.

"Do you want to talk?" she asked.

Matt shook his head, no. Jeez, she always knew just where to stand to be perfectly backlit. He could see her body through her gown, and he wanted her. Man, he wanted her. He had to get her out of here. This was just too difficult.

"I wanted to tell you that I'm not going out with Dan," she said, pushing her hair back behind her ear and sitting on the very edge of the wicker chair. "It would just be...too weird."

No, Matt knew he should say, *it's okay. Dan's a good man. You should go.* But he couldn't make himself say it.

Maggie rolled her eyes. "I started thinking, what if my mother calls when I'm out? If you answer the phone, what are you going to tell her? Maggie's out on a *date?* She thinks we're married."

"But we're not," Matt said tightly. He forced himself to turn away from her and instead stared sightlessly out the window.

"The truth is, I told you I was going to have dinner with him, because I was hoping you'd be jealous."

Oh, God. It had worked. However, it had also worked to convince him that Maggie deserved someone more like Dan—and less like Matt.

''You should go back to bed,'' he said, his back to her, praying that she wouldn't say anything else. ''Please? I really don't want to talk right now.''

We don't have to talk, Maggie wanted to say, but the words stuck in her throat.

''Please,'' he said again. It was little more than a breath, an exhale, but it held all the emotion of a cry of pain. ''Go.''

And there she went. Running away. Too scared to speak out, to speak up.

Matt didn't turn around as she left the room.

Maggie lay in the darkness, looking up at the shadowy canopy that was draped above her bed, calling herself names.

Chicken. Coward. Scaredy-cat. Baby. Wimp. Only a wimp would have run away like that.

The digital numbers of her alarm clock switched from 1:59 to 2:00.

Maggie swore softly. Sleeplessness had never been a problem for her before. Of course, she'd never loved anyone the way she loved Matthew.

And she did love him.

So why was she lying up here all alone?

Because she didn't want to ruin their friendship? It was no longer a good excuse, because, face it, their friendship was already affected. She wasn't going to pretend to herself that she didn't feel anything for him, because damn it, she did. And she wasn't going to hang back anymore, careful to stay his buddy. She wouldn't be able to bear watching him find some other woman to spend time with.

So where did that leave her?

She knew that if she went to him and openly asked him to spend the night with her, he wouldn't refuse her.

But how would she feel in the morning?

That was a question that only the morning light could bring the answer to. The question facing her right now was, how did she feel tonight?

Maggie shivered, remembering the sensation of his lips on hers, of his body against hers. She wanted him, and she knew he wanted her. She'd seen the way he'd looked at her when she'd walked into the bathroom. She'd seen hunger in his eyes.

She stood up and crossed to the door. Taking a deep breath, she put her hand on the knob and turned it, swinging the door open.

And oh, dear Lord, Matt stood there, his hair down around his shoulders, his handsome face unsmiling. Even though the night had turned cool, he wore only his running shorts, and she could see the taut muscles in his chest rise and fall with each breath he took

Gazing up into his beautiful eyes, Maggie knew that the desire she saw there mirrored that in her own eyes. She wondered if he could hear her heart pounding from where he stood.

She wasn't sure who moved first, but he reached for her as she fell into his arms.

Matt kissed her, desperately, ferociously. And she clung to him, her mouth demanding, her arms wound tightly around his neck as he pulled her closer to him. Her tongue was in his mouth, and his hands swept the length of her body, and he knew that he shouldn't be doing this, but he couldn't make himself stop.

Their legs intertwined, and she rubbed herself against him. And still he couldn't stop himself from reaching down to lift her up so that her legs encircled him.

He pulled back then to look into her face.

She gazed back at him, her cheeks flushed from the heat they'd created, and he felt giddy. He buried his face in her neck, breathing in her scent. She smelled like Maggie—clean and sweet. How many times in his life had he stood close enough to inhale her fragrance, close enough to drive himself mad with wanting her?

She pulled his face up and kissed him.

But again he pulled back. "It's not too late to stop," he said, his voice sounding breathless to his own ears. He prayed that she wouldn't agree.

"Says who?" she countered, tightening the grip of her legs around him, then laughing at the expression on his face.

Another kiss propelled them across the room and they tumbled together onto Maggie's bed, Matt kissing her again and again in an explosion of need and desire.

"I came up here to talk," he tried to tell her.

"I can't talk right now," she said, kissing his cheeks, his eyes, his lips. "I'm busy."

He laughed. She kissed his neck, and he closed his eyes, his laughter turning to a sigh of pleasure as he touched her, as he filled his hands with her breasts, as he stroked the smoothness of her soft skin.

"It's important," he breathed.

"I'm listening." She trailed kisses down his chest to his stomach.

Matt felt her tugging at the waistband of his shorts, and he grabbed her wrist. He spun her over and pinned her to the bed with his body, his hands holding her arms above her head.

"Now I'm really listening." She smiled up at him.

Unable to resist, he brought his mouth down to hers and kissed her slowly, sweetly, deeply. When he pulled back, she was trembling.

And he was, too.

"I really tried to stay away from you," he confessed. "I know this is selfish, but I couldn't help myself because..." He took a deep breath and said it. "I love you, Mags."

"You don't have to say that," Maggie said quietly.

"But I do," he told her. "I'm crazy in love with you. I have been for years. It's important to me that you know that."

She looked searchingly into his eyes, her expression dubious. "Matt, I'm not one of those women who have to think that you're in love with them before they'll—"

"No. Mags, I know that," Matt said. "This isn't a line. I love you. You have to believe me. God, I've never been more sincere in my entire life."

She shook her head. "It doesn't matter—"

"It does to me. Damn it, I love you! You *better* believe me."

Maggie stared up at Matt. His eyes held a glint of determination she'd only seen since he'd begun improving the business, and suddenly, she realized that he was serious.

He was serious.

He *loved* her.

It was a good thing she was lying down, or she'd fall over. "I believe you," she whispered.

Relief and satisfaction flared in his eyes before he leaned forward to kiss her again. His mouth caressed hers, gently at first, then with greater need. He was on top of her, and she wrapped her legs around him, pulling him even closer to her.

She was on fire. Everywhere he touched her, she burned. He stopped kissing her, and she pulled her arms free, reaching up around his neck to bring his mouth back to hers.

But he resisted. "Maggie…" His face was so serious.

She pressed one finger to his lips. "Matt, I love you, too," she told him with a tremulous smile. "Make love to me."

But he didn't smile back. In fact, he looked even more troubled. "There's more I have to tell you."

Maggie pushed him off of her. "No."

Well, *that* surprised him.

"Not now." She crossed to the dresser and dug through her purse. Matt sat up slightly, leaning back on one elbow, watching her. "You just told me that you love me." She found what she was searching for and crossed back to him, picking up his free hand and slapping the little package into it. "Use this and prove it."

He looked at her in amazement. "You carry condoms in your purse?"

Maggie crossed her arms. "Oh, great," she said in mock anger. "Now you want to talk about that, too?"

He pulled her down onto the bed with him and kissed her. Maggie wasn't sure exactly how it happened, but when she came up for air, she was no longer wearing her nightgown.

He ran his hands and his eyes over her body, and Maggie felt the familiar rush of heat to her face as she blushed. Then a deeper, more powerful heat infused her as his mouth found her breast.

She ran her fingers though Matt's long, shiny hair, arching her hips up toward him. She could feel him through his shorts, but that wasn't good enough.

He clearly thought the same thing, rolling over and, in one quick motion, he yanked them down and kicked his legs free.

Matt had dropped the condom on the bed, and now he reached for it and put it on. He really didn't need it—there was no way he could get her pregnant, and he hadn't been with anyone else in—God, it was years. But it would take too long to explain, and Maggie *had* been adamant about this not being the right time for conversation.

He lay beside her and kissed her, intending to take his time. He'd waited so long for this moment. Every minute, every second was going to count.

But when she opened her mouth to him, when she threw one leg over his hips, he knew he couldn't wait. And she was just as eager. He was surprised by her strength as she pulled him on top of her.

She reached for him, guiding him and then…

Oh, *yes.*

She moved with him, breathing his name, kissing him, touching him, surrounding him.

Time stood still and there was only Maggie, only these incredible sensations she was making him feel. His desire for her blazed through him, his heart pumping fire through his veins. His need consumed him and he heard himself call out her name as she exploded around him, as the rush of his own release nearly stopped his heart.

She kissed him, so sweetly, so completely, and he knew without a doubt that he would love her until the day that he died.

Please God, don't let it be too soon.

Matt rolled over, pulling her with him so that her head rested on his shoulder. He kissed her again and again, kisses for the sake of kissing, delighting in the softness of her lips, the sweetness of her mouth.

Her eyes were so filled with love, he nearly wept.

"I love you," he whispered.

She smiled. "I believe you. You're a good actor, but you're not *that* good."

Matt laughed, but it faded away as he realized what he had to do now. There was no putting it off any longer. "We have to talk."

Maggie sighed, running her fingers across his chest and arms, already starting to make him crazy again.

He couldn't do this here. Not like this. "Why don't we go into the kitchen?" he suggested. "Make a cup of tea?"

Something in his voice must've telegraphed his anxiety, because she sat up. "I'm listening," she said. "Really."

"Can we go downstairs?" he asked.

She nodded and reached for her nightgown.

Twelve

After putting the kettle on the stove, Matt pushed the kitchen windows closed. The night air had gone from cool to cold, with the wind blowing off the sound. Maggie had a sweatshirt on over her nightgown, but she still shivered slightly.

He sat down at the table, across from her, fiddling with the napkin holder as he tried to figure out how to start.

"Now that we're down here," he said with a laugh, "I'm not sure how to say this."

She reached across the table, putting her hands on his. "Whatever you have to say, it can't be *that* terrible, can it?"

He met her eyes. "Mags, it's about when I went into the hospital. And yes, it's terrible."

She looked down at their hands for a moment, and when she looked back up, into his eyes again, there was so much love on her face, it nearly took his breath away. "You know there's nothing you can say that will make me stop loving you. *Nothing.*"

"I had cancer," he told her. There. He said it.

Maggie couldn't breathe. She stared across the table at him, waiting, hoping, *praying* for it to be a joke. Any minute now he'd tell her the punchline.

"I was diagnosed," Matt said softly, "with Hodgkin's disease."

"Oh, my God," she whispered. It was indeed a joke, a cruel, horrible joke of fate. "Was? Past tense?"

"Well, yeah," he said. Then he shook his head. "No, I don't want to lie to you." He looked up at her, his face apologetic, his eyes dark with unhappiness. "The truth is, I hope it's gone, but I don't know for sure. It's been almost a year since I had my last treatment of chemo. The odds of a recurrence are pretty high for the first year—"

"How high?" Tears were slipping down her cheeks.

"Fifty percent," he said. "Sixty percent, maybe more. I'm on the high end, because my cancer's already recurred."

How could he sit there so calmly and tell her that the odds of his cancer returning were so terribly high?

"But you know, instead of saying I've got a sixty percent chance of dying, I say there's a forty percent chance I'm going to live to be an old man. And that's great. That's... There was a time during my second round of chemo that my chances of surviving barely broke double digits," he said quietly.

"You had chemotherapy," Maggie said, pulling her hands away to wipe her eyes and cheeks. "For how long?"

"Two six-month courses. The second was intensive and kind of experimental."

"God, Matt, why didn't you tell me?"

"Before we made love? I tried to—"

"No, damn it!" Maggie hit the table with the palm of her hand and the flower vase came perilously close to toppling. "When you were in the hospital!"

The teakettle began to whistle, and they both stood up. Maggie reached the stove first, switching off the gas. She turned back to Matt and glared at him. "Why didn't you call me?"

He shook his head. "I couldn't. Besides, what was I supposed to say? Hi, how are you, it's been ten years, and oh, by the way, I have cancer?"

"Why not? God, do you know how it makes me feel that you were in that hospital, and I didn't even know? I was living my stupid, mundane life, completely unaware that any minute you were maybe going to *die?*"

She began to cry again, and Matt wrapped his arms around her, holding her close.

"I didn't die," he told her. "I'm not going to die. Not now. Especially not now."

She glared at him. "Cancer isn't something you can wish away."

He shrugged, pushing her hair back from her face. "Hey, why not? I'm willing to try anything. And wishing is relatively inexpensive and pain-free." He kissed her gently. "Tonight was so perfect. I'm sorry I had to ruin it."

"What, now you're apologizing for having had *cancer?*" With her arms wrapped around his waist, he felt so solid, so vital. She could hear his heart beating, steady and strong. It didn't seem possible that cancer was growing inside of Matt's perfect body. "I'm so glad you finally told me."

"I had to," he said.

"No, you didn't." She tilted her head back to look at him.

"Yeah, I did. If you love me, you deserve to know. I just…don't be scared, okay?"

"I'm not scared," Maggie told him. No, she was terrified. She reached up to touch his hair. "When you had chemo…"

His smile turned rueful. "Yup. I was balder than Yul Brenner. Except I didn't look as good as he did."

"You probably haven't cut it since…"

"Only to even it out." Matt sat down, pulling Maggie onto his lap. "Or to trim the ends. I kind of have this superstition. It's silly…"

"Tell me."

"It's dumb," he admitted, "but after my hair started growing back in, I kind of saw it as a symbol of life. And I got this crazy idea that if I didn't cut my hair, the cancer wouldn't come back. I know it's ridiculous, but it's gotten to the point where it's become like a superstition or a good-luck charm. It's kind of like lifting your feet and touching the roof of the car when you cross railroad tracks, so you'll have good luck. Deep down you know it's not going to matter one damn bit, but you still do it—just in case."

She fingered his hair again. "Gee, if you're never going to cut it, it's going to get pretty long. In about five years, you're going to have to hire someone to carry your hair around behind you."

"I hope so," Matt said.

His eyes were sober as Maggie gazed into them, and she realized with a jolt of fear that there was a very good chance Matt wouldn't be alive in five years. "When will you know?" she asked.

He knew what she meant. "I'm flying out to California at the end of next week."

"California?"

"Yeah, I suppose I could go into Yale New Haven Hospital, but I'd rather go back to the doctor who treated me," Matt told her. "We know each other pretty well. They'll do a series of tests to find out if I'm still clean."

"And if you are?" she asked. "What then?"

"Then I get happy." He traced her lips with his thumb. "Then I come back and we make love for the rest of our long, happy lives."

Maggie started to cry.

"Whoa," Matt said. "Mags, that was the *good* part."

"I love you," she said. "Don't you dare die!"

Matt held her close, his heart squeezing with pain, knowing that he couldn't make her any promises.

* * *

Maggie turned on the light in the late Mr. Stone's ostentatious office and went straight to the bookshelf. It didn't take her long to find what she wanted—she'd seen the books before, even though she hadn't realized their significance. She pulled the big *American Cancer Society's Cancer Handbook* off the shelf, along with several others.

As she looked through the books, she realized that her suspicions were true. Mr. Stone had these books because he knew about Matt's cancer. He had used a pink highlight pen to mark the sections on Hodgkin's, and she silently thanked him as she leafed through, reading the marked pages.

She was still sitting there an hour later, books spread out in front of her on the huge desk, when Matt came in. His breezy steps slowed as he saw what she was reading.

"Sometimes it's scarier to read about it," Matt said. "The books tell you only so much and make you realize how many unanswered questions you have. And if they go into any kind of detail, you need a medical degree to understand—"

"There's a lot you didn't tell me." Maggie tried hard to keep her voice from shaking. "You didn't tell me that even if there's no sign of a recurrence, that doesn't mean the cancer's gone. All it means is that you have a better chance of living five more years. And if you live the five years without a recurrence, all *that* means is you have a better chance of living *another* five years. And it just keeps on going. Forever."

"Mags, people who live for five years without their cancer returning are virtually cured."

She was silent, just watching him. He stared down at the red carpeting for a moment, then back up at her. His expression was unreadable, his eyes guarded. "Look, I know how tough it is to come to grips with this. If you don't want to deal with it, with *me,* I understand—"

"No!" Maggie stood up fast and the big leather chair rocked wildly behind her. "I just need to know *everything.* Don't hide stuff from me, okay?"

He nodded, watching her pace. "Okay. Then there is something else I should tell you."

Maggie froze, gripped with a sudden rush of fear. "What?"

"The chemo and radiation made me sterile," he said. "I'll never be able to have children." He laughed without humor. "At least not the regular way."

Relief flooded through her. She'd thought he was going to tell her that he felt sick again, that he thought the cancer was coming back.

"I've got some deposits in a sperm bank," he said, "but that's not very romantic—"

"I read something in here that scared me," she interrupted him. "I read that one of the symptoms of this kind of cancer is sleep problems. Night sweats and—"

"No," he said. "The problems I'm having sleeping now is different. It's in my head, Mags. I don't sleep much because it's important to me not to waste any time." He stood up, crossed behind the desk and threw open the heavy shutters. Sunlight streamed in, and then cool fresh air, as he opened the big window. He turned to face her. "I don't kid myself. I know I might not be here this time next year."

"How do you live with that?" she asked softly. "Tell me, so I can learn how to live with it, too."

He smiled at her. "You start by believing in miracles. You know, when I was diagnosed, they gave me seven months, tops. But here I am, three years later." He put his arms around her, kissed her sweetly. "Every day I wake up, Mags, I think of as a gift. I've been given one more day to live, and I'm not going to waste it."

"But don't you feel it's not fair? Don't you feel cheated?"

"*Cheated?*" He laughed. "No way. I've been given a second chance. I won big, Maggie. They told me I was going to die. I was dead, it was a given. But miracles happen." He kissed her again. "I'm more convinced of that than ever after last night. Not only am I not dead, but I'm living my dream. How incredibly great is that?''

He kissed her again, and she clung to him.

''Let's go back to bed,'' he breathed into her ear.

She made herself laugh instead of crying. ''Taking a nap in the middle of the day,'' she teased. ''Doesn't that fall into the 'waste of time' category?''

He laughed, a glint in his eyes. ''Absolutely not.''

Matt took her hand and pulled her out of the office, into the main part of the house, all the way up the stairs to his tower room. The blinds were up and the windows were open wide, letting in the sun and the ocean breeze. The sky was a brilliant blue—it was like being on top of the world.

He undressed her slowly, taking his time to touch and kiss her, as she did the same to him.

And there they were. Naked in the sunlight.

They took their sweet time, falling together back on his bed, touching, tasting, exploring.

He would have spent hours in foreplay, but it was Maggie who grew impatient.

She pushed him back on the bed, straddling him, plunging him deeply inside of her.

She laughed at his gasp of pleasure, smiling down at him as she moved on top of him, setting him on fire.

''Hey,'' he tried to slow her down. ''If you keep doing that, I'm going to lose control.''

''I know,'' she said. ''I like it when you lose control.''

Oh dear God, what she was doing to him… But… ''Mags, I'm serious—''

''Hey,'' she said, pretending to frown at him. ''Who's on top?''

He had to laugh. ''You are. Mistress.''

She laughed at that. ''Damn straight.'' God, she was so incredibly sexy. ''Tell me when,'' she ordered him.

Matt could see her love for him in her eyes, in her smile, on her face, radiating from her, and he knew that all the hell he'd been through had been worth it—if only to live for this one moment. And there would be other moments like this one, he knew, not just making love, but sharing their love.

She loved him. Maggie *loved* him. And it was all over for him.

"When," he gasped, and just like that, she dropped out of warp speed. She didn't stop moving, she just made each stroke last an eternity, and he crashed into her in slow motion. And then she was coming, too, and he couldn't believe how incredible it felt.

She collapsed on top of him, and he held her tightly, their two hearts pounding.

"I like it when you lose control," she whispered again.

Matt laughed. "Yeah, that kind of worked for me, too. Where did you, um, learn to…?"

She lifted her head to look down at him, her eyes sparkling with restrained laughter. "I'm extremely well read." Her smile was devilish. "I liked the *mistress* thing."

Oh, dear Lord, it was possible he was the luckiest man in the world. "I love you so much," he told her.

And just like that, she started to cry.

"Oh, Mags," he said, his heart breaking. "God, please don't cry." He kissed her. "Don't be sad—"

"I'm not," she told him, kissing him, too. "I'm crying because I'm so *happy*. Oh, Matt, I'm so glad you didn't die."

He held her close. "Me, too, Maggie," he whispered. "Me, too."

Thirteen

Maggie sat in the theater, looking up at the stage.

Matt was rehearsing a song that his character sang with a vocal quartet. The soprano, a woman named Charlene, was flirting with him, standing too close, her hand lingering far too long on his arm.

He glanced over at Maggie, caught her eye, and made a face.

"Some things never change," she mouthed to him, and he laughed. "Behave," she added, with a mock frown.

"Yes, mistress," he mouthed back, heat in his eyes.

Oh, dear Lord, it was hot in here. And when would this rehearsal end?

The soprano was watching them, and Maggie smiled sweetly up at her. Tough luck, Charlene. Matt was taken.

"Time to take ten, no *fifteen*," Dan Fowler shouted, and the cast scattered, knowing that the director was serious about the small amounts of time he allotted for breaks. "Stone! It's time to deal with your hair."

"Yeah, sorry, Dan." Matt dug into this pocket for a pony-tail holder and pulled his hair back from his face. "I'll keep it pulled back if you want."

"I want it cut." Dan's nasal voice echoed in the auditorium. "I got a friend here tonight who cuts hair down in New York. She's ready to cut your hair right now."

Matt froze. Maggie watched him make himself relax, one muscle at a time before he spoke.

"Tell her thank you," he said, "but I'm not going to cut my hair."

"Hello," Dan said. "Cody works for one of the biggest advertising firms in Manhattan. He doesn't have long hair."

"I'm sorry," Matt said, "but we're going to have to work around this. I'll tie it back and put it under my shirt. I'll wear a wig if you want me to."

Dan walked to the stage, followed by a woman in a black stretch jumpsuit. "Come on, Stone. It'll grow back. Getting your hair cut isn't going kill you. Don't make me treat you like some rude child and tie you down—"

Matt backed away. "No," he said, his voice sharp.

Dan stopped short. "Jeez, I was kidding."

Maggie quickly climbed on stage and moved to stand beside Matt. She took his hand, squeezing it, and he glanced at her.

"What's with you tonight, Stone?" Dan's eyes narrowed. "You seem a little… I don't know. Strung-out?" He turned toward the rows of seats. "Hey, Dolores!"

Dolores appeared instantly, as if Dan had conjured her up. She held a plastic specimen cup in her hand.

Matt exhaled loudly. It was similar to a laugh, but it held not a drop of humor. "I just don't want to get my hair cut," he said. "That doesn't mean I'm on drugs."

"Take the cup. You know what to do."

"Are you saying that I can't disagree with you without having to take a urine test?" Matt's voice rose in volume despite his efforts to stay cool.

"This is not a disagreement," Dan said. "This is weird behavior. Go do your thing, and then get back here and get your hair cut. Dolores, go with him to the men's."

Matt didn't move. He just stared at Dan.

"What, you're not going to do it?" Dan asked. "Then get off my stage."

Matt still didn't move.

"You think you're irreplaceable? Well, you're wrong. I'll take over your part myself. No sweat. In fact, it would be a real pleasure." Dan's gaze flicked over to Maggie just long enough so Matt knew exactly what he meant.

Two little words were on his lips. Two little words that would tell Dan Fowler exactly what he should do with himself.

But Maggie was watching him, and he closed his eyes instead. He took a deep, deep breath in through his nose. He held it, and then exhaled in a large swoosh through his mouth. Eyes still closed, he drew in more air.

"What's he doing?" Dan asked.

"I think he's trying not to kill you," Dolores said dryly.

Matt took three or four more deep breaths, then slowly opened his eyes. He took the specimen cup from Dolores, and even managed to give her a smile. "I'll take your drug test," he said quietly to Dan, "but you're not going to cut my hair."

Dan Fowler's face was expressionless as Maggie explained why Matt didn't want his hair cut.

But then he laughed. "You really believe this crap, don't you?"

Maggie's mouth dropped open. "Are you saying that you *don't?*"

"Yeah, I think it's fiction. Stone is what I call a pathological actor," Dan told her. "When you deal with him, it's impossible to tell where reality ends and fiction begins. I'm not sure he's able to tell the difference himself." He laughed again. "So much for you and him not being involved, huh? When did that happen?"

She didn't answer.

"I suppose that's what I get, making you guys practice all that kissing at home," he continued. "Stone's playing some kind of game with your head, Maggie. Cancer—my ass."

Maggie stood up, spitting out the very same words she knew Matt had worked so hard not to say. "You may have no trouble replacing Matt," she added, "but keep in mind that if he goes, I go, too."

"Relax," Dan said. "We'll work around the hair thing. I don't want either of you to quit, okay? I just think you shouldn't take everything Stone says as the absolute truth. Did he say which hospital he was in?"

"Yeah. The Cancer Center at the University of Southern California. Maybe you should call and check, make sure he really was there, Dan."

"Maybe I will. Oh, and in case you were wondering, his urine tests have all come up clean. So far, anyway."

"It must really suck to be you," Maggie told him.

He nodded, turning back to the papers on the table in front of him. "Yeah. Right now I wish I were Stone—imagine that." He glanced up at her. "I'll be here if you need me, you know, when you wake up from this dream you're living in."

"I won't need you," she said, seething with indignation as she walked away.

Fourteen

When the alarm went off at eight o'clock, Maggie was already awake.

Ever since Matt had left for California two days ago, she'd been unable to eat or sleep. The only thing she could actually do was work, so she'd dug in, working late into the night on the monthly accounts, searching for some legal principle to fall back on if they couldn't increase profits.

Stevie and Matt had had their heads together for over a week now, working on something that Matt didn't want to show her until they'd done some more research.

Maggie was still trying to get her hands on that mysterious codicil—tracking it down had been much harder than she'd thought.

She got out of bed, showered quickly and was soon downstairs in the office, wishing for the nine millionth time that she'd been able to talk Matt into letting her go with him.

But he'd been adamant she remain in Connecticut. ''I want to keep then and now completely separate,'' he'd said to her the evening before his flight. He'd smiled at her lazily as they lay in his bed. "I think of it as something out of science fiction—the time I spent there was kind of an alternate reality. If that and my present reality ever meet—boom. The whole world will explode."

Maggie had rolled her eyes. "Matt, get serious."

And he did. "I left behind an awful lot of pain and fear at the Cancer Center," he told her. "I know they saved my life—at least they gave me some extra time—but it's not a nice place. The tests aren't a lot of fun. And waiting for the results…"

"That's why I want to go with you," she said.

"And that's why I don't want you to come," he said. "Please. I don't want you to see me there, like that."

So here she was, waiting for him.

He'd called when his flight landed in L.A., and again several times over the past few days. He'd told her he wouldn't have any test results until Tuesday night.

It was finally Tuesday.

Maggie looked at the clock.

Eight-thirty in the morning.

It was going to be another long day.

The telephone finally rang at nine o'clock that evening.

"Hey, Mags." Matt sounded exhausted.

Maggie closed her eyes briefly, taking a deep breath. "Matt." Tell me. *Tell me, tell me, tell me.*

"Sorry I couldn't call earlier," he said. "You wouldn't believe what I had to go through to get to a phone."

If he were okay, he would have told her without any delay, wouldn't he? Maggie tried to still the fear that was rising into her throat. "Tell me," she said.

"Well, there's good news and bad news," he said. "I thought I was going to be able to catch the red-eye home tonight—"

"Oh, God," she breathed.

"No, that's the bad news," he said.

"Then tell me the good news."

"The good news is that there's no definite bad news," he said. "The test results came back…weird. They want to re-test before telling me anything."

"Weird how?" she asked.

"I don't know," he said. "I just know we're back in wait mode. If you want to know the truth, I think there was some kind of error in the lab and they're just afraid to tell me. I wish they would. It's better than thinking—"

"Matt, I'm going to fly out," she said.

"No," he said. "Don't. I've been picturing you sleeping in my bed, or working downstairs and… It's been a great focus for me, Maggie. I need you there, waiting for me." Over the line, she heard a murmured voice talking to Matt. "I have to go," he said. "I'll call you as soon as I know anything. I love you."

"I'm coming out there," she told him, but the connection was already broken.

The earliest flight to LAX left Bradley Airport several hours after midnight.

Maggie bought a ticket online, and then went about the business of getting through the day.

She had to file more papers in New Haven in an effort to get a look at that damned elusive codicil to Mr. Stone's will. And there was a rehearsal starting at seven. She'd have to leave a little early to get to the airport on time.

The day passed interminably slowly. Maggie waited in line after line, dealing with disinterested, apathetic clerks as she tried to find out what had gone wrong with her petition to release that codicil.

She ate a tuna fish sandwich standing up in a dreary deli, then went back to slug it out with more bureaucrats. At three o'clock, after demanding to speak to a supervisor, she found out that there was a form missing from the paperwork she'd submitted, and she had to get Matt's signature before anything else could be done.

She went out to join the wall of traffic on Route 95.

Back at the house, she hurried inside, only to find that she'd gone out without turning on the telephone answering machine. Matt might have called her, but she would never know. Bitterly disappointed, she sank down on the living room floor and cried.

Dan had taken the news that Matt wasn't at rehearsal and that Maggie was going to leave early in surprisingly good form. He made arrangements for one of the men in the chorus to read and walk through the part of Cody for the evening.

They were running the second half of the second act, starting with a solo Maggie sang, alone in Lucy's bedroom. The scene immediately following the song was the same one she and Matt had auditioned with—the scene with that brain rattling kiss.

It didn't matter how many times they practiced it, Matt still left her breathless. God, she missed him.

Rhonda, the accompanist, started to play, and Maggie tried to focus on the song. It was a plaintive ballad, in which Lucy, after becoming engaged to Cody's rival, wonders why she's feeling so miserable when she should be happy. Maggie didn't have any problem calling up feelings of misery this evening.

Please God, let Matt and me have a happy ending.

Finally, quietly, the song ended, and Maggie closed her eyes, following Dan's blocking.

"Lucy, are you still awake?"

That voice was unmistakable, and Maggie's heart leapt as she snapped her head up.

Matt stood on the other side of the stage, wearing his familiar blue jeans and high voltage white T-shirt. His face looked tired and maybe a little pale, but he was smiling at her.

"Matt!"

Two long strides brought him toward her, even as she launched herself at him. His arms went around her, and then she was kissing him—hungrily, breathlessly, impatiently, thankfully.

She pulled back to look up into his eyes.

He'd cut his hair. It was short—similar to the way he'd worn it in high school. She tried to swallow her fear as she wondered if he'd cut his hair because it hadn't worked as a good luck charm.

"I'm okay," he told her. "Maggie, I'm clean. The cancer hasn't come back."

The rush of relief was so intense that she swayed. He held her tightly, kissing her again.

"Uh, people." Dan's voice penetrated Maggie's euphoria. "This little reunion is deeply moving, but it's not getting us any farther along here. Do you mind sticking to what's in the book?"

Still holding Maggie close, Matt looked out at the director. "Please, can we take ten?"

"You've already taken five," Dan said grumpily. "We've got a scheduled break coming up in about twenty minutes. Let's keep it going."

"There's so much I want to say to you," Matt whispered to Maggie. He gave her one more kiss before crossing back to his mark on the other side of the stage.

They ran through their lines almost automatically as Maggie kept her eyes on Matt. She was afraid to blink, afraid he'd vanish as quickly as he'd appeared.

His hairstyle brought out the exotic planes and angles of his face. He was more handsome than ever. And as he turned his back to her slightly, she saw that he'd only cut the top and sides of his hair. The back was still long, pulled into a ponytail at his nape. He could stick it under a shirt and no one would ever know he had hair halfway down his back.

"And you're wondering what it would feel like," Matt

was saying, "if you brought your lips up, like this…" He moved her face up toward him, and Maggie caught her breath at the love she saw in Matt's eyes.

He didn't say anything for several long moments. She could feel his heart beating against hers, he was holding her so tightly.

"Oh, Christ." Dan's voice echoed in the room. "Line! Somebody give him his line!"

"And if I brought my lips down, like this…" Dolores prompted from the edge of the stage.

But Matt didn't seem to hear. "Maggie," he said, his voice husky. "Will you marry me?"

She caught her breath. *Marry* him. As in forever. As in the rest of his life. As in, he now believed his life would last long enough for him to share it with her.

Joy and relief flooded through her. There was nothing Matt could have done to convince her more that he believed his cancer was truly gone.

And as for *marrying* him…

"Yes."

With a shout of laughter, Matt kissed her.

The cast broke into a round of applause.

"Oh, Lord," Dan's bored voice cut over the clapping. "I guess we better take a break."

Fifteen

"**S**tevie's late," Maggie said.

"No, he's not," Matt said calmly. "We're early."

"Aren't you even the tiniest bit nervous?" she asked him. This still seemed unreal. They'd applied for the marriage license, waited the short time it took to get it processed, and now here they were, standing in a church, about to get…

Married.

Matt smiled down at her. "No."

With her hair piled up on top of her head, dressed simply in a white sundress, Maggie was the most beautiful bride he'd ever seen in his life. No, he wasn't nervous. Thankful, happy, joyous, excited—yes, he was all those things, but not nervous.

When he'd been in the hospital, when no one would give him a good answer as to why he needed more and more extensive tests, he'd been so sure his luck had run out.

Then, finally, he'd gotten a straight answer from his puzzled doctor. He was not only clean, but a precancerous condition in his lungs had vanished. No one could figure out what had happened. And the doctors hadn't told him earlier, because they didn't want to get his hopes up—they needed to be sure that somehow the tests hadn't been botched, that the results hadn't been switched with that of another patient's.

Especially since they'd been so sure this time last year that he wasn't going to survive. Yet, there he was, passing all the tests with flying colors, in apparent good health.

For now, at least.

Matt didn't know if "for now" was to last five years, ten years, or one hundred years, but he did know that he wanted to spend every moment of his life with Maggie.

No, he wasn't nervous.

But Maggie was.

"Are you really sure you want to do this?" she asked. "It's so...permanent. And sudden."

"Mags, I've loved you for over a dozen years," he reminded her. "It's not sudden. But it's definitely permanent." He laced their fingers together. "You're my best friend," he told her. "And the love of my life." He had to smile at himself. "That sounds so corny, but..."

"It's not," she said. Her eyes were luminous. God, she was beautiful.

"I know," he said, and kissed her.

"Yo, aren't you supposed to wait until *after* the vows for that monkey business?" Stevie interrupted them.

"You've got to work on your timing," Matt told him with a grin.

"Oh, great elder ones," Stevie said, bowing with a flourish. "Allow me to humbly introduce my friend Danielle Trent."

This was the girl who was providing Steve with so many sleepless nights. Tall and slim with short blond curls, her face wasn't really so much pretty as it was friendly, with a smattering of freckles across her nose. Her eyes were lovely, though—an odd shade of violet with thick, dark lashes. She underwent their scrutiny solemnly, then exchanged a look with Stevie and smiled. Her smile transformed her face, and she became suddenly, freshly beautiful. Matt found himself liking the girl instantly.

"I've heard a lot about you guys," Danielle said. "When Stevie asked me to come to your wedding, I couldn't resist. I hope it's really okay."

"Of course it is," Maggie said.

"Actually, you're a vital part of the action," Matt told her. We can't get married without you—we need two witnesses."

"You *are* eighteen, right?" Maggie asked.

"Just," the girl said.

"Excellent," Matt said.

The pastor of the church came in through a heavy set of double doors. He shook hands with all four of them, his round face beaming. "I haven't done a small wedding like this in years," he said as he led them to the front of the church. "We'll go through the vows and exchange rings here in the sanctuary. Then you can all come back to my office, and we'll do the paperwork."

"Rings," Maggie said in dismay. "I knew we forgot something!"

But Matt held out his hand and Stevie dropped a blue velvet jewelry case into his palm. "I took care of it," he told her. "The rings aren't sized or engraved, but I figured we could use them temporarily."

Maggie gazed at Matt, realizing again how much he had changed from the reckless boy she'd known in high school. He stood there, tall and strong and calmly in control, and she knew without a doubt that agreeing to marry him was the smartest decision she'd ever made in her life.

"Ready?" the minister asked with a smile.

Maggie looked into Matt's eyes and smiled. Yes, she was ready.

Their gaze held as the man began to speak, talking of love,

of commitment, of trees growing stronger with their roots entwined.

Then he turned to Matt and began the vows.

Matt didn't look away from Maggie once as he repeated the words that would bind them together. His voice rang out clear and true in the empty church, echoing among the beams and rafters of the high ceiling. There was not even the slightest trace of doubt on his face, nor the slightest glimmer of uncertainty in his voice.

Matt slipped the ring, a plain gold band, onto her finger and smiled at her, adding his own ad-lib to the well known lines. "I promise I'll love you forever, Maggie."

Forever.

The word had special meaning to them, since they both knew well that Matt's forever might not be as long as most. Maggie felt tears spring into her eyes, but she smiled up at him.

Her own voice trembled a little as she pledged and promised herself to Matt. She pushed his ring onto his finger, then held tightly to his hand. "I promise I'll love you forever, Matt," she added, too.

"I pronounce you man and wife." The minister smiled. "You may kiss the bride."

Matt leaned down and brushed her lips with his, then wrapped his arms around her as he kissed her more thoroughly.

"You're mine now," Matt whispered to her. "*You* are *mine.*"

He picked her up and twirled her around, laughing, right there in the front of the church. "All right!" his joyous shout echoed.

Stevie looked at the smiling minister, one eyebrow raised. "I dunno," he said. "I think he kind of likes her."

Maggie stirred and slowly opened her eyes to see Matt smiling down at her.

The silvery light of dawn was streaming in the windows of the tower room. Maggie caught her breath as she saw, once again, the hundreds and hundreds of roses that sat in vases on every available surface. Those roses were the reason Stevie and Danielle had been late to the church. But they'd done a wonderful job. The flowers had given the room a fairy-tale-like quality by candlelight, a quality that survived in the pale light of the morning sun. Even after two days, the room looked gorgeous, and the scent of the roses perfumed the breeze that wafted in through the open windows.

"What time is it?" she asked Matt, lazily stretching her arms above her head.

"Almost six."

"How long have you been awake?" she asked, snuggling against him.

"A little while."

Maggie gave him a look. "What, only two hours or only four hours?"

He shrugged, smiling.

"I wouldn't mind if you got out of bed when you can't sleep."

"I know," Matt said. "But I didn't want to get up. I wanted to be here. With you."

"Do you just lie awake and think?" she asked, feeling the familiar rush of desire as her legs intertwined with his.

"Sometimes," he said. "I like to spend some time every day centering myself—you know, keeping my perspective about what's a big problem and what's a little inconvenience. Actually, much earlier this morning, I went downstairs and got my briefcase. I was reading about the great controversy between using foil bags or plastic to package the chips."

He rolled his eyes and Maggie laughed.

"After we win this inheritance thing," Matt said, pulling her closer and running his hands down her body. "Let's give the plant manager a big fat raise and tell him to hold down the fort while we go on a honeymoon to some exotic, tropical paradise where we can run naked on the beach.''

He kissed her, and she could feel him, heavy and hot against her.

''Or maybe Europe,'' he said, his voice soft, hypnotizing. ''I've always wanted to go to Europe. How about you, Maggie Stone?''

Maggie *Stone*. She sighed with pleasure as he—

The telephone rang shrilly, and she jumped, then caught Matt's arm. ''Don't answer it. Please? Let the answering machine pick it up.''

Matt looked at her. ''Who don't you want to talk to?'' She kissed him, trying to distract him again, but he pulled back. ''Who else would be calling at six in the morning? Angie, right?''

Maggie sighed.

Matt laughed. ''Mags, there's no way Angie could have found out we got married on Friday. Steve and Danielle swore they wouldn't tell anyone and—''

''My mother thinks we've been married for almost two months now,'' Maggie said. ''It's something she would mention if Angie called, looking for me.''

''Maybe Angie knows, maybe she doesn't.'' Matt studied her face. ''I think you should call her and tell her about us. Then you can stop feeling guilty.''

''I don't feel guilty.'' Her voice rose with indignation.

''Yes, you do.''

''No, I *don't*.''

''Look at you—you've got guilt written all over your face.'' Matt grinned. ''You can't feel guilty about going to bed with me anymore because we're married. We're supposed to be doing this.''

Maggie closed her eyes with a sigh of pleasure as Matt's hands and mouth continued to roam.

''Call her, Mags,'' he said. ''Today.''

''Oh, okay.''

"Promise?"

She opened her eyes, looking down at him. "No fair. I'd promise you anything right now."

He smiled and kissed her again. "Then maybe this is a good time for us to talk about that invitation we have to dinner at your parent's house this afternoon."

"Oh, no," she said faintly. "Do we have to go?"

"Yes," he said firmly. "We can use the opportunity to tell them we're married. Of course, we'll probably have to show your father our marriage certificate as proof."

"You mean the new, *unlaminated* one?" Maggie said.

Matt laughed and kissed her, and they both stopped talking, for a little while at least.

"Hello?" Angie picked up the phone on the second ring.

"Hey, Ang." Maggie's stomach churned with dread. Whoever called this morning hadn't left a message on the machine, but deep down she knew it had been Angie. Somehow her friend had tracked her down. "It's me."

"Maggie." Angie's voice was cool, with a distance that had nothing to do with the fact that she was on the other side of the Atlantic Ocean. "'Bout time I heard from you. How's *Matt?*"

"Funny you should ask—"

"You know I always thought you were the smartest person I knew, because out of all my friends, you were the only one who never let Matt get to you. Damn, Mags, what are you thinking? *Living* with him? You know, your mother told me you're *married,* but I knew you wouldn't be *that* stupid—"

"Angie—"

"Or even that naive to think Matt would ever commit to marriage. The man is a *snake,* Mags. He may be handsome, he might be good in bed, but you cannot trust him. He'll promise you the moon, then he'll walk away and find somebody else."

"No, Angie—"

"He lies. He's a liar and a cheat—he doesn't have a soul. I swear, Maggie, get out before it's too late—"

"Stop! Angie, just *stop,*" Maggie shouted into the phone.

She could hear her friend breathing hard on the other end of the line. Her own voice shook as she started to speak, so she cleared her throat and started again. "I don't know what he did to you," she said quietly, "but he's never been anything but kind and honest to me."

"Oh, please—"

"Stop talking," Maggie said forcefully. "For once in your life, be quiet and listen to *me.*"

Silence.

"I love him."

Silence.

"And two days ago, I *did* marry him."

"*What?* Oh, God, you *idiot*—"

"He's good and kind and funny and smart, and I'm crazy about him," Maggie spoke right over her.

"I thought you were in love with that jungle man from the health club."

"Matt is the jungle man. I didn't recognize him at first."

"Oh, come on! You didn't *recognize* him? God, I should have told you to marry Brock. I don't know why Matt's married you, but he must have some ulterior motive."

"Gee, thanks a million." Maggie's voice shook with indignation. "Like what? Tell me what on earth his motive for marrying me could possibly be!"

"I don't know—"

"How about because he loves me? How's *that* for an ulterior motive?"

"No," Angie said. "Matt doesn't know how to love. You're just a prize."

"What?"

"A *prize.* You're something he always wanted but couldn't have. Now he's the winner. Except now that he's married to you, every other woman on the planet is something he can't have. How long 'til he goes after some other prize? One month or two?''

"No." Maggie gripped the telephone so tightly that her knuckles were turning white. "He loves me, Angie. He's my husband now, whether you like it or not.''

"I don't like it. Damn you, Maggie—how could you do this to me?''

"To *you*? What is your problem? You sound jealous, like you're still in love with him. Is that what this is about? You're angry because I got what you couldn't have?''

"No!''

"Damn right, no! You didn't want him. You married somebody else, remember? It's not like I slept with your boyfriend—''

"Did you?'' Angie asked hotly.

"What?''

"Did you sleep with him when he was my boyfriend?'' Angie's voice was rough with anger. "Jesus, all this time I was trying to protect you from him, and maybe *you* were the one who started it.''

"I can't believe you're accusing me of—''

"And I can't believe that you could do something like marry that lying bastard and expect us to continue to be friends as if nothing was different," Angie spat.

"I won't talk to you if you're going to call him names.''

"Then obviously, we have nothing more to say to each other," Angie said tightly. "Have a nice life, Mags. With luck, he'll die young and you'll still have a chance at happiness.''

There was a click as Angie hung up the phone, leaving Maggie staring sightlessly at the walls.

What a horrible thing to say—even more horrible, considering the circumstances. Angie didn't know about Matt's battle with cancer, but that was still no excuse to say such a thing.

Tears flooded Maggie's eyes and she cried.

* * *

Maggie stood in her mother's kitchen, cutting up tomatoes for a salad when Stevie breezed in.

"Hi, y'all," he said. "Am I late?"

Maggie thrust a cucumber at him. "Wash this," she said. "And your hands."

"I know, I know." Stevie pretended to be insulted. "What kind of skeevy type do you think I am, you have to tell me to wash my hands?" He looked at her over his shoulder from the sink. "How's Matt? You bring him along, or is he locked in the office, reading financial reports from the 1960s?"

"He's in the living room, talking to Dad," Maggie said.

"You tell Mom?" Stevie asked.

"Tell me what?" Mrs. Stanton asked.

"Nothing," they both said in unison, Maggie with a dark look at her brother.

"Maggie, please go find out what Matt and your father want to drink with dinner," her mother said. "And where is Vanessa?"

"Where *is* Vanessa," Stevie echoed, with a humorous look at Maggie. "Funny how she always disappears right before dinner, when there's work to do...."

Maggie rolled her eyes, as she dried her hands on a towel and went into the living room.

Her father sat along in a chair, reading the newspaper.

"Dad, beer?" Maggie asked.

He looked up at her and smiled. "Please."

"Have you seen Matt?" she asked him. "Or Van?"

"I think they're out on the deck." Her father got to his feet. "I better go see if your mother needs any help."

Maggie crossed to the sliding glass doors that led out to the sun deck. She could hear Matt's voice, talking quietly.

Looking out through the screen, she saw him sitting up on the railing. One cowboy boot was hooked around the bottom rail, the other foot swung loose.

Van was standing next to him. "...married probably next summer," she was saying. "After the divorce is finalized."

"You sure you want to jump into another marriage right away?" Matt asked her. "It seems to me you might want to take your time."

Van snorted. "You're a good one to give advice. I can't believe you and Maggie are married." She laughed, and just as Maggie was about to open the screen and join them, she said, "Do you remember that night we were up at Wildwood?"

Maggie's heart stopped. Matt and Van? At Wildwood—Eastfield's version of Lover's Lane, where kids went to party and make out?

"How could I ever forget?" Matt's voice was dry.

Maggie went back into the kitchen, feeling dizzy.

Matt had gone out with Vanessa. When? And why hadn't she known about it?

How *could* he? He'd always disliked Van. Or so he'd told Maggie…

She sat at the kitchen table, trying to calm herself. It didn't matter. It had happened ten years ago. Matt loved *her*. He'd married *her*.

Out on the deck, Matt gazed at Vanessa. "You were lucky it was my car you climbed into that night. If it had been someone else's…"

She laughed. "I was so drunk." She shook her head. "I couldn't believe Bill Fitch dumped me. *He* dumped *me*. It was…mortifying." She looked at him. "I would have slept with you, you know."

He nodded. "I know."

"You were in love with Maggie, though. Even back then, weren't you?"

Matt nodded again. "Yeah."

"She is so lucky," Vanessa said. "Did I ever thank you for driving me home that night?"

He laughed. "Not exactly.

Stevie came to the door. "Dinner is served."

Van caught Matt's arm. "Thank you," she said. "Be good to my sister."

He smiled at her. "I will."

Maggie was silent in the car on the way home. Matt glanced at her. "That wasn't so bad, was it?"

No, it was *terrible.*

"Now that your folks know we're married, we can tell the rest of the world," Matt said. "I want to shout it from the mountaintops. Although, have you noticed that Connecticut is seriously lacking in mountaintops?"

Maggie couldn't manage more than a wan smile. Try as she might, she couldn't get the picture of Matt with Vanessa out of her head.

Had they made love in the back of Matt's car? It was ancient history and it shouldn't matter. But it did. And she had to ask him about it.

As they went into the house, Matt pulled her into his arms and kissed her. *Ask him,* she ordered herself.

"If you don't mind, I'm going to do some work," he told her. "I haven't finished reading that crap on packaging. There must be three more files I haven't even looked at yet."

"Matt." Maggie's voice sounded breathless to her own ears. "Did you ever…"

Sleep with my sister? It was what she wanted to know, but she couldn't ask. Not like that. Not point blank.

He was watching her, waiting patiently for the end of her sentence.

"Did you ever go out with Vanessa?" A better start. Much less difficult to ask. And although she already knew the answer—she'd heard him say as much—they could go from there, and—

"No," he said. He was laughing, as if he found her question amusing.

Maggie stared at him, shocked.

"I never did," he said. "I didn't think she was that attractive. I still don't. She's so desperate, you know?"

"Not even once?" she managed to say. God, was he actually lying to her?

Matt smiled, his eyes so warm and sincere. "Not even once."

Do you remember that night we were up at Wildwood? Maggie heard an echo of Van's voice. And, *How could I ever forget?* had been Matt's reply.

If he couldn't forget just a few hours ago, it wasn't likely that it had slipped his mind right now.

He was lying.

To her.

Lying.

He opened the door to the office and turned on the lights. "You coming?" he asked.

"I have to get something upstairs," Maggie fabricated an excuse as she hurried away.

"Do me a favor and bring those files on packaging down from the bedroom, will ya?" he called after her.

She didn't answer, taking the stairs two at a time, wanting to get away from him, needing to think.

She sat for a few minutes on Matt's bed, looking out the windows, at the setting sun.

Matt had lied to her.

Even more frightening was the thought that if she hadn't already known the real truth, she never would've suspected he was lying. His voice and expression had been so sincere, and his eyes...

Dan Fowler's words came back to her. *Matt is a pathological actor. Don't believe anything he tells you.*

And Angie had been adamant, calling Matt a liar again and again.

But Maggie loved him. And he loved her.

Didn't he?

She couldn't believe he would lie about something like that. He'd *married* her, for crying out loud.

She stood up, resolving to ask him again, and to tell him what she had overheard. There must be a good explanation.

Turning, she gathered up the files Matt had asked her to bring him. Three files, right? But only two were out on the bedside table.

Maggie opened his briefcase and quickly leafed through the file folders he had inside. None of them were labeled, so she opened the top one and flipped through the papers, hoping to identify its contents quickly.

She scanned an official-looking document. Then with growing shock, she read it more slowly.

It was the codicil to the will. Matt had had a copy all along. Why hadn't he given it to her?

It was a wordy and lengthy document that boiled down to one thing: If Matt were to get married before the end of the fiscal quarter, he would automatically inherit.

The bedroom, still adorned with all those roses, began to spin.

Maggie sat down. The codicil specified conditions to the marriage—the woman Matt chose had to be over twenty-five years old, with a graduate degree. She had to be an upstanding member of the community, and preferably a longtime resident of Eastfield.

Maggie was that woman. The description fit her perfectly. Too perfectly.

Angie's words of warning about Matt's ulterior motive came back with a force that nearly knocked her over. By marrying her, Matt would inherit a fortune.

He didn't love her. He'd never loved her. He had only married her because she was willing and available and met the conditions of the will.

Her mind lined up all of the facts and the implications, but still she denied it.

No.

Matt loved her. He *loved* her.

No one could lie so absolutely, so perfectly, so consistently.

Could they?

The phone on Matt's bedside table rang.

Maggie picked it up.

"Hey." She could tell from his voice that he was smiling. "You get lost up there or something? Where are my files? More importantly, where's my *wife?*"

"I'll be right down," Maggie heard herself say.

Maybe it wasn't the real codicil. Maybe the real one was different. Maybe it didn't have anything to do with marriage. Maybe…

Tomorrow the real codicil was going to be released by the court. Please God, Maggie prayed, let it be different. Let this be one big mistake…

"Tomorrow I'll pick up our wedding rings at the jewelers," Matt said as they walked across the parking lot outside of the community theater. "We might as well wait to tell everyone that we're married 'til then. Is that okay with you?"

She didn't answer, and Matt laughed. "Mags, hey, where are you?"

Startled, she looked up at him, then tripped over a crack in the driveway. Matt caught her arm to keep her from falling. "You okay?" he asked.

She nodded, but he could see the strain around her eyes, and tension in her mouth.

"Dinner with your parents really blew you away, didn't it?" He pushed a stray strand of hair out of her face. "I'm sorry. You didn't want to go, and I talked you into it."

"Matt, do you love me?" she asked.

What? "You know that I do."

She nodded, but her smile was forced.

"You don't…" Matt cleared his throat and started again. "You don't doubt me, do you?"

"Don't be silly," she said and went inside.

* * *

Toward the end of the rehearsal, when Matt was up on stage for one of his solo numbers, Dan Fowler slipped into the seat next to Maggie.

"The Cancer Center at USC?" he said without any greeting.

Maggie felt the muscles in her face freeze. "Yes. That's where he was."

"No, he wasn't."

She looked at Dan, but he was staring up at the stage, at Matt. "All right," she said, her heart starting to pound. "What are you accusing him of now?"

Dan finally looked at her. "I'm not accusing him of anything." His voice was mild, but his eyes were flinty. "All I'm saying is that I called to verify his cancer story, and there was no record of a Matthew Stone ever having been at USC's Cancer Center." He shrugged and stood up. "I'll leave all the accusing to you."

Sixteen

Maggie's hands shook as she dialed the telephone. It had been torture, waiting until noon—until nine o'clock California time.

Matt and Stevie were in the kitchen, making lunch, and she was thankful for the privacy that gave her to make this call.

A call that would prove Dan Fowler wrong.

An elderly woman answered the telephone. "Cancer Center at USC. May I help you?"

"Yes." Maggie's voice shook, and she took a deep breath. "My husband was there a few weeks ago, and I need to check the exact dates of his previous stay for our insurance forms. Can you put me through to someone who can help me?"

"I should have that information on my computer," the woman answered. "What's your husband's name, dear?"

Maggie told her.

"Hmm," the woman said, and Maggie's stomach began to hurt. "*S, t, o, n, e,* right?"

"Yes."

"I don't have a Matthew Stone," she said. "Not this past month or any other time. Perhaps you're confusing us with the hospital at UCLA?"

"I'm sorry," Maggie said, hanging up the phone.

Lies. It was all lies.

"Yo, Mags." Stevie came back into the office. "Matt made you a salad. You want it out here or in the kitchen?"

Maggie just shook her head.

"Hey, ho." Her brother crossed to the door. "Mail call! Here's big Joe, the friendliest mailman in the Western Hemisphere."

He opened the office door and took a pile of mail from the dour elderly man.

"Hey, homeboy," Stevie greeted him, holding out a hand. "Gimme five."

Joe slapped a certified letter into his outstretched hand. "Sign for this one." He pointed to the form. "There and there."

At least Matt didn't have cancer. At least he wasn't going to die.

"Yo, Mags," Stevie said, closing the door behind Joe. "Looks like this is that legal thing you were waiting for."

She put her head on the desk and burst into tears.

Stevie stared. "Well, gee, I get kind of emotional when Joe leaves, too, but, he'll be back tomorrow, so—"

"How could Matt do this to me?" she said. "How could he put me through this? Pretending to go into the hospital, making me think he actually might die?"

"Is this another one of your acting things?" Stevie asked worriedly. "I hope?"

"Give me that goddamned letter." Maggie snatched the envelope from his hand. She tore it open and with shaking hands spread the document out on the table.

It was the codicil—and it was the same as the one she'd found in Matt's briefcase.

He didn't love her. He was just using her.

Correction—he *had* used her, but that was going to stop right now.

"Do you have your car?" she asked Stevie, reaching for a tissue and blowing her nose violently.

"Yeah, why?" Her brother looked very nervous. "What's going on?"

"I need a ride," she told him.

"Oh, yeah?" Matt came into the room, all smiles. "You going someplace?"

Maggie turned to look at him. How could someone who looked so beautiful do something so ugly? And how could she have been such a fool as to believe him?

His smile faded as he gazed at her. "What's the matter?" he asked.

"I know the truth," Maggie told him. She was *not* going to cry in front of him, damn it. "You son of a bitch."

Total confusion was on his face. "What?"

"God, you're good," she said. Taking a deep breath, she forced back her tears. She'd have time to face the hurt later. Right now, all she let herself feel was anger. It shot through her icy and cold. "But you can skip the act, Matt. The codicil to the will came today. You don't have to fake it anymore. Obviously, you've won."

"Maggie, you're scaring me," he said. "What are you talking about?"

She scooped the certified letter off the desk and slammed it against his chest. "It's all right there in the codicil. But you might as well cut the crap. I know that you've already seen a copy of this."

He frowned, pretending to skim through the document.

"Or maybe you only *think* you've won," she told him, her voice shaking. "But maybe you lose. I'm going to file for an annulment."

Stevie's mouth dropped open as he looked from Maggie to Matt and back.

"What are you talking about?" Matt said again. He looked stunned, confusion and disbelief alternately crossing his face. "Maggie, you can't be serious."

"I'm dead serious."

"What does this say?" Matt shook the document at her. "You know I can't understand this legal stuff...."

"You know damn well what it says." She headed for the door.

He lunged after her, catching her arm.

"Let go of me!" Maggie bit each word off clearly.

"Yo guys, I think I better go," Stevie said.

"No!" Maggie said.

"Yes," Matt countered. "Steve, go outside, all right. Give us some privacy, will you?"

"If I don't come out in fifteen minutes," Maggie told her brother, "call the police."

Matt staggered back. "Oh, my God, do you really think I'm going to *hurt* you?"

"You already have," she told him.

"How?" he asked, his eyes searching her face. "Christ, Maggie, tell me what this is about."

She went out of the office and up the stairs.

"Maggie, talk to me," he pleaded, following her to the room where she kept her clothes. "I love you, and you loved me. We're *married—*"

She spun to face him. "Not anymore."

"Why not?" he shouted, desperation in his face, the codicil to the will crushed in his fists. "Damn it, Maggie, you tell me why the hell not!"

"Okay, fine," she said. "We'll play this your way. Play the whole game out. The codicil states that you automatically inherit if you get married before the end of the fiscal quarter. But you can't marry just anyone. The conditions are listed quite clearly in the fifth paragraph."

He smoothed the crumpled paper, and read. And realization crossed his face.

"Oh, bravo," Maggie applauded. "One thing I can say about you, Matt, is that you truly are a brilliant actor. But save it for the Academy Awards, because I know you've already seen this codicil. I found a copy in your briefcase."

"If it was there, I didn't know it," he protested.

She laughed. "You know, I might've believed you. But combined with the rest of it…"

"What rest of it?" He was mad as hell now, too.

"All the lies." She roughly wrestled her gym bag from the top shelf of the closet. As she spoke, she began pulling her clothes from the drawers and piling them on the bed. "All this time they were right, but I was stupid enough to believe *you*—"

"*Who* was right?"

"Angie—"

"*Damn it!* I should have known she was somewhere behind this!"

"*And* Dan Fowler."

"He's not exactly the president of my fan club, either," Matt shouted. "So come on, I'm dying to hear. What did they tell you?"

"That you're a liar," Maggie shouted back. "And they're right! You *lied* to me, you bastard. You used tricks and lies to get me to marry you!"

"God, Maggie, you don't really think that, do you? I thought you believed in me, that you trusted me.…" He voice shook and he broke off. Tears glistened in his eyes. "Damn it."

The pain on his face was only an act. A tear escaped and slid down his face. It, too, was just part of his crap. "I never lied to you," he said.

"Gee, I don't know," she said as she packed as much as she could into her gym bag. "I'd call telling someone that you have cancer when you really don't more than a little white lie, wouldn't you?'' She turned to face him. ''I called the Cancer Center, Matt. They never heard of you. You were never there.

''You told me that you never went out with Van, but I heard you talking to her about going parking at Wildwood!'' She stopped to take a deep breath. ''You *lied* right to my face when I asked you about her!''

''No,'' he said, ''I can't believe that's what you think—''

She plowed right over him. ''But the biggest lie of all was when you married me.'' It was harder and harder for her to hold back her tears. ''You said you loved me, but I know that's not true. I know why you married me, and it has nothing to do with love.''

The look on his face would've broken her heart if she hadn't known it was all an act.

''But you know what?'' she whispered. ''I lied, too, when I told you I'd love you forever. Because I sure as hell don't love you anymore.''

Matt turned and walked out of the room.

He came back a moment later, carrying an empty suitcase. He set it down on the bed. ''I'll get Stevie to help you carry your things out,'' he said quietly. He was almost out the door when he turned back. ''I thought you believed in me, Maggie. I thought you had faith in me. But why should you be different from anyone else?''

Seventeen

As Maggie walked into the auditorium, she saw Matt immediately, standing by the stage. He was dressed all in black, and he was surrounded by most of the female cast members. Still, he looked up at her as if he had some sort of sixth sense and could tell when she was around.

A wave of misery descended upon her, and Maggie knew in a flash that she would have to move away. She couldn't stay in town with Matt living here, too. It would be horrible to be reminded constantly of what a blind fool she'd been.

''Places!'' called Dolores. ''We're doing a complete run-through tonight, and we're taking it from the top.''

Maggie dumped her bag into a seat and tiredly climbed the stairs to the stage.

Aware of Matt's eyes on her as he watched from the wings, she found it difficult to concentrate on the show. God, any minute he was going to come out, and she was going to have to kiss him.

She had to stay mad. If she could stay good and mad at the bastard, she'd be able to get through this.

Matt watched Maggie and felt like crying. When had it happened? When had she begun to doubt him? Or had she mistrusted him all along?

If that was the kind of person she was, then he didn't want her. Good riddance. She'd done him a favor by leaving.

Up on the shoulders of the men's chorus, Maggie smiled dazzlingly.

Desire stirred, and he closed his eyes, angry at his reaction to her. She didn't trust him—and he *still* wanted her.

And in less than a minute, he was going to have to kiss her.

Damn it. He couldn't do this.

But the stage manager gave him his cue, and he went out onto the stage. The lights hit him, and there he was. Standing right in front of Maggie. Their gazes locked. Somehow his mouth opened and the lines he'd memorized came out.

She seemed so unaffected, so calm.

But as he pulled her in for the kiss, he saw a flash of anger in her eyes. His own anger began to build, and he kissed her hard, too hard, hating himself for still wanting her, and knowing that before the night was through, he was going to go to her and beg her to come back to him.

Maggie sat in one of the dark corners backstage, praying for the fifteen minute break between acts to end. She was using every ounce of her energy just being on stage with Matt—she didn't want to use it up confronting him offstage.

But he found her. "Maggie."

He was backlit, and his face was in the shadows. She stood up, prepared to move out into the auditorium—anywhere, to get away from him.

But he caught her arm. "We have to talk."

She pulled away. "There's nothing to say."

He followed her onto the stage, out into the light. "There's a hell of a lot to say. Come on. At least give me a chance to defend myself.''

''Just leave me alone.''

''Maggie, God, *please*. I love you.''

She looked up at him and saw his eyes filled with tears and all of her anger came roaring back.

''Good delivery. You sound *very* sincere. But the tears are a little too much, don't you think?'' She pushed her hair off her face, working hard to keep her hand from shaking. ''Give up, Matt. I don't believe you. Besides, you don't need me anymore. I won't file for an annulment. We'll get a divorce— after you've gotten the inheritance.''

''You really think that's what this is about?'' he asked. ''Money?''

She didn't say a word.

He nodded. ''You loved me enough to marry me,'' he said. ''You owe me at least the chance to tell you—''

''I owe you nothing,'' she said.

''How can you say that?'' Matt felt sick. Did she really believe that? ''You should talk to your sister. If you don't believe me, you should ask her. And I'll call my doctor at the Center—he'll call you. Or you can call him. I *was* there—''

''Forget it, Matt,'' Maggie told him. ''I just don't care.''

Matt stared at her. She didn't care. He was ready to beg, to plead, to *crawl*, but damn it, *she* was the one who had done him wrong. She was the one who didn't trust him. He was even ready to accept that she'd found him guilty until proven innocent if it meant he'd have her back.

But she didn't care.

The last bit of hope that he'd been carrying evaporated, and his heart broke.

Eighteen

"Where the *hell* is he?" Dan Fowler stormed. "I knew it. I *knew* I should never have trusted that bastard with the lead to my show!"

"My brother works with Matt," Maggie told him. "I just spoke to him on the phone—he says he hasn't heard from him all day."

Outside, a storm was raging, and thunder crackled deafeningly, directly overhead.

"Beautiful, just beautiful." Dan groaned. "You guys had a fight, didn't you?"

"We split up," Maggie said, and saying the words aloud made her sick.

"And now he's gone." Dan started to pace as he swore. "The understudy is awful. We'll have to modify the dance numbers...."

"I think you should just take a deep breath," Maggie said, "because Matt wouldn't just blow off the show. He's going to be here."

Dan stopped pacing and stared at her. "You look like you've been run over by a truck. This guy does *that* to you, and still you defend him?"

"I just don't believe he would desert us one day before opening night," Maggie insisted. "He'll be here."

"Jeez, somehow I didn't expect *you* to be my champion."

Maggie whirled around to see Matt standing behind them. He looked exhausted. And he was soaking wet.

Dan swore at him, loud and long. "You're late. We're paying our orchestra by the hour, damn you. Where the hell have you been?"

Matt finally stopped looking at Maggie. "We're getting tidal flooding from this storm. I've been organizing work crews at the factory—sandbagging. I should have called, but for the past hour I've been on the verge of getting into my car and coming over here. But there was always one more person who needed to talk to me. I apologize for being late."

"Places!" Dan was already yelling. "Get Stone into costume and makeup! Now!"

After the dress rehearsal ended, Maggie reached over her shoulder to unzip the evening gown she wore for the show's closing number. She pulled the zipper down as far as she could, then reached around behind her, struggling to find the tiny pull.

A warm hand on her shoulder stopped her, and she felt the zipper slide all the way down.

Holding the dress to her front, she turned to face Matt.

Matt.

Tonight she'd run out of anger. All she could feel was the hurt. And boy, did it hurt bad. Because despite everything he'd done, she still loved him.

His eyes were angry, the way they'd been all night long, but his face and words were polite, cordial. "You did well tonight."

Maggie laughed humorlessly. "I know exactly how well I

did. This is an endurance test for me, Matt. I can't wait until it's over.''

He nodded then, his eyes dark with misery now. "Yeah, me, too." He cleared his throat. "I just wanted you to know that I'm going to go back to California after the fiscal quarter. I've already contacted a divorce lawyer and… I want you to have the house.''

She stared at him.

"There's no way I could stay in town with you living here, too," he said quietly. "I know you love it here, and…''

"That's…that's insane," she said. That house had to be worth millions.

"It's no more insane than any of the rest of this," he told her as he walked away.

Maggie stood backstage in the dark, listening to the sounds of the people who had begun to fill the seats of the auditorium.

It was ten minutes to curtain on opening night.

Matt was in makeup, already in character, joking and laughing with everyone in sight.

She closed her eyes, wishing it could be that easy for her, too, wishing she could just snap her fingers and become someone else, if only for a little while.

But Lucy, her character, was too much like herself. It wasn't enough of an escape.

"Yo, Mags," came a whispered voice.

She turned to see Stevie. He was wearing blue jeans that were crusty with dried mud, and a T-shirt that was no longer white.

"Well, gee," she said. "You got dressed up for the occasion.''

He grinned. "I'm coming to the show tomorrow night. With Danny." He laughed. "We actually have a real date. Matt's even letting me borrow the Maserati.''

"A date?" Maggie said. "You mean you finally—''

"Yeah, I finally took your advice," Stevie said. "See, we were out with the gang, and I just couldn't stand it another second. I said, 'Danny, I'm madly in love with you, and if you don't kiss me right this second, I'm gonna die.'"

"You did?" Maggie laughed. "Oh, my God."

"So she laughed at me," Stevie told her, "And I'm mortified, thinking, 'Wow, how totally humiliating.' But then—" he paused dramatically "—she kissed me. Boom. Right there. In front of everyone." He smiled. "She actually loves me, too."

"That's so great," Maggie said.

"So I came down here to say thank you and break a leg."

"Thanks."

"You and Matt patch it back together yet?" he asked.

She shook her head. "I don't think that's going to happen."

Stevie rolled his eyes. "You are such a fool. He loves you, Maggie."

"He married me to get his inheritance," she told him. But even as she said the words, they sounded so wrong. And Stevie was looking at her as if she were the village idiot.

"You don't *really* believe that, do you?" he said.

"I don't know," she admitted.

"Yes, you do," Stevie said. "You know him, Mags. He's a good guy. A little flaky with the weirdo diet and the strange sleep patterns, but…you *know* him."

She'd thought she did.

"He's been hanging out at the law library for very unhealthy periods of time," her brother told her. "He's working on something that would probably take you five minutes to do. He could use your help, you know. I mean, unless you don't care if he makes himself sick…."

Maggie gave him a look. "That's laying it on a little thick."

"Will you please just talk to him?" Stevie said. "If not for him, if not for you, then for *me?*"

She just shook her head.

"Places!" Dolores said.

Her brother backed away, pointing to her leg and making a breaking motion with his hands, then miming a telephone, mouthing the words, "Talk to Matt."

And tell him what?

Taking a deep breath, Maggie moved out into the center of the stage, to the mark where she would be standing when the curtain opened. She closed her eyes and bent her head, forcing her body to relax.

Tonight, her character, Lucy, was going to have a happy ending.

Maggie would give anything to have one of her own.

The cast went wild behind the curtains after the final bow. The show was a huge success—the audience had laughed at all the jokes, and the applause for the musical numbers had been deafening.

Laughing, Matt picked up Maggie and swung her around and around. She was smiling up at him, her arms around his neck and, without thinking, he kissed her.

Oh, God, he was kissing her. Her mouth opened willingly beneath his, and he drank her in, wishing he could slow this moment down, but too afraid even to move, for fear of breaking the spell. He could feel his heart pounding.

She pulled back, and he released her immediately. Their gazes locked, and Maggie cleared her throat.

"Cody and Lucy always did get a little carried away," she said.

Cody and Lucy. Not Matt and Maggie. "Sorry," he said.

"You were great tonight," she told him.

"You were, too."

The rest of the cast was making so much noise around them. Someone ran past with an open bottle of champagne.

"I don't want your house," Maggie said quietly.

"Too bad," he countered.

"Seriously, Matt," she said. "Stevie said you were working on something, but you don't have to do that. We can go into court some time in the next few weeks, and show them our marriage license. You've already won."

He laughed his disgust. "You call this *winning?*" His temper flared and he walked away from her, but then walked back. Breathe. He had to breathe, but he couldn't get the air into his lungs. "I'm not just giving you the house," he told her. "I'm giving you half of my share of the business, too."

She looked shocked. "Matt—"

"Hey, like you said," he told her harshly, "I won. And I wouldn't've been able to do it without your help. The house is your payoff for that. The half of the business is yours because—believe it or not—I really did think of you as my wife. But if you're more comfortable with it, you can think of it as payment for the sex."

Her eyes flared. Ooh, that got her mad. Stupid, stupid, stupid. He should have just kept walking away.

In response, Maggie actually uttered words he'd never heard her say before. At least not in this decade.

But it wasn't until he was in his car and driving—too fast—out of the parking lot, that he realized he wouldn't have been able to get a rise out of her if she truly didn't care.

Maybe he was going about this all wrong. Maybe instead of trying to show her how calm and collected he was—how much he'd changed over the years—maybe he should show her…

For the first time in days, Matt actually had hope.

He headed, fast, for Sparky's—where the entire cast was meeting to toast the opening of the show. He wanted to get there first.

Maggie pushed open the door to Sparky's feeling much less than enthusiastic.

But it was a tradition with the theater group to drink a

toast to the show, and this year, because they'd had no volunteers willing to host a party, the party was here at the bar.

Maggie was only going to stay for the toast, and then run for home as fast as she could.

As she went inside, she saw Matt was already there—sitting at the bar. Charlene, the flirtatious soprano, was next to him. She leaned in close to tell him something. And, God, he actually had his arm around her.

Maggie looked away, but not before she'd met Matt's eyes in the mirror.

He actually had the audacity to smile at her.

She found herself staring at the old-fashioned jukebox sightlessly, blinded by tears of jealousy. No, tears of anger. She wasn't jealous, she was mad.

She couldn't believe what he'd said to her after the show. Payment for sex... And now he was here, like this, with *Charlene*...

She glanced up to see Matt standing right behind her.

Quickly, she blinked back her tears and fished in her pocket for a quarter. She pushed the coin into the slot and pretended to be absorbed in choosing her song. But he reached over her shoulder and pushed the numbers for an old Beatles song. "P.S. I Love You."

"Dance with me," he said.

Maggie gazed up at him, suddenly beyond exhausted. She'd danced with him all night long, and that hadn't solved a thing. "Why don't you dance with Charlene?"

"Look, she sat down next to me. What am I supposed to do?"

"She made you put your arm around her?" Maggie couldn't stand it anymore. "I think it's kind of obvious that it's over between us," she said forcefully. "Why don't you just relax and have a beer and a cigarette and *Charlene* while you're at it."

"Is that really what you want?" Matt said. God, she was playing right into this entire scene. It was perfect. And he was right about her still caring. Oh, man, she cared so much. He wanted to kiss her. Instead he shrugged. "Fine. You got it."

He remembered the way he'd used to act, back in high school, before he'd learned to control his anger. It wasn't hard to get back into character—the bad boy was a part he'd played for years. He'd already started, over at the bar with Charlene.

He spun now, nearly colliding with a waitress. He took one of the oversized mugs of beer from her tray, ignoring her protest, and crossed to a table where some of the cast members were sitting. He put down the beer, took a cigarette out of a pack on the table and, holding Maggie's gaze, he very slowly and deliberately lit it.

He picked up the beer and crossed back toward her, taking a long pull on the beer and then an equally long drag off the cigarette.

Christ! He had to work hard not to cough. God, he hated the taste of both, but he didn't let her see that.

"This is more like it." He exhaled the smoke as he gazed at her. "Isn't it? It's what you expect from me, right? God forbid I should ever actually *change*."

He took another long swig of beer as, from the corner of his eye, he saw Dan Fowler watching them with horrified fascination.

Maggie's eyes were filled with tears. "Matt, stop."

"Gee, I don't know, Mags," he said, his voice rising in volume. "I mean, you got me pegged for this role. I'm a liar and a cheat, right? At least according to Angie and Dan. A liar who smokes and drinks too much. And let's not leave out Charlene. I think she'll be glad to go home with me, don't you? Oh, but wait, maybe not after she sees *this!*"

He pretended to chug the rest of the beer, but really just poured it down his shirt. "Or this!" he shouted, and slammed the mug down with such force on top of the jukebox that the record skipped with a wild screech. The music stopped.

The noisy bar was silent.

But Matt dropped character as he stubbed his cigarette out in a nearby ashtray.

"You're ready to believe all that about me," he said softly as he looked up at Maggie, "but you won't believe that I love you. If that's really true, then go to hell, Maggie. I don't want you anymore."

He turned and walked out of the bar, knowing all too well that his words had made him exactly what she thought he was.

A liar.

Maggie followed Matt out into the parking lot.

And found him on his hands and knees in the grass next to his Maserati, throwing up.

"Oh, my God," she said.

He swore. "Go away."

She dug in her purse for some tissues, crouching down next to him.

He took them from her, wiped his mouth, and sat up with his back and head against the side of his car. "Remind me never to smoke again." There was dark humor in his eyes as he looked at her. "Well, *that* sucked. So much for the tough guy act, huh?"

"Do you want me to drive you home?" she asked.

He shook his head. "No, I'm okay. It just was… I haven't had nicotine in so long, and, God, it just made my stomach…"

"That was impressive in there," she said. "Making the jukebox shut off that way…"

"Too much?"

"No," she said, starting to cry. "It was perfect."

"That's not me anymore," he told her.

Maggie nodded. "I know. I know." She couldn't bear to

look at him. His words were echoing in her head. *I don't want you anymore.* "Oh, Matt, will you ever forgive me?"

"I'll think about it," he said. He pulled himself to his feet and unlocked his car door. He had a bottle of water in the cup holder and he took a swig, rinsing his mouth and spitting it out.

She wiped her face, her eyes. "Stevie told me you were working on something…?"

Matt looked at her. "Yeah. I'm not, um… I'd prefer not to use our marriage as a way to win this thing," he told her. "I mean, if it comes down to it, I will—all those jobs are at stake. But I didn't marry you because of that fricking codicil. I didn't know I had that document in my briefcase."

"I know," she said. "Oh, God, I'm so sorry."

"What'dya do, talk to Vanessa?" he asked.

"No," she said.

"You call the Cancer Center? I gave them permission to give you whatever information you wanted."

"No," she said.

He was surprised. "You don't want proof that—" He laughed. "Did Stevie show you the thing I'm working on?"

"Stevie doesn't know what you're working on," Maggie countered. "He told me you were doing something and you could probably use some legal help. That's all he said to me."

Matt was trying to be casual, but for someone who was such a good actor, he was doing a truly lousy job. "So you just, like, decided that you believe me?" he said. "No proof, no…"

"It was actually something Stevie said tonight," Maggie admitted. "He reminded me that I knew *you.* That I knew you. Matt, please, *please* forgive me. All those awful things I said…"

She met his eyes, and as she looked at him, she could see tiny reflections of her face in the darkness of his pupils. She belonged there, in his eyes, and she knew she had to do whatever she could to stay right there.

But he reached for her, and as she held him, she started, again, to cry.

"God," he said, "no matter what I do, I seem to make you cry."

She looked up at him. "I'm madly in love with you, and if you don't forgive me, I'm going to die."

Fire, life and tears sprang into Matt's eyes simultaneously. He held her tightly as he laughed. "Yeah, like there's any doubt I'm going to forgive you."

"You said you needed to think about it."

"I was kidding!" He laughed. "Hey, if this failed tonight, I was going to fly my doctor out from California, and pay him to follow you around until you believed me. I was going to take a lie detector test. I was going to—"

"I love you, Matt," she said. "Do you still love me?"

"For always and forever," he promised her.

She would have kissed him, but he turned his head. "I'm not kissing you," he said. "I just barfed. But if you want to come home with me, and let me run upstairs and brush my teeth, you can try that line of Stevie's again, verbatim this time, and I guarantee it'll work as well for you as it did for him."

She held him tightly. "I think I vowed to love you in sickness and in health."

Matt laughed. "Get in," he said.

Maggie got in.

And he took her home.

Nineteen

Maggie sighed as she lay with Matt in his bed. *Their* bed. It felt so good to be home.

"I was such a jerk," she said.

"Yeah," he said. "You were."

She narrowed her eyes at him. "You're not supposed to agree with me."

"I'm not going to lie," he told her as he touched her face. "Not even about something like that. I'm never going to lie to you, Mags."

"I know," she whispered.

He kissed her and she felt herself melt. And then she started to laugh.

"What?" he said.

"I'm madly in love with you," she said, "and if you don't go down on me right this second, I think I'm going to die."

He shouted with laughter. "Can't have that," he said. "God, I missed you…"

* * *

Maggie woke up to find Matt sitting up in bed, reading the papers in a file.

The clock read 5:34.

"Hey," he said, smiling at her.

She stretched. "Did you sleep at all?"

He shook his head. "I think I was afraid if I fell asleep I'd find out that your coming home was just a dream."

Oh, Matt.... "It's not," she said.

He nodded. And handed her the file. "You awake enough to put on your lawyer hat?"

She sat up, arranging her pillow behind her. "My lawyer hat seems to have disappeared with the rest of my clothes."

He grinned at her. "I meant figuratively. And as long as we're leaning heavily toward all honesty all the time, I should probably tell you that the idea of your giving me legal advice while you're naked appeals to me in a very decadent way."

"Do I need to call you Mr. Stone?" she asked, opening the file and starting to read and...

She closed the file. And looked at Matt. "Are you serious about this?"

He nodded.

She opened it again. He'd outlined his plan for improving the company. It included on-site day care and a fitness room. It also included joint ownership in the company for every single employee from the managers to the cleaning staff.

Maggie flipped through his notes. "You're proposing to give the employees all but twenty-five percent of the company." She looked up at him. "You're just...giving it to them?"

He actually shrugged. "These people are the ones who've worked so hard to make this company successful. Can you imagine how much harder they'll work if the company actually belongs to them?"

She kept flipping through his notes. "And what's this? A grant program and..."

"Scholarships, too," he said. "Funded through the sale of

some of my father's assets. I'm going to keep only two of the cars—I mean, thirteen cars? Come on. Some of those are antiques and worth a ton of money. I'm going to put it all into a trust. I've worked out the preliminary numbers—I need you to check my math. But I'm pretty sure that with the bulk of the cash inheritance included in the trust, there'll be about three million in interest each year—to give away.''

''And you're going to run the grant's foundation,'' she saw.

''With you,'' he said, ''if you'll take the new position.''

Maggie looked up at him. ''Matt, this is…''

''Crazy?'' He shrugged again. ''I never really wanted my father's money—I told you that from the start. I was trying to save the company. I mean, don't get me wrong—my twenty-five percent will keep me very comfortable. I'm not going to give it *all* away.''

She closed the file. ''Well.'' She frowned slightly, tapping it with her finger. ''I guess my legal advice to you would be… Let's try it. Let's go for it. Let's set it up, and present it to the court. I can't tell you for sure if they'll accept this as the kind of improvement your father intended, but I'm willing to argue it—I think I can put up a good fight. And we do have a failsafe—our marriage certificate. I know you don't want to use it, but, like you said, you want these people to have their jobs come next Christmas.''

She reached for a pen from the bedside table, and started making notes right on the manila folder. Matt took both from her hands, and kissed her.

''We can work out the details later,'' he said. ''One thing I want you to do today is go through my briefcase, make sure there aren't any other unpleasant surprises hiding in there.'' He kissed her again. ''Will you do that for me?''

''I don't need to,'' Maggie said.

''But I want you to,'' he told her as he pulled her on top of him. ''Later.''

''Later,'' she agreed.

* * *

Matt's briefcase was filled with roses.

Roses and his hospital records from California.

He'd also written out an explanation of the night he'd gone up to Wildwood to a party, telling her how Vanessa had come into his car, falling down drunk after breaking up with her boyfriend. She'd come on to him, but he'd taken her home. End of story.

There was a note from Dan Fowler, too, apologizing for giving Maggie misinformation, explaining that Matt had chosen a privacy option at the Cancer Center, which meant that all information about his illness—including information he himself requested—had to be optained via mail, in writing.

And there was a copy of an e-mail from Angie.

"Dear Mags," her friend wrote. *"Matt e-mailed me a few days ago. I've spent some time thinking about it, and I've come to the rather earth-shattering conclusion that I was wrong.*

"I'm not going to tell you everything Matthew said to me (I wouldn't want it to go to your head!), but I do believe that he truly loves you. He's loved you for a long time, and I suppose I'm mostly to blame for you guys not getting together before this.

"You were right—I was jealous. Even now, even married, even completely in love with Freddy. I'm a bad person—if I couldn't have Matt, I didn't want you to have him, either. I think I knew back in high school that his feelings for you went way beyond my own relationship with him. Hell, they went beyond my relationship with you. I think I was afraid that if you and Matt got together, neither of you would have anything left to give to me.

"I know now that that's not true. I love Freddy as much as Matt loves you, and love like that is like a fire. It just keeps spreading, it keeps burning brighter and bigger.

"I'm sorry for the things I said to you. I hope you'll find it in your heart to forgive me.

"LOL! I know you will. I know you—you've already for-

given me. You're such a pushover. You need to work on that all right?

"So stay good and mad at me another week—God, I'm such a rotten bitch—and then call me and tell me that you still love me, okay?

"I love you.

"Love, Angie."

Maggie looked up to find Matt standing in the office door.

"I didn't need any of this," she told him. "I didn't need proof or permission from anyone to—"

"I know," he said.

She went through the pockets of the briefcase, but they were all empty.

"That's all that's in there," Matt said. He'd made sure of it.

"Are you positive?" she said.

Uh-oh. "Did I leave something out?" he asked.

She sighed. "I was sure you were going to ask me..." She stood up. "I guess I'm going to have to ask you." She took a rose from the bunch, and crossing to him, got down on one knee. "Matt, will you not unmarry me?"

He laughed.

She did, too, but back there, in her eyes, he could see that she wasn't entirely kidding.

"Oh, Mags." He got down on his knees, too, and kissed her. "Yes," he told her. But then he looked at her. "Wait, maybe I need to consult with my lawyer. The wording of that question was a little complicated. Yes, I won't unmarry you," he figured it out. "Yes. Definitely, yes."

Maggie kissed him. She kissed his face, his neck, his jaw, his cheeks, but then stopped, with only a whisper of space between her lips and his.

"I want," she said, and he could feel her warm, sweet breath against his face, "my wedding ring."

He kissed her—a long, lovely, heavenly kiss—then pulled

back and reached into his pocket. He'd carried the jeweler's box with him for days now, hoping...

Opening the box, he removed the two golden bands. Hers was so small, so delicate, compared to his. But both were engraved on the inside with the same inscription. "Maggie and Matt. Forever."

Maggie looked at Matt as he took her hand. His face was serious, but his eyes were soft. She felt the world fade around her as she lost herself in his eyes.

"I promise I'll love you forever," he said softly, repeating the words he'd said at their wedding, so many long days ago. He slipped the ring on her finger.

She looked down at their hands and she knew she was never going to doubt him again. No matter what the future brought, she would stand by Matt's side.

She held out her hand, and he placed his own ring on her palm. It was so big and solid, just like Matt himself. Yet she hesitated. "Matt," she said. "I lied to you." She forced herself to look up at him. "I lied when I told you that I didn't love you anymore. I was so angry, and I tried to stop loving you, but... I couldn't."

"We both said a lot of things in anger," he told her gently. "It's okay."

"I wanted to be sure you knew I didn't break my promise to you. I promised to love you forever, too, Matt, and it's a promise I intend to keep." She pushed the ring onto his finger and kissed the palm of his hand.

"I'm madly in love with you," Matt said, smiling at her despite the glint of emotion in his eyes, "and if you don't kiss me right this second, I'm going to die."

Maggie laughed. And then she kissed him.

And kissed him.

Forever.

*　*　*　*　*

A BACHELOR AND A BABY

by
Marie Ferrarella

MARIE FERRARELLA

earned a master's degree in Shakespearean comedy and, perhaps as a result, her writing is distinguished by humour and natural dialogue. The RITA® Award-winning author's goal is to entertain and to make people laugh and feel good. She has written a large number of books for Silhouette. Her romances are beloved by fans worldwide and have been translated into Spanish, Italian, German, Russian, Polish, Japanese and Korean.

To
Joan Marlow Golan,
with thanks
for the homecoming.

One

Rick Masters wasn't given to cruising around in his car. Certainly not in what was considered to be well past the shank of the evening.

It wasn't as if he was at loose ends with nothing to do. A stack of reports waited for his perusal, a pile of documents needed his signature and hundreds of people had lives on the cusp of being rearranged, all on his say-so once he made up his mind about the relocation of the present corporate headquarters for Masters Enterprises.

This wasn't the time to be driving around aimlessly on deserted streets.

Well, not aimlessly.

He hadn't been aimless in a very long time. And no matter what he tried to tell himself, he knew exactly where he was going. He'd finally given in and looked her up in the telephone book an hour ago.

She still lived there. In the old house. The one he still dreamed about on balmy nights when his mind gave him no peace.

Like tonight.

Maybe it was a mistake, coming back. Maybe this was the one challenge he should have turned his back on.

Too late now.

Besides, leaving a question unanswered was too much like letting the challenge win. Ever since he could walk, he'd always been too competitive to allow that to happen.

He'd taken that light a little too fast. Rick raised his dark eyes to look in the rearview mirror. No dancing blue and red lights approached.

He had to be careful, he told himself. There was no sense in letting his emotions run away with him, stealing away his tendency to be careful.

The way they once had, leading him down a path where he was vulnerable.

It seemed like a million years ago.

It seemed like yesterday.

He glanced along the silent, sleeping streets where he had grown up. It felt strange, being back. Stranger still to know that she still lived here in Bedford. When he'd left, he'd purposely never asked about her. Never given in to his curiosity about just what path her life had taken. It was enough that it was away from him.

Out of sight was supposed to be out of mind.

Right now, the only thing that appeared to be out of mind was him, he thought. Ironic amusement curved his generous mouth as he turned right at the next corner. There was a shopping mall now. He could remember when it was just an orange grove.

Bedford had done a lot of growing up in the last eight years. Why not? He had.

And yet, had he? Part of him didn't feel like the successful VP of Masters Enterprises. Part of him still felt like that young boy, head over heels in love with the wrong person. Except that then, he hadn't thought she was the wrong person.

But he had learned.

Learned a lot of things. Mostly how to take the helm of his father's company. He'd gotten to his present position on merit, not by coasting there because he was the boss's son. If he'd coasted, no way would he have been able to take over operations after his father's heart attack last October. The transition in management from father to son in the last six months had been an incredibly smooth one. And why not? All he did was live and breathe business these days. There was nothing else for him, not since he'd been betrayed by the last person in the world he would have thought capable of it.

Served him right for leading with his heart rather than his head. First and last time. It wasn't as if he hadn't been warned. Both his parents had told him that someone in his position had to be careful about the friends he made, the women he cared for.

Well, he'd learned all right. The lessons that you paid for dearly in life were the ones that stuck.

So what was he doing driving through her part of town, driving onto the winding streets of her development, threading his way toward her block?

He really didn't know.

He didn't turn back.

Self-torture had never been his way. He'd always been the philosophical one. Things happened. You got over them and moved on. And he had. Moved all the way across country to Atlanta, Georgia, the place that, until a month ago, had been the headquarters of his father's company. Georgia, where his grandfather had originally been from. But certain economical circumstances had arisen in the last year that made that arrangement no longer as advantageous as it once had been. Almost fully recovered from his heart attack, Howard Masters wanted to have the home office of his company moved to Southern California so that he could be closer to its operations. Tax advantages were no longer a factor. Only control was.

The old man still wanted to exercise control over the company his great-grandfather had begun in the back of a barn. Rick couldn't fault him. Keeping control had something to do with extending a man's mortality and Rick could sympathize with that.

Even so, he'd resisted the move at first. But then, he'd challenged himself to face up to his demons. After all, he'd been in love with Joanna a long time ago. He was smart enough now to know that love wasn't something to build a life on.

If he doubted that, he had only to look to his parents. Two icons of the social world who'd looked perfect together on paper, in photographs, everywhere but in real life.

Love, that wild, heady mysterious substance he'd once believed to have taken command of his soul, was only the stuff they wrote songs about. It had no place in the real world, and he was part of the real world.

What he did or didn't do affected thousands of people. Heavy burden, that.

He should be turning back. It was late and he had things to do.

The April night was crisp and clear and unusually warm, even for Southern California. He'd left the windows of his classic 64 Mustang down. His father had urged him to get a car more suitable to his present station, so he drove a Mercedes to work, but he'd refused to get rid of his Mustang. He wanted the car. Even though it had been the one he'd been driving the night he'd wanted to elope with Joanna. Even though they had made love in that car.

Or maybe because of it.

Rick shook his head as he retraced his way through a maze of ever-climbing streets. Hell of a time to be playing shrink with himself.

The houses here all lined one side of the street, their faces looking out onto carefully manicured vegetation that hid the backs of other houses as they progressed up the hill.

One more block and then he'd be passing her house.

Dumb idea, Rick upbraided himself. He needed to be getting back. Those contracts weren't going to review themselves and he believed in being a hands-on executive.

Hands. He could remember the way his hands had felt on her warm, supple flesh, remembered how it felt to lay her down on the cool spring grass and make love with her in the meadow behind his parents' summer home. It was just the two of them there. The two of them against the world.

Until he discovered what she was really like.

Rick wrinkled his nose. An acrid smell wove its way into the stillness.

Probably just someone using their fireplace. Some people didn't care if it was warm or not. It was just the beginning of spring and a fire in the fireplace was romantic.

His mind started to drift back again, remembering.

He knew he shouldn't have come this far. Annoyed with himself, Rick looked around for some place to turn his car around and go back the way he'd come.

The smell didn't go away.

Instead, it intensified with each passing second. He wasn't sure exactly what made him push on instead of turn around, but he kept going.

Like someone hypnotized, he pressed his foot down on the accelerator, urging his car up the incline and toward the smell.

And then he saw it.

The sky was filled with black smoke.

Joanna felt herself rebelling.

The dream was back to haunt her. The one where everything and everyone was obscured. The one that had her running barefoot, in her nightgown, through an open field enshrouded in fog and mists.

Everything was hidden from her. Hidden and threatening.

But this time, it wasn't fog, it was smoke that curled around her legs and crept stealthily along her body.

It didn't matter, the effect was the same.

She was lost, so very lost. And then she began

running faster, desperately searching for a way out. Looking for someone to help her.

There was no one.

She was alone.

Every time she thought she could make out a shape, a person, they would disappear as she ran toward them. The resulting emptiness mocked her.

It was a dream, just a dream, she told herself over and over again as she ran. Her heart twisted within her, aching in its loneliness.

She'd be all right if she could just open her eyes. Just bridge her way back into the real world. Over and over again, she told herself to wake up.

With superhuman effort, she forced open her eyes.

They began to smart.

Joanna woke up choking. Her lungs began to ache. Had the nightmare taken on another dimension? Groggy, she sat up in bed. Her bulk prevented her from making the transition from lying to sitting an easy one. She felt as if she'd been pregnant since the beginning of time instead of almost nine months.

Your own fault. You asked for this.

Her eyes were seriously tearing now. This wasn't part of her dream. She smelled smoke, felt heat even though she'd shut the heat off just before she'd gone to bed more than an hour ago.

And then she realized what was happening. Her house was on fire.

Stunned, her heart pounding as she scrambled out of bed, Joanna grabbed the long robe that was slung over the footboard. She was hardly aware of jamming her fists through the sleeves.

Barefoot, Joanna hurried to her bedroom doorway,

only to see that her living room was flooded in smoke. A line of fire had shadowed her steps, racing in front of her. It was now feeding on the door frame, preventing her flight.

Flames shot up all around her.

Something came crashing down right in front of her, barely missing her. Backing up, she screamed as flames leaped to the bottom of her robe, eating away at the hem. Working frantically, Joanna shed the robe before the flames could find her.

Driving quickly, Rick took the next corner at a speed that almost made the Mustang tip over. He jerked his cell phone out of his pocket and hit 911 on the keypad with his thumb.

The instant the dispatch came in the line, he snapped out his location, adding, "Two houses are on fire, one's almost gone."

As the woman asked him to repeat what he'd just said, he heard someone scream from within Joanna's house. Rick tossed the phone aside. It landed on the passenger seat as he bolted from the car. He barely remembered to cut off the engine.

The scream echoed in his brain.

Somehow he knew it wasn't her mother, wasn't some renter or some trick of the imagination.

That was Joanna's scream.

She was in there, in that inferno. And he had to get her out.

The last house on the corner, next to Joanna's, was already engulfed in flames. It looked as if the fire had started there and had spread to Joanna's house. So far, from what he could see as he ran toward the building, only the rear portion was burning.

That was where the bedrooms were, he remembered. And she was in one of them.

Racing to the front door, he twisted the knob. It was locked and there was no way he could jimmy it open. His talents didn't run in those directions. But he could think on his feet.

Stripping off his jacket, Rick wrapped it around his arm and swung at the front window as hard as he could. Glass shattered, raining down in chunks. Moving quickly, Rick cleared away as much as he could then let himself into the house.

He stopped only long enough to unlock the front door. He left it open, a portal to the outside world. He had a feeling he was going to need that to guide him out. Inside, the inferno grew.

"Joanna!" Cupping his mouth, he yelled again. "Joanna, where are you?"

The flames had momentarily frozen her in place as her mind raced on alternative routes of escape, trying to assimilate what was going on.

Was she dreaming?

She had to be. Why else would she be hearing Rick's voice calling to her? Rick was gone. Had been gone for eight years.

Without a word to her.

Maybe she was already dead. Maybe the smoke had gotten to her and she was having some kind of out-of-body experience.

A fireman. It had to be a fireman. She only thought it sounded like Rick.

"Here," she screamed. "I'm in here." Smoke crowded its way into her throat, slashing at her words, sucking away her breath. "In the back bedroom." Eyes smarting, she couldn't make out the doorway anymore. "I can't get out. Help me!"

Like a behemoth, the fire snarled and groaned, playing tricks on his ears, his eyes. He was sure he heard her, heard her voice, muffled but still strong, calling out. Flames belched out of the rear of the house now.

Despite the temperature, his blood turned cold in his veins.

Think, damn it, think.

And then an idea came to him. Running to the kitchen, he passed through the dining room. Rick stopped only long enough to grab the tablecloth and yank it off the table. He soaked the entire cloth in the sink, then hurried with it to the rear of the house.

Toward the sound of her voice.

There were curtains of fire everywhere. He couldn't see more than a foot in front of him. "Joanna? Joanna where are you?"

"Here, I'm here," Joanna called out. She couldn't get out the door and when she ran toward the window, she found her way blocked there as well. There was no way to get to the window. The rug beneath her feet was burning.

And then suddenly, something came rolling in on the floor, crashing through the flames. As she stared, the figure took shape, rising up to assume the full height of a man.

The room began to spin. She thought she saw Rick

Masters, her tablecloth wrapped around his head and shoulders, reaching out to her.

The next moment, she felt herself being wrapped up in the tablecloth. He was pressing it to her face, over her mouth. It was dripping wet. Joanna tried to drag in air and only felt smoke clogging her lungs.

"Let's go!"

The order echoed in her head, sounding so like Rick. She was going to die in some stranger's arms, remembering Rick.

The man's arms were around her as he urged her blindly on through what felt like an entire wall of fire.

Joanna tried to protest that she couldn't make it, but the words never rose to her lips. The man who looked like Rick was pushing her.

She felt herself stumbling. Falling.

The next moment, she felt his arms encircling her. And then suddenly, she was airborne. He was carrying her, carrying her through the inferno.

The heat was everywhere. She could hear it, feel it. And there was pain everywhere as well. Pain that was radiating not from the outside, but from within.

Something was tearing her in two.

Joanna bit down on her lip, but the scream came anyway. It shook her body, traveling down toward the center, toward the source of the pain. The pain wouldn't stop.

And then suddenly, the heat was gone.

She was being lowered.

Grass, there was grass beneath her.

Desperate, Joanna clawed her way out of the singed fabric enclosure that was still over her head and face.

And then it was off, lying in a heap on the ground next to her.

Gulping in air, Joanna looked around frantically, trying to get her bearings, trying to clear her head of the hallucination that insisted on sticking to her like a second skin.

She blinked several times, but the man sitting on the front lawn beside her, panting, with the smell of smoke clinging to every surface of his body, didn't resume his shape.

Didn't transform from who she thought she saw to who he really was.

He stayed the same.

Was she dead? Was that it? Was that why she was still staring up at Rick Masters?

There didn't seem to be any other possible explanation for it.

Rick dragged air back into his lungs. The house next to Joanna's was encased in flames. He saw no signs of anyone having escaped. His legs shook as he rose to his feet. He felt her grab his arm, pulling him back.

He looked at her over his shoulder. "Let go, I've got to see if I can get anyone out."

"There's no one there," she gasped out. "They're away on vacation." Her eyes still burned and she squeezed them shut for a moment, then opened them again. He was still there.

"How about in your house?"

She thought she shook her head. She wasn't sure if she did or not. "Nobody."

Rick sank down on the ground again. His heart was

slamming madly against his chest. "Are you all right?" he demanded.

He sounded angry. They hadn't seen one another in eight years and he sounded angry. Why? If anything, she should have been the one who was angry. Angry because he hadn't come after her the way she'd hoped, prayed that he would.

But he couldn't be here. Could he? Was she losing her mind?

Shaken, her head spinning, she stared at him, still afraid to believe that she wasn't somehow hallucinating all this.

"Rick? What are you doing here?"

The desire to hold her in his arms, to kiss her and make the world back off, was almost overpowering. But it was at odds with the renewed feeling of betrayal that seared through him. He might not have moved on with his life in the full sense of the word, but she obviously had. Moved on, married and was now carrying some other man's child in her body.

The sting he felt was unbelievably sharp and deep. Though he'd never talked about it, he'd thought of having children with her. Lots of children. Children with her face and his sense of logic.

Damn it, Joey, why did you do this to me?

"I asked you a question," he said his voice harsh with anger, with hurt. "Are you all right?"

Her mouth fell open. She wasn't dead. She was alive. And he was real. He was here. After all this time, he was here. Looking at her the way she never wanted him to look at her. She'd walked out of his life just to avoid that look in his eyes.

And yet, after all this time, here he was, looking at her as if he hated her.

She started to say something, and had her breath stolen away before she could utter an intelligible sound. What came out of her mouth was a purely guttural cry.

Joanna's eyes widened as her hand flew to her abdomen. The pain she'd been peripherally conscious of intensified, pushing itself to center stage and demanding attention.

"What? What's the matter?" On his knees beside her, concern pushed aside his anger.

Rick strained to hear the sound of sirens approaching, but there was nothing. Not only that, but there didn't appear to be any activity, or even any lights being turned on from the three other houses on the immediate block.

Where the hell was everyone? Had he and Joanna just slipped into some private twilight zone of their own?

Joanna clutched his arm, her nails digging into his flesh, her face drained of all color. She wasn't answering his question.

This couldn't be happening, she thought, frantically Not now. She wasn't due for another two weeks. The doctor had promised her.

Promises were meant to be broken.

The promise between her and Rick had been.

"The baby," she gasped, pushing the words out as best she could. "I think the baby's coming."

Two

Dumbfounded, Rick could only stare at her. "You mean later."

She couldn't be saying what he thought she was saying. Rick looked from her face to her abdomen and then back at her face again. That had to be the panic talking, he decided.

Joanna could almost feel her knuckles breaking out through her skin as she clenched his wrist.

"I mean *now*." The word rode out on a torrent of pain.

Crouching beside her, Rick carefully peeled her fingers from his wrist. She'd almost cut off his circulation. "Hang on, the paramedics have got to be getting here soon."

Instinctively she knew that they'd never make it in time.

Joanna shook her head violently from side to side, the pain all but cracking her in half. "Unless they're invisible and already here…they're going to be too late." She looked up at him. God, but life was strange, bringing them together like this, now of all times. "You're going to have to help me."

There were a great many things he'd learned how to do, felt comfortable in undertaking. Delivering a baby was not one of them. "Me?"

Even with the throbbing sound echoing in her head, Joanna could hear the wariness in Rick's voice. She couldn't very well blame him. This wasn't exactly her idea of ideal circumstances, either.

"I don't…like this any better…than…you do, but this baby…is coming…and I need…someone…on the other end." It was getting more and more difficult for her to talk, to frame complete thoughts. The pain kept snatching away her breath, railroading her mind. Panic was attempting to push its way into her consciousness.

Desperate, Rick looked over his shoulder at the other three houses on the block. They were all dark. Why hadn't any lights gone on? Why wasn't anyone home?

Where the hell *was* everyone?

Where they were didn't matter. What did matter was that he was here and so was she. And she needed him.

It occurred to him that for the second time in his life, he hadn't the slightest idea what to do. And both times had involved Joanna.

Someone had to be home on the next block. "Hold

on,'' he told her, beginning to rise to his feet. ''I'll go get help.''

The death grip tightened on his wrist, yanking him back down to her with a strength he didn't think she was capable of.

''You *are* help…'' She raised her eyes to his. ''Please.''

Damn it, she still knew just how to rip into his heart. Even after all this time. Rick knew he had no choice.

''Okay. I—'' He saw her jerk and stiffen, her eyes opening so wide, they looked as if they could fall out at any moment.

Joanna bit down on her lip so hard, she thought she tasted blood. A scream welled up in her throat, its magnitude nearly matching the agony assaulting her. It felt as if she were a holiday turkey and someone had taken a buzz saw to her body.

''I have to push…I have to push…I have to push.'' The words came out in a frantic rush.

He knew next to nothing about what was involved in delivering a baby, but it had to take longer than this. She had to be wrong. ''Are you sure?''

Clutching his hand as if it were her very lifeline, Joanna managed to pull herself up into a semi-sitting position. ''I'm sure…oh God…I'm sure.'' How did someone feel like this and still live?

Fear gnawed at her. Belatedly, recalling something Lori had said to the Lamaze class about not being able to pant and push at the same time, Joanna began panting hard. Praying that the action would at least temporarily divert this overwhelming urge she had to push the baby out.

Nothing she'd read or heard had prepared her for the reality of this. Before she'd ever walked into the sperm bank, she had read about every possible scenario that could happen at this juncture.

Every bad one now flashed before her, stealing away her courage.

She'd been so sure about this. So sure. She hadn't even regretted her decision when the local school board had tactfully "suggested" that she take an unpaid leave of absence until after her baby was born. Since she was a high-school English teacher, her condition in the somewhat conservative town was a source of discomfort and embarrassment to a number of the parents. But even then, she'd been sure about her choice to go this route alone.

Now she wasn't sure about being alone or even the route itself. Now there was only a sense of panic tearing into her with steel claws.

Here she was, her house in flames, her life in shambles, giving birth to a fatherless baby on the front lawn with the only man she'd ever loved inexplicably standing over her.

She felt as if she'd lost her grasp on reality.

"Ricky…I'm…scared."

"Yeah, me, too," he admitted.

His words echoed back to him. Joanna had been the only one he'd ever let his guard down with, the only one he'd ever allowed to witness his more human, vulnerable side. To the rest of the world, even from a very young age, he'd always presented a strong, unflappable front. It was expected of him. He was a Masters. Only Joanna had seen him as Ricky, as the boy he'd been and the man he was struggling to be.

But all that was behind him. Years behind him.

Rick squared his shoulders. He had to set the tone. What was there to be afraid of, anyway? Taking her hand, he looked down at Joanna. "Babies get born every day, right?"

Yes, but this one was different. This one was coming out of *her*. Shredding everything in its path. "Not this one."

He needed a blanket, a sheet, something. Feeling helpless, Rick looked around. There was nothing available except for the tablecloth he'd used to shield Joanna's face. Taking it, he tucked the material under her as best he could.

"Not exactly sterile, but better than the grass," he explained when she looked at him with huge, questioning eyes.

Oh lord, here came another one. Joanna wrapped her fingers around the long blades of grass, ripping more than a few out of the ground as she arched her back, vainly trying to scramble to a place where the pain couldn't find her.

But there was nowhere to go. The pain found her no matter how she twisted and turned, found her and constructed a wall all around her, imprisoning her.

There was no escape.

Panting again, Joanna tried to recall what she'd learned in her Lamaze classes. Nothing came to her. All she could remember was that the four of them, she, Chris Jones, Sherry Campbell and the instructor, Lori O'Neill, referred to themselves as the Mom

Squad, four single women who'd bonded because they were facing life's most precious miracle alone.

None of that helped now.

She froze, hardly hearing what Rick was saying to her, her body enveloped in one huge contraction.

What was it that Lori'd told the class the last session? Relax, that was it. Relax.

Right, easy for Lori to say. Of the four of them, she was the one who had the longest to go. Lori didn't know what it felt like to be a can of tuna with a jagged can opener circling her perimeter.

But she did.

Joanna let loose with a blood-curling scream as another contraction, the hardest one yet, ripped into her on the tail of the last one. There was no end in sight. She was going to keep on having these contractions until she died.

Rick jerked back, covering his ear. She had risen up and screamed right against it. He could still feel the sound reverberating in his head.

"Good thing I've got two ears. I'm not going to be using my left one for a while."

He shouldn't be the one here, helping her give birth to another man's baby, he thought. This should have been their child fighting its way into the world.

A sadness gripped his heart. He looked at her. "This is all wrong."

With what little strength she had, Joanna dragged her elbows into her sides and struggled to raise herself up again.

"What…? What's…wrong? Something wrong… with…my baby?"

"No, no," he assured her, pushing her gently back

down. "Just that your husband should be here, not me." *Or at least the paramedics,* he added silently.

"Don't…have…one," she gasped. She felt light-headed and fought to keep focused and conscious. Here came another! "Now, Rick, now!"

Rick saw her face turn three shades redder as she screwed her eyes shut.

This was all happening too fast.

He didn't have to tell her to push. He didn't have to tell her anything at all. Suddenly, whether he was ready or not, it was happening. The baby was coming.

Rick barely had enough time to slip his hands into position. The baby's head was emerging. He could feel the blood, feel the slide of flesh against flesh.

Wasn't giving birth supposed to take longer than the amount of time it took to peel a banana skin back?

And why hadn't the fire trucks arrived yet? Were they the last two people on the earth?

It felt that way. The very last two people on earth. Engaged in a life-affirming struggle.

"Pull…it…out!" Joanna screamed. The baby was one-third out, two-thirds in. Why had everything stopped?

She fell back, exhausted, unable to drag in enough air to sustain herself. Beams of light began dancing through her head, motioning her toward them.

Toward oblivion.

In mounting panic, Rick realized that she was going to pass out on him. One hand supporting the baby's head, he leaned over and shook Joanna's shoulder, trying to get her to focus.

"I can't pull it out," he shouted at her. "You can't

play tug of war with a head, Joanna. You have to push the baby out the rest of the way.''

''You…push it out…the…rest of…the way. It's…your…turn.''

And then she felt it again. That horrible pain that she couldn't escape. It bore down on her, tying her up in a knot even as it threatened to crack her apart. It didn't matter that she had no strength, that she couldn't draw a half-decent breath into her lungs. Her body had taken over where her mind had failed.

''Oh…God…it's not…over.'' How was she going to do this with no strength left? How was it possible?

Panting, gasping for air, she looked at Rick. He was right. This was wrong, all wrong. She should never have decided to have this baby, never agreed to leave Rick without explaining why.

Too late now for regrets.

The refrain echoed in her brain over and over again as heat surrounded her, searing a path clear for more pain.

The tablecloth below her was soaked with blood. ''Push,'' Rick ordered gruffly, hiding the mounting fear taking hold of him. What if something went wrong? Should there be this much blood? She couldn't die on him, she couldn't. ''C'mon, Joanna, you can do this!''

No, she thought, she couldn't.

But she had to try. She couldn't just die like this. Her baby needed her.

From somewhere, a last ounce of strength materialized. She bore down as hard as she could, knowing that this was the last effort she was capable of making. If the baby wasn't going to emerge now, they were just going to bury her this way.

Fragments of absurd thoughts kept dancing in and out of her head.

She thought she heard sirens, or screams, in the background. Maybe it was the fire gaining on them. She didn't know, didn't care, she just wanted this all to be over with—one way or another.

She felt as if she was being turned inside out and still she pushed, pushed until her chest felt as if it was caving in, as if her very body was disintegrating from the effort.

And then she heard a tiny cry, softer than all the other noise. Sweeter.

Her head spinning from lack of oxygen, Joanna fell back against the tablecloth, the grass brushing against her soaked neck. She was too exhausted even to breathe.

Rick stared at the miracle in his hands. The miracle was staring back, eyes as wide and huge as her mother's. He felt something twist within him. He was too numb to identify the sensation.

"You've got a girl," he whispered to Joanna, awe stealing his voice away.

He dripped with perspiration, but he knew it was chilly. There was nothing to wrap the baby in. He stripped off his shirt and tucked it around the tiny soul. The infant still watched him with the largest eyes he'd ever seen.

Several feet away from him, a fire truck came to a screeching halt. He hardly acknowledged its arrival. All he could do was look at the baby he'd helped to bring into the world.

Joanna's baby.

The scene around them was almost surreal. People were shouting, firefighters were scrambling down from the truck, running toward them. Running toward the fire.

In the midst of chaos, an older firefighter hurried toward them, his trained eyes assessing the situation quickly. Squatting, he placed a gloved hand on the woman on the ground as well as one on the man holding the newborn. "You two all right?"

"Three," Rick corrected, looking down at the new life tucked against his chest. "And we're doing fine." The smile faded as he looked at Joanna. "I mean—" She'd gone through hell in the last few minutes. He might be fine, but she undoubtedly wasn't. "She needs to get to a hospital."

Rising to his feet, the firefighter nodded. "I can see that." Turning, he signaled to the paramedics, who were just getting out of the ambulance. The firefighter waved them over, then glanced back at Rick as the two hurried over with a gurney. He nodded toward the burning buildings. "Anyone else in there?"

"I don't know." Rick looked to Joanna for confirmation. She shook her head. "I don't think so. I just got here myself," he explained.

"Not just," the firefighter corrected, looking at the baby in Rick's arms.

Rick had no time to make any further comment. A paramedic took the baby from him. He felt a strange loss of warmth as the child left his arms.

"We'll take it from here," the paramedic told him kindly. "Thanks."

The firefighter and a paramedic had already lifted

Joanna onto the gurney. Strapping her in, they raised the gurney and snapped its legs into place.

"You the father?" the first paramedic asked.

Rick was already stepping back. He shook his head in response. "Just a Good Samaritan, in the right place at the right time."

He avoided looking at Joanna when he said it.

She and the baby were already being taken toward the ambulance. The rear doors flew open. Rick remained where he was, watching them being placed inside. For one moment, he had the urge to rush inside, to ride to the hospital with her.

He squelched it.

He was in the way, he thought, stepping back farther as hoses were snaked out and firefighters risked their lives to keep the fire from spreading.

"Lucky for the little lady you were in the neighborhood," the older firefighter commented, raising his voice to be heard above the noise.

The rear lights of the ambulance became brighter as the ignition was engaged. And then it was pulling away from the scene of the fire.

Away from him.

"Yeah, lucky."

Rick turned and walked toward his car. Behind him, the firefighters hurried about the business of trying to stave off the fire before it ate its way down the block and up the hillside.

There was no doubt about it, Rick decided. He should have his head examined.

After he'd gone out to look over the proposed site for the construction of the new corporate home office, instead of returning to the regional office he was temporarily working out of, he'd taken a detour. Actually, it had been two detours.

He'd gone to see just how much damage there'd actually been to Joanna's house. He was hoping, for her sake, that it wasn't as bad as it had looked last night.

In the light of day, the charred remains of the last house on the block—a call to the fire station had informed him that the fire had started there with a faulty electrical timer—looked like a disfigured burned shell. But the firefighters had arrived in time to save at least part of Joanna's house. Only the rear portion was gutted. The front of the house had miraculously sustained a minimum of damage.

Still, he thought, walking around the perimeter, it was going to be a while before the house was livable again.

With a shrug, Rick walked back to his car and got in. Not his problem. That problem belonged to her and her significant other, or whatever she chose to call the man who had fathered her baby.

As far as he was concerned, he'd done as much as he intended to do.

For some reason, after Rick had gone to what was left of Joanna's house, he'd found himself driving toward Blair Memorial Hospital, where the paramedics had taken her last night.

Joanna didn't look surprised to see him walk into her room.

The conversation was awkward, guarded, yet he couldn't get himself to leave.

He had to know.

"You said last night that you weren't married."

He'd promised himself that if he did go to see her, he wasn't going to say anything about her current state. The promise evaporated the moment he saw her.

"I wasn't. I mean, I'm not."

"Divorced?" he guessed.

"No."

"Widowed?"

She sighed, picking at her blanket. Had he turned up in her life just to play Colombo? "No, and I'm not betrothed, either."

She was playing games with him. It shouldn't have bothered him after all this time, but it did. A great deal.

"So, what, this was an immaculate conception?" Sarcasm dripped from his voice. "What's the baby's father's name, Joanna?"

She took a deep breath. "11375."

He stood at the foot of her bed, confusion echoing through his brain. "What?"

"Number 11375." She'd chosen her baby's father from a catalogue offered by the sperm bank. In it were a host of candidates, their identities all carefully concealed. They were known only by their attributes and traits. And a number. "That's all I know him by."

Trying to be discreet, Joanna shifted in her bed. She was still miserably uncomfortable. No one had talked about how sore you felt the day after you gave birth, she thought. Something else she hadn't come across in her prenatal readings.

She raised her eyes to Rick's. His visit had caught her off-guard, but not nearly as much as his appearance in her bedroom last night had. All things considered, it was almost like something out of a movie. A long-ago lover suddenly rushing into her burning bedroom to rescue her. After that, she doubted very much if anything would ever surprise her again.

What kind of double talk was this? "I don't understand. Is he some kind of a spy?"

"No, some kind of a test tube." She saw his brows draw together in a deep scowl. He probably thought she was toying with him. This wasn't exactly something she felt comfortable talking about, but he'd saved her life last night. He deserved to have his question answered. "I went to a sperm bank, Rick."

If ever there was a time for him to be knocked over by a feather, Rick thought, now was it. Maybe he'd just heard her wrong. "Why?"

"Because that's where they keep sperm."

This was an insane conversation. *What are you doing here, Rick? Why are you eight years too late?*

She ran her tongue over her dry lips. "I wanted a baby."

For a second, he couldn't think. Dragging a chair over to her bed, he sank down. "There are other ways to get a baby, Joanna."

Suddenly, she wanted him to go away. This was too painful to discuss. "They all involve getting close to a person."

Memories from the past teased his brain. Memories of moonlit nights, soft, sultry breezes and a woman in his arms he'd vowed to always love. Who'd vowed to always love him.

Always had a short life expectancy.

"They tell me that's the best part," he said quietly.

She looked away. "Been there, done that."

Her flippant tone irritated him. It was on the tip of his tongue to ask if there'd been money involved in this transaction, as well. But the question was too cruel, even if she deserved it. He let it go.

Rick rose, shoving his hand into his pockets as he looked out the window that faced the harbor. "So there's no one else in your life?"

"My baby." Her baby would make her complete, she thought. She didn't need anyone else.

Rick looked at her over his shoulder. "Someone taller."

She knew she should be fabricating lovers, to show him that she could go on with her life, that it hadn't just ended the day they parted, but she was suddenly too tired to make the effort.

"Not in the way you mean, no."

Funny, whenever he'd thought of her in the last eight years, he'd pictured her on someone's arm, laughing the way he loved to see and hear her laugh. It had driven him almost insane with jealousy, but he'd eventually learned how to cope.

Or thought he had until he'd seen her last night, her body filled out with the signs of another man's claim on her.

He turned and looked out on the harbor again. The sky was darkening, even though it was only two in the afternoon. There was a storm coming. Unusual for April. Boats were beginning to leave. "I went by your house this morning."

Her house. Her poor house. Joanna held her breath. "And?"

There was no way to sugarcoat this, but he did his

best. "It was only half destroyed by the fire." Rick turned to look at her. "But it's not habitable." He saw the hopeful light go out of her eyes.

"Damn, now what am I going to do?"

He approached the matter practically. "Well, it's not a total loss. It might take some time to rebuild— you do have coverage, right?"

Yes, she had coverage, but that wasn't why she was upset. Fighting back tears, she sighed. "That's not the point. I was going to take out a home loan on it." The appointment had been postponed from last week. She fervently wished she'd been able to keep it. Now it was too late. "Nobody gives you a loan on the remains of a bonfire." Joanna struggled against the feeling that life had just run her over with a Mack truck. She'd been counting on the money to see her and the baby through the next few months until she could go back to work and start building their future. "Now I don't have the loan or a place to live."

Rick studied her face for a long moment. And then he said the last thing that she expected him to say. The last thing he must have expected himself to say.

"You can come and stay with me."

Three

She stared at Rick, momentarily speechless.

As far as she knew, prenatal vitamins did not fall under the heading of hallucinogenic drugs and she'd had nothing else to throw her brain out of alignment. Why, then was she hearing Rick make an offer she knew he couldn't possibly have made?

"What did you say?"

Her eyes were even bluer than he remembered, bluer and more compelling. He had to struggle not to get lost in them, the way he used to.

"I said, you can come and stay with me—until you get on your feet again," he qualified after a beat, feeling that the offer begged for a coda. This wasn't meant to be a permanent arrangement by any means. He was just temporarily helping a friend. For old times' sake.

If she could have, Joanna would have walked away. As it was, all she could manage was a pugnacious lift of her head.

"I'm sorry, but I don't take charity."

He felt as if she'd insulted him, insulted the memory of what had once been between them. Or had that only been in his own mind? Right at this moment, the chasm that existed between them seemed a hundred yards wide. Sometimes, it was hard to remember how it had gotten this way.

"It would have been charity if I'd just put a wad of bills in your hand and told you not to pay it back." He shrugged, struggling to rein in anger that had materialized out of nowhere. "This is just putting a couple of empty rooms to use."

She assumed by his offer that he was staying at the estate. It was the last place she wanted to be. Not with the past vividly rising up before her. "I really don't think your father would exactly welcome the invasion with open arms."

"One woman and an infant are hardly an invasion—or an intrusion," Rick added before she could revise her words. He guessed at part of the problem. His parents had never treated her with the respect that he'd felt, at the time, that she deserved. His mother was gone now, but there was still his father. "And my father is Florida on vacation." An extended one, he thought. His father hadn't been back to California for several months, actually.

A vacation meant that the man was returning. "So, what's that, a week, two?"

"More like three months or more." With things like teleconferencing, there was not as much need to appear in the flesh anymore, Rick thought. He couldn't say that he disliked the arrangement. The less he saw of his father, the better.

Her mouth curved with a cynicism that was ordinarily foreign to her. "Oh yes, I forgot, the rich are different from you and me—" She glanced up at him. "Well, from me at any rate."

He heard the bitterness in her voice. Was that directed at him? Why? He hadn't said anything to trigger it. But then, as his father had once pointed out, he really didn't know Joanna at all.

Something within him made him push on when another man would have just shrugged and walked away. He wasn't even sure why.

Maybe because, despite the bravado, she looked as if she needed him. Or at least, someone. "Mrs. Rutledge is still there."

At the mention of the woman's name, Joanna's face softened. She and his parents' housekeeper had gotten on very well during the days when he had invited her to his house.

"How is Mrs. Rutledge?"

Like a fighter returning to his corner between rounds, Rick gravitated toward the neutral topic. "Still refusing to retire. Still thinking that she knows what's best for everyone."

Joanna smiled, remembering. "She always reminded me of my mother."

More neutral territory. Rachel Prescott had been the woman he'd secretly wished his mother could have been. He'd spent a great deal of time at Joanna's house over the three years that they went together.

He'd half expected to find her in Joanna's room when he came to visit. "How is your mother?"

"My mother died last year." Joanna looked down at her hands, feeling suddenly hollow. Thirteen months wasn't nearly enough time to grieve.

The news hit him with the force of a bullet. "Oh, I'm sorry." What did a person say at a time like this? How did he begin to express the regret he felt? The world was a sadder place for the loss. He looked at Joanna, his hand covering hers in a mute sympathy be couldn't begin to articulate. "She was a very nice woman."

"Yes, she was." Joanna fought the temptation to stop this awkward waltz they were dancing and throw herself into his arms, to tell him that she'd really needed him those last few months when she had stood by her mother's side, watching the woman who had been her whole world slip away from her. Instead, she looked up at him and said, "I read about your mother in the paper. I'm sorry."

Rick shrugged, letting the perfunctory offer of sympathy pass. It was sad, but he really didn't feel the need for sympathy. He'd never been close to his mother, not even as a child, and consequently, hadn't felt that bitter sting of loss when she died. He'd returned for the funeral like a dutiful son, remaining only long enough for the service to be concluded before flying out again. The entire stay had been less than six hours.

In part, he supposed, he'd left so quickly because he'd wanted to be sure he wouldn't weaken and do exactly what he'd done last night. Drive by Joanna's house. Looking for her.

Joanna tried to fathom the strange expression on his face. She had almost gone to his mother's funeral service at the church, hoping to catch a glimpse of him. But somehow, that had seemed too needy. So instead, she'd shored up her resolve and remained strong, deliberately keeping herself occupied and staying away.

There was another reason she'd kept away. To come to the service would have been to display a measure of respect and she had none for the deceased woman, none for her or her husband. Not since the two had joined forces that August day and come to her bearing a sizable check with her name on it.

All she had to do to earn it was to get out of their son's life, they'd said. To sweeten the pot, they'd appealed to her sense of fair play, to her love for Rick. Between the two of them, they'd projected the future and what it would be like for Rick if he married her. They were adamant that he would grow to despise her. He belonged, they maintained, with his own kind. With a woman from his social world, with his background and his tastes. Someone who could be an asset to him, not a liability. They'd even had someone picked out. A woman she knew by sight.

They argued so well that she'd finally had to agree. She hated them for that, for making her see how much better off Rick would be without her.

"Actually," Rick commented on her original protest, "if there is any charity being dispensed, you'd be the one doing it."

He always was good with words, she thought. But he had lost her this time. "Come again? I think I pushed out my hearing along with the baby."

The laugh was soft. He began to feel a little more comfortable. Despite the hurt feelings that existed between them like a third, viable entity, Joanna had always had the knack of being able to make him relax.

"If Mrs. Rutledge finds out that you're homeless," he explained, "and that I knew about it, she'll have me filleted."

"I'm not homeless," she protested. "Just temporarily unhoused."

It was an offer, she supposed in all honesty, that she couldn't refuse. She knew she could probably crash on any one of a number of sofas, but she would also be bringing her baby and that was an imposition she wasn't willing to make. Babies made noise, they took getting used to. It was an unfair strain to place on any friendship. Rick had the only house where the cries of a child wouldn't echo throughout the entire dwelling. Where she wouldn't be in the way as she struggled to find her footing in this new world of motherhood.

Joanna chewed on her lip, vacillating. "You're sure your father's away?"

For a moment, Rick was transported back through time, sitting in math class, watching her puzzle out an equation. He smiled, fervently wishing he could somehow go back and relive that period of his life.

But all he had available to him was the present.

"I spoke to him this morning via conference hookup. He's having a great time marlin-fishing off the Florida Keys."

Joanna tried to picture the stuffy man sitting at the stern of a boat, a rod and reel clutched in his hands, and failed. "Marlin-fishing? Your father?"

He knew it sounded far-fetched, but it was true. Howard Masters had undergone nothing short of a transformation. "The heart attack turned him into a new man. He might not be stopping to smell the roses, but he is taking time to do almost everything else."

The man had always been consumed with making money. She'd heard that he'd only taken one day off when his wife died. "What about the business?"

"Mostly, it's in my hands." He wondered if that made her think that he'd become his father. The thought brought a shiver down his spine. "He likes to look over my shoulder every so often and make 'suggestions.' But mostly, he leaves it all up to me."

She wondered if Rick would eventually turn into his father. There was a time when she would have said no, but that was about a man she'd loved. A man who had failed to live up to her expectations. "Is that why you're here?"

Eyebrows drew together over an almost perfect nose. "In the hospital?"

"No, in Bedford. Did the family business bring you to Bedford?" He nodded. She knew she should leave it at that, but she couldn't help asking, "And why were you outside my house last night?"

He gave her the most honest answer he could, given the situation. "I'm not really sure."

Fair enough. Joanna blew out a breath, shifting slightly again, trying not to pay attention to the discomfort radiating from her lower half. *This too, shall pass.*

"Well, I can't say I'm not glad you were." She

raised her eyes to his. "Otherwise—" her voice, filled with emotion, trailed off.

He stopped her before she could continue. "I've learned that 'otherwise' is not a street that takes travel well." There was nothing to be gained by second-guessing. "You get too bogged down going there."

He heard the door just behind him being opened. Welcoming the respite, Rick turned and saw a nurse wheeling in a clear bassinet. Inside, bundled in a pink blanket, sleeping peacefully, was possibly the most beautiful baby he'd ever seen.

"Someone's going to be waking up soon and it's feeding time," the woman announced. Her smile took in both of them.

Rick moved out of the way as the nurse brought the bassinet closer, his eyes riveted to the small occupant. "Wow."

The single word filled her with pride. Joanna couldn't help smiling. "I believe that's her first compliment."

"But not her last," Rick guaranteed. "She cleans up nicely."

"You got to see her at her worst," Joanna pointed out. She didn't add that he'd seen her at possibly her worst as well.

Rick sincerely doubted that the word *worst* could be applied to a miracle. Something stirred within him as he watched the nurse lift the infant from the bassinet and hand her over to Joanna.

He was in the way, he thought. "Well, I'd better be going." He began to edge his way out.

Suddenly, she didn't want him to leave. Not yet. "Would you like to hold her?" Joanna asked.

Somehow, the baby looked far more fragile now than she had last night. And his hands were large and clumsy. "I already did."

"I mean now that she's not messy." Joanna read his expression correctly. "She won't break, you know. Not if you're gentle."

"I won't slam dunk her," he promised. The quip was meant to hide what was really going on inside him. There were emotions there that he wasn't sure he understood or knew what to do with. Certainly none that he could label properly.

Very carefully, he slipped his hands under the baby's back and neck, making the transfer. He unintentionally brushed his fingers against Joanna's breasts. Their eyes met and held for a moment before he backed away from her, holding the infant to him.

The nurse looked on and nodded with approval. "You're a natural."

"He should be," Joanna told her. "He's the one who held her first."

The woman's smile brightened. "Oh, are you her father?"

"No." The nurse's innocent question dragged him away from the formless region he'd momentarily found himself inhabiting and back to the real world. He wasn't the little girl's father and that was the whole point. "I'm not." He handed the infant back to Joanna. "I'll be back before you're discharged."

There was a formal note in his voice that she didn't understand or like. The temporary bridge between their two worlds was gone and they were back to being wounded strangers again.

"We'll see," she called after him. She had the satisfaction of seeing him momentarily halt before continuing out the door.

Like a commando unit making a beachhead, the three other women who comprised the Mom Squad descended upon Joanna as one later that afternoon, brightening her spirit as well as her room.

They came bearing gifts, and, more importantly, they came bearing good will and cheer. Something she was finding temporarily in short supply.

The baby was awake and alert and seemed very willing to be passed from one woman to the other like a precious doll.

Sherry Campbell, newly returned to the working world as a reporter for the *Bedford World News* and a brand-new mother in her own right, was the first to hold her. The baby was almost as big as Sherry's own three-month-old son. But then, Johnny had been a preemie.

"She's beautiful." She beamed at Joanna. "Of course, that's not a surprise. Look at her mother."

Chris Jones, a special agent with the FBI, coaxed the baby out of her friend's arms. She tucked the newborn against her, partially resting the infant against her own rounded stomach. "Too bad we don't know what the father looks like."

Lori O'Neill laughed. "Well, he was obviously not a frog."

Sherry frowned thoughtfully as she looked at the others. Joanna's method of becoming pregnant was a matter of record. "Do sperm banks allow ugly men to contribute their um, genes?"

"Apparently not," Chris cracked. She handed the infant over to Lori and then moved around to the side of Joanna's bed. She perched on a corner, though it wasn't easy. "So tell me, was it awful?"

"Was what awful?" Joanna asked.

Chris hesitated. "Giving birth. Was it like getting shot?"

Joanna pressed her lips together, trying not to laugh at the question. She knew that Chris was nervous about this unknown territory they all had to face on their own. "I've never been shot, so my field of reference is a little limited."

Chris backtracked. "Okay, was it like what you imagine getting shot is like?"

Lori rolled her eyes. She'd never given birth herself, but she'd talked to scores of mothers. The comparison was unusual, to say the least. "Chris—"

"Well, I've been shot," Chris insisted, "and that was the worst pain I've ever physically had, but it was okay." She looked at the others, feeling herself grow defensive. "I'm just trying to put things into perspective here."

Sherry pretended to shake her head as she leaned in to "confide" to Joanna. "You'd think that a woman who was with the FBI, who'd gone through some pretty scary situations and lived to tell about it wouldn't be so afraid of giving birth."

Chris tossed her long blond hair over her shoulder. "I'm not afraid of giving birth, I just want to be prepared, that's all. The first thing you learn as an agent is never to walk into a room you don't know how to get out of—"

"The only way to 'get out of' this particular 'room'

at this point is to give birth," Lori told her, "so you'd just better resign yourself to that. Relax," she gave Chris's shoulder a playful pat, "it's not as bad as you think."

"Why didn't you ask Sherry?" Joanna asked. After all, the vivacious reporter had been the first of them to go through childbirth, and if anyone could fill Chris in on the darker side of giving birth, it was Sherry. She'd delivered her baby in a desolate mountain cabin with only a dog and a reclusive billionaire in attendance. Lucky for her, the man had been a jack of all trades, up to and including being a one-time pre-med student.

Chris sighed, picking at the design on the blanket. "Because all Sherry'll tell me is the official party line." Chris rolled her eyes and parroted the famous edict uttered by mothers since the beginning of time: "You forget all about the pain as soon as you hold the baby in your arms."

"Well, you do," Joanna insisted. And she had already—for the most part. "Except when you try to shift your bottom."

Sherry and Lori laughed, but Chris looked at her seriously. "So it's awful?"

"Awful?" Joanna repeated, examining the word. "No, not really. It's not exactly something I'd recommend doing for pleasure," her eyes slid over toward the baby, who was back in Sherry's arms, "but it is definitely worth it. Trust me."

The baby began to fuss a little. Sherry patted the tiny bottom and the fussing stopped. "So, I hear you didn't make it to the hospital, either."

Joanna laughed shortly. "I almost didn't make it

anywhere. My house was on fire when I went into labor."

Lori's eyes widened. "Oh my God, we didn't know. How's your house?"

Joanna remembered how terrified she'd been as they put her into the back of the ambulance. The last thing she saw as they closed the doors was the wall of flames closing in around her house.

"Still standing, they tell me. The fire chief came by to see me earlier today and said they managed to save part of it, but right now, it's not habitable."

There but for the grace of God, Sherry thought. She knew all about Joanna's situation and her financial predicament. Like Joanna, she'd been eased out of her job. Hers had been a high-profile position as lead anchor woman for the local news station. If it hadn't been for some string-pulling that had landed her on the newspaper, she would have been in the same place as Joanna now. Unemployed. The only difference being she had her family to lean on. Joanna didn't.

Sherry leaned over and squeezed Joanna's hand. "You can come and stay with me." Sherry grinned. "We can start a baby co-op."

But Joanna shook her head. "You have a new baby and a new man in your life, the last thing you need right now is another woman with a newborn."

Lori was quick to interrupt. "You can crash at my place."

Joanna laughed. She knew Lori meant well, but it wasn't possible. "I've seen your place. It's a broom closet. Not even *you* can really crash there."

Lori knew she had a point. She'd been looking at

apartment rentals ever since she'd found out she was pregnant. "I'm looking for a new place."

"Well, there's always me," Chris offered. "My place is bigger than a bread box," she pointed out.

Joanna had already made up her mind, however. "Thank you, all of you, really, but I have a place to stay."

Sherry second-guessed her. There were times that Joanna had just too much pride. "You can't stay at a hotel. They charge exorbitant rates and—"

Joanna cut her off. "It's not a hotel. It's the Masters estate."

The other three exchanged looks. Chris was the first to recover. "What? How did this happen?"

Joanna decided to go with the abridged version. No one knew about her and Rick and, for the time being, she wanted to keep it that way. Maybe for all time, she thought. "It happened when Rick Masters rescued me from my burning bedroom."

Lori recalled seeing something in the newspaper. "Didn't I just read that he was spending time in Florida?"

Joanna nearly choked. She could just see Howard Masters rushing in to save her. "Not the father, the son."

A slow, appreciative smile curved Sherry's lips. She'd seen photographs of Richard Masters. Definitely not a face that stopped a clock. A heart, maybe, but not a clock. "Oh, the son."

Chris was familiar with the man. "Wow, talk about a fairy-tale meeting—"

"It wasn't our first." The words had popped out before she could stop them.

Lori made herself comfortable on the bed. "Have you been holding out on us?"

"Just someone from my past." Joanna shrugged dismissively.

"Details, we want details," Chris begged. She exchanged glances with Lori. "You know how hungry for romance pregnant women get."

Joanna searched for a tactful way out. "It all happened a long time ago."

"Doesn't matter," Sherry urged her on, "tell us."

Oh, what the hell did it matter? After all, these were her friends, women who had already shown, more than once, that they cared about her. "We were supposed to get married."

"And?" all three cried almost in unison.

She sighed. The memory still bothered her, even after all this time. "And his parents convinced me that I was all wrong for him. That Loretta Langley was the woman he should build his future with."

"Hate the woman already," Lori told her. "Who was she?"

"Someone from his side of the tracks."

"Tracks don't matter unless you're a train," Chris told her firmly. "I hope you told those people where to go."

Maybe she should have, but her mother hadn't raised her that way. And besides, Rick's parents had been very, very persuasive and thorough. "No, like I said, they convinced me."

"But not him," Chris told her.

The matter-of-fact tone had her pausing. "What do you mean?"

"Well, you do the math. He just 'happened' to be

there to rescue you, right?'' It didn't take a profiler to see through this case. ''Unless the man's a demented pyromaniac who sets up his own heroic scenarios, I'd say he still had a thing for you.''

Joanna waved away the conclusion. She wasn't about to set herself up for another fall, not after all this time. ''I doubt it.''

But Sherry backed Chris up. ''He offered to let you stay with him, didn't he?''

''He could offer to let the population of Scotland stay with him and not really notice. It's a very big house,'' Joanna insisted when she saw the others exchange looks.

Her own husband's house had been virtually empty before she'd come into his life, Sherry thought. Size had nothing to do with it. It was who was there to fill it that mattered. ''I'd say the lady doth protest too much, wouldn't you?'' She looked at the others, who nodded.

Sherry's comment fell on deaf ears as far as Joanna was concerned. They could say whatever they wanted. It still didn't change what was. For whatever reason he'd shown up in her life now, Rick had gotten over her a long time ago. To believe anything else would just be deluding herself and right now, she thought as she looked at her baby, she had more important things to think about.

Four

Never mind that he'd already made two appearances in her life in the last two days, the first of which would always rank as spectacular, each time Joanna saw Rick walking toward her, it didn't fail to surprise her, at least to some degree.

This time, he actually came with a surprise of his own as well. Nodding a greeting at her, Rick deposited a large rectangular box on top of her blanket-covered legs.

Despite the fact that the logo on the box proclaimed it to be from a department store that catered predominantly to a clientele whose incomes began in the six-figure range, Joanna stared at it blankly. There was no wrapping paper, no card to declare its purpose, not even a ribbon to proclaim a feeble attempt at festivity. He just placed it before her and then took a step back, like someone admiring his own handiwork.

Not touching the box, she raised her eyes to his. "What's this?"

Rick curbed his impatience, telling himself that what was inside was utilitarian and not a gift. But a sense of anticipation refused to abate. He wanted to see the expression on her face when she opened it. "It's a box."

"I can see that." She fingered it tentatively. Was he giving her a gift? Was he trying to say he was sorry for not coming after her eight years ago? No, that was stupid. She was sure he probably didn't think about that at all. Not the way she did. "What's in it?"

He almost leaned over and opened the box for her, but at the last minute, he shoved his hands into his pockets. "Only one way to find out that I know of—unless you've acquired X-ray vision along with that suspicious mind of yours."

She raised her chin, a hint of defensiveness evident in the motion. "I am not suspicious."

Rick laughed shortly. From where he stood, it felt as if she was questioning all his motives. "Then what would you call it?"

"Being cautious." Joanna shrugged carelessly. The sleeve of her hospital gown went sliding off her shoulder and she pushed it back up. "Once burned, twice leery, that kind of thing."

He didn't want to go where she was leading. There was no point in going over that ground. "You were burned by a box?"

Joanna pressed her lips together. He knew damn well what she was saying. "No, by a feeling."

He looked at her. What was she implying? He'd

been the one to get hurt back then, not her. She'd made a tidy profit out of it as well. "Well, maybe that makes two of us."

Exasperated, he gave up waiting. Rick reached over and lifted the top of the box for her, shaking it slightly so that it would come loose. The bottom rose with it, then separated. As the box fell, its contents came tumbling out, revealing a two-piece red suit.

He remembered, she thought, stunned. There'd been a red suit she'd once pointed out to him, saying that she loved the way that it looked. This suit was almost identical to that one.

But that was eight years ago. It had to be a coincidence.

And yet…

"Clothes?" She tried to read his expression. There was no indication that he knew what the red suit meant. "You bought me clothes?"

He picked up the pale cream blouse that had been packed under the suit and had slid off the bed when the box opened. He placed it next to the outfit. Rick nodded at what she was wearing.

"Well, you're being sprung soon and I didn't think the hospital was going to let you keep that fetching gown they issued you. I happen to know for a fact that there are laws on the books against parading around in public without any clothes—even with a body like yours."

She ran her fingers over the fabric. She knew the kind of price tags that went with outfits like this. There was no way she could have afforded to buy it for herself. But somehow, she was going to find the money to pay him back. She was her own person and not to be bought, even by acts of kindness.

Joanna laughed shortly at his comment. "Thanks for the compliment, but it's been a while since you've seen this body."

She knew, to the day, just how long it had been since they'd been together as lovers. How many years, how many months, how many days. No matter how many other things she filled her head with, that information somehow always managed to remain.

He wondered if she even remembered pointing out that red suit to him. Probably not. He was being too sentimental. Funny, he would have thought that there was no sentiment left in him. All it took to bring it out was being with her.

Rick shrugged. "There was that encounter a couple of days ago," he quipped.

Color shot up to her cheeks. "You know what I mean."

"Yes, I do and yes it has been a long time since I admired your body in the very best sense of the word." His eyes swept over her. "But I'd still be willing to bet that you look better than ninety-eight percent of the female population."

Her eyes filled with amusement. "Ninety-eight percent, huh? My, you have been busy. When did you get any time to pay attention to business?"

"Slight exaggeration," he allowed, sitting down in the chair beside her bed. "The kind, if I recall correctly, that you used to be given to." It was a throw-away line. He recalled everything there was to remember about her. That was his curse, the reason he could never get himself to settle down and start a family the way his friends all had. The way his parents kept insisting that he do. He nodded toward the box. "That should fit you."

She glanced inside the jacket. It was the right size. "You've got a good eye."

"More like a good memory. I did buy you that sweater one Christmas."

A sadness waft through her. The sweater had been retired to a keepsake box, along with every single word he'd ever written to her and every photograph of the two of them she'd had. The box had been in her closet. It was undoubtedly a casualty of the fire. It was as if she wasn't even allowed to hang onto her memories.

She tried to keep the tears back.

"What's the matter?"

"Nothing," she sniffed. "Allergies."

He scrutinized her face. She was lying. "I don't remember you having allergies."

Joanna waved her hand vaguely. "It comes and goes." Very carefully, she placed the jacket back into the box on top of the skirt. She folded the blouse, leaving it on top of both, then closed the lid over them. "Thank you."

He took the box from her, placing it on the shelf against the wall. "You're welcome."

He was still thoughtful. It was nice to know that some things hadn't changed. "I hadn't thought about what I was going to wear," she confessed. Her daughter, on the other hand, was all taken care of. All she had to do was choose an outfit from the gifts that Lori, Sherry and Chris had brought her.

He had a feeling clothes had slipped her mind.

When he'd gone back to her house a second time to closely assess the damage, he'd also taken inventory of her clothes. Nothing had been spared. It was just sheer luck that he'd found her purse on the living-room coffee table. Aside from the smoke damage, it was still intact.

"You were never detail-oriented."

"No," she agreed, "that was always your department." That was what had made them so perfect together, they complemented one another. Whatever trait one lacked, the other possessed. It was as if they were meant to be one whole person. Or so she'd tried to tell herself at the time.

Had she ever really been that innocent? To actually believe in soul mates?

For a moment, Rick sat there in silence, looking at her and wondering what had happened to them. Why had things gone so wrong? They'd had so much going for them.

And then he laughed to himself. He knew the answer to that. In part, he blamed his family for what had happened, but he couldn't help blaming her as well. All she'd had to do was love him, to have faith in him and know that he would have made everything right.

But she'd allowed herself to be lied to. To be bought off. That had been the real end of any dreams that might have been. She'd allowed money to come between them. Just as his parents had predicted.

The touch of her hand on his had him pulling out of the daze his thoughts had taken him into. She was staring at him. "What?"

He had such a strange expression on his face. As if he were a million miles away. "Where are you?"

"Right here," he said shortly, embarrassed at being caught. "I was just thinking, that's all."

And she had a feeling she knew about what. "Having second thoughts about the arrangement?"

"No." The denial was sharp. He forced a smile to his lips, or what might have passed for one, had she not known what he was capable of. "Just thinking," he repeated.

He was shutting her out. Well, what did she expect? That they would suddenly pick up where they'd left off eight years ago? Did she expect him to sweep her off her feet, tell her that nothing else mattered except that he loved her and would always love her?

She wasn't twenty anymore, wasn't naive anymore. There was no such thing as happily ever after, not for her and Rick at any rate.

Still, she heard herself pressing, wanting him to be truthful with her. "About what?"

About how something wonderful could have turned out so badly. He rose to his feet. "What time are they signing you out tomorrow?"

Mentally, she retreated to her corner. His kindness had thrown her off for a minute, but she was okay now. Able to handle things as they came. "Before noon. My insurance won't cover another day."

He frowned. Something didn't sound right. "I thought the teachers' union had a good insurance plan?"

"They do." And she wished she could still have it. But the COBRA payments that would have allowed her to carry on her insurance after termination had been far too expensive for her even to consider. "Mine's an individual policy." She took a breath before telling him. "I'm not a teacher anymore."

He stared at her. When they'd been together, all she could talk about was becoming a teacher. It had been her goal ever since she'd been six years old. And one of the things his mother had found abhorrent. "You loved being a teacher."

"I still do." She struggled to keep the note of bitterness out of her voice. Like everything else, this was just a hurdle she had to get over. "But the one thing I failed to factor in when I made my decision to become a single mother was that the local school board would be uncomfortable with my single state coupled with my distended body. Simply put, they didn't feel that I was setting a good example for the children. So, they asked me to 'go on an extended leave of absence.'"

"No money," he guessed.

"No money."

She was as feisty as he remembered. Another woman would have crumbled in her situation. "So you're unemployed."

Joanna preferred to put her own spin on it. Raising her chin, she told him, "I am temporarily between positions."

He laughed, shaking his head. "Damn, but you are unsinkable, aren't you?"

"I try to be. Things have a way of working themselves out." She looked at him pointedly. "Who would ever have thought you'd come charging through the flames to rescue me?"

"Who would have thought," he echoed. Taking

out a PalmPilot, he pulled up his schedule and made a notation with his stylus. "I'll be here before eleven," he promised, then tucked the PalmPilot into the pocket of his jacket. He saw her smiling and shaking her head. "What?"

"I just had a flashback." She grinned. "Remember how you used to say that you were never going to be anything like your father?"

Momentarily stepping into the past, he couldn't help recalling other things he'd said to her. Like pledging his undying love. It sounded hokey now, but he'd meant it then with a fierceness that had taken even him by surprise.

Life had a way of changing things.

Rick brushed his fingers along the outline of her cheek. "I used to say a lot of things." And so had she. He dropped his hand to his side. There was no point in going there. He'd learned his lesson. Words were usually empty, forgotten moments after they were uttered. "Times change."

She raised her eyes to his. *Maybe I was wrong to believe your parents, maybe I was wrong to leave you, but you were wrong, too. You didn't come after me, didn't try to make me change my mind.* "Yes, they do, but people don't have to."

He deliberately turned his thoughts to the business world. "They do if they want to grow. If you don't move forward, you slide backwards."

That was his father talking, not him. Had he become his father these last years? She didn't want to believe it, didn't want to think of him that way. "Not necessarily. There's nothing wrong with standing still."

There is if you're trying to stay one step ahead of memories that can undo you. He looked at her for a long moment. "I'll see you tomorrow." With that, he turned away and began to walk out.

She felt a pang squeeze her heart. What was she doing, trying to torture herself? She still had some money saved. "Rick."

His hand on the door, he stopped and looked over his shoulder. "What?"

"I can still go to a hotel."

"Mrs. Rutledge is expecting you. I'll see you tomorrow."

And with that, he left.

She glanced over to her sleeping daughter, and fervently prayed that men found a way to evolve in the next fifteen years, before her baby got involved in her own whirlwind.

"Sometimes, Rach, men are more trouble than they are worth."

But even as she said it, Joanna knew she didn't really believe it.

It felt as if every cloud in Southern California had converged above Bedford the next day. The storm began at around six in the morning and promised to continue until the evening without any letup.

"If it'd rained like this three days ago, my house would still be standing," Joanna commented as she took the seat beside Rick in the Mercedes.

Behind her, Rachel lay strapped into a baby seat. Joanna had been surprised to see that he had thought to get one for the baby. The tab on the items she owed him for was growing.

If it had rained like this three nights ago, he would have just kept going after passing her house. There would have been no need to rescue her, no need to deliver her baby. And no need to bring her into his life, however temporarily.

Fate was a very strange thing. It both took and gave.

He glanced toward her. She was quiet. He couldn't remember her ever being quiet. "Tired?"

"A little." And more than slightly apprehensive that she was making another wrong decision.

"We'll be there soon," he promised.

"I remember the way."

She remembered far more than that, she thought, and that was part of the problem. How insane was it, to walk back into the past like this?

But it wasn't the past, not really. She was a mother now, and he had moved on with his life, too. They were just two people who'd once shared a past, nothing more.

Despite the storm and the frantic rhythm of the windshield wipers, Joanna could make out the form of a tall, thin woman standing at the entrance of the house, a huge umbrella in her hand, poised to go into action at a moment's notice.

The instant she saw them, Mrs. Rutledge opened the umbrella and hurried toward the passenger side of the car, prepared to protect and serve to the best of her ability. Some things, Joanna thought with a surge of warmth, *didn't* change.

"There's Mrs. Rutledge," Joanna heard herself saying. "Won't she catch cold?"

He wondered if Joanna was aware that she sounded excited. "No germ would dare try to incapacitate Mrs. Rutledge. I've never known her to be sick a day in her life. Or at least, not a day in mine."

The next thing Joanna knew, her door was being opened. The scent of vanilla dueled with the smell of the rain and won.

"My dear, how pale you look." The woman's light-green eyes shifted accusingly toward Rick before becoming compassionate again as she looked at Joanna.

"Hello, Mrs. Rutledge." Joanna smiled warmly at her. There was no evidence of any change in the housekeeper. She still had iron-gray hair, worn short, still dressed in a light-gray shirt-front uniform that came mid-way down her calves. "How are you?"

"Ready to bring a little color back into your cheeks, you can count on that."

After over fifty years, there was still just the barest hint of a Southern drawl in her voice. Nadine Smith Rutledge hailed from South Carolina, the seventh of fifteen children born to a coal miner and his wife. They'd all gone on to earn their own way in the world as soon as they were old enough to work. Only Nadine had made it out this far west. She'd come to work for Rick's grandfather and stayed on through the generations, making herself indispensable along the way.

The housekeeper peered into the back seat, her face softening considerably. "And this must be your little one. One forgets how tiny they start out." She looked over at Rick. She took on the tone more suitable for a headmistress than a housekeeper. "Well, don't just

sit there, come around to my side and hold the umbrella while I help Miss Joanna and her baby out.''

''Yes'm.'' Tolerant amusement surrounded the single word. Rick hurried out of the car, rounding the
hood. He took the umbrella from the older woman,
holding it aloft as Joanna got out. It was large enough
to provide shelter for all three of them.

Mrs. Rutledge carefully unfastened the straps
around the infant. Cornflower-blue eyes opened wide
to watch her. ''She's got your eyes, Miss Joanna. And
your fair skin.'' With gentle hands she drew the baby
out of her seat. ''Going to be a beauty, she is, mark
my words. Oh my,'' she murmured as she brought
the bundle of softness to her chest. ''I haven't held a
little one in my arms since I took care of Mr. Rick
here.'' Mrs. Rutledge glanced over her shoulder at
him. ''Hard to believe he was ever this small, isn't
it?''

Rick cleared his throat. ''Could we get Joanna and
her baby out of the rain before we go traveling down
memory lane, Mrs. Rutledge?''

''Hope your baby's got a better disposition than
that one,'' she commented to Joanna.

With her arms wrapped firmly around her small
charge and Rick holding the umbrella over her head,
Mrs. Rutledge led the way to the front door. Joanna
pressed her lips together, trying not to smile. The
woman made her think of Queen Victoria strolling
about Windsor Castle.

Castle was the word for it, Joanna thought a moment later.

Or maybe *mausoleum* was a better one. She'd always felt that the house where Rick had grown up

had all the warmth of a stone. Nothing seemed to have changed. If anything, it felt even colder.

"I know, I know," Mrs. Rutledge commented, glancing at her face. "It has all the hominess of a cave, but now that Mr. Rick is here, I suspect there'll be some changes made. Won't there?" She peered at him pointedly as he shut the front door.

After closing the umbrella, Rick deposited it in a large metal umbrella stand his mother had bought on one of her frequent shopping trips to Paris. It was shaped like an African elephant. Water cascaded along the elephant's face, making it appear as if it was crying.

He felt absolutely no attachment to this place. "I'm here to set up a new corporate home office, Mrs. Rutledge," he reminded her, "not to redecorate the house."

"Still, if you're moving back here, you're going to need to make some changes. Make this more of a home." Her eyes sparkled as she turned them toward Joanna. "I've been making up this list of renovations for the last few years."

Joanna looked at Rick. He'd told her his father was away on vacation. "Doesn't Mr. Masters still live here?"

Mrs. Rutledge dismissed the obstacle with a wave of her hand. "He's hardly been here in the last six months. He's become a changed man since his heart attack."

"So I've been told."

"Enough about that, you two need to rest. Let me show you where you'll be staying," Mrs. Rutledge said. Turning on her heel, she led Joanna to a room located on the first floor in the east wing of the house.

Since Mrs. Rutledge had taken over, this was his cue to leave, Rick thought. But he decided he could spare a few more minutes. Besides, he wanted to see the expression on Joanna's face when she saw the nursery.

Moving around them, Rick opened the door to the first room and then allowed Joanna to go in ahead of him. "It's yours for as long as you want."

Done in pale blues and whites, it looked like a bedroom out of a dream. He'd remembered that blue was her favorite color, she thought, or was that its original color and she was just reading too much into it?

"The nursery's right through here." Mrs. Rutledge opened the door to a small adjoining room. "This gets the morning sun," she told her. Right now, rain pounded against the panes. "When it's available."

Joanna crossed to the crib, looking at it in awe. It was an antique. Mrs. Rutledge placed the baby in it, then covered the infant with a blanket.

Joanna looked at the woman. "Where did you—?"

"This used to be Mr. Rick's. I had it taken out of storage when I heard you would be staying with us."

"Temporarily," Joanna interjected.

"We're all here temporarily, Miss Joanna," Mrs. Rutledge replied. "On our way to other places." She smiled warmly. "No reason we can't be comfortable while we're here, is there?"

Joanna slanted a glance toward Rick. Damn, but her heart was going to be in jeopardy again, she just knew it. "That depends on what that comfort costs."

"Not a dime, Joanna, not a dime."

She turned to him. "You know I can't accept all this."

"We'll discuss it later," he told her. "I've got to be going." She still looked frail to him somehow. Squelching the protective feeling stirring within him, he drew Joanna aside. "You'll be all right?"

"I have Mrs. Rutledge, how could I not be?" She looked around her. "You really didn't have to go to all this trouble, you know."

Maybe not, but he'd wanted to. Maybe she still had some kind of hold on him, despite everything. "I didn't," he lied. "All I did was tell Mrs. Rutledge and she did the rest." He caught Mrs. Rutledge looking at him. The woman, he knew, didn't approve of lies.

He was lying, Joanna thought. She could always tell when he was lying. His tone changed. Moved, she brushed a kiss against his check. He jerked back as if she'd burned him.

Flustered, she took a step back herself. "Sorry."

"Don't be." Stupid to overreact that way, he upbraided himself. It was just that he didn't want to start anything. *Then why did you bring her here?* "It's just been a while, that's all."

Despite his resolve, Rick couldn't hold back the warmth that insisted on spreading through him. There'd been women since Joanna had left his life. A host of women. In the beginning, he'd tried to lose himself in them, to engage in hot, mindless sex intended to burn away her very memory. It didn't, and he'd learned soon enough how futile that effort was.

Even so, for a year after he'd left Bedford, he'd

forced himself to remain active on the social scene until he'd finally abandoned the futile effort.

No one had ever affected him the way she had.

You never forget your first love. Mrs. Rutledge had told him that. Mrs. Rutledge had an annoying habit of being right.

"I leave her in your capable hands, Mrs. Rutledge," he said to the housekeeper. With that, he left the room.

"He's never been the same, you know," the woman confided once Rick was safely out the door. "Not since you left." Mrs. Rutledge silently closed the nursery door and gently ushered Joanna to her bed. "I just thought you'd want to know that."

Joanna didn't want to talk about this, didn't want to feel guilty about doing something that had cost her more than anyone could ever guess. "Mrs. Rutledge—"

The woman held up her hands. "I'm not asking you why you broke it off with him. I'm sure you had your reasons. It's none of my affair what happened between the two of you." She drew back the comforter and waited for Joanna to sit down. "I just think you should know that you were the only ray of sunshine this house had seen in a very long time and when you left, the light went out. Out of the house and out of his eyes."

She spread the comforter over Joanna much the way she had over the baby, then crossed to the doorway. "I'll just be down the hall. Call me if there's anything you need. *Anything,*" she underlined.

Suddenly exhausted, Joanna was having trouble

keeping her eyes open. ''I just want to close my eyes for a few minutes.''

The woman nodded her approval as she slowly eased the door closed.

Five

The sound of persistent tapping made its way into Joanna's consciousness, rousing her brain and lifting it from the depths of sleep. Raindrops, she realized. Raindrops were hitting the window panes.

Joanna forced her eyes open. The room was nestled in darkness.

She wasn't alone.

She bolted upright, a sense of fear blanketing her. The shape she'd vaguely discerned took on form. Rick was standing beside the bed, looking down at her.

"Wha-what are you doing here?"

He grinned, the left corner of his mouth rising a little higher than the right. She'd teased him more than once about his lop-sided grin.

"You keep asking me that. My house, remember?"

It took a second, but she did remember. Remember everything. The fire, Rachel being born, Mrs. Rutledge. She sighed. "Oh, right. I remember."

"You feel up to dinner? Or do you want me to have Mrs. Rutledge bring you a tray?"

She couldn't allow herself to be waited on, no matter how tempting. "I'm not an invalid."

"I'll take that as a no." Rick crossed to the doorway. "Mrs. Rutledge is right outside. I'll see you in the dining room," he told her as he left.

She felt foolish. She'd only meant to close her eyes for a few minutes. How long had she been asleep? She glanced at the clock on the night stand.

"Omigod," she cried out loud, "it's almost six o'clock. I slept over five hours."

Mrs. Rutledge stuck her head in from the nursery. "Certainly looks that way."

When Rick had said the housekeeper was outside, she'd thought he meant the hallway. She didn't realize he was talking about the nursery. Joanna quickly swung her legs down from the bed. "The baby—"

For an older woman, Mrs. Rutledge knew how to move fast without giving the impression of moving at all. She was beside her before Joanna could finish her sentence, placing a hand on her shoulder to keep the new mother from leaping up and possibly hurting something.

"She's fine, dear. I've been in to check on her several times." She smiled warmly at Joanna. "You, too. You were easier. You didn't need any changing or feeding."

It was her responsibility to care for the baby, not the housekeeper's. Some mother she made. Joanna dragged her hand through her hair and looked at the other woman, guilt nibbling away at her. "You changed her?"

Because it was already dark, Mrs. Rutledge went to the windows and began drawing the drapes.

"I'm from a large family, dear. Took care of my share of babies. Things haven't changed all that much. One end eats, the other eliminates." She saw Joanna looking toward the next room. "You can reassure yourself about Rachel's condition and even have enough time to freshen up before dinner."

"Dinner," Joanna echoed, trying to straighten out the jumble in her head. "Rick said something about that just now."

She wasn't altogether sure she was up to facing him over a meal. She'd had some pretty erotic dreams just now, all of which had involved him. With their effect still hovering over her brain, it became rather difficult for her to remember to keep her distance from him.

Mrs. Rutledge crossed back to her, folding her hands rather primly before her.

"He arrived home half an hour ago." She smiled. "He came in and checked on you himself, couldn't believe you were still sleeping. He also took over Rachel's last feeding."

She stared at the housekeeper as if the woman had just told her Rick had sprouted wings and flown over the house. "He fed Rachel?"

The woman nodded. "Didn't do that bad a job of it, either." Mrs. Rutledge smiled. "Man's a natural. Some men should be fathers," the housekeeper said pointedly, looking at Joanna.

"Mrs. Rutledge—" This was going into territory she didn't feel up to dealing with tonight.

Like a seasoned stock-car driver negotiating a track, Mrs. Rutledge effortlessly changed the course of the conversation. "There's a fresh dress for you hanging in the closet."

"Fresh dress?" Surprised, Joanna turned and looked over her shoulder toward the mirrored closet.

"Mr. Rick picked it up on his way home. If you ask me, the man's got a flair for shopping as well. Not many of those around these days." Her work here was finished. Mrs. Rutledge crossed to the doorway. "Dinner's in the dining room at six-thirty."

Still sitting on the bed, Joanna scooted back and pulled her legs up to her, encircling them with her arms as she leaned her head against her knee.

This had to be a dream, she thought. A housekeeper who doubled as a nanny, new clothes that magically appeared when she needed them. And a Prince Charming who fed and burped babies. A dream all right.

She slowly shook her head. It was tempting, so tempting to pretend that things could go back to the way they had once been.

But they couldn't. Too much had happened, too much time had gone by. You could go home again, but only to visit, not to stay.

Needing to center herself, to touch base with the reality that was her life, Joanna got up and went to see her baby.

The dress fit.

But then, she'd never doubted that it would. After

all, Rick had picked it out and he had always had an eye for color, for sizes. For everything that mattered. He was, she thought, pretty nearly perfect.

And not hers anymore. He might have saved her, might have brought her here for old times' sake, but she couldn't allow herself to confuse kindness with what they'd once had.

And didn't have anymore, she reminded herself.

As she'd slipped on the light-blue dress, the fabric felt soft and feminine against her skin. It made her feel the same.

Joanna smiled at her reflection in the mirror as she brushed her hair into place. Blond waves fell, framing her face. How was it that he always knew just what to do? Except once, of course, she amended.

But that was all in the past and it had to stay there. For both their sakes.

Ready, she tiptoed into the next room. Rachel was asleep again.

She felt a tug at her heart, seeing the baby in what had been Rick's old crib. This was the way things should have been.

But they weren't, and she should be grateful for what was, not regretful about what wasn't.

Joanna looked down at Rachel a moment longer, before stealing off. Best baby in the whole world, she thought. Of course, her first night alone was still ahead of her. That would be the real trial by fire.

So would going in and facing Rick over dinner, she thought.

The irony of the situation struck her full force. There was a time, she mused, when it wouldn't have been necessary to brace herself in order to see him.

There was a time when she would have raced into the dining room on winged feet instead of leaden ones.

"I can do this," she told herself as she left the room.

After taking one wrong turn, she found her way to the dining room. Rick was already seated, sipping a glass of wine. He rose in his chair when she entered.

"Your manners always were impeccable," she told him as she walked in.

The dining room, like the rest of the estate, was formal, with a long table designed for entertaining large parties of people. There were four tall, white tapered candles, set in silver, with flames softly teasing the air. Her place setting, she noted, was opposite his, all the way at the other end of the table. She wondered if she needed to drop bread crumbs to find her way back.

"Training," he murmured. His eyes swept over her, appreciating the silhouette she cast. If there were any remnants of her pregnancy, he certainly couldn't detect them. She was as trim as he remembered her. As trim as she appeared in his dreams. He banked down the ache he felt in his loins. "The dress looks nice on you."

As if she were bringing out the best in the dress instead of the other way around. Her mouth curved. The man had always known his way around a compliment.

Seating herself, Joanna looked down at the garment. "Thank you. Again."

"Wine?" he asked. He held his glass aloft when she didn't seem to hear. "Or are you—?"

She shook her head. "No, I'm not nursing her."

Her voice seemed to disappear into the atmosphere. She raised her voice. "Rachel's perfect in every way, but she has an allergy." She gave a small shrug. "To me, it would seem, or at least to my milk. The doctor said she's better off with a formula." She saw that he was beginning to rise and guessed at his intent. "But I'll pass on the wine right now. It'll just make me sleepy."

Although, sitting here, looking at him, was making her anything but sleepy. Anticipation seemed to be jumping through her veins, even though she knew there was nothing to anticipate.

He sat down again. Joanna toyed with her thoughts for exactly two seconds before giving voice to them. "You know, you can't just keep buying me things."

It appeared to her as if he was looking at her pointedly, although at this distance, she wasn't sure. "There was a time I would have bought you anything."

She lowered her eyes to her plate. Prime rib. Her favorite. Mrs. Rutledge had outdone herself. "And there was a time I would have let you, but right now, I'm beginning to feel like an indentured servant."

After taking another sip, Rick set down his glass. "If I recall my history correctly, the bargain was usually for seven years. Recalculating that to take in approximately two hundred and fifty years of inflation, I'd say the length of time would probably be extended to something like thirty-two years now."

Her fingers tightened around her fork. Was he saying that he wanted her in his life? No, that was only wishful thinking on her part.

"I'll pay you back in cash, if you don't mind."

Was he frowning? She certainly couldn't tell. The candles weren't giving enough illumination and the light from the chandelier had been dimmed. "I could have worn the suit you bought."

"You fell asleep in that," he pointed out. "The alternative was to have Mrs. Rutledge unearth one of my mother's dresses for you out of the attic." He knew exactly how she would have reacted to that. It was no secret that his mother had never had any use for her. "I don't think you would have wanted that."

"No, you're right." She saw him cock his head. He hadn't heard her. "I said, you're right." She frowned. "You know, I'm beginning to think I know why your parents drifted apart. It was this table. It's longer than the boundaries for Rhode Island."

Picking up the corners of her place setting, Joanna abruptly rose to her feet and slid the setting along the surface of the table until she reached the last chair directly to his right. Leaving her place setting there, she went back to retrieve her glass. She put it next to her plate and sat down triumphantly.

"There."

He'd watched her in amusement, remembering how her very presence had brought a freshness into his life that he had been utterly unaware was missing. Until she came. "I thought you might be more comfortable over there."

"I was getting hoarse over there," she contradicted. "I couldn't see your eyes from where I was sitting."

"And that's important?"

"Haven't you heard? Eyes are the windows to the soul." She realized that her eyes were smiling into his. God, but she had missed him. Missed him with every fiber of her being. It wasn't easy being noble. "Did your parents always eat like that?"

He shrugged. "When they ate together at all, yes. But most of the time they weren't even here. My father kept late hours and was away on business a great deal. My mother had her clubs, her charity work, it pretty much kept her out of the house. The only time they were here together was when they entertained." He looked around the room. It had always felt cold to him, even in the dead of summer. "I took a lot of my meals alone in here."

She could see him, a lost boy hungering for more than food at mealtimes. Something else to hold against his mother. Why did women have children if they didn't want to be with them? What organization could possibly have had a better claim to her time and her heart than her own son? "Charity begins at home."

Joanna said it with such fierceness, he had to struggle not to smile. She hadn't lost any of her feistiness, he noted. He realized that it pleased him. "My mother always thought that a very trite saying."

Joanna took a long sip of cold water, not trusting herself to answer right away. Maybe it was disrespectful to speak ill of the dead, but there was nothing about the late socialite that Joanna had liked.

"No offense, but your mother always had a way of belittling people and making them feel as if they were beneath her."

This time, he did smile. "None taken. She wasn't exactly cut out of the same cloth that Mother Teresa was." It was something he'd made his peace with as a young boy. He'd actually thought that everyone's mother was like this. Until he'd met Joanna's, and in Joanna's case, the apple hadn't fallen far from the tree. "I always envied the bond you had with your mother."

"I was lucky." Joanna smiled. Her mother was probably her favorite topic.

Her wording struck him as ironic. "Not many people would have said that—" He stopped abruptly, realizing what he'd almost said.

He was referring to her mother's circumstances. The reason his parents had come to her and said what they had. She raised her chin defensively. She wasn't ashamed of who she was.

"In my place?" she guessed, concluding his thought. "Why, because my father did the proverbial disappearing act right after my mother told him she was pregnant? Because my mother had to raise me alone?"

The scenario had been so classic, but she still ached for her mother whenever she thought about it. Her mother had been seventeen and afraid, but, she'd assured Joanna, she'd loved her from the first moment she knew she was carrying her.

When Joanna had been a great deal younger, she'd fantasized that her father would just show up one day, begging their forgiveness. He'd ask her to be a flower girl at their wedding. When Joanna was nine, her mother had heard from a friend of a friend that her father had died in an automobile accident, and that was the end of that fantasy.

But even though she'd had no father, she counted herself extremely lucky to have had her mother in her life. Besides, what if her father had turned out to be a man like Rick's father? She was convinced she was better off this way.

There was no way Rick wanted Joanna to think that he pitied her. Nothing could have been further from the truth.

"No, I was just commenting on the fact that you always saw the glass as half full and about to be filled to the top no matter what. I always thought that was one of your best attributes."

"That, too, was a gift from my mother." Her mother had been the most upbeat person she'd ever known. And she'd always liked Rick, Joanna remembered. "A positive attitude is what gets you through life."

Rick nodded. He could remember sitting in Joanna's kitchen, hearing her mother saying that. He looked at Joanna. "How long…?"

When he hesitated, she knew what he was asking. "Has she been gone? A little over thirteen months."

The loss of Joanna's mother filled him with a great deal more sadness than the loss of his own had. "I'm sorry she couldn't have lived to see her namesake."

That was probably her biggest regret, Joanna thought. That her mother wasn't there to share all these things with her. She saw motherhood from a whole new perspective now that she was one. There was so much she would have wanted to tell her mother.

"Yes, me too."

He had to ask. "Why did you decide to have a baby now?"

It had come to her one evening, sitting alone in her

empty house. "Well, after my mother died, I just felt I needed someone to love. I had all this love to give, and there was no one around to take it. So, I decided to have a baby."

He could understand that part of it easily enough, it was the way she went about it that didn't make any sense to him. It wasn't as if Joanna was hearing her biological clock ticking loud and clear. She was only twenty-eight. There was plenty of time left.

"Why that way, though? Most women would have tried to find the right man first."

There was no point to that. She raised her eyes to his. "I'd already found him."

Was she trying to tell him there'd been someone else in her life? That she'd broken it off with someone else as well? "Who?"

Sometimes, she decided, men could be very, very dense. Even intelligent ones. "Fishing for a compliment? You, you idiot."

The words came out before he could stop them. "If that was true, then why did you do what you did?"

There it was, the white elephant in the dining room. They'd acknowledged its presence. She supposed it had to come to that sometime.

She looked away. The terrain was painful, even after all this time. She supposed it always would be. "I did it for you."

"For me?" he echoed.

His tone was cynical and it rankled her. Anger rose up in her chest. "Well, I didn't do it for me. It was the hardest thing I'd ever done."

"Was it? Was ripping out my heart really hard for

you? Or did accepting the bribe make you forget all about that part of it?''

''Bribe?'' Her appetite gone, she pushed her plate away. ''What bribe? What the hell are you talking about?''

He could taste his anger as it rose up in his throat. All those years, wasted, because she didn't believe in him, didn't believe that he could rise above anything his father threw his way and take care of both of them. ''Don't act dumb, Joanna, it doesn't become you.''

She drew herself up, her eyes flashing. All the emotion that had been pent up for so long threatened to come pouring out. ''Don't you dare tell me how to act. I can be dumb if I want to, especially when I have no idea what you're talking about.''

She was lying to him. After all this time, she was lying. How could she? Didn't she think he knew? ''My father told me all about it.''

She just bet he did. Joanna crossed her arms before her. ''Enlighten me. *What* did he tell you?''

He had the urge just to get up and walk away. And keep walking.

But he'd done that once and it had brought him back here. This time, he was going to confront her, get it all out. And defy her to talk her way out of it.

''That he told you if you married me, he'd disown me and there wouldn't be a penny for us, but that if you left me, he'd give you a check for fifty thousand dollars. And you took the money.''

Joanna's mouth dropped open. Did he actually believe that? ''I did what?''

''You took the money,'' he repeated. It took effort

not to shout at her, not to demand to know why she'd thrown everything away like that. "I saw the check with your endorsement on the back. I refused to believe it until then, until he showed me the proof."

For a second, Joanna was just too stunned to speak. It never occurred to her that people would go to such lengths to pull off a deception. Never occurred to her because she would have never done anything like that herself. She didn't believe in lying.

Shaking her head, she blew out a breath. "I guess your father can add forgery to his list of talents. Forgery as well as lying."

"You're telling me it never happened?" It was a challenge, even though he knew better.

Her eyes held his for a very long moment. "I'm telling you that not all of it happened. Yes, your parents came to me, and yes they told me that if I married you, they'd disown you. And yes, there was an offer of a check." Her eyes darkened. "But that's where the story changes. I tore the check up in front of them. That was when your mother took me aside and painted a very vivid scenario of how you would grow to hate me because you had to face an existence without all the things you were accustomed to. And that it would be because of me."

It was his turn to stare at her, not knowing whether or not to believe what she was saying. "And you believed her?"

Joanna sighed. Angry tears rose in her eyes at the memory.

"I didn't want to, but she was very, very persuasive and I was afraid that there was more than just a germ of truth in what she was saying. I could live with struggling to make our way in the world, I'd done it all my life. But I didn't know if you could and I didn't think it was right for me to be the one to deprive you of all your 'creature comforts,' as your mother put it.''

Suddenly the walls were down and it was eight years ago. She had to tell him now what she couldn't have told him then. ''I would rather have died than to have you hate me. And in a way, I guess I did.''

''You never took the money,'' he repeated slowly, letting the words sink in.

''I never took the money.'' Why did she have to convince him? He'd loved her once, how could he not believe in her? ''You want to hook me up to a lie detector?'' she asked cynically.

He swallowed an angry retort. ''Why didn't you come to tell me all this?''

He should have known the answer to this, too. ''Because if I came to you, I *wouldn't* have been able to tell you all this. You wouldn't have let me walk away.'' *And even if you had, I wouldn't have been able to.*

''Damn right I wouldn't have.''

''And every day, I would have lived in fear of seeing you slowly begin to resent me, then hate me.''

Rick couldn't believe she was saying this. ''Didn't you know me any better than that?''

Joanna shrugged. Maybe she should have trusted him, maybe she should have trusted herself. But his mother had been so confident....

''I thought I did, but I didn't want to risk it. I was twenty years old and, by your parents' standards, very naive. You meant the world to me and I wanted you to be happy.''

He'd been everything but that. ''So you left me.''

''So I left you,'' she echoed. It had been the single most unselfish thing she'd ever done and it had almost killed her. ''Your parents said that Loretta Langley was much better suited for you.''

He remembered his parents' efforts to push the two of them together right after his father had dropped the bombshell about Joanna taking the bribe. ''Loretta Langley was a shallow, narcissistic cardboard figure my mother could easily lead around by the nose. I didn't want a puppet, I wanted you.''

Tears burned her eyes. She blinked them back. ''Then why didn't you try to come after me? Why did you just pick up and leave?''

''Because I was hurt.''

His parents had done a stellar job of ruining two lives, she thought. ''Because you believed I could be bought. How could you?''

He answered her question with one of his own. ''How could you believe that I'd actually pick my empty lifestyle over you?''

''I guess your father's a better salesman than either of us ever thought.'' She laughed shortly.

He couldn't believe it. All those years lost because of lies. ''So now what?''

Too much time had gone by for them to pick up where they'd left off, she thought, even though she wished it was otherwise. There were things to resolve, trust to rebuild. Once it was lost, trust was a very hard thing to find again. It was like learning how to walk again after a car accident had denied you the use of your legs.

Maybe, eventually…

"Now we finish our meal," Joanna proposed, moving her plate back in front of her, "and take it one step at a time." Her eyes widened as Rick abruptly stood up. The legs of his chair scraped loudly along the marble floor. "What are you doing?"

Taking hold of her wrist, Rick brought her to her feet and pulled her to him. "I've just decided what I want my first step to be."

Six

She didn't get a chance to ask "What?"

The question was unnecessary anyway.

She knew.

One look into his eyes and Joanna knew. He wanted exactly what she wanted, what she'd thought about, dreamed about these last long years without him.

Rick dove his fingers through her hair, tilting her face up to his. Bringing his mouth down to hers.

The torrent of emotion, secured behind dams that had been weakening these last few days broke loose, flooding both of them.

Oh, but she'd missed this, missed him.

Wrapping her arms around his neck, Joanna pressed her body against his, absorbing that old, familiar heat and reveling in it as it shot through her at the speed of Mach 8.

Who said you couldn't recapture the past, at least for a moment? Kissing Rick erased all the years, all the heartache. She was twenty again, and in love.

Desire surged through him with a vengeance that all but rattled his teeth. She still had the power to weaken his knees and reduce him to a pile of needy ashes in the space of a few seconds. No other woman could ever do that. No other woman even came close.

But then, he'd never loved anyone but her. The others who populated his social life were there due to sheer physical attraction alone, an attraction that quickly waned, leaving as abruptly as it came. Once he slept with a woman, the pull was no longer there. He was, he knew, subconsciously searching for someone to take Joanna's place.

But this, this was different. It always had been. The more he kissed her, the more he wanted to kiss her.

If there was such a thing as a soul mate, then Joanna had been his. Once.

Desire slammed into him, demanding release, demanding that he act on it. But even if there wasn't Joanna's condition to think of, this was too soon. He felt it in his bones.

You couldn't recapture the past and turn it into the present just because you wanted to.

Could you?

Logic disintegrated, leaving only rubble in its wake. All that remained was need.

Rick could feel every fiber of his body wanting her. In another moment, he wasn't sure if he could rein himself in.

Pulling his head back, he framed her face with his hands and looked at her.

"Damn, but you still have the ability to knock my shoes off."

She glanced down at his feet and then raised her eyes to his. "Figuratively speaking." Her mouth curved as she tried very hard not to tremble.

His own smile faded. He wanted her so badly, he was surprised that he didn't go up in smoke.

"How long?" he asked. She cocked her head and looked at him, confused. "How long before you're able to make love with me?"

Her smile, so reminiscent of the girl he'd once known, went straight to his heart. "Cutting right to the chase?"

His throat felt dry. "It's been eight years, Joey, there's no cutting to anything."

Joey. It was a nickname only he used. It brought back a flood of memories. She could almost feel him whispering it against her ear as they lay in one another's arms, enshrouded in darkness and the contented afterglow of lovemaking.

She closed her eyes as he pressed a kiss to her throat. Wishing she could go back and change things. Wishing that they hadn't lost all the time that they had.

Joanna shivered as desire teased her very core. She opened her eyes and looked up at him. "Soon, I hope. Very soon. The doctor said I was making great progress and there weren't any complications. I've heard some women can do it as soon as two weeks after they give birth. And I've always been very, very healthy."

He brushed the hair from her face, reluctant to let her go. "Two weeks," he murmured.

"It might be longer," she cautioned.

"It already is." He brushed a kiss to her forehead, holding her to him for a moment longer. He felt his body quickening, rebelling against his resolve. But he'd been without her all this time, he could wait a little longer. From a safe distance.

Dropping his arms to his sides, Rick took a step back, then moved his chair into place. If he didn't leave now, he wasn't sure if he could keep from touching her.

Was he leaving? In the middle of dinner? "Where are you going?"

"To take a long, cold shower. I've got a feeling I'm going to be taking a lot of them in the next couple of weeks. Or longer," he tacked on.

Turning to leave, Rick suddenly swung around again. His hand against the column of her throat, tilting her head back, he pressed a quick, deep kiss to her lips. One for the road. "I'll see you tomorrow."

"Tomorrow?" She looked down at his plate. He'd only half finished his meal.

Rick nodded. "It's going to be a very long shower." He nodded at her plate. "You'd better finish that or Mrs. Rutledge is going to take it as a personal insult. She tells me she spent a lot of time preparing your favorite meal."

She didn't have much of an appetite. He'd stirred things up in her, making her ache for him. "You didn't finish yours," she pointed out.

He laughed shortly. "She's used to that." And then he winked at her. "Besides, I've got a feeling you'd better build up your strength."

With that, he turned and walked out of the dining room, leaving her to her meal. And some very erotic thoughts.

By the time Rick stepped out of the onyx-tiled shower, he felt almost waterlogged. He'd remained in the enclosure for a very long time, not only trying to cool off desires that felt almost insurmountable, but also to try to get a handle on his anger. Anger against his parents and especially his father. The sense of betrayal was almost overwhelming.

Had it only been his mother who had come to him with the story of bribery, he would have been highly skeptical and far more inclined to get to the bottom of it himself. He knew his mother didn't approve of Joanna, that she had set her sights on his marrying "within his class," whatever the hell that was supposed to mean.

But his father was another matter. His father had always kept clear of his mother's machinations. He rubber-stamped a lot of things, ignored others. Rick had the feeling that his father might have even liked Joanna, at least a little. He'd never echoed his mother's feelings about her, never looked down on Joanna because her family weren't "people of substance." So when the man had backed up his mother and even produced the endorsed check, Rick had felt he had no choice but to believe that Joanna had been bought off.

He'd thought they'd gotten somewhat closer these last couple of years, he and his father, shedding the roles of two strangers. He'd been at his father's side right after the heart attack.

So why hadn't he told him about his deception?

Was everything in his life a lie?

It was hard for Rick not to feel bitter.

Getting out of the shower, he toweled his hair furiously as he crossed to the telephone next to his bed. He tossed the towel aside and hit the speed dial for his father's cell phone.

It rang twenty times before the metallic voice came on to tell him that his father was either out of the area, or not picking up.

"No kidding, Sherlock," Rick muttered.

He hurried into his clothes, then, his hair still wet, Rick went downstairs to his office. He kept a phone book there of all the important numbers he might need. Taking the book out of the top drawer in his desk, he flipped through it and found the phone number to his father's house in Florida.

It was past eleven on the east coast, but this matter wasn't going to wait until morning. It had waited long enough.

Rick heard the answering machine pick up. Frustration flooded him as he waited for the short, utilitarian message to be over. "Dad, if you're around, pick up. You there, Dad? Pick up, it's important."

Nothing. Muttering a curse, Rick had begun to hang up when he heard a noise on the other end of the line.

"Hello? Richard? Is that you? What's wrong? Something happen to the negotiations for the new headquarters?"

Jerking the receiver back to his ear, Rick's fingers tightened around it.

"What's wrong?" he echoed, barely keeping his

fury in check. "I'll tell you what's wrong, old man. You lied to me."

There was an uneasy pause on the other end. "Richard? Have you been drinking?"

Rick dragged his hand through his wet hair, pacing back and forth around his desk. "No, I haven't been drinking. I also haven't been seeing things clearly, either."

"I don't understand."

"Neither do I." He blew out an angry breath. Damn it, he'd thought he could at least trust his own father. "I could see why Mother would have lied to me. She always wanted things her way, wanted to control my every move just the way she did yours. But you, Dad, you forged that check and made me believe something that tore me apart. Didn't you give even a small damn about me?"

There was another long pause on the other end.

"How did you find out?" Howard asked as he realized it was finally over, finally out in the open. The subject was one that had never been completely buried for Howard Masters, even though he'd tried to put it out of his mind over the years. It felt as if a huge weight had been lifted from his shoulders.

Rick was surprised that there wasn't even the vaguest attempt at denial on his father's part. He didn't know whether that made him angrier, or relieved that he was finally going to confess.

"I did what I should have done eight years ago. I talked to her."

Howard Masters had been preparing himself for this ever since he'd made the suggestion that the home office be moved from Georgia. It had been his way of orchestrating things. "I'm glad it's out in the open." He only hoped his son believed him.

"Glad, are you?" Rick sincerely doubted that. He struggled to keep his voice down. If he started shouting, he knew Mrs. Rutledge would hear him. Though she was more family to him than either of his parents ever were, he didn't want to bring her into this. "Then why the hell didn't you tell me yourself? These last couple of years when we were working together, why didn't you say something?"

"I tried. More than a few times." His conscience had kept goading him to tell Rick. "But things got in the way."

"What things?" Rick demanded. What could possibly have kept his father from telling him the truth after his mother was gone?

"Business." Howard hesitated, then told him the truth. "Cowardice, I suppose. We were getting closer and I valued that. I didn't want to risk losing you. And before that, there was your mother to reckon with." Opening that can of worms would have caused an even greater schism in the family.

That was a poor excuse. "Mother's been dead for three years."

"You seemed to be happy with your new life," his father said lamely.

"Happy?" he demanded. "Dad, I've never been happy a day in my life, except when I was with Joanna."

"If it means anything, I'm sorry." Howard sighed. "Ever since the heart attack, I really have been trying to find a way to tell you. I decided the best way was to make you come back to Bedford for more than four hours. I knew Joanna still lived there. I was hoping circumstances might bring you together.''

Some of the anger left. Rick realized that his father had deliberately decided to move company headquarters out of Georgia. His father had insisted on it, even when Rick had balked and said it wasn't a good idea. His protest had been drowned in a sea of statistics his father had sent to him showing why the move was advantageous.

Rick dropped into his chair and tilted it back. ''This doesn't get you off the hook, you know.''

''I know. That'll take time. I hope I'll have it.''

In the last year, his father had come face-to-face with his own mortality and no longer took for granted that he had an infinite amount of time. It was a far cry from the man who'd once acted as if he was going to live forever.

Rick thought he heard a woman's voice in the background, calling his father's name. ''Who's that?''

''Someone who's made me realize more clearly that I should have never stood in the way of your happiness, no matter how convinced your mother was that it didn't lie with that girl.''

''She has a name, Dad. Joanna.'' Rick paused. It had never occurred to him that his father might find someone. The relationship with his mother had been such a failure, he would have thought that would have stopped his father from ever venturing out on the field again. ''What's the name of the woman with you?''

''Dorothy.'' Rick could hear a smile in his father's voice as he said the name. ''Richard, maybe someday you can find it in your heart to forgive me.''

''Yeah, maybe.''

But not now, not yet. It was going to take him time to work through this. Time to resolve everything in his life. It was the second time that his parents had upended everything for him, and it was going to take a while before things could get back to some semblance of normalcy.

"We'll talk later." He didn't trust himself to say anything further right now.

Rick replaced the receiver. He sat, staring at the telephone for a long time.

The sound of crying roused him. Rick realized that he must have dozed off. Small wonder. Going over quarterly reports was guaranteed to put anyone to sleep. He'd sought refuge in work the way he always did when his thoughts began to crowd in on him. Once, when he'd left Bedford for the east coast, it had been his saving grace.

His mouth felt like cotton. Rick stretched, his muscles aching from sleeping in an easy chair. The thick binder that had been on his lap slipped to the floor. He bent over to pick it up.

The crying got louder.

The baby was crying. Joanna's baby.

Joanna.

He nearly stumbled as he got up. Rick tossed the binder onto his desk and left the room, stopping only to shut off the light behind him.

Making his way to the rear of the house, he knocked on Joanna's door, the wonder of everything seeping into his system all over again. She was here, in his house, with a child, after all this time. There was happiness, but there was a sense of unrest as well, that he couldn't quite banish.

It was all new, he counseled himself. He had to give himself time.

When there was no answer, he tried the doorknob. The door wasn't locked. He opened it slowly, not wanting to intrude, but wanting to be there for her if she needed him. Wanting her to know he was there. Because of pain and altruism, they'd both hurt each other before. He wanted her to know that somehow, things would be right this time. This was one of the small steps in getting there. Helping her out in this new position she found herself in.

He saw her standing by the window, moonlight and a small night-light from the other room mingling to create a surreal atmosphere in the room. She was wearing the nightgown he'd gotten her, and he could feel his gut twisting at the sight of her.

The black nightgown was far from practical, made of lace, nylon and unfulfilled dreams. The light from the moon was thrusting its way through the material, highlighting her body just enough to make him ache. Just enough to make him remember.

Her hair was loose about her shoulders, tousled as if she'd just gotten out of bed. He longed to run his hands through it, through it and over her, reclaiming what had once been his.

Maybe he should leave, he thought, before she saw him standing there.

But she was holding the baby to her, trying to soothe her. Mother and baby both looked distressed. "What's wrong?"

She turned, startled. She hadn't heard him come in.

Her attention had been completely focused on the baby. "I didn't mean to wake you."

He smiled, crossing to her. "You didn't. The baby did."

She still thought of them as a unit, she and the baby. Or maybe she wasn't thinking clearly at all. She'd had a nightmare just before Rachel's crying had woken her. A nightmare in which Rick's parents were surrounding her, larger than life and saying over and over again that she wasn't good enough for their son, that loving her would only bring him down. After all these years, she supposed a part of her still believed that.

"Sorry."

"Don't be sorry." He looked at the tiny wailing human being scrunched up against her chest. "How long has she been fussing?"

"A while now." She'd done all the right things, why wasn't Rachel going back to sleep? She'd been so good up until now.

Had she done something wrong?

Joanna looked tired, he thought. He brushed her hair back from her face. "Want me to get Mrs. Rutledge?"

"No." The word came out more fiercely than she'd intended. She lowered her voice. "Rachel is my responsibility. What kind of a mother would I be, handing her off to a nanny every time she made a sound or needed something?"

His mother, he thought, but kept the response to himself. Joanna wasn't anything like his mother and making the comparison would only upset her. So instead, he said, "A mother who knows how to accept help."

She was tired and frustrated, but it was something she was going to have to learn how to deal with. Her mother used to have a saying. No one ever fell from heaven pre-taught. That went for mothers, too.

"Mrs. Rutledge has been helping ever since I walked through the door. She deserves to sleep."

"So do you." He looked at the fussing infant. "Did you change her?"

"Of course I changed her." She realized she was snapping and amended her tone. "Sorry. I fed her, too."

"Then maybe all she needs is to be rocked a little." He held out his hands. "Here, give her to me."

She hesitated. She so wanted to do this right. "But it's late, you should be in bed."

He lifted a shoulder, letting it drop carelessly. "Nobody to be there with. I could stand a little companionship." Not waiting for Joanna to give him the infant, he took the baby from her. "Here, I won't drop her. I'm the one who held her first, remember?"

Reluctantly, she surrendered Rachel to him. She would never have thought he would want to bother himself with a baby. It made her realize that there was a lot about him she still didn't know. "Mrs. Rutledge told me you fed her earlier."

He smiled down at the bundle in his arms. "Mrs. Rutledge talks too much."

"She dotes on you, you know."

"The feeling's mutual." He sat down in the rocking chair in the corner and nodded toward the bed. "Why don't you lie down for a while? I'll take over."

"You don't have to do this." Even as she protested, Joanna sat down on the bed and slid back. "I mean, it's not as if you were her father."

His eyes met hers across the room. "No, but I could have been, if I believed in making donations. Don't argue with me. Lie down."

"Just for a second," she murmured.

It was the last thing she said. She fell asleep watching Rick rock the baby in the chair where Mrs. Rutledge had once sat, rocking him.

The last thought she had before she drifted off was that it was nice to have traditions in your life.

Seven

Rick's cell phone rang just as he was hurrying into his car. In deference to his position as vice president of Masters Enterprises, he was driving his Mercedes rather than his beloved Mustang.

It was a compromise. His father had wanted him to use the chauffeur-driven limousines, the way he had. The senior Masters maintained that it was more fitting. But Rick preferred being in the driver's seat himself. Preferred being in control. He supposed he got that from his mother. He considered it the only positive link between them.

He put his key into the ignition, then pulled the cell phone out of his pocket. Flipping it open, he paused before starting the car. "Masters."

"Mr. Rick, it's Nadine Rutledge."

There was no need to introduce herself. No one else

called him Mr. Rick or had quite that soft, Southern lilt in her voice.

Apprehension tightened his stomach. The last time he had heard from Mrs. Rutledge via telephone, it had been to inform him that his mother had died. His first thoughts were of Joanna and the baby.

"What's wrong?"

As always, Mrs. Rutledge's voice was low-key, soothing. "I'm not all that sure whether something is wrong, Mr. Rick, but Miss Joanna left."

"Left?" Echoes of the past came hurdling at him. Mrs. Rutledge couldn't mean that Joanna had left permanently. "Left where? Where did she go?"

"To her house, or what's left of it."

Relief was short-lived. What could Joanna have been thinking, going there now? He'd already given her a report on the condition of her house, brought her purse to her with her credit cards and wallet in it. Why this sudden need to go? Or, if she had to see it for herself, why hadn't she at least waited for him to get home?

"Did you try to stop her?"

It was evident by her voice that although Mrs. Rutledge was the one who ran everything in the house and had done so for his father after his mother's death, she didn't feel that it was her position to deter Joanna physically from doing what she wanted.

"I told her she shouldn't be doing this, but she insisted. I gave her my cell phone." It was clearly her way of compromising.

Frustration waltzed through him. Had Joanna taken his car? "Is she even supposed to be driving yet?"

He vaguely recalled Joanna saying that her doctor had warned her against it.

"That just pertains to a week after delivery. It's been almost two weeks," Mrs. Rutledge reminded him. "But she's not driving, she took a cab there."

"Damn it," he muttered. Exasperated, he glanced at his watch. He was meeting with the architect for the new home office in half an hour. Well, that was just going to have to wait. Joanna's well-being was more important than steel girders and Doric columns. "Do me a favor. Call my office and tell Celia to re-schedule my meeting with Donnelley and Sons. Have her tell them something came up and I'll see them at their office this afternoon at two."

"Consider it done."

"I already do."

Ending the conversation, Rick flipped the phone closed. He tossed it on the seat next to him, not bothering to waste time putting it away.

He couldn't help wondering what was going on in Joanna's head. Damn it, why was she doing this to herself? Seeing everything she loved destroyed would only be hard on her.

He turned the key in the ignition and pulled out of his parking spot. She'd been so busy this last week and a half, learning her way around this new phase of her life. Learning to be a mother. He'd thought that, beyond making an appointment with her insurance agent for sometime later in the week, Joanna had put the fire and its consequences out of her mind. At least temporarily.

Apparently not.

Just showed him he had no idea what went on in her head. He didn't know if he liked that or not.

For the last week and a half, despite the fact that Masters Enterprises was an international corporation and that if he was going to remain a hands-on leader, there was enough work to keep him busy around the clock, he found himself ending his days early. Coming home just to share the experience of parenting with Joanna, or watching quietly from the sidelines, absorbing the essence of mother and daughter.

When he'd seriously thought of their future while they'd been going together, it had never really included this phase of it. He'd envisioned the two of them flying to exotic locations, making love in all four corners of the world. Attending the elegant parties that were so much a part of his world. Enjoying life and each other. Alive with excitement. The thought of babies had only remotely entered into the scenario. Babies meant tedium, his parents had taught him that.

But babies weren't tedious. They represented a completely new, completely different kind of excitement. One marked with joy. And although he tried not to give it too much thought, sharing his days with Rachel and Joanna was bringing him in, centering him in a way he'd never thought he'd be centered.

He didn't want just to be a spectator, he wanted to be part of it all.

Was it the newness that was pulling him in like this? The feeling of recapturing the past in a whole new, different way? Would this exhilarating feeling and his involvement ultimately fade as he became accustomed to what was going on?

Rick turned down the next street, away from the building. He didn't try to fool himself. He was a different man than he'd been eight years ago. He'd grown in different directions, grown without Joanna at his side. She'd grown as well. He'd only had to look at this turn of events and her choice of single parenthood to know that she had.

Could the two halves fit together again, after all these years?

He didn't know.

What he did know was that rooting around in the ashes of what had been her home since childhood couldn't be good for her.

Rick pushed down harder on the accelerator, going faster as he kept an eye out for any police cars that might suddenly appear behind him.

Speed had never been particularly alluring to him. He ordinarily kept within the legal ranges without giving it much thought. But he found himself having to ease back on the accelerator now, flying through lights that were about to turn from yellow to red.

He made it across town to her development in record time.

Approaching her block, he could still detect a very faint smell of smoke even after all this time.

Or was that just his imagination?

His imagination had never been a particularly vivid one, except whenever Joanna entered into the picture. Everything that had to do with her was amplified, always just a little larger than life,

There was no sign of a cab on the block.

Maybe Mrs. Rutledge had been mistaken. Maybe Joanna had just gone to meet one of her friends for an early lunch, or decided to go shopping for clothes. She'd absolutely forbidden him to buy her any more things. Maybe she'd decided to replenish her nonexistent wardrobe on her own.

And then he saw her.

He'd almost missed her because she was down on her knees, sifting through charred ashes. Pulling up at the curb, Rick quickly shut off the ignition and jumped out of the car. Joanna gave no indication that she even knew he was there. Wrapped in her thoughts, she seemed to be completely oblivious to everything outside of the circle immediately around her.

For a moment, he thought of just leaving her with her thoughts and waiting until she rose and turned around.

But the sight of her form, so obviously enshrouded in grief even from the back, moved him so incredibly, he could feel tears of his own gathering in his eyes. She shouldn't have to be going through this. No one should.

Very softly, he came up behind her, not wanting to intrude, not wanting her to go through this alone.

"Joanna?"

Startled, she turned and looked over her shoulder. Her face was stained with tears.

The hell with standing back and giving her room to grieve. He erased the last few steps between them as he hurried to her. Crouching, he took her into his arms and raised her to her feet.

"Oh God, Joanna, why did you come here?"

She wasn't going to cry anymore, she wasn't, she told herself fiercely.

"I had to." She tried very hard to sound flippant. "I knew the mailbox had to be getting full." She nodded toward the structure at the curb, a cheery-looking miniature of the house that had once been whole. The mailbox was completely untouched by the tragedy that was behind it. She'd had it made as a gift to her mother one Easter. "I never left a forwarding address for the mail carrier," she explained with a slight shrug of her shoulder.

He framed her face with his hands and kissed her lightly. It had never even occurred to him to come by and check for mail, or to arrange for the mail to be delivered to his house. He'd see to it immediately. "I should have thought of that."

She shook her head, drawing away. Part of her was rebelling, calling herself weak for not standing on her own two feet. For leaning on someone, even if it was Rick. She was supposed to be stronger than that. She had to be strong because life had a way of running you down if you weren't.

"You've been thinking of everything else." She looked at him almost defiantly. "You're not responsible for me, Rick."

He took her hand, stopping her from moving away. "But I want to be."

She couldn't give up her independence, even to him. "I'm not fragile, Rick. I can take care of myself." And then she bit her lower lip as a fresh wave of tears came to her, threatening to undo everything she'd just said. "They're all gone."

He wasn't sure he knew what she was referring to. "What's all gone? Memories?" he guessed. "They're still there in your head, Joey.'' Lightly, he touched her temple. ''They always will be.''

She pressed her lips together. He undid her resolve by calling her Joey. She blinked hard to keep the dam inside from bursting, to keep the tears from washing over her face again. She didn't want to cry, she wanted to be strong. Had to be strong.

But so much had happened in her life this last year and a half. First her mother's illness, then her death. Then the board politely telling her she was an embarrassment and letting her go. And now part of her house was taken away from her. It was as if she couldn't be allowed to hold onto anything.

Was it always going to be that way? It made her afraid to rely on anything, least of all happiness.

''My photographs are all gone.'' Her voice was shaky and she paused to gather her strength to her. ''My mother's albums were stored in the living room and I found those. But the ones of us…'' She looked up at him, trying to remember him the way he was the first time she'd seen him. His hair was far more unruly and longer then. And there'd been a rebelliousness about him that time had taken away. ''The ones of you…were in my bedroom closet.''

She looked back at what had once been the rear of the house. It was hard even to pinpoint where the closet had been. That half of the house was now just a blackened shell, its frame barely standing.

He didn't know what to say, how to comfort her. He knew what photographs meant to her. When they'd begun going together, she'd insisted on snapping pictures almost constantly, capturing moments and freezing them for all time.

"Where are your mother's albums?" he asked.

Rather than answer, she took him by the hand and led him into the house. It felt funny, being able to enter through what had once been the dining room.

Joanna stopped at a large maple hutch that had sustained some smoke damage, but for the most part, was untouched by the fire. She opened the bottom doors. There were at least fifteen albums nestled against one another, arranged by years.

Seeing them, Rick couldn't help but smile. "She was a very orderly person."

"Yes, she was." Joanna's voice caught in her throat. And then she saw him begin to remove the albums one by one. "What are you doing?"

"I'm going to take them back with us. Bedford isn't known for having looters, but you can never be too safe with something as precious as these."

She knew he was saying that for her benefit, that he didn't care about photographs himself. He'd told her he never kept any. She brushed a kiss against his cheek. "Thank you."

It took three trips to move the albums from the hutch to the trunk of his car. He left the lid open. "Anything else?"

Joanna turned to look at the house. It reminded her of an illustration she'd once seen of Dr. Jekyll and Mr. Hyde. Half stately, half grotesque. "Everything," she replied with a heavy sigh.

He wasn't sure if she was kidding, but this was Joanna. He was willing to humor her. "We could come back with a truck."

With a small laugh, she shook her head. "I wasn't being serious, just sad. The photographs are the most important thing. That,'' she turned toward the mail-box, her mouth curving with self depreciating humor, ''and the bills.''

Crossing to it, she opened the small door, trying not to think of anything at all. She emptied the mail-box and placed the contents on the floor behind the passenger seat in the car. She didn't bother sorting through the large pile. She'd deal with all that later.

Rick was right beside her. ''Where's the cab, by the way?''

''I sent the cab away. I didn't know how long I was going to be here and I couldn't afford to have the driver standing there with the meter running.''

That sounded almost flighty, especially for her. ''How did you plan to get back?''

Reaching into her pocket, she pulled out a cell phone and held it up. ''Mrs. Rutledge gave me her phone so I thought I'd call a cab when I was done feeling sorry for myself.'' She put it back in her pocket.

Rick slipped his arm around her shoulders, drawing her closer to him, mutely giving her support. It meant the world to her, even though she told herself not to become dependent on it.

''You weren't feeling sorry for yourself, Joanna,'' he told her. ''You grew up in this house. You have every right to grieve because part of it was de-stroyed.''

For a moment, she let him protect her from every-thing. Let him make it all right. Turning her head against his arm, she looked up at him. ''When did you get to be so sensitive?'' The old Rick had been sweet and loving, but this was a level of compassion she wasn't familiar with.

"There's this program they have at work," he teased. "They make me take it for my own good." He brushed his lips against her forehead. "Ready to go home? Or do you need a little more time?"

She'd gotten everything she'd come for. "No, I don't need more time. You're right. What's most important is in here," she tapped her forehead the way he'd done earlier.

And in here, she added, thinking of her heart. A heart that was filled with love for her baby.

And for him.

But something kept her from voicing her feelings, a small, undefined fear that made her believe that things were not the way they had once been. They couldn't be. They weren't the same people they'd been then and she had come to learn not to expect anything.

When you didn't expect things, you weren't disappointed.

Holding the passenger door open for her, Rick picked up his cell phone from the seat and helped her into the car. He rounded the hood and got in behind the steering wheel. Strapping in, he glanced at his watch. With his meeting pushed back, he had some time on his hands. Returning to the office held no appeal to him. The work could wait.

Inspiration came out of nowhere. It had been a long time since he'd done anything on the spur of the moment. Rick started the car and pulled away from the curb. "Do you feel like going shopping?"

She stopped watching the house get smaller in the side mirror. "What?"

He took a right turn at the end of the block. "I seem to remember an old saying or joke that went 'Whenever I'm down in the dumps, I go shopping.' I thought there might be a kernel of truth in it." He was hoping that doing something familiar like that might cheer her up a little. "You do need more clothes, you know. Three outfits do not a wardrobe make."

She knew he meant well, but this had to stop. She wasn't his mistress, to be showered with gifts. He'd found her credit cards for her, but she was saving those for living expenses.

"I thought I told you not to buy me anything else."

"You did," he said matter-of-factly. Rick slanted her a look before making another right turn, this time onto a major street that led out of the development. "I take lousy instructions. Besides, I won't be picking them out this time, you will be. How about it?" When she didn't respond immediately, he asked, "Tired?"

"No, not at all." She'd been feeling more energetic lately. The baby hadn't learned how to sleep any longer, but she'd developed a pattern of being able to manage on less sleep herself. "But I really should be getting back to Rachel."

If that was the only reason, they were in the clear. "Don't worry about that. Mrs. Rutledge is having a ball with her. I'll just call her and tell her that you're all right and that we'll be a couple of hours late. She called me. She was worried," he explained, answering the silent question in her eyes.

"That explains what you were doing here." She

was seriously beginning to entertain the idea that he just materialized every time she needed him.

Shopping. Why not? Maybe something a little more normal might be in order after all. And this way, if she was there, she could keep a lid on the spending.

"All right," Joanna agreed impulsively, leaning back in her seat, "let's go shopping."

She felt like Cinderella.

Or maybe it was Julia Roberts in *Pretty Woman* she was thinking of. Whatever the comparison, Rick was making her feel like a princess.

Warning her ahead of time that he would leave her stranded in the middle of Los Angeles National Forest if she uttered a single negative word about cost, Rick took her to several exclusive shops in Newport Beach. With an unfailing eye, he selected just the right clothes for her, both casual and elegant, turning a deaf ear to her protests that all she needed before she was on her own was perhaps just a couple more *simple* items.

Since money had never been an obstacle in his life, Rick spent it as if it meant nothing. Joanna couldn't help thinking that he was every woman's dream when it came to generosity.

When it came to other things as well, but she wasn't going to allow herself to go there. If she didn't dream, she insisted silently, she wouldn't feel deprived when she woke up.

She had to all but drag him out of the third store before he bought her a complete wardrobe. The only thing that stopped him was that he had to be getting back to work.

Boxes and shopping bags had joined the pile of mail in the back seat, threatening to overflow into the front.

"I'm keeping a tally on this, you know," she informed him as she got into the car. She pulled her seatbelt around her, buckling up. "And at this rate, I'm going to have to turn over my next three years' salary to you."

Provided she could talk the board into taking her back now that her rounded abdomen was no longer a source of embarrassment to them, she thought.

He didn't want to hear about payback. "Joanna, let me make you a present of them."

It was too much and he knew it. "There's a difference between getting a present and buying a whole person," she pointed out.

He smiled as he guided the car back onto MacArthur Boulevard. "If you're determined to make some kind of payment," he glanced at her, "we could work it out in the barter system."

Tiny pinpricks of anticipation traveled through her. "What kind of barter system?"

His smile broadened considerably. "I'll think of something."

That they were going to make love was a foregone conclusion. But that had nothing to do with her owing him for all these things that he had insisted on doing for her. She prided herself on always paying her own way.

"It's going to be nothing less than cash and carry," she informed him.

He winked at her before looking back at the road. "We'll talk."

She knew they'd be doing more than that.

Eight

It felt good to take control of things again and not just drift, not just let life move her around as if she were a chess piece on some giant board. A pawn with no say in what was happening to her.

With each day that passed, Joanna felt a little stronger, a little more confident about herself as a mother, a little more confident about the direction her life was going to be taking.

At least in the practical sense.

She'd been to her gynecologist and gotten a clean bill of health. All systems were go, and her body had bounced back to where it had been nine months ago. She'd gone to see her home insurance agent—alone over Rick's protests—and filled out all the necessary paperwork in order to get the rebuilding on her house going.

She'd even been in contact with the head of the local school board.

That was where she had gone this afternoon, to see Amanda Raleigh, the head of the school board. Though she'd arrived at the local unified school district building with a considerable number of butterflies flapping madly in her stomach, the meeting had gone extremely well. Better than she'd anticipated. She hadn't had to wage a verbal war to get her old job back. Mrs. Raleigh had been very cordial, very accommodating. Not a bit like she'd been four months earlier when the woman had all but volunteered to sew a scarlet *A* on her dress.

But all that was behind her now. Two minutes into their meeting, Mrs. Raleigh had informed her that a position at a new high school would be waiting for her in the fall.

That just meant she had to get through the spring and summer somehow.

Joanna was already making plans. There were temporary agencies she could turn to during that time. Someone had to be able to make use of her abilities until she was teaching again in the fall.

All in all, she thought as she drove her car up the winding path to Rick's estate and into the garage, she was feeling pretty good about herself.

There was only one area that still resounded with question marks. An area that neither she nor Rick were willing or ready to broach.

Just where did they stand beyond the moment?

Before his parents had successfully conspired to pull them apart, she and Rick had been ready to face the future together for all time. With the confidence of the very young, they had made plans to get married in the spring.

Would that be in the future again? Would they get married? Would they even have a relationship once she left the confines of his estate?

She didn't know.

She did know that any thoughts about the future, other than the practical ones about providing for herself and Rachel, left her with an unsettled feeling. It was the same nervous feeling that had caused her to shy away from the myriad of men with whom her friends insisted on setting her up. Over the last few years, one of her friends was always touting someone "who's just right for you."

How many times had she heard that phrase? Too many to count.

But despite accolades to the contrary, the "someone" was never right. There was always some flaw that pushed her away before a second date could come about. Joanna knew damn well that she was probably not being fair to any of the men she'd gone out with, but she just couldn't help it.

Fear was a powerful deterring factor and while she thought herself fearless in so many aspects of life, she knew herself well enough to admit that she was afraid of getting hurt again.

So afraid that she didn't even want to venture into the field again.

So afraid that even now that her "perfect someone" had materialized in her life again, she didn't know if she had the courage to tread over the same terrain with her heart exposed to the elements.

It had been all she could do to pull herself together

the first time. The only reason she'd succeeded was because she'd had her mother to lean on. Rachel Prescott was the strongest, bravest person she knew. Her mother understood what it meant to pull yourself upright after love had all but disintegrated your heart. Though her mother had never once spoken ill of him, Joanna knew that her father had broken her mother's heart. He'd left her abruptly the moment he'd found out that she was pregnant, virtually disappearing from the scene.

Her grandfather, a strict disciplinarian, had thrown her mother out because she'd refused both of his ultimatums: abort her baby or give it up for adoption when it was born.

Her mother had been all about love, and because of her, because of her unwavering support, Joanna had found her own courage to go on after she had left Rick and he had left town.

Without her mother in her life, Joanna didn't know if she could do it a second time, if she could recover if things didn't go right. Under the circumstances, it was best not to test her at this point in her life. Her own daughter needed her and the baby came first.

The bottom line was that she couldn't allow her heart to go there, couldn't let herself dream and hope. She refused to live beyond the moment when it came to Rick.

Getting out of her car, she noticed that the Mercedes was parked beside the Mustang. Rick was home.

Once, when he'd had her over while his parents were away in Europe, the garage had been filled to capacity with his father's collection of automobiles.

His father had always loved displays that touted his wealth, his importance.

The collection was all but gone now. Three of the vehicles had found their way to Florida, his father's other residence, and two were still here for when he lived on the west coast, but for the most part, the car collection had been given to charity. That, she knew, had been Rick's doing. She'd heard from Mrs. Rutledge that Howard Masters now believed that there were more important things than money.

Would wonders never cease?

Too bad he hadn't felt that way eight years ago.

She closed her door, looking at her own small foreign car. Rick had had it brought over last week. It looked completely out of place here amid the other cars. Like a poor relation allowed to eat at the table because it was Christmas.

Kind of the way she probably would have felt if she'd married Rick, she thought.

She supposed she could see his parents' side of it, why they had balked at having a daughter-in-law whose parents hadn't even bothered to get married, much less been able to have their lineage traced back through noble bloodlines.

The years had brought her insight she fervently wished she didn't have.

In the absolute sense, his parents were right. Rick had a great future before him. He needed "his own kind" as his mother had put it, beside him, not someone who was a bastard in the old sense of the word. A man should be proud of his wife, not embarrassed by her.

And that was what she would have been to him. An embarrassment.

"Did you run into a problem?"

The sound of Rick's voice coming from the entrance to the garage startled her. Joanna turned around. The sun was behind him, framing him in golden rays as if he were the Chosen One.

She couldn't help smiling. Maybe he was at that, she thought.

The Chosen One, but not chosen for her. He'd assumed the helm of his family's business with ease. And in that time, he'd only become better-looking. She'd thought of him as beautiful to start with, but the years had tempered that beauty with a ruggedness that was almost irresistible. She couldn't help wondering why he wasn't married by now. What had happened to the woman his mother had chosen for him? The one she'd stepped aside for?

Didn't matter. That wasn't her concern. She banked down her thoughts and responded to his question. "No, why?"

"I heard the car." Crossing to her, he nodded at her vehicle. "When you didn't come in, I thought maybe something was wrong. You were frowning."

She dismissed his observation. "Just thinking."

Taking her chin in his hand, he tilted back her head. His eyes searched hers for a clue. She'd become a great deal more closed-mouth than she'd been when they had been together. "About?"

"Thoughts. And to answer your question, nothing's wrong. The school board told me that, after reviewing the matter, they're willing to have me come back."

She wasn't telling him anything he didn't already

know. He slipped his arm around her shoulders, beginning to usher her toward the house. "Very gracious of them. Maybe they don't like facing the possibility of a lawsuit."

She looked at him, puzzled. "Why would they think I'd sue them?"

There was a note in her voice that warned him to keep his part in this under wraps a while longer. "Everyone sues these days."

Joanna stopped walking and shrugged his arm away from her shoulders.

"Did you have something to do with this?" Now that she thought about it, Mrs. Raleigh had looked a little uneasy. All things considered, the woman had seemed a little too eager to reinstate her.

"I didn't talk to anyone there."

She knew him. He was being deliberately evasive, deliberately telling her small truths to fabricate a larger lie. He hadn't talked to anyone *there,* which meant that he *had* talked to someone somewhere about her situation.

Joanna felt her temper emerging. "Who *did* you talk to?"

Rick's shrug was charmingly noncommittal, but she was in no mood for charm. "I talk to a great many people every day."

He was playing games. She pinned him with specifics. "About me."

He waved his hand in the air, tossing her a diversion. "I asked Mrs. Rutledge—"

Joanna fisted her hands on her hips. "Rick!"

He wasn't about to lie outright to her. Besides, he wasn't ashamed of what he'd done. It was all very reasonable, all very aboveboard. It was the school district who had been in the wrong, not him. "I had my lawyer talk to them."

She should have known. Angry, she curbed the urge to slug him. Given his physique, he wouldn't have felt it and it might have even injured her knuckles. But that didn't negate the desire.

"Damn it, Rick, how could you?"

Why was she getting so angry? He tried to appeal to her logic. "Joanna, it's discrimination. In this day and age, an unmarried pregnant woman—"

"—can fight her own battles." Didn't he get it yet? His mother had been an independent woman. Did he think that was only a trait reserved for the rich? "*I* wanted to fight my own battles. Win my own battles." She blew out a breath. "Now I can't go back."

He didn't see the connection. "Why? Because I did what you were going to?"

How dense was he? Or was he just patronizing her? "Because you did it *for* me."

He studied her for a moment. "Since when did ego become such a big thing with you?"

It wasn't about ego. It was about self-esteem. Apparently he couldn't distinguish the difference between the two. "Since I wanted to be my own person." She wanted him to understand. She wasn't being ungrateful, she was being herself. She didn't want to lose that sense of self, not even for him. It carried too big a price.

Her voice softened a little as she told him, "I can't have someone else charging into battle for me, I can't start relying on that."

It didn't make any sense to him. "Why?"

She closed her eyes for a second, gathering strength together. He really didn't see, did he? She spelled it out for him.

"Because when you lean on something and that support suddenly crumbles, then what happens? You fall flat on your face. You fall hard enough and you're not going to get up again."

She was talking about herself, he realized. Funny, they'd grown apart, grown in different directions, and yet, they shared this. The fear of abandonment. He would have preferred being able to share something else.

"Not you, Joey." He tucked a strand of hair behind her ear, the way he used to do. And she shook it loose, the way she used to do. A smile curved his lips. "You always get up again. It's one of the things I liked about you." She'd been soft, but she'd never clung. She didn't need him to be strong constantly. But he found himself wanting her to need him a little. "I also liked the fact that you used to let me do things for you once in a while." He framed her face with his hands, trying to secure her complete attention. "People need to be needed, Joey, just as much as they need to feel invincible."

Placing her hands over his, she slowly removed them from her face. "I don't want to feel invincible, Rick, I just want to stand up on my own two feet."

"And you are." A touch of exasperation filled his voice. "I wasn't threatening the board, trying to make them take back a shoddy teacher, I was trying to make them see the error of their ways and take back a wonderful teacher." Couldn't she see the difference?

He was just saying that, she thought. That hadn't

been his reasoning then. People in high positions get accustomed to having their wishes obeyed without question.

"How do you know I'm a wonderful teacher?" she challenged. "You've never even heard me teach."

"Because you're a wonderful everything else." His gaze washed over her, making her feel warm all over. She felt herself losing the thread of the argument. "I figured why should teaching be any different?"

She wanted to remain angry, to make him understand, but it wasn't easy. "You're making it hard to argue."

His grin teased her. "That was my intent."

She had to make him understand why it was important to her. "But I want to argue. Don't you see—"

He slipped his hands around her waist. "Do you know, trite as it sounds, that you're beautiful when you're angry?"

She sighed, knowing she was tottering on the edge of defeat. "Rick—"

"Of course," he said philosophically, "you're beautiful when you're laughing so I suppose that's not much of an accomplishment."

The man was utterly impossible. And incredibly irresistible. She could feel the heat of his body traveling through hers. "Rick—"

He shook his head, then kissed her forehead. "Sorry, you're not going to make me apologize for doing what's right."

Backing away from him, she threw her hands up. "You've got to stop doing this, Rick. Stop buying me things, being my bully—"

"Bully?" Now there was something no one had ever called him before. He paused, pretending to roll the image over in his mind. "I've never thought of myself as a bully. I'm more of the Sir Lancelot type, don't you think?"

If he was the first knight of the realm, where did he see her in all this? "And I'm Guinevere?"

He smiled into her eyes, drawing her to him again. "Yes."

But she shook her head. "I don't want to be Guinevere, the romance ended very badly."

He thought it over for a second. "Well, you're too pretty to be Merlin and if you're King Arthur, that takes this relationship into a whole other realm that I'm not prepared even to consider." For a moment, they were back in the past, sitting on her mother's porch, fantasizing. He grinned at her. "Okay, who would you like to be?"

"Me, Rick," she insisted, and then her voice softened. "Just me."

He nodded. "A very good choice. I vote for that, too." His hand around her waist, he began to usher her toward the inner garage door. "Now come into the house, I have something for you."

She sighed, exasperated. "Aren't you listening? I just told you I don't want you spending any more money on me."

"I swear, you are the hardest woman to shower with things. But don't worry, this didn't cost anything." For good measure, he crossed his heart, the way he used to.

It was like experiencing déjà vu. She shut the feeling and its accompanying sensations of nostalgia away. "You stole it?" she scoffed.

He thought of the box in his room. "No, I unearthed it." He opened the door leading into the house and waited for her to walk in first.

Now he had her curious. But first, she wanted to look in on her daughter. She'd discovered that being away from Rachel for more than a couple of hours at a time filled her with a sense of longing. It was going to be difficult once she went back to work—one aspect of independence she wasn't looking forward to.

"Let me just go in and check on Rachel first before you start 'showering.'"

He laughed. "Why don't we do it together? See the baby I mean, not shower—although—"

This time she did hit him, but she laughed as she did it. "You know, this isn't over with yet."

"I sincerely hope not." There was a look in his eyes that completely unsettled her.

She looked at him pointedly. "I mean this discussion."

Mrs. Rutledge came out to greet them the moment they entered the house. Her proximity to the inner door had allowed her to hear almost everything.

"I was beginning to wonder if I was supposed to bring out the swords for you two." She was referring to the two ancient samurai swords that hung over the fireplace in the den. "And a referee." She looked at Joanna. "Did everything go all right at your meeting with the school board?"

Joanna in turn slanted a look toward Rick. "That depends on who you ask." She supposed, in his defense, from Rick's point of view, he was only trying to help. A lot of women would have killed to have someone in their corner. The problem was, he wasn't in her corner, he *was* the corner.

"You'll work it out," Mrs. Rutledge assured her with unflagging cheerfulness. She saw the two begin to go toward the rear of the house. "I just put the baby down. Mind you don't wake her."

Joanna shook her head as the woman walked away. "I'm starting to wonder whose baby this is," she murmured to Rick.

"She tends to be a little protective," he told her, and then added as he looked at Joanna, "There's a lot of that going around."

Tiptoeing into the nursery, Joanna saw that Rachel really was asleep. She'd been hoping to find her awake. But she didn't have the heart to rouse her.

Standing here, looking down at her daughter, raw emotions found her. She was still in awe of the fact that she was a mother, that this tiny life had entered hers and that she was responsible for it.

It both humbled her and filled her with a great deal of love.

"She looks like you."

She felt his breath along her cheek as he spoke and struggled not to shiver. "No, she doesn't."

Maybe she'd misunderstood what he meant. "When you were a baby."

Drawing away from the crib so as not to wake Rachel, she looked at him. "How would you know?"

"I sat up last night, looking through your mother's albums." He nodded toward the open door, indicating that they should take the conversation out of the room in case it might wake the baby.

"Why would you do that?"

"I was just curious." He eased the door closed and followed her into the hallway. "You're not seriously going to turn the board down because of your pride, are you?"

"My pride?" Stunned, she looked at him. "What does my pride have to do with it?"

"Everything from where I'm standing. For some reason, you feel as if you have to do everything yourself. The world's not like that, Joanna."

She'd watched her mother struggle to provide a living for them. There'd never been anyone to help her and she'd never complained. It was just something she did and it was a trait she'd passed on to her.

"It is for me."

He shook his head. "The world is about networking, about doing favors and having them done for you. You're being noble in your own way, but you're also being damn stubborn in a way that only you can be."

She frowned. "What's that supposed to mean?"

But he only grinned at her. "That's okay, I like stubborn women." He kissed her temple. "Now come with me." He took her hand, threading his fingers through hers. "I still have something to show you."

Nine

The moment he started walking with her toward the staircase, his cell phone rang.

Joanna looked at his jacket. "I think your pocket wants you."

Rick sighed, stopping. He wasn't in the mood for interruptions. "I'm going to have to remember to turn that off when I come home."

"There's always the regular phone," she pointed out. One of the rooms served as his office. "Your fax, e-mail. They'd find you."

She was right. There was no getting away from responsibility. He hoped that this was something that could be settled quickly. Pulling out his phone, he saw that Joanna was about to walk away, probably to give him some privacy. He held up his finger, indicating that he wanted her to stay.

"Masters."

Joanna watched his face as he listened to the person on the other end of the phone. His brows slowly drew together like dark clouds gathering before a storm. "Can't you handle it, Pierce?"

Whoever Pierce was, Joanna thought, his answer was obviously negative. Rick's eyebrows almost touched over the bridge of a nose that sculptors had been immortalizing for centuries.

"Fine, I'll be there in twenty minutes." Annoyed, he slapped the lid shut. He was frowning deeply as he replaced his phone in his pocket. The frown faded slightly as he apologized. "I'm going to have to go out for a little while."

From what she'd seen of him these last few weeks, she wouldn't have expected anything less. He was in full command of the company, not just his father's right-hand man. That meant that business would take up most of his time. She was surprised that he could come home early. "A man's gotta do what a man's gotta do."

He ran his hands up and down her arms, his eyes on her face. "What this man wants to do is spend the evening with you." Impulse had him forming plans as he went along. It had been a long time since he'd felt spontaneous within the confines of his own life. "I wanted to take you out and celebrate your rehiring. You haven't been out since Rachel was born."

If only he knew. "Far longer than that," Joanna laughed.

There was something in her voice that made him want to ask her questions, made him want to find out what life had been like for her these years they'd been

apart. Had there been anyone else after him? Someone who'd captured her heart? What other men had
held her? Had made love with her?

Or had she been like him, alone in her heart if not
in reality?

He knew he had no right to ask, but that didn't
change the fact that he wanted to. That he wanted to
know.

Taking her hands in his, Rick looked into her eyes,
losing himself there for just a moment.

"I won't be long," he promised. "When I come
back, we'll go out. Does dinner and dancing sound
good to you?"

Joanna grinned. "Right now, a hamburger and a
jig sound good to me." *Any place,* she thought, *as
long as it's with you.*

"It'll be more than that. Maybe this'll hold you
until then. Take it as a retainer."

Rick meant only to brush a fleeting kiss to her lips,
nothing more. He didn't have time for more. Pierce,
his chief assistant, brought with him from Georgia,
sounded harried. It looked as if one of the divisions
of Masters Enterprises might have a wildcat strike on
their hands.

But touching his mouth to hers only made Rick
want to kiss her again. Life had a way of wantonly
turning things inside out without giving any notice.
He knew that now. Gathering her into his arms, he
kissed her as if he wasn't coming back. As if she
wouldn't be here when he did. As if the world was
going to end in the next five seconds and all they had
available to them were these precious few moments.

He was draining away her soul. As he drew his lips

back, Joanna had to hold onto his arms just to steady herself. If she'd been an old-fashioned galleon, she would have sworn that she had just been broadsided and breached.

Still holding on to his arms, she pretended to shake her head to clear it. It was only half in jest. "Wow, if that's a retainer, I can't wait to find out what the whole payment is."

He brushed the back of his hand against her cheek, a bittersweet feeling filtering through him. All the warnings he'd issued to himself were temporarily on hold. He just wanted to enjoy the sight of her. "Just be ready when I come back."

"I'm not sure if that's possible," she murmured as he left the house. She was beginning to think that nothing would prepare her for him, not at this level of intensity.

She couldn't help wondering if he'd forgotten all about that mysterious "something" he'd alluded to earlier. She knew she'd told him to stop giving her things, but he'd made her curious.

Passing a mirror, she grinned at her reflection. Rick still had the ability to make her feel as if she were no more than twenty.

Rick unconsciously tightened his hands around the steering wheel as he took a turn. It took effort to make himself relax and loosen his grip. He glanced at the clock on the dashboard. Eleven-oh-two. He had to work hard to rein in his anger and curb it.

The quick meeting had been anything but that. It definitely hadn't gone as planned. What should have taken no more than an hour had stretched out into four, then five, threatening to go well into the pre-dawn morning until he'd finally called a halt to it, promising to reconvene the next day.

Obviously he wasn't as on top of things as he'd originally thought, otherwise the workers at the Pasadena plant would not be threatening to walk if certain terms were not met.

When it rained, it poured. As if his life wasn't hectic enough with the home office transfer, he was now in the middle of a work arbitration.

The meeting felt as if it were a million miles away. Right now, all he was concerned about was finding a way to make it up to Joanna. He didn't want her to feel that he was taking her for granted, that he expected her to stand on the sidelines, waiting until he could spare a moment for her.

He'd called her twice from the office, pushing back the time until there wasn't any time to push back.

He felt really awful. There weren't enough hours in the day, but somehow, he intended to find them. Or create them if he had to. There had to be a way to be a conscientious businessman while still maintaining some kind of a private life. He hadn't wanted one up until now, but things had changed, at least temporarily. He needed to find a way to be able to juggle both, he thought, getting out of the car.

It was after eleven. Too late to eat out. And probably too late to make it up to Joanna. The evening wasn't supposed to have gone this way.

Feeling drained and annoyed, Rick let himself in through the garage.

"So, how did it go?"

Glancing toward the living room, he saw her getting up from the sofa. She was wearing a robe and her hair was slightly tousled, as if she'd just been lying down.

He closed the door behind himself. "You waited up for me?"

She shrugged carelessly. The sash on her robe loosened slightly, the two sides parting a little. "I waited. I'm up, so I guess you'd be safe in saying that I waited up for you."

Crossing to her, he flashed an apologetic smile as he slipped off his jacket. This time, he'd made sure his cell phone was off. He dropped his jacket on the back of the sofa. "I'm sorry about tonight."

"Why, did it go badly?"

Her makeup was gone, and she looked as natural as sunshine. He could feel himself being aroused. "No, I meant about us not going out."

"Well, unless there's some kind of edict about closing down all the restaurants in the world by tomorrow morning, I figure you can make it up to me." There were still frown lines about his mouth and eyes. She feathered her fingers along his brow, pressing them away. "Did you get a chance to eat?"

He nodded, loosening his tie then slipping it off. It joined his jacket. "We sent out for sandwiches. How about you?"

"I got the better end of the deal." She threaded her arms around his. "I had Mrs. Rutledge." The woman had insisted on making her a full dinner. "There's some leftover beef Wellington in the refrigerator if you're interested." She waited to see if he wanted her to warm up a portion for him.

"Beef Wellington?" It was one of Mrs. Rutledge's

specialties. "You really did get the better end of the deal."

As far as food went, anyway, she thought. The evening had gone very peacefully. Rachel had been perfect company, sleeping for most of it. "Sometimes things turn out that way. So, are you hungry?"

"Yes." But as she turned to go to the kitchen to prepare a late meal for him, he caught her by the wrist and pulled her back. When she turned to look at him quizzically, he said, "I'm hungry, but it doesn't have anything to do with food."

"Oh?" She cocked her head, looking up at him. "What does it have to do with?"

Instead of saying anything, he pulled her closer to him and brought his mouth down on hers. The kiss began passionately and ended practically in flames.

By the time he drew his mouth from hers, they were both breathing hard.

"That," he told her.

She threaded her arms around his neck. Her eyes danced with mischief as she looked up at him. "Aren't you too tired for 'that'?"

He locked his hands behind her, his pulse beginning to accelerate. "Did it feel as if I was tired?"

She sighed, wishing the moment and this feeling would go on forever. Knowing it couldn't. "It felt like heaven."

He glanced toward the rear of the house, where the nursery was. "When was the baby fed last?"

"Twenty minutes ago."

One down. "And Mrs. Rutledge?"

Tongue in cheek, she said, "She ate about three hours ago."

He pressed a kiss to her throat, then another. Her pulse leaped up to mark the passage of his lips. "I meant is she asleep?"

"She said good-night at ten." It was hard to get the words out when her head was spinning.

"That's all I wanted to know."

His lips found their way back to hers again. He kissed her hard, the way he had earlier before he'd gone to his meeting. The way he'd wanted to all evening.

Joanna could feel her blood rushing in her veins as her whole body went on alert.

It wasn't going to end here, in the hall, with a kiss that curled her toes so hard she might never be able to straighten them again.

This was just the beginning.

Anticipation sang through her body, priming it. Making her ache so badly, she almost whimpered. Joanna wrapped her arms around him even tighter, raising herself up on her toes. Trying to absorb every nuance of his kiss, every nuance of his body. To sustain her later.

It wasn't easy, but he pulled his head back to look at her. "You sure it's okay?" he breathed.

It was more than okay, it was wonderful. The grin on her lips came into her eyes as she looked at him. "Well, if we make love out here, Mrs. Rutledge might see us if she wakes up and hears something."

He laughed, kissing her quickly before saying, "You know what I mean."

It touched her that he was so concerned about her well-being at a time like this. Another man would be ripping her clothes off by now. Independence not withstanding, it was nice to have someone worry about her, even if only fleetingly.

"Yes, I know what you mean." She brushed a kiss to each of his cheeks. "And the doctor said I'm fully operational."

The description made him laugh. "That makes you sound like an aircraft."

Her arms around his neck, she pressed her body tantalizingly against his, swaying just enough to make him crazy. Her eyes never left his as she said seductively, "Come fly me."

It was all he needed to hear.

The instant he kissed her again, needs that had been held back for so long broke free of their chains. He kissed her over and over again, changing the chemical composition of her body from solid to almost completely liquid. Heated liquid.

And then, it seemed as if her body was on automatic pilot. Her arms still around his neck, she jumped up, wrapping her legs around his hips and waist. Her mouth never broke contact with his.

He caught her, holding her to him. She could feel her inner core moisten and yet seem to be on fire. Her mouth slanted over his again and again.

All the years of longing pushed forward, fueling her desire, beating against her with fisted hands as they begged to be finally freed.

She was playing havoc with his restraint, bending it all out of shape until he didn't know how much longer he could contain himself. He could feel the inner heat emerging from her, hitting him square in the stomach, whetting his appetite and raising it to incredible heights. His mouth sealed to hers, his consciousness all but disintegrated, he was barely aware of walking with her.

Somehow, they made it into her room, though the logistics of how didn't completely register. All Joanna was aware of was the overwhelming desire that had taken her body hostage.

How many times had she dreamed about this, digging deep into her memory and reconstructing every time they'd been together? The first time, the last time, they'd all merged into one compelling memory, making her long so much that it hardly seemed humanly possible to feel this way and still live.

But she'd managed. Managed to survive for a long time without him. Without anyone.

But now that was at an end. She was going to make love with him tonight. She had to. Otherwise, she was going to self-destruct.

Joanna felt as if there were explosions going on all over her body.

Slowly, he drew her away from his body and laid her down on her bed. Her robe parted. The nightgown she had on exposed more than it covered. His mouth became as dry as the Mojave in summer.

As he lay down next to her, he could feel his entire body pulse to a rhythm that had been set down before time was recorded.

He tugged her robe from her shoulders. Joanna raised her hips to accommodate him and he felt in danger of swallowing his tongue as he pulled the robe off the rest of the way. The silken material slid unnoticed to the floor.

Covering her mouth with his, Rick took his assault to two fronts, his lips reducing her to the consistency of tapioca pudding left out overnight while his hands delved beneath her nightgown, finding places that had existed only in his dreams. Places that had once been his.

Joanna drew her breath in sharply against his mouth as she felt his fingers spread out over her hip, caressing her softly over and over again. Regaining possession. She turned into his touch, savoring it, then abruptly pulled away.

When he looked at her in confusion, she breathed, "No fair."

Before the words could penetrate the growing haze around his brain, before he could ask her what she meant, Joanna began making short work of the clothes he was wearing.

Understanding, he leaned back and quickly undid the buttons of his shirt.

But she was the one who pulled the tails out of his waistband, the one who pushed the shirt off his shoulders as she craned her neck in order to capture his mouth with her own.

The next to go were his pants. Wiggling almost beneath him, she undid the button, then the zipper, her hand delving inside the space that was created to touch him lightly before she continued removing his pants.

He moved to help her, but she was clearly in charge. A woman with a mission. "You've done this before," he teased.

He could have sworn there was a twinkle in her eyes. "I've practiced on mannequins."

He didn't want her to think that he was prying. She had the right to be her own person, the right to her privacy. As much as he wanted to know, he wouldn't ask. He wanted her to know that.

"I'm not asking about your past, Joey."

"There is no past, Rick." Hot with her breath, the words echoed against his mouth. Unable to rein in her emotions, she yanked away his underwear. "There's only you."

He didn't know if she meant that, if there'd been no man in her life since they'd separated. But true or not, he wanted to believe it.

So, for now, he did.

The flame within him raised ever higher.

Pressing her back against the soft comforter, he began to make slow, methodical love to every inch of her, beginning at her toes and working his way up as she twisted and sighed beneath him.

He lingered over every part of her, satisfying his own ever-increasing desire with the sounds and movements she made as he pressed kisses to her instep, to the back of her knees, to the insides of her thighs. Cataloging dusky tastes in his brain.

Remembering.

Finding the very heart of her, his tongue teased her, bringing her up to her first climax.

Joanna grasped fistfuls of the comforter, scrambling closer to the sensation that was exploding within her as his mouth branded her. Making her completely his, as she always had been.

She bit down hard on her lower lip to keep from crying out.

Panting, she fell back, only to be quickly brought up to the promise of a second explosion.

She reached for him, wanting to touch him, to possess him as he did her, but he was merciless in his quest to bring her pleasure.

He kissed her belly, making it quiver, weaving the chain so that it descended again before he finally took it upward.

He anointed each of her breasts, hardening the peaks until she thought she would go insane. And then, he was over her, poised, ready, wanting.

She realized that her eyes had been squeezed shut. She opened them now and looked up into his face. The face of the man she had always loved.

Framing it with her hands, she raised her head and pressed her lips against his. The kiss that flowered between them was velvety and deep.

It cut through the last of his resolve. He'd wanted to prolong the moment, to kiss and tease her a little longer before he finally came to her. But there was no way he could physically hold back even a moment longer. She'd weakened him, weakened him with the look in her eyes, with the soft promise of her body as it yielded itself up to his.

Uttering a sound that was only marginally intelligible, Rick drove himself into her.

His eyes holding hers, he began to move, at first slowly, then more and more rapidly with each beat of his heart. He'd wanted to watch her, to take in every movement, every tiny glimmer of her expression.

But the need to kiss her, to savor her lips, was even greater. Just as his body was sealed to hers, he sealed his mouth over hers.

As their hips moved and the tempo increased, so

did the urgency of his kiss until both erupted in one final, all-surrounding crescendo.

Within the small eternity that followed, Rick found the spark, the ecstasy, the peace that had been eluding him for so long. He clung to it.

Ten

Nestled in the crook of his arm, she'd been quiet for a while now. Rick wondered if that was a good thing. Brushing a kiss against the top of her head, he asked, "What are you thinking?"

He could feel her smile as it spread against his chest. The warm feeling following in its wake was indescribable.

"That you must have been practicing." She looked up, her hair brushing against his skin. "I don't remember you being this good."

He laughed softly. "I was always this good." The smile faded slightly as he looked into her eyes. "And I haven't been practicing."

He watched as her smile turned into a grin. "Oh, then you're telling me you've lived like a monk all these years?"

"Of the highest order." Rick winked and then crossed his heart with his free hand. "Want to see my membership card?" He pretended to reach for it, then stopped. "Oh, sorry, this outfit doesn't come with pockets." When she laughed, another warm feeling curled through his belly, like smoke from a chimney on a crisp winter morning. His arm tightened around her as emotions he'd been so certain had left him for good filled his heart. "I've missed you, Joey."

She turned into him, the humor gone from her eyes. "Why didn't you come after me?" There was no recrimination in her voice. She just wanted to know. "I was in the same place I always was. Why did you just leave town like that?"

He shrugged. Looking back, he knew he shouldn't have. He should have laid siege to her house until the truth came out. "Pride, I guess." He lowered his gaze to take her in. "The same pride that keeps you stubbornly fighting off help at every turn."

She shook her head, her hair moving along his arm. Arousing him again. "Apples and oranges."

"Fruit salad," he countered.

She stared at him in confusion. "What?"

The grin began in his eyes, filtering down to his lips slowly. "I thought as long as we're lobbing fruit around, we can make a salad."

Laughing, Joanna swatted at his arm. "You're talking crazy."

"Right." He fitted her against him, his eyes intent. "Then shut me up, Joey. I don't want to talk about the past." He kissed the swell above her breasts and felt her begin to shift, "or anything else, except that

I've got a very beautiful naked woman in my arms and I've remained inactive far too long.''

She could feel his desire for her growing. The man was incredible. ''Again?''

The look on his face was pure innocence. ''Hey, being a monk lets you store up an incredible amount of energy, lady…'' Suddenly, he whipped her around, making her land flat on her back. ''I have only begun to make love.'' He raised and lowered his brows comically. ''Think you're up to it?''

Her heart was already beginning to race. ''Why don't you try me and see?''

He shifted so that his body covered hers. ''Exactly what I had in mind.''

It wasn't until nearly an hour later that she found her tongue again. She had all the energy of a de-stuffed rag doll. As if he wasn't already perfect enough, the man was an incredible lover.

With what she thought was her last ounce of strength, she turned her body toward his. It amazed her that he hadn't fallen asleep yet. She splayed her hand against his chest, finding infinite comfort in the feel of his heart beating beneath her palm.

''By the way, was that a ploy?''

''What?'' He raised his head just a tad to look at her expression. ''That I can make love all night under the right conditions?''

''No, that you had something for me.'' She pushed herself up onto her elbow and her eyes sparkled as they dipped low on his torso. ''Or was that 'it'?''

''A little more respect, please,'' he teased, stealing a kiss. ''And no, 'that,' as you so irreverently called it, wasn't 'it.'''

Her curiosity was roused all over again, despite her resolve not to accept another material thing from him. "Then what?"

He laughed, drawing her closer. "Getting mercenary on me, are you?"

"No," she protested with just enough indignity to have him guessing whether or not she was serious. "I just want to know when you're feeding me lines."

"I'd never feed you a line." Sitting up, he threw off the sheet and got out of bed. "Wait here."

She bolted upright. "Rick, you can't go out like that. What if Mrs. Rutledge sees you? She'll have a heart attack."

"I wasn't about to go parading up the stairs in my birthday suit." Rick grabbed his pants from the floor where they'd been discarded and put them on quickly. Pulling up the zipper, he didn't bother buttoning them. "Wait here."

"With bated breath."

Moving the pillows against the headboard, Joanna sank back against the bed, sighing. She felt exhausted, excited, energized all at the same time. All that and in love as well.

She knew she shouldn't be, that it was a mistake to fall in love with Rick all over again. She knew that what his parents had said was ultimately true. She and Rick belonged in totally different worlds. A temporarily out-of-work love child with next to no roots and a multi-millionaire with bloodlines that went back to the Thirteen Colonies had little in common. They could hardly be mentioned in the same sentence.

But for now, for tonight, Joanna thought, lacing her fingers behind her head, she could let the practical

world go and just pretend that she was still just
Joanna Prescott, twenty years old and wildly in love.

Because she was.

She glanced toward the doorway. Rick had returned
and he was carrying a rectangular, unwrapped, white
shirt box in his hands.

Unlacing her hands, she made herself comfortable.
"That was fast. Grabbed the first thing you could find,
did you?"

"No." But he had grabbed the first box he could
find in order to make it look like a gift. Rick sat down
on the bed next to her. "I grabbed the gift I had for
you. The one I was going to give you before Pierce
called in the middle of his heart attack." She looked
at him uncertainly. "Figuratively speaking. Pierce is
always having heart attacks. He enjoys being dra-
matic."

He put the box on her lap. As she moved forward,
the sheet began to slip from her breasts and she made
a grab for it. He stayed her hand.

"No, don't. Let it fall." He moved her hand away
from the sheet. "Let me have my fantasy."

She raised an amused brow. "Your fantasy is
drooping sheets?"

"No," he pressed a kiss to her shoulder and had
the pleasure of feeling her shiver ever so slightly,
"my fantasy is you." He nodded toward the box on
her lap. "Well, aren't you going to open it?"

She caught her lower lip between her teeth, looking
down at the box.

"Let me savor this. Sometimes, anticipation is the
best part." And then she looked at him. His hair was
still tousled where she'd run her fingers through it.

Joanna could feel her skin glowing just thinking about what they'd done. "Except for tonight," she said softly.

He curbed the temptation to run his hand along her breasts, reveling in the softness of her skin. Instead, he nodded at his gift. He wanted to see her face when she opened it more than he wanted to fulfill his erotic fantasies. "The box."

"The box." Joanna placed her hands on either side of the gift. "And you're sure this didn't cost anything?"

"Not a dime," he assured her, just the slightest bit impatient. "Even the box was one that was just lying around."

A grin played along her lips. "But you think I'll like this."

She was messing with him and she knew it. "Open it already. Here," he reached for the box, ready to open it for her himself, but she pulled it aside.

"No," she laughed, "I can open my own free gifts."

And then, as the lid came off and she held it in her hands, the laughter stilled.

There was an album inside. Its cover had been weathered slightly by the passage of time. She recognized it as one she'd given him years ago. She'd always thought he'd thrown it away.

Joanna said nothing as she carefully took the album out of the box and set it down on her lap. Then, very slowly, she lifted the cover and looked inside. There was page after page of photographs. The photographs that she'd lost in the fire. Tears filled her eyes.

"It's not free," she whispered, "it's priceless. But where did you get this?"

"From my closet. From deep in my closet," he added. "I couldn't make myself get rid of it." The album had been there all these years. He hadn't taken it with him when he'd left town, hadn't wanted to look at anything that reminded him of her.

She still didn't understand. "I thought you said you didn't care about keeping photographs, that you didn't need them."

Inside the album was every single photograph she'd insisted on giving him. Each time she'd had a roll of film developed, she'd made duplicates of all the shots that contained the two of them. And each and every time, he'd acted cavalierly, claiming he didn't believe in keeping photographs, even after she'd given him the album as a keepsake.

Rick shrugged. The truth was, he was far more sentimental than he'd ever wanted to admit.

"Saving photographs didn't sound macho. A twenty-two-year-old guy wasn't supposed to get sentimental over something like that. These are all the ones you lost in the fire." Craning his neck, he looked at her. "You're crying." A shaky sigh escaped as she nodded. Taking a corner of the sheet, he wiped away her tears. "Happy tears?" She nodded again. Rick shook his head. "That never made any sense to me. It's like *aloha* and *shalom,* words that can mean two completely opposite things."

Emotion welled up inside her. She carefully placed the album on the nightstand and then turned back to Rick. Wrapping her arms around his neck, she hugged him as hard as she could. "Thank you."

He kissed the top of her head, not trusting his voice at the moment. The heat of her body began working its magic again. He could feel himself becoming aroused just holding her.

He glanced over toward the nursery. "Think Rachel'll sleep a little longer?"

"She's been sleeping longer and longer these days." Mentally, Joanna crossed her fingers. "I think Mrs. Rutledge's been training her."

He could just barely remember what the woman had been like when he was growing up. Strict, but kind. "God bless Mrs. Rutledge."

She watched unabashedly as he rose and slid his pants from his hips. "What did you have in mind?"

Rick got into bed with her. "Round three."

She wiped the last of her tears away with the back of her hand, having absolutely no idea how much that aroused him. "Ready when you are."

"Ready," he declared.

Rick pulled her back down on the bed. He lost no time revisiting places he had gotten far more familiar with in this short space of time than he was with his own body.

Weaving a wreath of hot, open-mouth kisses along her quivering skin, he paused only long enough to say, "When it comes to you, Joey, I was born ready."

"Big talk," she teased, arching her body temptingly against his, savoring the burst of desire that erupted within her each time his mouth made contact. "Actions speak louder than words."

"Then prepare to go deaf."

Taking her hands, he held them above her head, locking his fingers through hers. His body was less than a hairbreadth away from hers, tantalizing her, making her yearn for the coupling she knew was to come. He moved against her just enough to make her crazy.

Joanna felt herself growing damp, could feel the throbbing need in her own loins. Two could play this game, she thought. She arched against him, then gloried in the smoky look that came into his eyes.

With one slow, teasing movement of her body, the warden had become the prisoner, the captor had become the captured.

She held him in the palm of her hand. He knew that in some ways, she always would. How had he lived so long without this woman, without feeling her supple body yielding itself to his? How had he been able to withstand the days without losing himself within her?

Containing himself as best he could, holding both her hands in one of his, Rick moved down the length of her, branding her with his lips, his tongue.

He was creating havoc within her very core. Joanna could feel the precursors of climaxes reaching up to greater and greater heights within her, wanting the final moment, the final triumph. And just when the climax threatened to erupt, he'd pull back just enough to keep the moment from happening.

It was torture, and she loved it.

Finally releasing her hands, he framed her body, lightly skimming his fingers along her skin even as his mouth reduced her to the consistency of quivering warm jelly.

"You're making me crazy." The words came in short, breathless spurts.

"Good," he murmured against the tender flesh of her stomach, his warm breath arousing her to almost a frenzy.

She bucked beneath him. "Now, Rick, now."

He wasn't sure if it was a plea or an order. Whatever the case, it came because she wanted him as much as he wanted her. And it came at the right moment because he knew he couldn't hold out much longer.

Pulling himself up along her body, her dampness exciting him, he stopped just short of entry. Poised over her, his eyes held hers for a long moment.

She felt as if time had suddenly been frozen.

There was so much she felt, so much she wanted to say. So much she couldn't say.

But he could read it in her eyes.

There was no need to part her legs, she was ready for him. Eager for him. He drove himself in, his breath catching in his throat from the start.

And then the dance began, not a waltz, but a wild tango, heated from the very start, pledged to get only more so before the music stopped.

The final explosion came quickly, draining them both. He held her in his arms as tranquillity descended, wishing that this moment *could* somehow be pressed within the pages of time, to be revisited, refelt, whenever he needed to remember what it was like to love someone so much that nothing else mattered.

He kissed her temple. "Loud enough for you?"

Joanna moved her head so she could look at him. "Eh? What did you say? I can't hear you, I've gone temporarily deaf."

He laughed and hugged her to him. And felt himself getting aroused all over again.

The woman was more than part witch, he thought. And she was all his.

The rest of the night was spent in further exploration, in testing the limits both of their endurance and the boundaries of their creativity.

He found himself doing things with her that had never even crossed his mind, found himself assuming positions that would have made a yoga master proud. And while she had always been an exciting lover, the years of deprivation had transformed her into an aggressive one.

More than once, she assumed the lead, making him the one who wanted to sit up and beg.

For mercy.

For more.

She teased his body, tempting it, tantalizing it, bringing it up almost to a climax and then knowing just how to retreat in order to heighten the experience when it finally came.

He was in complete awe of her.

In complete awe of his own body and how it responded to her.

And somewhere in the night, amid lovemaking and dozing, heat and contentment, all the doubts that had been plaguing him slipped silently away.

It was almost idyllic. As close to paradise as she would ever get, living or dead, Joanna mused at the end of the following week.

But on some level, she kept waiting for it to end.

For the serpent to make his entrance and cause her ultimate banishment.

Life was almost too perfect.

She had a wonderful new daughter, someone to help her out when she stumbled—the way her mother would have, had she lived—and a man she adored who came home to her every night. It was so much more than she'd ever had before.

Rachel had learned to sleep through the night, allowing her not to if she so chose. Since that first night together, she and Rick made love every night. The nights belonged to both of them, and the past as well as the present.

But with each day that passed, the thought that she had to be getting out on her own grew a little stronger, made itself known a little more. She couldn't keep putting it off, not if she wanted to keep her own self-respect. And that was as important to her as he was.

What cinched her resolve even more was the fund-raiser he took her to in the middle of the week. It was an annual affair to raise money for one of his mother's favorite charities. Rick felt obligated to make an appearance and he asked her to come with him. Against her better judgment, she agreed.

His friends, the people who inhabited the world his parents had so carefully crafted for him years ago, welcomed him back to Southern California with opened arms. Their arms, however, were closed when it came to Joanna. They left less than an hour after they'd arrived.

"You don't have to leave on my account," she told him, hurrying beside him as he strode out the door after a woman had nodded toward her and asked him if he was slumming. "Stay with your friends."

"I'm leaving on my account and those are not my friends. Those are just people I used to know. People," he told her firmly, "I don't want to know anymore. Not if they can't be civil to you."

All she could think of that night, as he made love with her and tried to make her forget the misspent hour and the unthinking comments aimed in her direction, was that his parents had been right after all. She didn't belong in his world.

That Friday, Rick came home early, full of plans for the two days that lay ahead. He wanted to take her to Catalina for the weekend, to make up for the fund-raiser. He knew that night still bothered her and he wanted to erase it from her life.

Rachel was old enough to be separated from her mother for a couple of days. The weather promised to be idyllic, and he'd personally booked passage and made hotel reservations on the island.

In an incredibly good mood, he came in the front door looking for her. She wasn't in the living room, but he found signs that she'd been there. The classified section was spread out on the coffee table.

Rick stopped to look at it. His smile faded. "Joanna?"

"In here," she called from the kitchen. When he came in, he was surprised to see her in an apron, surrounded by pots. There was something boiling on the stove. "You're home too early. I'm making dinner tonight and I just started." She stopped when she saw the look on his face. "What's wrong?"

"What's this?" Rick dropped the newspapers he'd found on the kitchen table. The page was turned to the rental section and there were several listings circled in bright red.

She shrugged casually as she reached for flour and spread it out on a plate. She'd told him when she came that she didn't intend to stay here permanently. "Apartments for rent."

He struggled to contain his anger. "Why are you looking for an apartment?"

"To move into," she replied. Joanna dusted the flour from her hands. "The check came from the insurance company today."

He frowned. "I thought you said you were rebuilding the house."

"I am." She took out a plate of chicken cutlets she'd prepared earlier. Closing the refrigerator, she placed the plate on the counter and began coating each piece with the flour mixture. "This check is for living expenses. I had a rider on the policy that if something happened to the house and I couldn't live in it for a while, the policy provided funds to allow me to rent a place while reconstruction was taking place." Turning away from him, she opened the cabinets and rummaged around for a suitable frying pan.

Rick placed himself in front of her. "Is this because of the fund-raiser? Because of what Alyssa Taylor said?"

"No," she said firmly. "This has nothing to do with Alyssa."

"Aren't you happy here?"

Taking the frying pan out, she put it on the stove.

"It's not a matter of being happy, Rick. It's a matter of taking charge of my life."

"Independence again."

She could hear him huff the word out behind her. Annoyed, she turned around and looked at him. Why was he so determined not to allow her to stand on her own two feet? Did he want her to be a clinging vine? "Yes, independence again."

He didn't care for her tone. "I haven't exactly kept you chained in the basement."

She sighed. She didn't want to lose her temper. He'd been good to her. More than good. But this was just something she needed to do. The fund-raiser had only reminded her.

"You haven't kept me chained at all. You've been wonderful." She went back to preparing the meal. "But I told you, I can't let myself get used to this."

He took the knife out of her hand and held her arms still. "Why?" He searched her face for an answer. "Why can't you let yourself get used to it?"

"Because this is *your* house."

"It could be yours, too."

A soft smile curved her lips as she shook her head, denying his assertion. "I don't think squatters' rights apply to mansions, Rick."

At times, she could be the most exasperating woman. "I'm not talking about squatters' rights. I'm talking about spouse's rights." He saw her eyes grow huge and moved in for the kill. "Marry me, Joanna."

It took effort not to let her jaw drop. "Just like that?"

"No, not just like that. We'll need a license, blood tests, a priest—"

She pulled her arms away from him and moved back. "Stop kidding around."

"I'm not kidding around. I'm serious." He turned her around again to look at him, then took her hands in his, half imploring, half trying to keep the edge out of his voice. "Marry me, Joanna. You, me, Rachel, Mrs. Rutledge, we'll be a family."

She wasn't buying it, wouldn't allow herself to buy it, not for one moment. He was trying to make up for what she'd endured. "I won't have your pity."

It wasn't easy hanging onto his temper. "There's nothing about pity in the marriage vows. They've even taken out the word *obey*."

Why was he making this so hard for her? Didn't he understand? What they had was wonderful, but it couldn't be permanent.

"Rick, your parents were right. I hated them for it, but they were right," she insisted, her voice nearly breaking. She refused to allow herself to cry. "I'm just a teacher, an out-of-work one at that until the fall. You're a jet-setting multi-millionaire." He was still being dense, she could see it by the look on his face. "I'm a mutt, you're a pedigree. People are going to keep reminding you of that."

Was that it? Was she afraid of what people like the ones at the fund-raiser would say? To hell with that. To hell with all of them. Didn't she know that?

"The kind of people who'd remind me of that are the kind of people I don't want to associate with," he insisted. As she tried to pull away, he held her wrists fast. "And as for 'pedigree,' I don't want to try to create thoroughbreds or show dogs, Joanna, I want to create a marriage. I thought you did, too."

This was breaking her heart. He had to see that, she thought.

"I'm not in your league," she insisted, knowing that eventually, the matter would come up. She needed to say it before he did. Before he resented her for all the things she wasn't.

"What 'league'?" he cried, his temper dangerously close to erupting. "We're not playing baseball here. I'm trying to forge a good life for myself. And you're part of that life. I lost you once because I was too stubborn to block out my pride and come after you. I'm sure as hell not about to let your pride keep us apart."

Joanna sighed. "Then maybe I'd better leave now so that you can see this clearly—"

"Damn it, Joanna, you're the one not seeing things clearly. You're the prejudiced one, not the insufferable, egotistical people you think will stand and wag their fingers in my face for having the good sense to fall in love with someone who's—"

He stopped abruptly when he saw the look on Joanna's face. She was looking toward the doorway. "We're not alone."

He swung around to see Mrs. Rutledge standing there. Her expression was unreadable. "Mr. Rick, there's someone to see you."

He wasn't in the mood for anyone. "Mrs. Rutledge, I'm in the middle of a hell of an argument right now." He waved dismissively, turning away from the housekeeper. "Tell whoever it is to come to the office on Monday."

"I don't plan to come to the office anymore, unless I'm invited, of course."

The familiar voice had Rick pulling up short. Stunned, he turned around again and saw that, as incredible as it was, he was right.

His father was standing directly behind Mrs. Rutledge in the doorway.

Eleven

Rick moved forward, putting himself between his father and Joanna.

He seemed oblivious to the protective gesture, but it wasn't lost on Joanna.

"Is this about the potential wildcat strike? Because if it is, that's over."

"Yes, I hear you handled that quite nicely. No, this isn't about the wildcat strike. I'm not here to look over your shoulder anymore."

"What are you doing here, Dad?"

Tall, gray-haired and just gaunt enough to be still referred to as suave, Howard Masters gave his surroundings a short once-over before answering. "Well, unless I miss my guess, until a short while ago, I used to live here."

Apparently her timing was excellent, Joanna

thought. She'd started looking for a place to rent just in time. "Are you moving back?"

Rick's father turned his gray-blue eyes in her direction. It was impossible to know what he was thinking, but the look in his eyes appeared kindly. "Would that be an inconvenience?"

"Not at all, sir." To make her point, Joanna picked up the newspaper from the table and folded the page she wanted, slipping it into the pocket of the apron as she looked at Rick.

There was a ghost of a smile on his father's lips. "Hire a new cook, Richard?"

Damn it, the old man knew what Joanna looked like. He took instant offense for her. "No, Dad," Rick said tersely, "this is—"

But Howard cut in deftly, his lips curving into a full-fledged smile as he looked at her. He inclined his head in a silent show of respect.

"Joanna Prescott, yes, I know. I was only teasing, son. I haven't had much practice at it, so I imagine it didn't come across that way. Perhaps my field is more in the area of deadpanning," he proposed, then gave a small half shrug. "At least, that's what Dorothy says." He looked from one to the other. "From the sound of it, I was interrupting something."

Joanna got back to her work. "Nothing that won't keep, Mr. Masters."

"Call me Howard. I've decided to become less formal in my remaining years." The announcement was met with stunned silence.

Obviously unmindful that he appeared completely out of his element, Howard wandered over to the large pot simmering on the stove. Three sets of eyes watched him with more than a little wonder.

Lifting a lid, he inhaled deeply. "Am I correct in assuming that you're making dinner?"

Was he toying with her for some reason? Should she be bracing herself for some kind of mind-blowing confrontation? "Yes."

He carefully replaced the lid before turning toward her. "May I stay?"

She was just thankful there were no gusts of wind traveling through the house, otherwise she was certain she would have been blown flat on her face. It took her a second to recover. "As you pointed out, Mr. Masters, it's your house."

It wasn't the answer he was after. "May I stay?" he repeated, waiting. His tone gave every indication that the question was genuine and not meant to bait her.

Joanna exchanged looks with Rick. He didn't appear to know what was going on any more than she did. "Yes, of course."

Enough was enough. If his father was playing some elaborate game to embarrass Joanna, it wasn't going to happen, not while he was here to stop him. "Dad, what's going on?"

Rather than take offense at the sharply voiced question, Howard looked at his only son affably. "Part of my new lease on life, Richard. I'm not taking anything for granted anymore." He looked at Joanna. "Do I have time to freshen up?"

He certainly looked like the man who'd tried to buy her off eight years ago, but he definitely didn't sound like him. "Dinner won't be ready for an hour."

Howard nodded, pleased. "Splendid. I'll see you in the dining room then." As he walked out of the kitchen and past Mrs. Rutledge, he gave her a nod of approval. "You're looking very good these days, Nadine."

"Thank you, sir." The words dribbled from her lips. Mrs. Rutledge's eyes shifted to Rick, silently questioning him. But he merely lifted his shoulders in a confused shrug.

"Positively eerie," Mrs. Rutledge murmured to herself after the senior Masters left the room. In all the years she had worked for the man, this was the first personal comment, much less compliment, that he had ever given her. Giving her head a quick shake to clear it, she turned to Joanna. "So, tell me, how may I help?"

It seemed odd to have a woman so capable in the kitchen willingly take a back seat and assume the role of assistant. But she had no time to waste arguing about who belonged at the helm here. Joanna glanced toward the end of the counter. "The potatoes need peeling."

Mrs. Rutledge went to wash her hands. "Consider them peeled."

"And what about me?" Rick asked. There was an edge in his voice. He still wasn't entirely convinced that his father was here purely for altruistic reasons, that he wasn't here to somehow sabotage his life, the way he had eight years ago. "What role did you have planned for me in all this?"

The comment about too many cooks spoiling the broth played across her mind. She went to find a colander. "You can play the part of the hungry but patient lord of the manor."

He knew how to read between the lines. "Which means get out of your way."

Joanna looked at him over her shoulder, grinning for the first time since he'd walked into the house. "Exactly."

She was using this as a respite from what they'd been talking about. She knew that he wasn't about to try to argue with her while Mrs. Rutledge was in the room and his father could walk in on them at any time. This was a private matter just between the two of them. Okay, he'd table it for now. He might be wounded, but he was by no means defeated. His mistake eight years ago was in not pushing. A man learned from his mistakes.

He leaned over her and whispered in her ear, "To be continued."

"I never doubted it," she murmured under her breath as he walked out. Putting the matter out of her mind for the time being, she looked over toward Mrs. Rutledge. "Thank you."

Long, spiral peels piled up beside the cutting board as Mrs. Rutledge made short work of the potatoes before her. She raised only her eyes as she continued peeling. "For what, dear?"

She knew that the woman was on top of everything, had heard everything. "For not asking questions."

"Not my place, dear," Mrs. Rutledge responded blithely.

But that was what it was about exactly, Joanna thought. Place. And hers was not beside Rick.

* * *

Howard Masters entered the dining room and took his place at the head of the table just as Joanna put down the last of the covered dishes on the table. He noted that there were only two places set.

He looked at her. "You're not joining us?"

Joanna avoided Rick's eyes. He'd asked her the same question less than a minute earlier. She'd just assumed that his father wouldn't want her at the table and after turning Rick's proposal down, she was in no mood to be placed in a position where she might be belittled.

She took a step toward the doorway. "Well, no. I thought that you two would want to eat alone."

"No, please," Howard countered, "join us." He looked at his housekeeper who had brought in the main course, chicken parmesan. "Mrs. Rutledge, please bring another place setting for the young lady." Before Joanna could protest, Howard pulled out the chair to his left, directly opposite his son. "Please," he coaxed Joanna, "sit."

She had no choice but to do as he asked, allowing him to push in her chair for her.

Taking his own seat, Howard smiled at her. "I see that you've brought the settings closer together." He nodded his approval. "Much better." He turned toward Rick. "Your mother and I always wound up shouting whenever we ate in here." Raising his wineglass to his lips, he took a long sip before setting it down. "Of course, that seemed to be the natural order of things. I suspect we would have wound up shouting even sitting as closely as this." He turned his attention to the dishes before him, helping himself to a sizable serving of everything on the table. "Everything looks very good, Joanna. I had no idea you were so capable."

This was a father Rick hardly recognized. He had half expected, after the confrontation they'd had over the telephone regarding the deception, that his father would reconnoiter and take the offensive again. This was completely unfamiliar territory for him. The heart attack really *had* changed him for the better.

Rick made an effort to clear things up and get back on stable footing. "You said something when you arrived about not going to the office anymore?"

"Yes." Howard paused to savor a piece of the chicken and then nodded his approval. "I've decided to retire. Officially. All my life, I believed that a man was defined by his family, his work. That ultimately meant having no identity of his own. No life of his own. At sixty-seven, I've decided it's high time I had one."

An identity, huh? Rick wasn't sure if he was buying into this new, improved model his father was purporting to be. "And just who are you, Dad?"

Howard's smile was stately, regal. Howard could see that his son didn't believe him. That was all right, there were times when he was surprised himself at this turn of events. Surprised and grateful for a second chance.

"I'm just discovering that, Richard. And the process, they tell me, is half the fun." He looked at Joanna. "Wouldn't you agree?"

Joanna felt as if she was shell-shocked. "Is that what you'd like me to do? Agree?"

"My dear young woman, I want you to do anything

you want to. Really.'' He knew that wasn't enough, that they weren't going to believe him, either of them, until he showed them how sincere he was. Laying down his knife and fork, Howard took a breath, bracing himself. ''I suppose this has to be gotten out of the way before anything can move forward.'' He shifted slightly in his seat, looking at Joanna. ''I apologize, Miss Prescott. I did you a great disservice eight years ago.

''I could, of course, blame it on Richard's mother. That would be the easy way out. Richard can testify that she was a very strong-willed, opinionated woman and she is gone, so she wouldn't be able to contradict anything I said.'' His smile was philosophical. ''However, since I did not have my spine surgically removed, that isn't really an excuse. No one can make you do anything, and the truth is, at the time I thought that a marriage between the two of you would be a great mistake.''

He saw that his son was about to interrupt. Holding his hand up, he quickly continued. ''You must understand,'' he addressed his words to Joanna, ''I come from a long line of blue bloods and snobs. We like to fancy ourselves a cut above everyone because, three hundred years ago, our ancestors had the good fortune to be sent to this country, crammed on a ship that was barely seaworthy. Never mind that they were most likely thieves and undesirables, the only creatures who came to the new world with a fair amount of regularity. They were forefathers and that was all that counted. Over the centuries, they were all whitewashed and elevated to a level just a little above saints and a half breath below God.

"What I am trying to say, in a very roundabout way, is that there *was* no excuse for doing what I did. Whatever my opinion regarding a proper spouse for my son," his smile was ironic, "lying, intimidating and forging should not have entered into it." He took Joanna's hand in his, strengthening his appeal. "I am truly sorry for what I did and can only hope that you will find it in your heart to someday forgive an old man his foolishness."

It took Joanna a moment to recover. The man had caught her completely off guard. And, as always, when confronted with an apology, any ill feelings she might have felt quickly disappeared.

Besides, she had already seen his side of it. Had made it known to Rick that she understood. "You were only doing what you thought was best for Rick."

Howard looked at his son. "I see what you see in her. Aside from beauty, she possesses compassion, a very rare quality indeed. It only makes me regret my actions more."

Joanna had never been the kind of person who enjoyed turning the knife in someone's heart. "There's no sense in harboring regrets about the past, you can't do anything about it."

"Other than learn from it," Howard agreed. "And I have. Life is too precious to waste dragging your feet or putting off anything that needs doing." He gazed at his son pointedly. "That's why I came here. To make my apology to you in person and to tell you that I am bowing out of the picture."

Howard raised his wineglass in a toast. "Masters Enterprises is all yours, Richard. Other than my stock

options and the annual shareholder's vote, I am di-
vorcing myself from the company entirely. Putting
myself out to pasture, so to speak."

His father had alluded to this during their last call,
but Rick had been certain it was just a passing
thought, soon to be glossed over and forgotten. "I
don't know what to say."

Howard placed his glass on the table. "Good luck
comes to mind."

"Of course." Try as he might, despite the last few
months, Rick couldn't see his father in the role of a
man on a permanent holiday. He'd always felt that
his father *needed* to work. "But aren't you being too
hasty? The company was always your life."

"And isn't that a sad thing?" Howard eyed his
glass, shaking his head. "Dorothy taught me that,"
he confided to Joanna. "The legacy we leave behind
is not a building, but deeds, people we've touched as
we pass through life. People who are better off because we've passed their way." His sadness melted
into a smile as he reacted to her expression. "Ah,
you're beaming. You agree with me."

"With my whole heart." He had just espoused her
own philosophy. She couldn't have been more surprised.

"Snap her up, Richard, or I might decide to beat
you to it."

Rick was still trying to come to terms with what
seemed to be his father's epiphany. "What would
Dorothy say?"

Howard laughed. "Dorothy Wynters is a wild, free
soul who doesn't want to get married. She says she's
happy enough just 'keeping company.'" His tone

dropped to one of confidentiality. "But I hope to change her mind soon." He reached into his pocket and took out a black ring box. Opening it, he held it so that Joanna could get a good look at its contents. "What do you think?"

She'd never cared that much for jewelry, but the ring, a three-carat heart-shaped blue diamond, took her breath away. "I think I should have worn my sunglasses." She grinned. "That has to be the biggest diamond I've ever seen."

Howard closed the box, returning it to his pocket. "Could a woman say no to this?"

"It would be hard," Joanna allowed. It seemed odd to her that the man was asking her reassurance. Never in a million years would she have ever imagined herself in the scene she was now in. "But coupled with you, I don't see how."

Howard laughed. The sound surprised her. Joanna distinctly heard an echo of the laugh she loved so dearly. Rick's laugh was a carbon copy of his father's.

"Charming, too. You are an incredible package, Miss Prescott."

The man was actually likable when he gave himself half a chance, she thought. "Joanna, please."

Going through the motions of eating, hardly tasting his food at all, Rick could only stare at his father. "Who *are* you?"

"As I've told you, I'm in the middle of discovering just that," Howard said.

As far as she was concerned, Rick's father had already found that out and was on his way to building a better life. "So, do you have a date in mind?"

"Any date she says yes to." Howard finished his

meal and leaned back with the rest of his wine. "You'll both come to the wedding, I trust."

"Absolutely." Joanna's enthusiasm was solitary. She slanted a look at Rick, raising her brow at his glaring silence.

Rick held his hands up, as if to slow down the assault of the words that were coming, fast and furious, his way. He shook his head. "I'm still having trouble absorbing all this. Just what kind of medication are you on, Dad?"

"The best. Love. I never thought it could happen at my age. Hell, I never thought it could happen at all." He paused, his eyes never leaving his son's face. "You must know that your mother and I weren't exactly a love match. More like a merger of two old families for the purpose of propagation." He shut his eyes and shook his head. "When I think of all the time that I've wasted—"

Howard opened his eyes when he felt a hand on his.

Joanna was looking directly into the older man's eyes. "No going back, remember? Just forward. Today is the first day of the rest of your life isn't just a trite saying, it's also true."

He smiled his thanks.

Howard remained for another hour. Joanna introduced him to her daughter when the infant woke from her nap. She was completely straightforward about the baby's conception.

Rick expected some sort of cryptic comment at the very least. His father stunned him by commenting favorably on Joanna's strength of character.

"You go after what you want. I admire that in a

woman." After glancing at his watch, Howard rose to his feet. "Well, as much as I hate to cut this short, I have a flight to catch and these days, they're advising us to arrive at the airport hours ahead of time." He surrendered Rachel to Joanna. "I only came to California to see my lawyer about what needed to be done in order to transfer the company to you, Richard, and," he looked at Joanna, "to make amends if I could."

They walked him to the door, flanking him on either side. Turning to face them, Howard took Joanna's free hand in his. "I've done you a grave injustice, Joanna, and you've been far more gracious to me than I deserve. That said, I hope that Richard comes to his senses and brings you into the family before someone else takes it into his head to snap you up." He placed her hand on his son's. "You two belong together and I had no right to try to change that. I realize that now."

Touched, Joanna leaned forward, as Rachel made bubbles and gurgled against her chest, and brushed a kiss on Howard's cheek.

He looked at her, smiling. "You are a true lady." Then he turned toward his son and surprised him by embracing him. "Take care of her, Richard."

Feeling a little awkward, Rick returned the embrace. "I'd like to, but she won't let me."

His hand on the door, Howard paused and looked at Joanna. "What's this?"

Shifting Rachel to her other arm, she patted the baby's bottom. "I believe everyone should take care of themselves."

Howard frowned. "That's all well and good when

it comes to 401K retirement plans. Otherwise, a little interdependence never did anyone any harm.'' He leaned forward and pretended to confide to Joanna, ''And men like to feel that they're still necessary for something. Take pity on us.'' He glanced at his son, then back at her. ''Humor us and allow us to ride to the rescue once in a while.'' He winked at her, then embraced his son again. ''Thank you for your hospitality and your forgiveness. I'll be in touch.''

With that, he let himself out. Joanna stood staring at the closed door a moment before turning toward Rick. ''Who was that masked man?''

Rick could only shake his head. ''Damned if I know.''

Twelve

Rick waited patiently, keeping the subject under wraps while they bathed Rachel and got her ready for bed. But once the baby was asleep, he felt under no obligation to hold back any longer.

The moment Joanna emerged from the nursery, he said, "I'll have that discussion now."

Well, it wasn't as if she didn't know it was coming. Joanna pressed her lips together, searching for strength. Rick was making it harder and harder to stick to her guns. Having him right there beside her helping to care for Rachel went a long way to disintegrating a resolve that wasn't made of steel to begin with.

But the memory of the fund-raiser was still very vivid in her mind. It was that image she hung on to in order to help her remain steadfast on rather wobbly legs.

Walking past him, she went into her room. It wasn't going to be hers for much longer, she thought. "There's nothing to discuss."

He followed her, closing the door behind them. Mrs. Rutledge had said something about retiring for the night, but voices carried.

"Then you don't love me."

She swung around, wounded by his assumption. If her whole course of action was going to depend on making him believe she didn't love him, then it was doomed from the start because no matter how resolved she was not to ruin his life, she couldn't tell him she didn't love him. It just wasn't in her.

"I didn't say that."

"You didn't have to." He blew out a breath, struggling to hang onto a temper that was badly frayed. "When a woman turns down a man's proposal, that's usually some kind of indication that she's not all that crazy about him."

Didn't he understand? They weren't children anymore. How many ways did she have to say it? "Love doesn't conquer all, Rick, society does. And like it or not, you're smack-dab in the middle of the social world."

Incredulous, he shook his head. "I feel like I've stepped into some kind of time warp, or a parallel universe or something straight out of *Star Trek*. My father sounds like you and you sound like my father."

Any minute now, she was going to cry. For years, in the small, sad wee hours of the morning, she'd thought about what she'd done, about what they could have had together. Now he'd asked her to marry him and she'd had to turn him down. For his sake. And it was killing her.

"Some things you just can't buck. Wasn't going to that party enough for you?" she cried. "I didn't even know what fork to use."

Rick stared at her, dumbfounded. "And that's it?" he demanded. "You're basing our entire future, the rest of our lives, on a fork?"

She threw her hands up. Why couldn't he just leave it alone? There was nowhere to go in her room, nowhere to escape. She went for the door. "You're twisting things."

He caught her by her arms and turned her around to face him. He wasn't about to let her run off.

"And I'll keep on twisting them until they're the way I want them to be. And no," he denied, one step ahead of her, "it's not about control, it's about happiness. And the shooting down thereof."

Releasing her, he dragged his hand through his hair, frustration chewing huge chunks out of him. "Damn it, Joanna, they have classes to teach you how to use a fork. They don't have classes to teach you to be you." He was shouting, he realized. With effort, he lowered his voice. "Stubborn but wonderful."

"I'm doing this for both of us." Her eyes pleaded with him to understand. He hated that. He wasn't going to benefit from having her refuse to be his wife, he was going to suffer because of it.

"And what my father said hasn't changed your mind?"

Life-altering epiphanies at his father's stage of the game didn't count. "He's lived his life. He has nothing to lose."

"And I do?" he shouted at her.

Rick didn't trust himself to keep a civil tongue in his head any longer. Abruptly, he turned on his heel and strode away from her.

Two minutes later, she heard the front door slam. The sound reverberated in her chest. Her first impulse was to run after him, to tell him she'd changed her mind. But she held herself fast. She couldn't allow herself to be weak. It was because she loved him that she was doing this and she had to remember that. So instead she sank down on her bed and remained in her room.

But God, it hurt.

She'd barely dropped off to sleep when she heard the knock on her door.

Immediately alert, her first thought was that something had happened to Rick. She'd spent most of the night pacing, praying. Waiting for him to come home. When he didn't, she'd thought of calling all the hospitals in the area to see if there'd been an accident.

By two o'clock she was beyond exhausted and had lain down on the bed, telling herself she needed to get some rest. After all, she was supposed to start apartment-hunting by nine.

Leaping out of bed, she ran to the door and swung it open, half expecting to see Mrs. Rutledge bearing some kind of dire news.

"What is it—?"

She nearly slammed into Rick.

Catching her balance, she stepped back, looking up at him. He was all right. Nothing had happened to him. Relief flooded through her.

The next second, anger caught up to her. How could he have put her through this? She hit his chest with the flat of her hand. "It's almost three o'clock in the morning. Where the hell have you been?"

He glanced down at the sheets of paper he had tucked against him. "Gathering evidence."

"Evidence?" Her eyes narrowed. "What are you talking about?"

Something his father had said earlier at dinner had triggered him. "I called my father at the airport and he gave me a list of names. I spent the rest of the time looking them up."

He'd completely lost her. And it was no excuse for storming out the way he had. "Names, what names? Rick what are you talking about?" She searched his face for telltale signs. "Have you been drinking?"

"No, but don't think I wasn't tempted." For the first ten minutes after he'd left the house, he'd seriously thought about doing just that, before a more productive course of action suggested itself. "But getting drunk wasn't going to solve my problem."

He was talking in circles, circles she wasn't following. "What problem?"

"You." Taking the conversation out of the hallway, Rick strode into her room and dropped the pages he was carrying on her bed. They fell like so many autumn leaves on top of her rumpled sheets. "Read that." He gestured toward the pages. "Pick any order you want to, it doesn't matter."

She looked at the pages. "What is that?"

Rick laughed shortly. "Those are my illustrious ancestors." Since she didn't look as if she was going to pick a page up, he did. He took the first one from the top. "Oh, here's a good one. Simon Greeley, born 1657 or thereabouts. Cutpurse." He looked up at her. "In case you don't know what that is, it's exactly what it sounds like. Someone who cuts the strings off your purse. In other words, a thief. Simon comes from my mother's side." He couldn't help grinning, thinking how aghast his mother would have been to know that there was someone like Greeley lurking in her family tree. "I'm sure she would have been thrilled to know that."

Discarding that one, he picked up another sheet. "Here's another one of my mother's people. Jenny Wheelwright. Street prostitute. No date of birth but she was shipped to Georgia in lieu of a death sentence in 1689." Tossing the page aside, he chose a third sheet. "Here's one of my father's glorious forebears, Jonathan Masters, common thief." He grinned broadly. "Notice the emphasis on the word *common?*" He began to reach for another. "There's more. Would you like me to go on?"

She didn't get it. Why was he deliberately berating his ancestors? "What are you doing?"

"I thought that was obvious. Showing you my bloodlines. After all, you've got a right to know what you're getting into. This—" he gestured at all the sheets littering her bed "—is my family.

"Oh, and in case you're interested, I also took the liberty of finding a few of Alyssa Taylor's relatives and a couple for some of the other people who attended the fund-raiser. Not one of them have clans that could exactly be called pure as the driven snow,'' he assured her. ''And then I did you.''

She stared at him. ''Me?''

He nodded, sitting down on the bed. He began pulling the pages together into one pile again. ''Took a little time. I only had your mother's name to work with. Since you've never told me it, getting your father's name was a little tricky.''

Where was all this coming from? And why had he gone to all this trouble in the middle of the night? ''How—?''

''Hospital records,'' he answered simply. ''His name is on your birth certificate.''

She knew that couldn't have been readily available to him. There was only one way he could have gotten the information. ''Since when did you become a hacker?''

''I'm not, but my assistant is loaded with a lot of hidden talents. Most are parlor tricks, but this one turns out to be very handy. When it comes to extracting computer files, Pierce is a veritable Houdini. I worked him to death tonight and left him facedown on his bed. But I digress,'' he told her, and he became serious. ''According to my information, you're the best one of all of us. Not a single thief, murderer or strolling lady of the evening in your family tree. Just a lot of good old-fashioned honest laborers and farmers.'' He shifted around on the bed so that he could take her hand. ''Maybe I'm the one who should be worried about you being ashamed of me.''

Joanna stared at the sheets of paper on the bed. ''You did all this for me?''

Tugging on her hand, he made her sit down beside him. "Well, you're the one who needs convincing, not me. I already know that you're the best thing ever to happen to me. And, if anyone ever makes you feel the slightest bit out of place, I'll just give them a peek at their family tree and I guarantee that you won't get a second haughty look out of them."

Joanna shook her head. This had to be the sweetest thing anyone had ever done for her. "I don't know what to say."

He cupped her cheek. "I believe the operative word of the day is still *yes.* As in, 'Yes I'll marry you.' 'Yes, I'll go to Catalina with you—'"

This was coming out of left field. "Catalina?"

In the excitement of his father's unexpected visit, he hadn't had a chance to tell her. "I booked tickets for us to go tomorrow—today," he corrected. "Oh, and yes, I've also got something for you."

She wasn't sure if she could take anything more. But before she could ask him what else he had up his sleeve, Rick took out a velvet box from his pocket and handed it to her.

She opened it and immediately recognized the ring. There couldn't possibly be two like that. She looked up at him, puzzled. "This is your father's ring." Joanna tried to give it back to him.

He pushed her hand gently back, closing her fingers around the box. "No," he corrected, "technically, it was to be Dorothy's ring."

She still didn't understand. "Then how did you get it?"

His father had slipped it into his pocket when he'd

embraced him at the door. The show of emotion had completely caught him off guard.

"He gave it to me just before he left, saying that he saw the way you looked at it and thought it might help me convince you." Rick searched her face. "Was he right?"

Didn't he know her yet? "I wouldn't marry you just because of a ring."

He knew that. The ring was just to sweeten the deal, a token to symbolize his affection. "Would you marry me just because you love me? Just because I love you?" And then he grinned. "And just because I won't give you any peace until you do?"

"You know they call that stalking, don't you?" It wasn't easy keeping a straight face. Or keeping herself from throwing her arms around his neck.

"They used to call it determination." Rising to his feet, he took her into his arms. "I don't care about labels, Joey. Or what 'society' says. I care about you, about your baby. About the kind of life we can have together. And the kind of life I'd have without you." He looked into her eyes. "I've already seen it and I don't like it. I had to keep myself busy twenty-four hours a day just not to think about you. And most of the time, it didn't work. Remember, you were the one who once told me that the most important thing in life is not what you do, but who you love and who loves you back." His arms tightened around her. "The most important part of my life is that I love you. And you've already told me that you love me. In my book, when people feel like that, they get married."

She no longer had the will or the energy to resist. "You're sure about this?"

"How many ways do I have to say it?"

She glanced over her shoulder at the pages on her bed. She laughed. "You've already found plenty of ways to say it."

"Now I only want you to say one thing."

She lifted her chin, struggling not to laugh. "One thing."

He nipped her lower lip. "Wise guy."

Her smile faded as she became serious. "Not so wise. I walked away from you once."

"And now?"

"I'm not walking anymore." *Ever again,* she promised silently.

Rick nodded, pleased. "Good, then I'll cancel the work order to put bars and deadbolts on all the windows and doors."

She laughed. "It wouldn't have gone with the style of the house anyway."

It was his turn to grow serious. "The only thing that I care about going with the house is you."

"Okay."

But he shook his head. The glib answer wasn't enough. "I want to hear this formally. Joanna Prescott, will you do me the supreme honor of becoming my wife?"

She could feel her heart swelling with love. "Yes, oh yes." Throwing her arms around his neck, she kissed him.

Just as the kiss flowered with the promise of passion, they could hear the sound of the baby crying over the baby monitor. Joanna drew back reluctantly. "My baby's crying, I'd better go to her."

"Our baby's crying," he corrected. "And we'll both go to her. In a minute."

He kissed her again, long and hard, just to seal the bargain.

*   *   *   *   *

If you enjoyed A Bachelor and a Baby, *you'll love the next book in Marie Ferrarella's exciting series* THE MUM SQUAD, *available in July 2004 from Silhouette Sensation:*

The Baby Mission.

Don't miss it!

0604/51a

▼ SILHOUETTE®

DESIRE™ 2-IN-1

AVAILABLE FROM 18TH JUNE 2004

CINDERELLA'S MILLIONAIRE Katherine Garbera

Dynasties: The Barones

Life was about commitments for hardworking chef Holly Fitzgerald—until she fell for sexy Joe Barone. Holly allowed herself just one night with him. But as the clock neared twelve, she knew one night wouldn't be enough…

THE LIBRARIAN'S PASSIONATE KNIGHT Cindy Gerard

Dynasties: The Barones

When Daniel Barone rescued Phoebe Richards from her aggressive ex-boyfriend, she could hardly believe it. He was everything a hero should be…and out of her league! Would Daniel give in to his own unexpected desire for this innocent librarian?

✥

SLEEPING WITH THE BOSS Maureen Child

When secretary Eileen Ryan had to share close quarters with handsome financial adviser Rick Hawkins, she vowed to stay professional. But before long, one kiss led to a night of passion…

THE COWBOY'S BABY SURPRISE Linda Conrad

After a year of searching, FBI Agent Carly Mills finally found her missing partner Witt Davidson working as a cowboy, with no memory of his past. Carly ached to remind Witt of the passion they once shared…and to introduce him to their child!

✥

HAVING THE TYCOON'S BABY Anna DePaulo

The Baby Bank

Liz Donovan wanted a baby and a donor could be her last chance, until sexy tycoon Quentin Whittaker offered to be the father—as long as she married him first. Forever hadn't been part of Quentin's game plan but once she had his baby, could he really leave?

A LITTLE DARE Brenda Jackson

Shelly Brockman had finally told her sexy ex, Sheriff Dare Westmoreland, that they had a son, a boy Dare had arrested that day! Will being so close again to Dare reopen Shelly's wounded heart, or will this be Shelly's final chance to win his love?

AVAILABLE FROM 18TH JUNE 2004

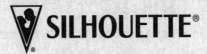

SILHOUETTE®

Sensation™

Passionate and thrilling romantic adventures

THE BABY MISSION Marie Ferrarella
ROSES AFTER MIDNIGHT Linda Randall Wisdom
TRUTH OR LIES Kylie Brant
FATHERS AND OTHER STRANGERS Karen Templeton
HEARTBREAK HERO Frances Housden
McIVER'S MISSION Brenda Harlen

Special Edition™

Life, love and family

THE MARRYING MacALLISTER Joan Elliott Pickart
THE RELUCTANT PRINCESS Christine Rimmer
MAYBE MY BABY Victoria Pade
MOON OVER MONTANA Jackie Merritt
ANNIE AND THE CONFIRMED BACHELOR Patricia Kay
A WINCHESTER HOMECOMING Pamela Toth

Superromance™

*Enjoy the drama, explore the emotions,
experience the relationship*

WHAT THE HEART WANTS Jean Brashear
BORN IN THE VALLEY Tara Taylor Quinn
THE THIRD MRS MITCHELL Lynnette Kent
SHE'S MY MUM Rebecca Winters

Intrigue™

Breathtaking romantic suspense

SPECIAL AGENT NANNY Linda O Johnston
KEEPING BABY SAFE Debra Webb
THE BUTLER'S DAUGHTER Joyce Sullivan
KANSAS CITY'S BRAVEST Julie Miller

SILHOUETTE SPOTLIGHT

Two bestselling novels in one volume by
favourite authors, back by popular demand!

Sometimes families are made in the most
unexpected ways...

Available from 18th June 2004

*Available at most branches of WHSmith,
Tesco, Martins, Borders, Eason, Sainsbury's
and all good paperback bookshops.*

0604/064

SILHOUETTE

Long Hot
Summer

A sizzling
summer read

Beverly
Barton

Lindsay
McKenna

On sale 18th June 2004

*Available at most branches of WHSmith,
Tesco, Martins, Borders, Eason, Sainsbury's
and all good paperback bookshops.*

0704/81/SH80

A
passionate
mission

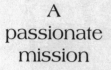

The Country Club

Book 8 available from 18th June 2004

COUNTRY/RTL/8

A
mysterious
Woman

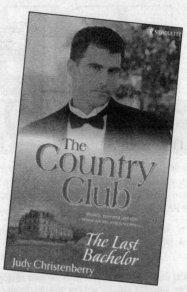

The Country Club

Book 9 available from 18th June 2004

COUNTRY/RTL/9

FREE
2 BOOKS
AND A SURPRISE GIFT!

We would like to take this opportunity to thank you for reading this Silhouette® book by offering you the chance to take two more specially selected titles from the Desire™ series absolutely FREE! We're also making this offer to introduce you to the benefits of the Reader Service™—

- ★ FREE home delivery
- ★ FREE monthly Newsletter
- ★ FREE gifts and competitions
- ★ Exclusive Reader Service discount
- ★ Books available before they're in the shops

Accepting these FREE books and gift places you under no obligation to buy; you may cancel at any time, even after receiving your free shipment. Simply complete your details below and return the entire page to the address below. *You don't even need a stamp!*

YES! Please send me 2 free Desire books and a surprise gift. I understand that unless you hear from me, I will receive 3 superb new titles every month for just £4.99 each, postage and packing free. I am under no obligation to purchase any books and may cancel my subscription at any time. The free books and gift will be mine to keep in any case.

D4ZEF

Ms/Mrs/Miss/Mr ....Initials...............................
                                                                                    BLOCK CAPITALS PLEASE

Surname...

Address...

....

....Postcode ....

Send this whole page to:
UK: FREEPOST CN81, Croydon, CR9 3WZ
EIRE: PO Box 4546, Kilcock, County Kildare (stamp required)

Offer valid in UK and Eire only and not available to current Reader Service subscribers to this series. We reserve the right to refuse an application and applicants must be aged 18 years or over. Only one application per household. Terms and prices subject to change without notice. Offer expires 30th September 2004. As a result of this application, you may receive offers from Harlequin Mills & Boon and other carefully selected companies. If you would prefer not to share in this opportunity please write to The Data Manager at PO Box 676, Richmond, TW9 1WU.

Silhouette® is a registered trademark used under licence.
Desire™ is being used as a trademark.
The Reader Service™ is being used as a trademark.